George

Sept 10 2013

An Air Navigator in World War Two, George Culling was successively a Head Teacher, Principal Lecturer in Education in a Polytechnic and Director of Schools and Teacher Training Department in the British Council. Later, he tutored and examined for the Open University and taught the piano.

His hobbies include piano-playing, listening to music, current affairs, reading, walking, gardening and writing.

PRITCHARD'S PARANOIA

I dedicate this novel to my wife, Maureen, a never-failing source of love, encouragement and support.

George Culling

PRITCHARD'S PARANOIA

AUSTIN MACAULEY
PUBLISHERS LTD.

A CIP catalogue record for this title is available from the British Library.

ISBN 978 184963 365 9

www.austinmacauley.com

First Published (2013)
Austin Macauley Publishers Ltd.
25 Canada Square
Canary Wharf
London
E14 5LB

Printed and Bound in Great Britain

Acknowledgments

I am grateful to Michael Foot, a one-time colleague in the British Council, who took the trouble to read and comment on my manuscript when it was in quite a raw state.

I would also like to record my thanks to those members of the Fulbourn Writers' Group, whose observations, written and oral, I found very helpful.

Contents

Explanatory Note – Fact and Fiction

The first open-air school in Europe was opened in the forests of Charlottenburg, near Berlin, in 1904, when tuberculosis was a major concern. It was the inspiration of a German doctor. The Prologue is otherwise fictional, as are all the characters in the novel.

The Charlottenburg School inspired the opening of similar schools in other Western countries, including Britain. London (the then LCC) opened twelve, and their pupils were categorised as delicate. Many suffered from eczema or asthma, and sometimes both. Altogether, ninety six open-air schools, with a variety of designs, were opened in Britain.

Newly-qualified, I taught in an open-air school, which had four bandstand-type classrooms, from 1950 to 1954 During part of that time I worked with a Head who was emotionally disturbed and erratic in behaviour. That was when the 'Bell-Ringing' incident occurred, almost exactly as described, and also something similar to the 'Round-Headed Scissors' affair.

There is an autobiographical element, in that, like Malcolm Brown in the story, I was an Air Navigator in a Lancaster in World War 2 and was subsequently selected for teacher-training under the Emergency Training Scheme, while I was serving in Burma. This Scheme involved only thirteen months training but we were committed to further study. Like Malcolm Brown I studied part-time for a B.Sc.(Econ.) of London University; then an M.A.

At a time when the testing of children is sometimes controversial, today's teachers, and others, may question whether standardised test of Mathematics and Reading (as used by Malcolm Brown) were really in use in the early 1950s. Yes, they were. I used those produced by the National Foundation for Educational Research, and so, like Malcolm Brown, obtained the mathematical age (or quotient) and reading age (or quotient) of all my pupils. I wanted each child to be challenged by work appropriate to his/her attainment level, so that they would all experience the joy of success.

George Culling

PRITCHARD'S PARANOIA

(abstract)

There was something very odd about Rupert Pritchard, the new Head Teacher. His small eyes darted restlessly from side to side and he exuded an air of nervous uncertainty coupled with a suspicious wariness.

From the outset, Pritchard isolated himself from the teachers, much to their concern, occasionally sending them memos which were usually both misconceived and irrelevant. He soon began to exhibit symptoms of paranoia, focusing on insignificant details while ignoring major issues and tasks. He seemed to be increasingly unbalanced, even informal gatherings of the teachers being perceived as a threat. No staff meetings were held and Pritchard's few contacts with the teachers often deteriorated into unpleasant and malicious altercations. He also nursed a delusion that a senior staff member was a rival, plotting his downfall. The staff became desperately anxious to save their school from Pritchard's malign influence and planned various counter- measures.

Fortunately, a General Inspection of the school brought matters to a head when it led to a critical report by the Inspectors. Their recommendations were passionately debated by the Governing Body and culminated in a dramatic intervention by one member, which finally persuaded the Board to recommend Pritchard's dismissal. That triggered his lurch towards insanity and an urge to take revenge on all those perceived as his enemies.

Perhaps Pritchard's delusions of persecution, switches of mood, suspicions, and homicidal /suicidal tendencies, suggest that he was a schizophrenic paranoid.

Prologue
1901 Berlin

Doktor Bernd Kleinhans was deeply troubled. His mind overflowed with disturbing images of the children he had just seen. Too many looked pale and undernourished; one could almost be described as emaciated. Some, with obvious symptoms of rickets, had white, spindly legs, curved outwards like those of a bandy jockey. Others were so undersized that they appeared to be up to two years younger than their chronological age. One poor little fellow had an old man's wrinkly face, almost as if he had skipped half a century of normal development. Kleinhans agonised over their plight:

Cases of tuberculosis are increasing every day among the young. Action must be taken very soon or these children will have a really poor start in life. They are part of our next generation. They are the citizens of tomorrow. I must do something for them!

The pupils he had just seen had been specially selected, drawn out of their classes, as children in a poor state of health; and assembled for his examination and recommendations.

These children don't need medicine as much as a complete change of environment. Above all they need plenty of fresh air, three good meals a day and regular exercise. A rest in the middle of the afternoon would help too – a siesta.

And then the idea for an ambitious project dawned on him, at first as vague, incoherent strands of thought, which coalesced gradually into a clearer picture.

He envisaged that all the children classified as delicate, drawn from a fairly wide area around Berlin, could be brought in daily, by coach, to be taught in specially-built, open-air classrooms set in attractive rural surroundings. The walls would be only a few feet high, but the roofs would have extended eaves to keep out rain and snow. If rain or snow threatened to blow through the gap, then some sort of canvas curtain could be fixed to keep it out. A nurse would make daily visits, and a doctor would carry out regular examinations. Each child's height and weight would be regularly measured and recorded, and other aspects of development carefully monitored. It would be a bold and radical project to deal with a critical situation.

He realised that such ideas might upset a lot of people. The Berlin authorities, though probably sympathetic to his aims, might throw out his scheme on the ground of cost. They were controversial in other respects, too. Parents and some prominent citizens, might protest that he was proposing a 'kill or cure' scheme for the most vulnerable children, rather than the kind of finely-gauged programme needed to cater for the wide range of disabilities and conditions of such delicate children. Trying to see his plans from their point of view, he reflected on their likely reaction:

The poor kinder will surely catch colds, or perhaps influenza; some might die. How, in the open air, could they survive a German winter, which always brought freezing cold weather and heavy snowfalls?

He appreciated that there were many gaps in his plans. He really needed inputs from another doctor to help him fill in the missing details. He decided to consult his colleague, Doktor Dieter Sand, and outline his plan to him. Sand might help him to develop his ideas further. Perhaps they could then make a joint proposal?

He was going to be disappointed. Sand dismissed his ideas with something approaching contempt.

'My God! You can't be serious Bernd! The poor little sods will probably freeze in the winter!'

'Nonsense!'

'Of course they will. Would you like to spend a German winter in the open- air, Bernd?'

'That's not the point.'

'Yes it is. No-one in his right mind would contemplate such open – air madness.'

'Thanks, Dieter,' he smiled, 'but I assure you I'm perfectly sane, and I fully intend to explore ways of helping the poor kids.'

But Kleinhans was nevertheless quite downcast. He had depended on some help from his colleague and reflected on the reasons for his disappointment.

'Well, that's Dieter for you. His main concern is not to put a foot wrong, lest he spoil his chance of promotion. He knows that my scheme is going to be controversial. He's afraid of upsetting his superiors. No stomach for a bold initiative! Perhaps I'll get a more helpful response from Doktor Werner Friedrich, the senior physician in the Child Care Unit.

But Friedrich was nearing retirement. The last thing he wanted was to become involved in something even marginally controversial. He just wanted a quiet life during his last few years of service in child medicine; the years that would lead to a good pension and a quiet life, with plenty of fishing.

'This looks like a hair-brained idea to me,' he began. 'I want nothing to do with it! And I advise you to drop it before you make a fool of yourself. If you're determined to push ahead, I suppose you could put it to the Councillors in Berlin. But take my word for it, they'll be horrified. They'll reject your ideas and they won't thank you for wasting their time. And it may not do your reputation, and future career prospects, any good. Drop it! That's my advice!'

But Doktor Kleinhans had no intention of dropping his project. In fact, the more he thought about it, the more enthusiastic and determined he became.

Always on his mind was that unhappy image of pale, undernourished, undersized children.

He succeeded in arranging a meeting with the Councillors in Berlin. It was to be held in the large and rather forbidding Council Chamber.

On the appointed day he found himself confronted by a group of about twenty five men and two women. He looked down on them from his dais. They appeared rather stern and intimidating. Here and there he detected expressions of indifference, boredom and cynicism. A formidable task lay ahead.

However, Doktor Kleinhans had very carefully honed and polished his arguments. He described one heartbreaking case after another, involving pallid, undernourished, and often malformed children, whose life-span could be shortened significantly unless radical action were taken. Specific disorders and disabilities were outlined and he spared his audience no upsetting detail. He used every argument he could muster, even an appeal to their patriotism. His audience listened with rapt attention; some with moistened eyes.

He emphasized the vital importance to healthy child development, especially for delicate children, of fresh air, good food, exercise and rest. In the environment of the pinewood forest in Charlottenburg, which was his favoured location for such a school, the pupils would be in close proximity to nature where there would be so much to learn and discover. He was convinced that the vast majority of the children would benefit to some degree. They would be happier and healthier. Every child's health and academic progress, he promised, would be carefully monitored. Individual cases would be regularly reviewed and if any child appeared not to be benefitting, he could easily be transferred back to a normal school.

His presentation over, the Doktor rested his case and braced himself for an onslaught of penetrating questions and negative comment. To his astonishment nothing of the kind happened. He was thanked for bringing the 'dire situation' to the notice of the Council, and told that it would shortly find time for a full discussion about it. In due course, they would be in touch with him.

Afterwards, exhausted by his efforts, Kleinhans reflected on how his presentation had been received.

Well, I'm glad that's over. It went much better than I thought it might. The councillors received me very well. They were polite and listened attentively to my arguments. However, I mustn't get too carried away. I don't really know what was going on in their minds while I was rabbiting on. I'd be foolish to be too sanguine. They'll probably ask their financial people to draw up an estimate of cost and that may prove to be the stumbling block.

Doktor Kleinhans had underestimated his powers of persuasion. He had been much more successful than he could have hoped. Within a few weeks, the Berlin Authority arranged for an architect to liaise with him and to draw up suitable plans for what was seen as a bold social experiment in both education and medicine.

The first open-air school for children from six to sixteen, was opened in 1904, and located, as Kleinhans had proposed, in the pine forest of Charlottenburg. A more favourable environment could hardly be imagined. Situated amidst the trees, grass and wild flowers were four attractive wooden classrooms, each built in the style of a bandstand. Each small class had a wide age-range of pupils and the character of a village school, necessitating a great deal of one-to-one instruction and small-group work.

As planned, both the medical and the educational progress of the children were carefully monitored and recorded. A nursing sister was always on the premises and a doctor called every week to examine particular children.

Visitors noticed, even after a few months, their healthy complexions and happy demeanour. And they definitely did not want to leave their open-air school!

Obviously some children did not make as much progress as others; a few, with serious organic problems, or chronic conditions, made very little progress at all. Nevertheless, Berlin's Chief Medical Office, to whom the Doktor made regular reports, was delighted with the results. Both local and national newspapers carried enthusiastic articles, including photographs of the School and the happy faces of its pupils. There were also full accounts and photographs in foreign newspapers

The Charlottenburg Forest Open-Air School became a model, not only for open-air schools in Germany but also for others in the Western world. They included several in various parts of Britain, and twelve in London.

Part One: A New Broom

Chapter 1
September 1954, London

Haselmere Open-Air School for Delicate Children was near Streatham Hill, in South London. Like most of the other eleven in London, it had been modelled on the Charlottenburg prototype, except that instead of a forest environment, the four, well-spaced, bandstand-type classrooms were situated among extensive lawns, fruit trees and flower beds. A beautiful and tranquil oasis, located in a suburb of the city, it was surrounded by a high wall, which largely sheltered it from noise and traffic pollution. The whole area had once been the garden of an Edwardian music-hall star, whose spacious house had been destroyed in 1943 by Hitler's bombs. The old two-storey stable block had survived, the upper floor now housing the Head Teacher's study and a stock room, while the ground floor contained the school kitchen. In the furthest corner of the grounds stood a charming eighteenth century gardener's cottage, now occupied by the resident caretaker, Sammy Goodman, its walls covered by wisteria and its surrounding garden filled with flowers of every hue.

Apart from the classrooms, one other building had been added: an assembly hall which, like the classrooms, had dwarf walls and extended eaves.

Among the ninety five pupils, the major medical problems included eczema, malnutrition, asthma and other respiratory conditions. Sometimes such medical problems were compounded by partial deafness or visual defects, emotional disturbance (only two), and other complications. Tests of both verbal and non-verbal intelligence, administered throughout the School, had revealed a close match with a curve of normal distribution – so there was an average proportion of the bright and the dull.

A critical situation had arisen at the end of the Summer Term, with the sudden death, following a haemorrhagic stroke, of the Head Teacher, William Rogers, a man universally loved and respected: warm, courteous and considerate, and blessed with the skills of unobtrusive leadership.

The four teachers regarded him as irreplaceable and had been disturbed to discover that a new Head Teacher would be appointed as soon as the very beginning of the Autumn Term.

All four looked far from happy as they waited in the hall for the arrival of the new Head. It was just after eight in the morning of the first day of Term. They had assembled in good time so that they could exchange views about the situation that had developed while they had been on holiday.

Mary Prince, an experienced teacher in her mid-thirties, had a round, pleasant face, crowned with wavy, reddish hair. Today she was neatly dressed in a woollen two-piece suit. Mary stood next to Tom Bates, the senior teacher: fiftyish, muscular, with a healthy red/brown complexion. His serious expression could not conceal the crinkly lines of humour around his eyes. Normally he was casually dressed in a polo-necked pullover, but in deference to the occasion, he now wore a collar, tie and suit, in which outfit he looked far from comfortable.

'Tom, I can't believe this is happening. William died such a short time ago, and now, right at the beginning of a new term, we're going to meet his replacement, whom we've never even seen! The whole thing has been rushed, hasn't it?

'Yes, I suppose it has.'

'But why? You were a very effective Acting Head during, and after, William's illness, and you should have been re-appointed until the proper procedures had been followed to appoint a permanent Head. Or they could have made you the Head.' She looked at him appealingly, for confirmation. 'Don't you think?'

Tom smiled.

'Actually, Mary, they couldn't do that, because I didn't even apply for the post. Why? Because I'm much happier in the classroom. I'm not a manager or administrator and I love teaching. About your other point, the Governors decide these things. They wanted an immediate advertisement. The Special

Schools' Inspector and probably his superior, Dr Mitchell, then went through the applications to select a short list, and finally the Governing Body carried out the interviews.'

'Were the inspectors present at the interviews?'

'I'm sure that one of them, Ronald Parham, would have been there.'

'But most teachers were on holiday while all that was going on, so they won't even have seen the advert!'

'Probably not, but some evidently did.'

'So we might have a Head Teacher selected from a small, unrepresentative pool. Don't you think?'

'Possibly, Mary.'

'Oh, my God! Perhaps he was the sole applicant!'

Tom chuckled. 'That's highly unlikely.' He was thoughtful for a moment; then was suddenly serious.

'Mary, you're fair-minded. Let's face this new chap with an open mind. Give him the benefit of the doubt. Yes?'

'I suppose so. It's just that running a school such as Haselmere requires someone rather special, someone with the right human touch, a leader everyone can look up to.'

'Absolutely right. Perhaps we've got someone like that.'

'Maybe. But I still think that because this School has been run so well up to now, the governors should have given themselves plenty of time to find a first-class replacement.'

'Perhaps. But it was their prerogative to make the decision to press ahead – and, as I say, we may find we have just the kind of Head Teacher you have in mind!'

Malcolm Brown had heard the last words exchanged. In his late twenties, tall, athletic and full of energy, he had been a wartime air-navigator in a Lancaster. Just after the War he had been accepted for training as a teacher, under the Emergency Training Scheme. This was his second post. He indicated his full agreement with Mary's views. So did his pregnant wife Caroline, the infant teacher, a strikingly attractive brunette.

'Look,' Tom added, facing all three of his colleagues, 'our new Head Teacher has never worked in an open-air school before and he must know that he has a lot to learn. He'll see you as the experts you are. He'll want to pick your brains. I'm sure we'll all want to help him to settle in and give him every assistance.'

'You're right, Tom,' Mary acknowledged. 'It's just that I really do feel that there was no excuse for rushing things. The governors should have waited. But now that we have a new Head, yes, we must give him all the help we can.'

***

Not far away, the caretaker, Sammy Goodman, had just left his pretty cottage and was on the way to fix a loose shelf in one of the classrooms. Sammy, of indeterminate age, was short and wiry with a small, nut brown face, etched with deep wrinkles which could re-arrange themselves magically into a smile of such kindness, charm and beauty that nearly all who met him were captivated. His handyman skills were much appreciated and he excelled at keeping the school 'ticking over,' but his humanity, humour and goodwill were valued even more than his practical expertise. He was, everyone agreed, a lovely man.

Chapter 2
September 2nd 1954

Ronald Parham, the Special Schools Inspector, strode into the hall alongside Rupert Pritchard, the new Head Teacher. The Inspector, a tall, commanding figure, with penetrating blue eyes, a clipped moustache, and hair best described as 'short back and sides', had been a colonel in a tank battalion during the Second World War, and a 'desert rat' in the North African Campaign. He had a distinguished wartime record. A regular visitor to the School, he was well respected in spite of having a somewhat pompous manner at times.

His height and bearing emphasized the modest stature of the man by his side. Rupert Pritchard, short and stocky, was dressed very formally and immaculately in a dark blue, pinstripe, serge suit. He wore a blue tie with a gleaming tie-clip, and had black, highly-polished shoes. He was almost completely bereft of hair, with a few long strands arranged with scrupulous care across his balding scalp. He had obviously prepared himself with fastidious care, but he did not appear at all assured. In fact, blinking behind his thick-rimmed spectacles, he looked distinctly hesitant.

Malcolm was not favourably impressed, though he told himself that appearances can deceive.

He looks a bit out of his depth and more like a solicitor than a Head Teacher, and I don't like those eyes. They dart about everywhere –he's hardly looking at us – and he seems so unsure of himself. Nor does he seem at all happy to be amongst us! Still, I'd be wrong to make up my mind too soon. Let's hear what he's got to say. He is, after all, the <u>successful</u> candidate. He must have particular skills and abilities – as well as valuable experience. He's probably very nervous on his first day.

Mary almost gasped with dismay but kept her emotions in check.

Oh my God! This confirms my worst fears. He looks a wimp! How could the governors have foisted someone like this on us! No..... I'm wrong. I mustn't jump to conclusions. We promised Tom we'd be fair-minded, keep an open mind and give Mr. Pritchard every assistance. As Tom said, we are the experts, and I'm certainly prepared to give our new Head my full co-operation.

It was true that Rupert Pritchard looked apprehensive, restless and uncertain, and those ever-darting eyes made little appeal to the onlookers.

But now Parham, straight-backed and gazing penetratingly at his audience, opened the proceedings, in his brisk and no-nonsense manner. The colonel was addressing his troops.

'Good morning. It's nice to see you all again. I hope you've all enjoyed a good Summer Break (hand to mouth while he cleared his throat). I've come here today to introduce you to the new Head Teacher of Haselmere Open-Air School, Mr Rupert Pritchard. (slight smirk on the Head Teacher's lips) Mr Pritchard has been a very effective Deputy Head at Rosemount School for Educationally Subnormal Children for eight years (smirk widened to a beam). He is therefore well acquainted with special educational needs. Mr Pritchard knows that you all had a very difficult time during the Summer Term, with the illness and then death of a much-loved Head Teacher. I am sure that he is well equipped to help the School to settle down again after that very worrying period.

I am also sure that you will give him the same support and loyalty as you gave his predecessor (staring challengingly at his audience) when he introduces the next phase of the School's development.

Perhaps you would now like to say a few words, Mr Pritchard?'

For a fleeting moment the new Head Teacher looked taken aback, with an expression of acute anxiety, but he recovered quickly, held his head as high as his height allowed, and began to address the group. It was obvious that he had carefully rehearsed his introductory words for there was a complete absence of spontaneity, his speech being delivered in a laboured manner, while conveying no sense of genuine conviction or warmth.

'I was very pleased to be appointed Head Teacher of Haselmere, about which I have heard many good things. It is a school that I know has achieved a great deal in the past, not only in helping children to overcome their disabilities but also in terms of their educational progress. Inevitably there will be some changes here as we all respond to new challenges and changing circumstances. But whatever the future holds, your loyalty and support will, of course, be essential, and I look forward to working with you all.'

Such a formally correct but rather dull, robotic presentation did nothing to lighten the proceedings. Sensing that, Ronald Parham was keen to move on to the next stage. He proposed that Pritchard might now like to meet his colleagues individually. Malcolm noted that again the Head Teacher looked irresolute, though he managed to smile and nod in agreement.

Tom Bates was invited to step forward, and the inspector introduced him as a very experienced teacher who had been a tower of strength to William Rogers, and had done an excellent job as Acting Head towards the end of the previous term.

Tom, like Malcolm, had been studying Pritchard closely and noting those flickering, restless eyes, and the general air of nervous apprehension. There was something else, too: a look of wariness and even suspicion, especially when Parham praised Tom's work as an Acting Head. Nevertheless, Tom shook his hand warmly.

The other teachers, and the nursing sister, were then introduced, with a brief word, and shook hands.

Altogether it had been a boringly dull affair: no liveliness, no humour and no lifting of the spirits. Its participants were therefore relieved, visibly so, when the proceedings came to an end.

Meanwhile two coaches had arrived. Children spilled out of them and made for the playground where they enjoyed themselves until the bell rang. Morning exercises had been cancelled, so it was time for breakfast. Mr Pritchard had disappeared, presumably to go to his study.

It was not until the mid-morning break that the four teachers had an opportunity to exchange views. Malcolm summed up his reaction when he met Mary.

'I'm afraid I wasn't at all impressed with him. He looked so unprepossessing and insignificant.'

Mary nodded. 'Yes, didn't he? In both appearance and manner.'

'And he hardly seemed right for Haselmere. Or am I being too hard?'

'Not at all, Malcolm. This is a special school in every way. We need someone with a warm personality who can establish a good rapport with staff, parents and children. Someone with humour and humanity. Someone fit to follow William. Someone who can take the lead in what has always been a well-run, happy school. Quite honestly, Mr Pritchard doesn't look to me the right person to take charge of Haselmere. And those eyes! He gives me the willies! But Malcolm, I know that I must guard against making up my mind before the poor man has had a chance to show us what he's made of! It's quite wrong of me to talk like this at this early stage.'

Caroline looked quite worried. 'Well, it really is, Mary. And I don't entirely agree with Malcolm.' She turned briefly towards her husband. 'Sorry dear! I think we must guard against the notion that we should have as Head Teacher a kind of William Rogers Mark Two. Human beings come in all shapes and sizes. Different people make different kinds of contribution. Mr Pritchard has been chosen by the governors, so I suppose he seemed better than the other candidates. And don't forget that he's had experience as a Deputy Head in another type of special school. He must be better than he seemed today. Perhaps he was just nervous on his first day. Let's give the poor bloke a chance!'

Tom decided it was time to intervene. 'You're right, Caroline. Parham says that Rupert Pritchard's been an effective Deputy Head, and we should take his word for it. Don't be too influenced by what we've just seen. I expect he was rather nervous. Who wouldn't be in the circumstances? He came in alongside Parham.' He laughed. 'Our much-respected Ronny has many excellent qualities, but that military bearing makes him appear quite intimidating. No doubt Mr Pritchard found it difficult to express himself in such a formal situation. It can't have been easy for him. Let's all give him a fair crack of the whip, shall we?'

The others agreed. In any case there was no time for any other observations as the break had come to an end and the children were drifting back to their classrooms.

***

As a group of children from Malcolm's class made their way to their classroom, they exchanged views on their (short) experience of the new Head Teacher. One particular group consisted of a few children whose severe and chronic conditions had led to frequent visits to hospitals and clinics, with some long stays in the former. Their schooling having been constantly interrupted, they were well behind other children in both numeracy and literacy. They were, however, a lovable and good-natured crowd. To Malcolm, they were "The Scallywags," though he was careful never to use that term openly.

Their leader was Billy Green, aged ten. His eczema was ignored for years in a large, dysfunctional family. When he arrived at Haselmere six months earlier he had looked a pathetic sight: large patches of rough, red, itchy skin, with some cracking, flaking, blistering and oozing. Yet he was always cheerful and spirited.

Regular applications of ointment, combined with a good diet and plenty of fresh air, had effected a significant improvement, though much remained to be done.

'It's a funny old world, init?'

'What d'ya mean?' Tony Seymour, aged nine, a fellow sufferer.

'Well, first poor old Mr Rogers popped off, and that was sad, don't yer think?'

'Course it was. Very sad. I liked him.'

'And then Mr Bates took over, and 'e knew how to run the School, like Mr Rogers, in a proper way, didn't 'e?'

''e did. Well 'e'd been a teacher 'ere a long time. 'e knew everybody and everythink, didn't 'e?'

''e did. 'e done a good job. I like 'im, too.'

'I like 'im, too.'

'And now we've got someone else. Why's that? What was wrong with Mr Bates?'

'I dunno. Ask me another?'

'Well, this Mr Pritchard seems a funny geezer to me.'

'Why's that?'

'Well, 'e spoke to some of us just after breakfast. It was funny. 'e didn't ask us f'instance 'ow we liked being in an open-air school, or anythink like that – what you'd expect. 'e just wanted to know what time the coaches arrived this morning – 'ow'd I know that? – And were they ever early or late? I 'adn't a clue. I said, 'Sorry sir, I ain't got a watch.''

Lucy Pym, aged nine, had been listening. She had inflammation of the bronchial tubes with some trapped mucous and had trouble breathing out.

'I don't like the look of 'im,' she said, pulling a face. 'It's them funny eyes. They give me the creeps!'

***

During the afternoon break, it emerged that no-one had seen Rupert Pritchard since lunch-time. Mary was indignant, and turned to Malcolm.

'Well, I thought he would visit all the classes – after all there are only four! – and have a relaxed chat with each of us. That would have been very nice and, really, meeting each of us informally, and speaking a few words to each class, should have been a priority shouldn't it?'

'Yes, but I suppose there's quite a lot to do in the office. He's finding his feet, isn't he?'

'Yes, and the best way to do that is to get to know us – and the children. He really should have spoken to them, with warmth and humour, and said a few encouraging words to all of us. We'll do our best to support him, but he's got to support us, too! This morning's affair was bound to be stiff and formal and he should have been anxious to show us the more relaxed, open and friendly side of his nature.'

'Yes,' Malcolm agreed with a grin, 'if he's got such a side!'

The others laughed. Tom, who joined in the laughter, now became more serious.

'But come on now. This was his first day here. We agreed to give him a fair chance. He probably wanted to familiarize himself with the stock books, medical records, accounting systems and the like. Admin matters, as I know, can be a worry and a pain in the neck. Anyway,' he added, with a twinkle in his eye, 'the day isn't over yet. Mr Pritchard may yet give you all a nice surprise and pop in just when you're clearing up and preparing to go home!'

Mary's response was close to a snort. 'I hope not. My two boys at home are waiting to be fed!'

They all chuckled as they returned to their classes for the day's final session.

***

In Malcolm's class, the last session of the day was not without incident.

Doris Thompson, a sweet-faced little girl aged ten, was normally placid, polite and co-operative, but in addition to her problems with asthma and eczema she had been diagnosed as *emotionally-disturbed.* Any apparently trivial incident could overwhelm her, and in a matter of seconds she could become a furious, screaming bundle of energy. In one of her wild, unmanageable tantrums, she would lash out at anyone within striking distance, unless restrained, until her dramatic eruption was exhausted.

No-one knew what sparked Doris's explosion of wrath on this occasion. Quite suddenly, with only twenty minutes of the lesson to run, it happened. She became wild, noisy and aggressive, and hit out at some children sitting near her. Then she jumped to her feet, rushed out of the classroom into the garden, and was soon out of sight.

Malcolm always marvelled at how understanding and sympathetic the other pupils were on such occasions. Doris, they decided, was having one of her *turns.* They wanted to help. One or two offered to find her and bring her back.

Malcolm thanked them but declined their offer. His first task was to check that no-one was hurt. Then he settled the children on a task and went out to search for his pupil. Perhaps, he thought, she had not gone far. She hadn't.

It was while hurrying through the gardens that he spotted two figures coming towards him, one of whom was a little taller than the other. As they drew nearer, he saw that one was Sammy, the caretaker, and the other was Doris. Regarding him as a friend, she had made a beeline for his cottage and he had come out to meet her, chatted to her in his friendly way, and helped her to recover her normal self.

Malcolm was delighted to see that they were both smiling happily, and he sighed with relief. Sammy had often appeared at critical moments and helped to resolve the children's personal problems. Malcolm mused that the title of *Caretaker* had a special meaning in Sammy's case, for Sammy *took care* whenever he could. And now he had performed his magic once again. How would they ever manage without him!

***

Rupert Pritchard, in his semi-detached house, a few miles from the School, was sprawled over his favourite armchair. He had just downed a second glass of 'The Famous Grouse,' swirling each gulp around his mouth, and feeling the golden liquid trickle down his throat. He grunted with satisfaction. It was his favourite whisky, and from now on, he told himself, he could afford to keep one or two bottles ready for his evening tipple.

He considered the day's events. He was now the Head Teacher of Haselmere Open-Air School. His appointment had come out of the blue. He had no particular qualifications or experience fitting him for the post, but he'd thought it might be worthwhile to have a stab at it. So he'd filled in an application form. At the interview, he reflected, he'd found it fairly easy to pull the wool over the eyes of members of the Governing Body – and then he was told that he would be offered the post! Nothing ventured, nothing gained!

He'd been a Deputy Head, but that didn't mean much. He'd had a class to teach full time and in a small school his DH duties were minimal – just a few routine tasks that the Head found rather boring! Like ordering pens, nibs, ink, paper, blotting paper and other consumables.

But I did it! I'm now the Head. I'm in charge, and the teachers had better come to terms with that. I'll have to show them that I've got the authority. I must demonstrate that I'm in charge. There's one of them, though, who might be a threat – Bates, who's been Acting Head. I think he resents being elbowed aside. I'm sure he wanted my job. I'll have to watch him – take him down a peg or two – or he'll threaten my authority. There'll be opportunities. I'm the Headmaster. I'm in charge! Yes, I'm in charge. And I'll make my mark. In my own way! In my own time.

Chapter 3
23 September 1954

Rupert Pritchard's low profile, or semi-isolation from the life and activities of the School, continued for the next two weeks of term. The teachers had no opportunity to discuss anything at all with him; nor did he visit any of the classrooms. While that continued to concern the teachers, they were so busily engaged with their pupils, that at first they were not unduly upset by what they would have normally regarded as bizarre behaviour.

The commencement of a new School Year involved the settling in of children who had been on holiday for six weeks, getting to know all those who had been promoted from a lower class, studying the health and academic records of those arriving from normal schools, etc. There were dozens of tasks that could not be postponed. It was by far the busiest time of the School Year.

As the days passed, however, the teachers became increasingly perturbed. Previous Heads and Acting Heads had, at all times, been very active around the School: visiting each class every day, talking to pupils and teachers – often spending part of each day teaching a class –; and generally building up an ethos of warm and friendly co-operation, kindness, good humour and helpfulness. Such inspirational activities were supplemented by regular appraisals. The School's Head Teachers normally devoted time to a sensitive monitoring of academic as well as medical progress and standards. Haselmere School, with its happy, well-motivated children, had long been one of the most successful open-air schools in London, and much of the credit for that had been due to enlightened leadership.

But now, the School had a Head Teacher who appeared to be singularly *inactive* and the teachers were bewildered. What were Pritchard's ideas? How did he plan to run the School? Did he want to change anything? When would there be a Staff

Meeting when they might learn something about how he saw the future development of the School? When would he talk to them about *anything?* When would he begin to make an impact? There were both medical and educational issues that needed to be discussed with him, including the problems and progress of individual children. Rupert Pritchard had been appointed to the Headship but the teachers were beginning to feel leaderless!

Walking one morning around the campus during a mid-morning break, Mary met Tom while she was examining the fruit trees dotted around the garden, noting how well the Cox's apples and Conference pears were maturing. Mary had a lot on her mind, and came straight to the point in her usual direct and lively manner.

'Tom, what's happening? Where's Mr Pritchard? Here we are in the third week of term and I have yet to have a chat with him – even a short one. We've got an invisible Head Teacher!'

Tom laughed. 'Well, not quite. If you keep your eyes skinned, you'll see him briefly from time to time.'

'All right. So he flashes past and if we're very alert and observant we might spot him! Good heavens! Is that really good enough? We have a new Head who knows nothing about this kind of school. Right?'

'Yes, that's true.'

'You have been Acting Head twice, and you've had a long experience here, haven't you?'

'Yes.'

'And you were a <u>very successful </u>Acting Head.'

'Now that's a really nice thing to hear.' He grinned. 'Thanks, Mary.' But he knew what was coming.

'You know almost all there is to know about running this school. So has Mr Pritchard done the obvious thing – spent any time at all picking your brains and finding out all he can from you about how the school ticks?'

'No, he hasn't – not yet. We naturally exchange the usual greetings when we pass near each other, usually first thing in the morning, but that's all.'

'That doesn't make sense, does it? In fact, it's incredible!' She looked at Tom rather imploringly. 'Don't you think?'

Tom shuffled rather uneasily, 'Well, I must say that I have been expecting him to ask me a few questions, and to have a chat about this and that, but it hasn't happened yet.'

'But Tom, that's not good enough! There's so much that we need to know, especially about his plans for the future. There are so many issues that should be discussed with him. Decisions must be taken. At the moment we're just carrying on as if he doesn't exist. Where's the captain?'

'Mary, I absolutely agree with everything you've said. The initiative for a talk should really come from Mr Pritchard, but I did approach him last week. I offered to run over one or two matters that he might find helpful, but his reaction was very lukewarm – he even looked rather suspicious – and I had the distinct impression that my intervention was not welcome. '

'Tom, that's very worrying.'

'Yes it is. But my hands are tied. I've been rebuffed. It's up to him, now, to make the next move.'

'Whenever that is.'

'Yes.'

'But suppose he doesn't?' We simply can't go on like this.'

'No, we can't. You're quite right. OK... I'll tackle him again in a day or two, unless something happens before then.'

'Thanks, Tom. I know that, in fact, you are even more worried about this lack of contact than we are.'

Later the same day, Mary briefed Malcolm and Caroline on her chat with Tom. Malcolm had been too absorbed with his class to think much about Pritchard. But now, his views chimed with Mary's.

'Obviously, Tom and Pritchard should discuss the management of Haselmere, the needs of our children, the curriculum, the changes that he would like to make, etc. I'm amazed they haven't yet done so. They're the two key people. We'd all feel much more confident about the future if we knew that they were having regular chats, and getting on well together.'

'Absolutely.'

And Caroline added,

'What we really need, Mary, is a full-blown Staff Meeting where we can all express our views freely. As Tom put it, we are the experts. Between us we've got a lot of valuable experience that we want to share. And Mr Pritchard must have expressed his own ideas at his interview. We'd like to hear about them!'

***

It was quite late in the afternoon when one of the gardeners delivered an envelope to each of the teachers while they were engaged with their pupils. Inside was a memo. as follows:

MEMO NO.1

From: Mr Rupert Pritchard, Headmaster

To: All Staff at Haselmere Open-Air School for Delicate Children

23 September 1954.

I have noticed during the past fortnight that there have been a number of variations in the timing of the daily programme. I would be glad if you would ensure that the following times are adhered to unless there are exceptional circumstances, when some minor modification may be justified.

8.45 a.m.	*Arrival of coaches*
8.55 a.m.	*Breathing exercises*
9.00 a.m.	*Breakfast*
9.45 a.m.	*Commencement of lessons*
11.15 a.m.	*Break*
11.30 a.m.	*Lessons*
1.00 p.m.	*Lunch*
1.45 p.m.	*Rest Period*
2.15 p.m.	*Lessons*

3.15 p.m.	*Break*
3.30 p.m.	*Lessons*
4.35 p.m.	*Children assemble for the coaches*

Signed... Rupert Pritchard, Headmaster.

At the end of the School Day, Malcolm saw Tom and Mary in conversation, and he and Caroline joined them. Rupert Pritchard's memo, his first 'contact' with them, dominated their conversation.

Mary was indignant. 'For Heaven's sake! We've been waiting for Mr. Pritchard to get to know us – as human beings as well as teachers – and he comes up with this! A memo! We've never been sent a written note of this kind. The very idea would have been anathema to William! This is a small, intimate community which flourishes when all of us are in regular face-to-face contact: sharing ideas, co-operating and supporting each other. Someone should tell His Lordship!'

Caroline agreed. 'It's very silly, and quite unnecessary.'

'To send a written note of this kind to four teachers in a small school, of which he knows next to nothing, is preposterous,' Malcolm commented.

Tom sympathised with the views of his colleagues. 'You can see what he's done,' he said. 'He's noted the normal times that we've been keeping, and has simply codified them!'

'But why on earth ...?' Mary's reddening complexion reflected her growing indignation and anger as her arguments tumbled out.

'Good Lord! There must be variations in the times sometimes. Coaches may be held up in traffic. We often have to deal with a sick child after a long coach journey. A child may fall over and be injured in the playground. Another might have an asthmatic attack at an awkward time. This is, after all, a *special school!* And can't we sometimes run a minute over time when rounding up a lesson? There are dozens of factors that may modify the framework of our daily time-table. At present it all works pretty well, but a degree of flexibility is essential. Yet although our Head Teacher knows very little about such matters, he sends us this stupid note! Why not discuss it with us first if he really thinks it's important. Personally, I don't think it is.'

'Yes,' Caroline said, 'and it comes after a wall of silence. This is actually his very first communication with us since his arrival.'

'It's crazy,' Malcolm added. 'Even if he'd made a real attempt to get to know us – and he certainly hasn't done that – sending out a formal note makes no sense at all.'

'It looks to me,' Caroline said, 'as if he felt that after more than a fortnight here, he just had to try to make his presence felt.'

The others laughed.

'That's about it,' Mary agreed. 'Well, there you are, Tom. We are united. We speak with one voice. But what's to be done?'

'I'm not sure, yet,' Tom replied. But as the senior teacher, he felt it was imperative that he should now talk to Rupert Pritchard to try to reach some sort of understanding. His colleagues had a number of legitimate concerns. He would go to Pritchard and convey their disquiet over the absence of Staff Meetings, the need for regular contact, and the question of time-keeping. Probably he would raise the last issue first – it was the least controversial – and work round to those topics requiring a more diplomatic approach.

'Leave it with me,' he said, 'and I'll see what I can do in the morning.'

***

Tom was as good as his word. He decided to visit Pritchard in his study the next day, 24 September at 8.30a.m., which was when he, and most other members of staff, usually arrived. He had been thinking long and hard about the views of his colleagues. They were anxious to learn something about Pritchard's ideas for the future development of the School, and what he expected of them. Once he had cleared up misunderstandings about the daily timetable, he thought, he could move on to the more fundamental issues. He reflected as he approached Pritchard's study.

They're all first-class teachers with very high standards. And everything they said was true. We must have a Staff Meeting. I suppose I should have emphasized to Pritchard, at the outset, the need for an early discussion on key professional issues ... But who'd have thought that he would need to be reminded of such an obvious point?

Tom knocked on Pritchard's study door a minute or two after seeing him arrive. There was no immediate response. He fidgeted, feeling increasingly uncomfortable. A few weeks earlier, he himself had occupied this study – not all the time because he had his own class to teach- but he had used it, before and after the school day, to deal with essential admin. work. And his door was always open for visits by the other teachers.

A minute later he knocked again. He had to wait about another ten seconds before he heard a rather high-pitched, 'Come in'. He entered the study.

'Good morning, sir,' he began.

Pritchard appeared to be concentrating on some papers, focusing his eyes, from time to time, on a typewritten letter. It was as if Tom had not entered or spoken. He frowned, turned over one or two other papers, and then looked up slowly. Tom felt sure that he detected the same guarded and suspicious look in his eyes that he had noticed on Pritchard's first day. He didn't feel at all welcome. Pritchard's opening question sounded terse and impatient.

'What is it, Bates?' Tom had never before been spoken to by a Head Teacher in such an unfriendly, almost hostile, manner; but he replied politely.

'I'm sorry to interrupt you so early in the day, sir, but there are a few matters I'd like to raise with you – if the time is convenient. It shouldn't take too long.'

'I'm glad to hear that. I was just about to review the carbon copies of recent stock orders, but I suppose that can wait a few minutes, if you really have something important or urgent to discuss. By the way, is it your turn to take breathing exercises today?'

'No, sir. Malcolm Brown will be in charge of that today.'

'Right. Now what is it?'

'Well, sir, yesterday you sent a memo setting out the normal daily time-table.'

'Yes. What of it?' Pritchard made no attempt to disguise his impatience.

'I wonder whether you would mind clarifying your reasons for sending it, sir.'

'Clarifying? It should have been clear enough. What is there to clarify?'

'Well, the content is quite clear, sir – and the times are those that the teachers usually follow. Am I therefore right in saying that it represents an endorsement of our normal practice?'

'No, Bates. Nothing of the kind. There have been one or two variations in timekeeping recently, variations for no apparent reason. I've set out the times I want followed.'

'Mr Pritchard, I appreciate your wish for consistency, but our colleagues have pointed out to me that sometimes things happen that disrupt the normal schedule. They would like to maintain their normal flexibility. A child may be sick shortly after arrival on the coach – and need immediate attention – and that could have a knock-on effect on later timings, delaying breathing exercises and breakfast for a few minutes, or there may be traffic hold-ups, and so on. You would not necessarily be aware of such incidents.'

As Tom finished, Pritchard flushed and stared at him in silence for a few minutes. As his colour deepened, he appeared to be controlling his emotions with difficulty. Then,

'Mr Bates, I do not need a lecture from you about the obvious.'

He then paused very deliberately for a few seconds.

My memo has a specific reference to 'exceptional circumstances' so you are making a non-point. You also seem to be questioning the very purpose of my memo. That surprises me. However, I will tell you. It is to achieve some regularity and certainty in our daily time-table, in order to ensure the smooth and efficient running of this School for which I am responsible. I have observed some quite unnecessary discrepancies, which have given me cause for concern. You, the senior teacher, who should be giving me strong and loyal support, have apparently come here to question my well-considered action. Perhaps you have persuaded the other teachers to accept your views. I will bear that in mind! And that's all I have to say on that subject.' He was now red in the face.

Tom was too taken aback to respond. He had always had a friendly, relaxed relationship with Head Teachers, with whom he had worked loyally and happily. Nor had he ever before had to respond to any situation remotely like the present one.

After a short pause, Pritchard continued.

'But there is another matter to which I should draw your attention – and that is the question of dress. All the teachers in my School should be dressed in a way that is appropriate for teachers, and contributes to their dignity and stature. Part of an acceptable dress for male teachers is the wearing of a collar and tie. You have been wearing an open-necked shirt on warmer days and a polo-necked sweater at other times. I would be glad if in future you would follow my direction in that respect. That is all, Mr. Bates. I must now attend to the task in which I was engaged when you arrived. Thank you.'

Tom had been dismissed before he had an opportunity to raise the key question of Staff Meetings or the crucial question of regular daily contact with all the teachers. He was going to have to return to his colleagues empty –handed.

As he turned to leave, he seethed with anger. Humiliated and frustrated, he strode quickly out of the room, along the narrow passage, down the stairs, and out into the open. It was good to feel the cool September air on his hot cheeks.

I am the senior teacher here and I've twice been Acting Head. That little bugger has had much less teaching experience than I've had – and he obviously knows nothing about how to treat his professional colleagues. He doesn't know much about running a school, either. He's a pain in the neck and he's got a bloody cheek speaking to me like that. But why did I let him get away with it? I suppose because he's the Head and I've always respected the Heads with whom I've worked – just as they've always respected me. I'm shackled by an in-built sense of loyalty. I wouldn't have minded listening to his ideas about a dress code, but the arrogant and dogmatic way he spoke! He's going to be a problem, and at the moment I'm not at all sure how I'm going to deal with him. God only knows how he was selected!

As he walked back, towards the other teachers, they became central to his thoughts.

Twenty yards ahead, my colleagues are standing there, hoping that I'll bring them some useful information about Pritchard's plans. I'd better decide now how much to tell them. They mustn't know how badly I've been treated; how I've been humiliated. That would make them very angry.

When Tom was only a few feet away from the group, he spoke as calmly as he could, keeping his inner turmoil well under control

'I've spoken to Mr Pritchard about the memo. 'He thinks that his reference to '*exceptional circumstances*' covers our concerns.

Mary was stunned. 'Is that all? I mean, does he understand why we're all baffled about his reasons for sending the memo at all? We don't understand its purpose, do we? Why not simply talk to us?'

'Well, I asked him why it was sent. His answer was that it was to ensure the smooth and efficient running of the School.'

'But it does nothing of the kind.'

'Of course it doesn't.'

'So where do we go from here?'

'Well, he's sent the memo and he's not going to back down. All we can do is to carry on as before, and see what happens. A rigid adherence to specific times is, we're all agreed, quite unrealistic. We know that. Apparently he doesn't. Perhaps experience will teach him!'

'And Tom,' Mary added,' did you have the chance to bring up anything else with him? The question of a Staff Meeting for instance, or the fact that we would like to hear his ideas on what and how we should be teaching?'

'I'm sorry, Mary. I'm afraid I interrupted Mr Pritchard when he was in the middle of something, so time was rather limited.'

The other teachers, nonplussed, then dispersed to join their pupils at breakfast. Tom felt very deeply that he had let them down; he was embarrassed and dejected. It wasn't until he approached his class that he began to recover. He knew that mixing with his lively adolescents would soon raise his morale. He loved teaching, and he enjoyed teaching this particular class. With them he had a friendly, easy relationship, and firmly believed that, on that basis, he could maximise their learning, and also their social development. But approaching his class, he couldn't quite rid his mind of the unpleasantness he had just experienced.

I'd prefer to keep my distance from that man, but I suppose I'll have to forge some kind of working relationship with him, though I've got very little respect for him now. I reckon I'll have to brace myself for further unpleasant scenes, too, because for some reason he's got his knife into me. And he seems determined to belittle me whenever he can. He's out to make my life a misery. I wonder why?

***

''As anyone seen our invisible Head Teacher?' Billy Green put the question to his mates in the playground.

''Course we 'ave,' Tony Seymour responded. 'And 'e ain't invisible 'cause 'e pops out for 'is grub whenever 'e gets 'ungry. Just like my 'amster!'

The others laughed.

Tim Owen, ten, whose severe asthma held him back in numerous ways, and who always struggled to keep up with his pals, now broke in:

'I miss 'avin' a proper Head Teacher,' he said. 'You know, someone who smiles and talks to us friendly-like, who takes an interest in us, who teaches us interestin' things, and who has a laugh with us sometimes As you said, Billy, 'e's a funny ol' geezer!'

***

During the afternoon break, Caroline sought Sammy, the popular caretaker. She wanted to report a leaking tap and Sammy's plumbing skills had been demonstrated before. The caretaker didn't appear to be working anywhere round the School so she went to his cottage and knocked gently at the door. There was no response. She knocked a little harder, but still there was no reply. Then, tentatively, she called out, but in vain. She was reluctant to enter the cottage without invitation, but was also becoming worried that something might be wrong. Suddenly, she made up her mind. Sammy would have no objection. Pushing the door fully open, she crept through the hall, still calling his name, and peered into the sitting room. Her eyes swept round it, noting that it was immaculately clean and tidy. At first she could see nothing unusual. Then she saw him. He was sprawled on the floor, flat on his back. He looked uncannily peaceful and, she decided, as tears rolled down her cheeks, quite beautiful. She knew that he was dead.

***

The news of Sammy's death spread rapidly throughout the School and left everyone in a state of shock. It was hard to comprehend, yet it dominated their thoughts. Some of the teachers and children had seen Sammy only a short time earlier and he had seemed his normal self, smiling and cheerful, as he exchanged a few words with everyone he met whilst going about his many tasks around the School.

The teachers knew how upsetting it was for the children, to whom Sammy had been a very special person. He had known them all by their first names and was unfailingly kind and helpful. Though upset themselves, they talked to the children about his death, answered questions and comforted and supported them.

Caroline found that an especially challenging task. Her little pupils, from six to eight years of age, had regarded Sammy as a kind of benevolent uncle. The reality of death was beyond their comprehension, as was the fact that they could not expect to see Sammy again. She did her best, and some of the children cried while her eyes remained red-rimmed and moist.

The teachers met during the next break. Tom said that Rupert Pritchard had asked him to contact a local undertaker and make all necessary arrangements for a funeral service. They chatted about Sammy's unique contribution to the School and Malcolm could not hold back an observation that was also in the minds of his colleagues:

'Last term we had an outstanding Head Teacher, and we also had a wonderful character in Sammy, our caretaker. Now they have both gone and we're so much poorer as a result, aren't we?

And Mary added, 'Yes, we've had two dreadful shocks – two deaths, both out of the blue – and I'm bound to say that the replacement for the first of them gives us cold comfort!'

Chapter 4
21 October ^t

The atmosphere of gloom in Haselmere, following the death of Sammy Goodman was exacerbated by the absence of any sign of positive leadership by the new Head Teacher. But this morning a major surprise awaited Malcolm on his arrival. In his pigeon hole was a message for him, as follows:

October 20th 1954
You are cordially invited to a sherry party in my room at 4.40 (or as soon as the children's coaches have departed) on November 3rd. 1954.
RSVP
Rupert Pritchard.

Malcolm could hardly believe his eyes and couldn't get his thoughts round such an unexpected development.

Our Head Teacher has avoided every type of social interaction for nearly six weeks, driving us all to distraction. And now he proposes to have a party! He cordially invites me! Astonishing! I hardly know him. Surely he's not going to act like a normal human being at last!

It soon became clear that his colleagues had received identical invitations: the four teachers, Mrs Jenny Martin, the School Secretary, and Sister Mears. And perhaps there were others. He hoped there wouldn't be too many. If the object of the exercise was to bring together staff and Head in order to foster closer co-operation and friendly working relations, then all well and good. But a small group was obviously desirable.

Not surprisingly, the invitations stimulated much curiosity and comment.

Mary's reaction summed up the general response.

'It looks as if we're going to have a drink and a cosy chat with our elusive Head Teacher. I suppose it's a small step in the right direction although it's no substitute for regular contact. There's a huge chasm between us at present.'

'There certainly is,' Malcolm agreed, 'and really the best way to bridge it is to talk to us regularly – to treat us as human beings. Just that!'

'Yes,' Caroline added, 'and he's putting the cart before the horse isn't he? Isn't it normal to make a few friends before you invite them to a party?'

The others joined in her laughter, and Mary continued,

'But he's not normal is he? Our Head Teacher is a very strange man – an oddball, who hasn't made a single friend since his arrival. Put like that, it's rather sad, isn't it? I feel almost sorry for him.'

'Don't be,' Malcolm said. 'We've been waiting for him to approach us, and he's chosen not to. ... But let's concentrate now on the invitation. It's come out of the blue, and we're naturally taken aback. But it may signal a change – a change in attitude. The sherry party must be intended to break the ice. It may usher in a new era!'

Mary burst into laughter. 'Some hope! You're getting carried away, Malcolm.

Tom had approached, and he had heard the last few comments. His own reaction to the invitation, coloured by Pritchard's recent behaviour towards him, was of amazement coupled with some apprehension, but he felt that he must express a degree of optimism that he didn't really feel.

'My reactions are much the same as all of yours,' he began,' though I'm inclined to agree with Malcolm. This invitation may signify some change in approach, though we can't be sure about that. I think we should accept it at its face value. It's just possible that Mr Pritchard realises that he hasn't made the best of starts here (derisive laughter all round) and wishes to get to know us a little better. Anyway, I'll tell him to count me in, and,' – with a broad grin – 'I'll communicate my acceptance by written memo – naturally.'

When the teachers met for their pre-lunch chat, Pritchard's proposed sherry party was temporarily forgotten, eclipsed by some disturbing news in the morning newspapers. Malcolm brought up the subject.

'Have you all heard there's going to be a national dock strike?'

'Yes,' Mary replied, 'isn't it depressing? We've got plenty of economic problems as it is. War-time rationing has only just ended. We're still recovering from the War, aren't we? We can't afford to have a strike of 51,000 dockers. The newspapers say that our trade will be cut in half.'

'They're probably right,' Malcolm said, 'and I expect they'll be a Balance of Payments crisis, too. We're having to import a lot at present because our factories still haven't yet got back to pre-War production.'

'No wonder,' added Caroline. 'Many of them were bombed and rebuilding them will take many more years. But really, I know nothing about the strike.' She smiled at Malcolm. 'Malcolm always monopolises the newspaper in the morning. ... But I don't think strikes are the right way to settle disputes. They should go to arbitration.'

Malcolm agreed. 'And do you know what this strike is about? No? Well, you'll hardly believe this. It's because the union *fears* that the dockers *might* soon face compulsory overtime. It's not over pay this time. I believe they're quite well paid at present.'

'They are,' Tom said, 'but don't forget that before the War some of them had a pretty rough time. Have you heard about the Casual Dock Labour Scheme? During the Great Depression some of them gathered every weekday morning outside the dock gates while a foreman pointed out those he wanted for work on that particular day only. Some of them stood on their toes to attract attention. Those not chosen would later collect their dole money. It was depressing and demoralising and created a lot of bitterness.'

'I'm sure that's all true,' Mary responded, 'but a lot of workers suffered during the '30s. Right now we're trying to recover from a crippling war. This is another fight for survival. And now we have this! It makes me furious . ...'

'Now,' Malcolm broke in, 'let me give you some good news!'

'Yes, please,' Caroline said, 'so long as it's not some sporting news.'

'Well, not quite sport. Athletics. Have you heard about Chris Chataway's great run? He's just beaten the World record for the 5,000 metres, and at the same time beaten Vladimir Kuts of the USSR. Do you remember him?'

Caroline shook her head, but Tom answered, 'Yes I do. How could I forget? Kuts is the Russian sailor who ran from the front, right at the beginning of an international 5,000 metres race. That wasn't the accepted way to win. Normally the winner was someone who tucked himself in and paced himself cleverly, leaving the leader to overstretch himself. In this case, all the commentators thought that Kuts would be easily overtaken towards the end of the race. Instead, he simply stayed in front throughout and won! It was an event that shook the world of athletics!'

'Absolutely right, Tom. What a memory!' Malcolm said. 'And now good old Chris Chataway has beaten him. That's terrific news! And since Chataway helped Roger Bannister to run a mile in under four minutes a few years ago – the first man ever to do that – he deserves to have his own success. That's really made my day!'

***

Malcolm noticed Tom's absence during the mid-afternoon tea-break.

'He's with Jenny,' Mary told him. 'I saw them deep in discussion in the garden a few minutes ago. They both looked very worried.'

'I can see Tom now,' Malcolm announced. 'He's on the way here, and I've an idea he has something to tell us.'

Tom was soon among them. He picked up a cup of tea as his colleagues gathered round him, took a couple of sips, and then began.

'I've got some news about Sammy,' he announced.

Their attention and concern was immediate. Tom continued:

'His doctor found that he had suffered a sudden and very severe heart attack.'

'It was certainly sudden,' Caroline commented, as the image of Sammy lying on the floor in his cottage floated through her mind, and her heart fluttered. 'But I didn't know that he had a weak heart.'

'No. I don't think any of us did,' Tom said, 'and I understand that while his doctor was aware of a minor heart problem, he was nevertheless very surprised that such a massive attack occurred without warning. Anyway, he decided to consult a colleague. The upshot is that Sammy's funeral is going to be postponed until after a post-mortem has taken place.'

'A post-mortem!' Malcolm blurted out. 'What on earth can that mean?'

'Well,' Tom replied, 'I suppose it's to ascertain beyond doubt the nature of Sammy's death. There's something else. I've been talking to Jenny. Evidently Rupert Pritchard wanted Sammy to do something for him on 24 September, the day he died, some time before the tea-break. Pritchard summoned Sammy to see him in his room and told him that he wanted him to put up some coat hooks that his visitors could use. Jenny was nearby, of course, and heard everything. Sammy explained that he would need to go out and buy the hooks. He said he couldn't do it on that day because there was no time to buy the hooks and also fix them. In any case, he explained, he had a full programme of work in two of the classrooms that would keep him busy until well after School had ended for the day. However, he said that he would go out the next day to buy them, and then put them up on his return.

Pritchard was not satisfied with that. He made it clear in no uncertain terms that he wanted the job done immediately.

Sammy became upset and pointed out that it would take a while to shop for the hooks, and there was now little time left for that. He would probably need to visit two or three shops to get just what he wanted.

Jenny became increasingly distressed when she heard Pritchard's raised voice, which she said, had a bullying tone which became louder and more insistent. Their argument continued for several minutes Finally, Sammy departed, looking red-faced and unhappy. Caroline entered his cottage about half an hour later, and found him on the floor, dead. ...'

'My God!' Mary cried out. 'If that man has brought about Sammy's early death. ...!'

Tom spoke quietly. 'It all sounds pretty disturbing, I know, but we shouldn't jump to conclusions. The coroner at the inquest will want to know as much as possible about Sammy's activities and experiences in the twenty four hours before his death. Jenny will, of course, give evidence and Pritchard, too. Let's wait until we hear the verdict.'

***

Later that afternoon Tom was handed a brief note by Jack Ford, one of the School gardeners. It was from Rupert Pritchard, requesting him to see him in his study at around 4.35 p.m, or when the children's coaches had left the School premises.

Tom reflected ruefully that fortunately he had no plans to go home as soon as the school day had ended, but that he might have arranged to meet his wife for a shopping trip or to go for a meal. Such possibilities seemed not to have occurred to Pritchard.

The Head Teacher's door was, as usual, shut, and as Tom knocked he could not help thinking about how brutally he had been put in his place on the previous occasion. Hearing a response, he entered, and was surprised to find Rupert Pritchard in a comfortable armchair, with an empty one nearby on which, with a sweep of Pritchard's arm, he was invited to sit.

'Mr Bates,' he began, with something approaching a smile, 'I have been thinking that we should have a little chat.'

Several thoughts rushed through Tom's mind:

I'm very curious about the sudden change of tone. It's a bit sudden and I'm suspicious. He may have realized that it's not a good idea for a new Head Teacher to trample over his senior teacher. He'll need to tap my experience sometimes. Of course, he may have already encountered a few problems on the admin side on which he needs my advice. But I don't trust him and I'll be on my guard.

Pritchard continued, in a quiet, reasonable manner.

'I believe that, as Acting Head, you were in charge here for a short period towards the end of last term.'

Tom didn't know whether to be amused or irritated by the question.

He knows all about that. What on earth is this leading up to?

'Yes, that was so, Mr Pritchard.'

'Did you enjoy being in charge?'

'Well, I didn't mind exercising that responsibility. I was "helping out" in a way, though I am actually happier teaching my class. I love teaching, and I'm not really an administrator or a manager.'

Pritchard reaction – a screwed-up expression compounded of disbelief, surprise, bewilderment and irritation – was one Tom found almost comical.

Several moments elapsed before the Head Teacher resumed, apparently having regrouped his thoughts.

'Now, Mr Bates, I am sure that, having been given that responsibility, you thought you stood a good chance of being offered the Headship, didn't you?'

'I know that sometimes happens, but. ...'

'Mr Bates, I think we should be frank with each other. You are an experienced teacher, and the Headship was available. You must have thought of yourself as the preferred candidate?' Pritchard's eyebrows were raised enquiringly.

It was Tom's turn to pause, as he considered the drift of the meeting.

This has developed into an interrogation and I don't like the way it's going at all. Obviously he thinks that while we're sitting down together in this cosy way he'll be able to pump more out of me. He's going to be disappointed! I'll just give him the simple facts.

I could hardly think that, Mr Pritchard, for two reasons: firstly, I had not even applied for the Headship myself, and secondly, I had no knowledge of the candidates – their experience or their qualifications.

Pritchard frowned.

'Quite so, Mr Bates, but for an admittedly short time you had overall responsibility. You were in charge. To revert to my previous point, I think that in spite of your love of teaching – which I do not doubt – you must also have found the job of Acting Head both enjoyable and satisfying.'

'Yes, Mr Pritchard, but....'

'It was natural that you should do so, Mr Bates, and you may well have thought that, while you were not one of the <u>official</u> candidates, you might have been elevated from your temporary position. You may have expected the Governing Body and the Special Schools Inspector to have thought that it was sensible to promote someone who, though not a short-listed candidate, was presumably already doing the job adequately.'

Tom's frustration and anger mounted.

I've really had enough of this. I've explained my position, but he doesn't want to listen. The man seems to make up his warped little mind about something, and then look for evidence to support his crackpot theories. He's impervious to all arguments to the contrary. His mind is shut. And I don't like the word <u>adequately.</u> If that word really described my efforts as Acting Head, I wonder what word would fit <u>his</u> as Head Teacher?'

Tom turned his head squarely to face Pritchard, and spoke firmly and evenly.

'I really cannot add anything substantial to the answer that I've just given you, Mr Pritchard.'

Pritchard was silent again, apparently considering his next line of approach, while Tom became increasingly restless and uncomfortable. He felt that he could never enjoy a moment's relaxation with this perverse individual. Once again, an interview with him was constantly shifting into unexpected and unwelcome channels . Pritchard continued:

'I just want us to understand each other, Mr Bates. You have to come to terms with the fact that I am the Head Teacher here. I am younger than you are but I am in charge of this School. Have you fully accepted that fact?'

Tom coloured, and his temper rose. He was too taken aback to think of an appropriate response immediately. Then he straightened up, confronted Pritchard, and allowed his voice to reflect his rising outrage.

'Mr Pritchard, I am not the least bit concerned about your age in relation to my own. What is really important for both of us is simply how well we perform our work, and the quality of our contribution to the life and work of Haselmere. I'm sure you agree.'

Pritchard flushed as he digested Tom's words, and his own anger rose. He swallowed and was momentarily silent. He had no intention of responding to what he regarded as an intolerable insult. Instead he returned to the attack; this time focusing on an entirely different goal.

'I have noticed, Mr Bates, that almost every day, you gather the other teachers together for a meeting.'

What a bloody cheek! He's referring to our get-togethers during our breaks; our free time!

'No, sir, I do not. I do nothing of the kind. I cannot imagine....

'I haven't finished, Mr Bates.' Pritchard's voice now rose in volume. 'I see you talking together in the hall at almost the same times every day. At such meetings you perhaps see yourself as some sort of *de facto* Head Teacher?'

Tom really had had enough now. He again turned to face Pritchard, his normally calm features now reflecting his growing anger.

'I'm afraid, Mr Pritchard, that you could hardly be more mistaken. In fact your suggestion is preposterous. Frankly, you're talking rubbish. Since you have not yet seen fit to arrange a single Staff Meeting, the teachers need to meet regularly to discuss essential matters concerning the welfare and progress of individual children. And many other professional matters.'

Pritchard was now furious, his eyes fluctuating wildly, while he dabbed the perspiration from his forehead.

'I doubt very much that you meet just for that purpose!' he shouted.

'You're quite right,' Tom shouted back. 'We also chat and joke together. And why not? We have no Staff Room. The teachers must relax somewhere. It's their free time for God's sake. Can't you see that? What the hell do you expect us to do in our own free time during a break?'

Both men were now on their feet, facing each other. Pritchard was furious.

'How dare you speak to me like that! I am in charge of this school, Mr Bates, and I order you to discontinue these unofficial meetings.' He paused and breathed deeply before spluttering out his next words. 'Should any meetings of staff become necessary, then I will arrange them, and I will be in charge of them. No more unofficial meetings, Mr Bates. Is that clear?'

And, without waiting for an answer, Rupert Pritchard rose, returned to his desk, sat down and began to shuffle the papers in front of him. Shaking with anger, he was also florid-faced, his hands quivering and his eyes still flitting rapidly from side to side.

Standing, Tom looked down on him contemptuously for a brief moment before turning on his heels and striding away. He was uncharacteristically enraged as he hurried downstairs and pushed open the door. Outside, all was quiet as the School was deserted. Everyone had gone home, except for the new school keeper, Angus McClure. It was refreshingly peaceful. He decided to take a walk in the grounds. As after his last confrontation with Pritchard, the cool autumn air was very welcome on his flushed cheeks, and the gardens were always beautiful. There was still a surprising amount of colour: the white and pink Japanese anemones, standing high on robust stalks; golden chrysanthemums; and the 'final' blooms on rose bushes of every colour.

But as he strolled, Tom's mind was flooded with images of the meeting he had just had, and what he now knew for certain about the man who was now in charge of the School.

Mary's judgment at the outset was spot on. The selection process was rushed, though it's a mystery how the Governors chose such an idiot. Of course, he's never had any management training. But much more serious is the fact that he's a crackpot. He's seriously unbalanced: obsessed with ideas based on fantasy and irrational suspicions. While harbouring his delusions he remains isolated from the life and activities of the School – and so they develop in his warped mind and it becomes impossible to hold a normal conversation with him. He's a psychological case! And he doesn't make much contact with the children, either. He's a terrible liability here. And we're lumbered with him! How on earth can we possibly preserve the quality of the work we do under his incompetent leadership?

We're due to go to his bloody sherry party. In the circumstances that's an absolutely weird idea. I've no idea how we're going to cope with him or keep up our standards while he reigns over us! God help us!

Tom sat on one of the garden seats. He felt ruffled, and needed to be alone. He looked at his watch and was surprised how late it was. He was about to move when he found himself contemplating the sky. Overall, it had a pinkish glow. There were patches of mackerel cloud and silky wisps of cirrus which, as the sun was setting, produced a palette of colours which coalesced as in a Turner skyscape. The beauty of the sky, the loveliness of the gardens, and the tranquillity of the atmosphere, moved Tom, and helped him to put his present problems in perspective. He rose and walked briskly out of Haselmere.

Chapter 5
3 November 1954

The great conundrum was that although their Head Teacher had invited them to a party, the staff still found him as coldly isolated from the life and activity of Haselmere as ever. There was no sign of a thaw. What was in his mind? Why did he want to have a party? What might they expect?

Caroline summed up their thoughts while she and Malcolm were having an early morning cup of coffee in their little flat.

'He never comes into our classrooms, he never chats to us, and he makes no impact at all on the day-to-day running of the School. He only attends our assemblies now and again, just to remind us of his existence! Most of the time, I suppose, he just attends to routine things, like ordering basic stock and paying non-teaching staff, etc.'

'And sending memos.'

'But he's only sent one of those.'

'True, but I suspect that he's establishing a pattern. They'll be more of them. Brace yourself!'

'But the first one didn't make much difference, did it? He really is weird, isn't he?'

'Too true. I'm afraid the Governors chose the wrong bloke!'

'Yes, and I really can't imagine what was in their minds.... But now I'm going to change the subject. In case you've forgotten, Malcolm, today is the day of the sherry party. We'll soon find out what it's all about; what it means for us.'

'Well, hopefully, a glass or two of Tio Pepe, and some happy banter and jollity. We're going to enjoy ourselves and our Head Teacher is going to unbend!'

'Oh, Malcolm, you're always the supreme optimist!'

Malcolm laughed. 'Perhaps. But here, Caroline, is something much more interesting, in today's newspaper. Four famous people have just died. All household names. The obituaries are well worth reading.'

'I'm sure they are. Who are they?'

'Well, there's Henri Matisse, the great modern artist, at 84; Lionel Barrymore, who was in dozens of films – in a wheelchair – as Dr Gillespie; George Robey, the comedian – and star of the Music Hall – in our parents' time; and Wilhelm Furtwangler, conductor of the Berlin Philharmonic. The obituaries are well worth reading.'

'I'm sure they are; obituaries are often the most fascinating part of a newspaper!'

**

At Haselmere, Tom, having decided to ignore Pritchard's request, had arranged to have a meeting of the teachers in his classroom, during the mid-morning break. He had some news that they had been anxious to hear.

'The Coroner's court dealt with Sammy's death at the inquest yesterday,' he began. 'His doctor gave evidence about his medical condition, and then the Coroner wanted to establish Sammy's state of mind on the day of his death. His wife stated that he had appeared to be perfectly normal in the morning. She was followed by Pritchard and then Jenny...'

'Why was Jenny there?' Mary asked.

'Because Pritchard said that she had seen more of Sammy than anyone else in the School – which I suppose is true. I'm glad she was; otherwise we wouldn't know exactly what had occurred. Jenny gave me a pretty full account of the proceedings.'

'And Jenny had some crucially-important evidence, didn't she?' Malcolm was thinking about the angry dispute that she had heard.

'Yes. But interestingly enough, Pritchard told the Coroner quite openly what had taken place – that he had required Sammy to carry out a task and that the caretaker had said that he was too busy to do it on that day.'

'And did he also give an account of how he raised his voice to Sammy and upset him,' asked Caroline.

'Not exactly that,' Tom replied, 'but apparently he did say that he made it clear that he was not pleased with Sammy's response, and that he was rather angry with him. I imagine he thought that his anger was entirely justified.'

'And what did Jenny add to that?' Mary wanted to know.

'Jenny explained that her office was next door to Pritchard's study and that she had heard the dispute through a thin partition wall. In response to a question from the Coroner, she acknowledged that Pritchard had sounded very angry, and that Sammy had seemed very distressed.'

'So,' Malcolm said, 'the Coroner was given a fairly clear picture of what took place. What was his verdict?'

'His verdict,' Tom replied, 'was that the death was accidental, that it followed a heated difference of opinion that evidently upset Sammy, whose death would not have occurred had he not had a heart condition that appeared to have been more serious than anyone realised.'

'And I suppose,' Mary observed, 'that the Coroner had no choice, but personally I feel sure that Sammy would still be with us if that heated quarrel had not taken place.'

'I'm sure that's right,' Malcolm said, 'except that I believe all the heat was on one side!'

'And tonight we're all going to a party hosted by him!' Caroline pointed out.

'Yes,' Tom said, 'and I'm sure we all feel pretty uncomfortable about that in view of what's happened. '

***

Just after the end of the school day, Malcolm and Caroline met outside one of the classrooms, and began to walk towards Pritchard's study.

'My God! Look, Malcolm. All those people walking ahead of us! We're all heading in the same direction. Surely they're not all going to Pritchard's party?'

'It looks like it. There's quite a procession forming.'

Tom and Mary were just ahead of them. But there was also Jenny Martin, the part-time secretary, Sister Mears, Dr Alan Hargreaves, the school doctor, Philip Thomas and Francis Burton, the peripatetic teachers, Ronald Parham, the Special Schools inspector, the two school Helpers, and the two gardeners.

There were others, too, who were less familiar to the teachers, and a few who were complete strangers.

'I think they must be governors,' Malcolm said. 'Good Heavens! There must be about twenty people ahead of us, all heading in the same direction. It'll be a terrible squash in Pritchard's study. It's not that big.'

'A squash is just what I don't want,' protested the pregnant Caroline. 'Look, let's hold back for a while. I don't want to be thrust into a tightly-packed queue in the corridor just outside Pritchard's study. I've come here for a relaxing evening! I'm not prepared to be pushed and shoved!'

'OK. You're absolutely right. Let's wait a bit. Let's sit on this bench for a while until all those people ahead of us have disappeared up the stairs.'

'And even a little after that.'

'Agreed.'

About ten minutes later, the couple rose and continued their stroll. Reaching the corridor leading to Pritchard's study, Malcolm's concern increased. Just ahead of them, there was some congestion near Pritchard's door, and half a dozen visitors were clearly finding it quite difficult to get through it.

'Damn!' Malcolm muttered. 'I'd hoped we'd managed to avoid that.'

As they stood wondering what to do next, a few guests staggered out of the room, clutching their sherry glasses and looking relieved at reaching the exit. They passed them as they moved along the corridor. Malcolm and Caroline were then able to move freely towards the door; and suddenly they found themselves inside the room. They were finally at the party!

Their hearts sank. It was much worse than they had anticipated. The noise had hit them as soon as the door was opened. The decibel level was so overwhelming that everyone's voice had to be raised several notches to stand any chance of being heard. Caroline looked with horror at a room tightly packed with people, many of whom were perspiring, while others smoked To someone in Caroline's condition, it was nightmarish.

'This is simply awful. It's a shambles!' she mouthed to Malcolm, who clutched her hand protectively. He was becoming increasing worried.

'We'll get out as soon as we can,' he whispered fiercely, 'but I suppose, for form's sake we'd better meet and greet our host.'

'Yes, but let's make it as brief as possible.'

Pritchard being one of the shortest people in the room, only half of his head was visible, which did not help identification from the other side of the room. The couple then struggled through the mass of bodies, shrouded in wispy clouds of smoke, to where the Head Teacher stood, apparently absorbed in conversation with Ronald Parham. He appeared to be entirely unaware of their approach and, as they drew nearer, his attention remained focused on the inspector, his only response to the new arrivals being to wave his hand airily towards the glasses of sherry on a nearby table. They were astonished, angry and indignant at the blatant rudeness, the absence of any form of greeting or proper acknowledgement. However, Malcolm took what he hoped was a dry sherry, and Caroline a sweeter one, and they looked about them for any space in which they might stand without being jostled by the constantly shifting bodies which surrounded them.

Having moved into a corner, they found themselves close to Mrs Mears and Jenny, both looking rather bewildered, and they had a brief conversation with them, though the overwhelming noise level ruled out normal conversation. Circulating was quite out of the question. Malcolm thought it was rather like standing up in a London tube train during the rush hour, except that there was no strap to hold on to. The smell of tobacco, combined with the cocktail of smells arising from too many bodies in a confined space, was suffocating and repellent.

Caroline indicated to Malcolm that she found the atmosphere unbearably congested and stuffy. Her heart was beating wildly. They must get out as soon as possible!

He began immediately the slow task of steering his wife, now increasingly distressed, towards the exit. Slowly they moved along, glasses held high, constantly asking other guests kindly to let them through, and finally they were able to squeeze their way out of the door.

Once outside, with the door shut behind them, it was as if a wall had suddenly descended to shut out the all-pervading noise and the hot and stuffy atmosphere. It was peaceful and, mercifully, there was room in the corridor to stand without being pressed on all sides. Malcolm glanced with concern at his wife.

'How are you dear? I'm so sorry to have let you in for this.'

'I'm alright now, but I don't think I could have stood much more of that. It was ghastly! But it's not your fault. None of us realised it would be like this. Look, Tom and Mary are over there. Let's join them.'

Mary was pleased to see them, but not at all pleased with her party experience.

'I had to ask a neighbour to look after my children so that I could be free for this,' she began, 'and what a hopeless shambles! A ridiculous number of people, absolute chaos, no friendly chats, and our Head Teacher giving all his attention to Rupert Parham and the governors, while completely ignoring his colleagues. We teachers were clearly a low priority. And this was supposed to be a party! Who was it for? Certainly not us!'

Malcolm agreed. 'I can't understand why he invited us. If he wanted to cement his relationship with the inspector and the Governors, for his own ends, he should have invited only them to his party and no-one else. That might have worked. Though, if he was trying to impress the VIPs I shouldn't think he was successful because, as you say, the so-called party was a shambles!'

Caroline, now clearly recovered, gave vent to her own indignation and anger.

'That,' she said, very emphatically, 'was simply awful, and no party. A party is where you can relax and chat with your friends. That was a travesty, a very unpleasant experience. Something of a bun fight.' She smiled. 'No. Actually it was worse than a bun fight because, so far as I could see, there was nothing at all to eat!'

Mary agreed. 'That's right. Nothing at all. Not even nibbles. I wouldn't have come if I'd had the slightest idea that it would be so dreadful. Really, I'm quite disgusted!'

'So are we all!' Malcolm agreed, 'so let's go home. And I don't think Caroline and I have the slightest inclination to express our thanks to our "kind" host for a "lovely evening". We couldn't be so hypocritical.'

The others felt the same way and they all went out together. They had finally escaped from 'Pritchard's Peculiar Party' as they afterwards referred to it.

Chapter 6
4 November 1954

Today it was Malcolm's turn to supervise the children's breathing exercises. He watched the coaches arrive and the children tumble out of them. They could hardly wait to get out. Some of them then ran *hell for leather*, making a beeline for the playground, while others, meandering in groups, continued with the spirited banter and laughter that had kept them amused during their coach journey. The School was coming to life! Malcolm was always impressed with the children's normality:

It's hard to realise that they all have some disability or serious medical condition, and that some of them have spent much of their lives in hospitals or clinics. Apart from those with eczema, they look absolutely normal. In fact some of them are so lively and have such rosy cheeks that they look more normal than normal children! And they are so happy! Open-air education definitely works!

He chatted with some of the children, went to collect the School bell, checked the time on his watch, and rang it three times. It made a loud, penetrating clang, to which the children never failed to respond whatever they were doing, and however much noise they had been generating. They all 'froze; there was a miraculous silence, with all the children's eyes on Malcolm. Having gained their full attention, he was just about to begin the morning's breathing exercises when he glimpsed, to one side, the figure of Rupert Pritchard striding purposefully towards him. As he approached, Malcolm noticed that his complexion was distinctly more florid than usual.

What's he doing out here? He's never appeared for this session before. There's trouble on the way because he looks like thunder. He's thoroughly worked up. What on earth's the matter with him?

He was soon to find out.

When they were face-to-face, Malcolm saw that Pritchard's whole demeanour was wildly uncontrolled and his expression distorted with fury. He looked ready to explode.

'What's this?' he demanded angrily. 'You have rung the School bell two minutes early!'

Malcolm, astonished at the absurdity of the complaint and the attitude and appearance of Pritchard, managed to stay calm.

'Oh, is that so, sir? Sorry. I did look at the time, and I thought my watch was correct. I intended to ring the bell at precisely 8.55. Perhaps my watch is a little fast.'

'Mr Brown, you will recall that on September 23rd. I gave specific instructions in regard to the daily timetable. Breathing exercises should, as you know, commence at 8.55 – no earlier and no later. You rang the bell at 8.53. You may not regard it as important that we should all adhere strictly to our timetable, but my view, as Head Teacher of this School, is that it is essential for its smooth running . And I intend to enforce it. Having received a memo about the daily timetable near the beginning of term, you cannot be ignorant of my requirements.'

What utter rubbish he talks. The pompous ass!

'Mr Pritchard. I have apologised. I'm afraid I forgot to check my watch this morning. It's easy enough to do so with the radio pips, and that is my normal practice.'

'I'm glad to hear that Mr Brown. You are a young and inexperienced teacher who is on probation. At the end of your first two years of teaching, it will be my responsibility to consider how well you have performed, which must, of course, include the question of time-keeping.' Pritchard's voice, on a rising crescendo, now approached its climax. 'You have been given "qualified teacher" status subject to a successful probationary period, he shouted. 'Do I make myself clear?'

That's all piffle! You have no idea how well I perform as a teacher because you never see me teach! And you certainly don't give this inexperienced teacher any support or encouragement, as you should! You're just throwing your weight about, though it's my bad luck that you have the power to make or break me – and you want to remind me of that.'

'Yes, Mr Pritchard, you have.'

'I'm glad to hear that. Now, I believe you have not been trained like a normal teacher. You are an 'Emergency Trained Teacher.' His lip curled. 'How long was your training?'

'Thirteen months.'

'So. Very different from the usual two years. Not really long enough. And I believe your academic qualifications are very limited, too?'

'That's true, sir. But I hope I'll soon graduate with a B.Sc.(Econ.) of London University.'

'But you're teaching here; you can't possibly be a student at London University.'

'That's right, it'll be an external degree. I'm studying with a correspondence college.'

Pritchard appeared unimpressed, and continued his harangue in a loud voice.

'One further point. You left my sherry party yesterday evening quite suddenly without even coming back to me for a final word of thanks. I am not unduly concerned about that on a personal level, but I'm sure that some of my special guests must have noticed – including members of the Governing Body and Mr Parham. They will not have been favourably impressed.'

Malcolm's patience was wearing thin.

To hell with your special guests and to hell with you! And surely they won't have been favourably impressed either, with your badly-organized shambles of a party!

'Mr Pritchard. As you know, my wife Caroline is pregnant. She found the very crowded room too stuffy and was feeling unwell. I had to take her home as soon as possible.'

'It is unfortunate that your wife felt unwell and had to miss part of the party, but,' – another rise in volume – 'there was certainly an absence of good manners on your part.'

And following his intemperate outburst, the Head Teacher stamped away, leaving behind a young teacher outwardly calm but inwardly fuming, and a crowd of bewildered children of delicate constitution, who had been standing still and shivering in the crisply cool November air for far too long.

Malcolm finally began the breathing exercises five minutes late! He hoped the cook would not mind that breakfast would also be delayed by the same interval, and that Pritchard might reflect that his intervention had probably completely upset his precious daily timetable!

***

Over breakfast the pupils chatted about the extraordinary scene they had just witnessed in the playground.

Billy Green as usual led the discussion.

'What did yer think about what 'appened in the playground. What a shocker! Mr Pritchard shouldn't speak to our teacher like that. It ain't right Mr Brown's a good teacher and 'e didn't do nothing wrong, did 'e?'

'Course 'e didn't,' responded Tony Seymour. Mr Pritchard made me feel nervous, and I didn't feel well. 'e upset me.'

'Me, too,' added Lucy Pym. 'Fancy making a fuss about two minutes! And what a cheek to shout like that at Mr Brown. I'm on Mr Brown's side!'

'So am I,' said Billy.

'Me, too' said Tony. I don't want to 'ave anythink to do with that man. I 'ope 'e keeps out of my way. I feel sorry for Mr Brown.'

'Me, too,' Lucy said. A nice man like Mr Brown shouldn't 'ave to put up with such a 'orrible bloke.

***

For the mid-afternoon break Tom called the teachers to a meeting in his classroom. It was shortly after the end of the school day. The other teachers had no idea about its purpose, but knew that it must be important.

Tom smiled apologetically at his colleagues. 'I'm sorry, I can only offer you the children's chairs, but at least, being designed for my adolescents, they're the biggest in the school.'

When the teachers were settled, he continued 'I'm also sorry for the short notice. The fact is, this morning I happened to see and hear something that I found very disturbing, something that made me really angry.'

'What was that, Tom?' Mary asked. 'You're not put out very often.'

'I saw Pritchard stride up to where Malcolm was standing in the playground – you won't mind my mentioning this, will you, Malcolm? – ready for breathing exercises, and the angry outburst he directed at him was offensive and unprofessional, especially as Malcolm is such a good teacher.' He smiled at Malcolm. 'And he shouted at him, sneering at his alleged inexperience and lack of qualifications – and that was all in front of the children, who had to stand there, bewildered and frightened. And they were getting cold too. Frankly, I was disgusted! No, Malcolm, you probably didn't see me, but Pritchard made so much noise and fuss that I couldn't help noticing what was going on. Now, that incident, following others – more about those in a moment – convinced me that we should now take a more positive stance with this unpleasant character who is supposedly our leader, take stock of our position and discuss our future strategy!'

'Hear! Hear! But what caused His Lordship's outburst in the first place? Mary enquired.

'The fact that I rang the bell two minutes early,' Malcolm replied.

'Two minutes early? He complained about that? That's incredible!'

'Yes, it was, as usual, something ridiculously insignificant,' Tom said. 'But it convinced me that from now on we must meet regularly. We should keep one another fully informed of all our dealings with Pritchard, so that we can decide our joint response in each case. We've got to work together, to follow a common strategy. We must always tell one another about any problems we have with Pritchard.

For example, I have never told you about my own altercations with him. Let me put you in the picture. When I went in to see him about your concerns regarding his memo, he was rude, uncooperative and dismissive, brushing aside our views. He went on to criticise my appearance – my clothing – and practically ordered me to wear a collar and tie.'

'What a damn cheek!' Mary commented.

'Yes ... well, the second time I went to him was on 21 October , the day he sent out his invitations to that awful sherry party. It was worse than on the previous occasion. He refused to believe that I didn't covet his job as Head, and said that I had to come to terms with the fact that, although he is younger than me, he is in charge. And then came the most preposterous accusation – that I have been considering myself as the *de facto* Head here, and calling you together regularly for unofficial Staff Meetings I told him that the idea was absurd and we ended up by shouting at each other.'

'The man's barmy!' Malcolm said. 'He is completely removed from reality. He lives in his own little capsule and nurses his own twisted ideas.'

'You're right,' Tom said. 'And that's why we have to adapt. We have all been far too patient and tolerant up to now.'

'Especially you,' Caroline said.

'Well, I wanted to give him a fair chance to settle in before getting too indignant about his obvious shortcomings and bizarre behaviour. But, like you all, my main concern is to try to preserve everything that's good about this School – to keep the children happy and to maintain both academic and medical standards, and also the wonderful ethos that William developed. It's not going to be easy and at some stage we may have to consider talking to Ronald Parham about our concerns. Meanwhile, with your agreement, I will do precisely what Pritchard has accused me of, and become a *de facto* Head, in that I am willing to take the lead in guiding you through the present difficulties. I'll be happy to tackle Pritchard about anything that worries us. His complete lack of respect for his staff is more than I can stomach. What do you think? I'd like to be sure that we're all completely as one about this.'

'Well, count me in. I very much welcome everything you've said,' Mary responded. 'I'm especially keen that we should share our experiences and act together. Always!'

Malcolm and Caroline indicated their agreement.

'It's a hackneyed expression, I know,' said the former, 'but unity is strength! Seriously, we have no leader at present, so please step into the vacancy, Tom!'

***

The crisis in human relations at Hasemere had reached a critical juncture. The teachers knew that in the long run, they would prevail, because every useful or valuable development depended on their efforts and their co -operation; and now that they had a real leader, and one they liked and trusted, they would seek jointly to thwart any negative or baneful influences or actions of their Head Teacher.

Chapter 7
2 December 1954

The weather in Britain never loses its capacity to surprise. For years the final weeks of the old year can be mainly mild, often with drizzle or fog. The really cold snaps are usually confined to January. But sometimes the calendar of weather patterns stands on its head; it can be freezing cold well before Christmas. This year was such a time. Crisp, powdery snow up to a depth of six inches had fallen during the night. The extensive gardens at Haselmere were camouflaged in a blanket of snow. Garlands of icicles glistened on the branches of fruit trees, pathways merged with adjoining lawns, sparkling spiders' webs mysteriously appeared on every shrub, and everywhere the wind had sculpted the snow in ridges and perfect curves which rose up the sides of the classrooms.

The coach drivers had not had an easy time, yet both managed to draw in to the School grounds only a few minutes late. As the children arrived, they gazed wide-eyed at the *winter wonderland* that was their School. It was hardly recognisable as such. Memories of the last cold snap flooded into their minds. Then, entranced, delighted and excited they bounded into action. Cries of undiluted joy soon floated across the playground from those involved in a snowball fight. Some children hastened to make a snowman, and were searching for objects to serve as eyes, nose and mouth. But the main attraction would soon be the slide. Some older children chose a traditional spot for it, and many leather soles glided rapidly over the snow until it was suitably flattened, compressed and polished. A couple of feet wide, and about eight yards long, its surface was soon a shiny pathway of steel, an invitation to the daring and the adventurous. A queue of children soon formed, waiting patiently to use it. They didn't have long to wait because each child skimmed along at an alarmingly breakneck speed – or so it seemed to Malcolm – their shoes polishing the surface even more, so that it became increasingly slippery. Most children flashed by upright, with slightly bent knees; others almost squatted, their bottoms sometimes scraping the ice. At the end of the slide they sometimes lost their balance and tumbled into the snow. Then, scrambling to their feet, they laughed happily even if they were slightly shaken up. Malcolm, enjoying the joyous scene, kept a close eye on everything that was going on – there was always a teacher on duty – but there were no problems. Watching their antics, he enjoyed them vicariously, and was as happy as they were.

It's wonderful to see these children, with such a wide range of medical conditions, playing so happily. They are wonderfully normal! All this activity will warm them up on this freezing cold day. The ink in the classrooms is frozen and the children will need to wrap themselves up in their blankets. I'll probably take them on a little walk round the garden to look at the glistening spiders' webs; watch the blackbirds, greenfinches and robins, etc. feeding; look at the footprints of birds and animals in the snow; and study the form and patterns of some of the undisturbed snow. There's plenty to see and to learn at first hand, as well as to enjoy, on a day like this. ...

***

The following day, before they left for Haselmere, Caroline rushed up to Malcolm, bursting with excitement.

'Darling, sorry to interrupt you, but I want you to come and feel my tummy.'

'Your what?'

'My tummy.'

Malcolm had been absorbed, as usual, in the morning newspaper, but Caroline's invitation was imperative, and he moved with alacrity from his comfortable armchair.

Caroline was now looking decidedly pregnant, with a well-rounded bulge which was not normally very evident under her maternity dress. But now she raised her garment, bared her tummy, and indicated where Malcolm should place his hand.

'Can you feel our baby?' she cried excitedly. 'No, not there! Here! He's kicking away impatiently. Isn't it marvellous?'

After a few moments of highly-focused concentration, while Caroline studied his face anxiously for an appropriate reaction, Malcolm was ready to respond.

'Yes to both questions, my love,' he answered while allowing his hand to be guided by Caroline to the crucial centre of activity that he had missed. 'It's wonderful. He or she is a bundle of energy! How long will it be now? The baby and I are keen to make each other's acquaintance!'

Caroline laughed. 'Not keener than I am. It's difficult to be precise about the date. I know that I was pregnant in June so my best guess would be March. By the way, dear, you know that I gave in my notice some time ago, and I'll be leaving the School later this month. Well, Mary has very kindly offered to hold a little farewell party for me at her house in Streatham. It'll begin at about 7.30, which will give her time to get everything ready after getting home from school.'

'A party? Not like the last one I hope!'

'Of course not. How could you say that?'

'Well, as a result of that experience, I've been put off parties for the time being.' He grinned.

'Idiot! Just be serious for a moment and I'll tell you what we have in mind.

It will be on 8 December ...'

'And who's coming?'

'All the teachers and their spouses will be invited, of course, and Rupert Pritchard. ...'

'But he's my sworn enemy. Must he be invited?'

'Yes, because he is our Head Teacher, whatever we think of him, and also I'd rather like to show him what a real party is like.'

'Fair enough.'

'There will also be Mrs Mears, Dr Hargreaves and Jenny. No-one else. It will be small and cosy, and we'll have a nice chat and plenty to eat and drink.'

'O.K. I expect I'll come.'

Caroline attempted to box his ears but her move was anticipated, and Malcolm skirted clear of the danger zone.

***

Arriving at School, they both found memos in their pigeon holes, which read as follows:

MEMO NO. 2

From: Mr Rupert Pritchard, Head Teacher

To: All Staff at Haselmere Open-Air School for Delicate Children

2 December 1954

During the present spell of bad weather, our pupils face certain dangers. Remembering that they are all classified as delicate, we should do everything we can to protect them. In particular, they should be discouraged from making and using slides or indulging in snowball fights, etc. I would like all teachers to ensure that such activities do not take place.

Signed... Rupert Pritchard, Headmaster

'And what do you think about the latest epistle from on high?' Mary enquired of Malcolm.

'Well, not much, actually. He's a spoil sport. Watching the children play in the snow yesterday was great. They had so much fun. They were wonderfully happy – really delighted. They love the snow, and they'll always remember cavorting in it, having snowball fights, and especially speeding along the slide. Even those suffering from asthma and various bronchial conditions, were having a go and enjoying themselves just as much as the others. It was really good to see them having so much fun. After all, it doesn't snow very often here, and when it does, I'm very glad that they make the most of it and have such a lovely time.'

'Well now, that must all be stopped.'

'Must it?'

'Of course. You've read the latest memo. '

'Yes I have, but I don't want to interfere with the children's play.'

'And nor do I. What do you think, Tom?'

'I think that the children will stop playing in the snow when it thaws – not before. As Malcolm says, they've been having a wonderful time. I wouldn't dream of stopping them. One of us will always be there when they are at play to see that no-one does anything too silly.'

'I think,' put in Catherine, 'that Pritchard should speak to all the children at Assembly about it if he wants to discourage play in the snow. But how many assemblies has he conducted so far. Two?'

'Yes, two,' said Malcolm, 'but how should we respond to this memo Tom?'

'I suggest we ignore it,' Tom replied. 'We are experienced teachers and we'll keep our eyes open, as we usually do. Any form of play in the snow that we think is reasonable, is fine. If Pritchard wants to challenge me about it, that will be fine, too. I'll tell him that he's gone about it the wrong way, that he should always discuss such matters first with his experienced teachers!'

The others happily agreed.

Fortunately, this new defiance by the teachers did not lead to any angry confrontations or threats because forty eight hours later Haselmere was looking rather different, and there was something else to distract attentions.

Chapter 8
4 December 1954

Two days after it arrived, the icy blasts from Russia, had moved away and been replaced by a trough of low pressure from the Atlantic. Overnight, the sky turned uniformly grey and during the morning there was a steady drizzle which, to the sad disappointment of the children, soon washed away the snow, the slide, the sparkling spiders' webs and all traces of the Arctic weather that had brought such joy to them.

It was much darker during the afternoon. The innocuous grey stratus cloud of the morning gave way to clouds of a deeper and darker complexion. The classrooms became gloomy, lights were switched on, and the drizzle expanded into a heavy downpour, rain bouncing up on the paths to a height of five or six inches, while the wind howled, and began to blow the rain sideways into the classrooms.

The teachers were well versed in the correct procedures to follow. Coping with the vicissitudes of the English weather in an open-air classroom was, for them, a normal aspect of life. Malcolm settled his pupils quickly with a series of English exercises of various levels of difficulty to match their wide range of attainment and ability levels. He then lowered canvas curtains on the three open sides of the classroom and tied them securely in position. Noise from the heavy plops of rain pounding the roof, the fierce gusts of wind, the billowing curtains and the rain splashing outside the classroom on the pathways, was potentially a major distraction for the children. But most of them had experienced something similar before, and they had tasks which required all their concentration – though their capacity for absorption never ceased to amaze Malcolm. Almost without exception, they were bent over their work, scribbling away, apparently oblivious of the noisy concatenation of sounds only a few feet away. Now and then, when there was a rising crescendo, a few looked up momentarily. Then, as if having reassured themselves that nothing dramatic had occurred, they re-focused on the work in front of them.

Then, in a moment, all was silent. The downpour had ended, the frenetic battering by wind and rain cut off so suddenly that children previously wrapped up in their work, now looked up in wonder, and glanced round uneasily. The sun struggled with some success to creep outside some still-scudding clouds, and lights were turned off. The timing was fortunate, for it was now break time, and once Malcolm had satisfied himself that, following the *cloudburst*, everything outside was reasonably normal, he signalled to his pupils, much to their enormous relief, that playtime had indeed arrived.

***

Before the end of the afternoon break, another memo. was delivered in pigeon holes.

MEMO. NO. 3.

From: Mr Rupert Pritchard, Headmaster

To: All Staff at Haselmere Open-Air School for Delicate Children

4 December 1954

I have been examining the records concerning non-consumable stock. I notice that an extraordinary number of round-ended scissors for the use of children have been purchased and issued over recent years. I do not understand the reason for that. Each pair of scissors should have a life of at least five years, so such regular replacement should not be necessary.

I would be glad if you would each count your existing stock of such scissors, and let me know the number as soon as possible, so that I can compare that with what the records show about issues to each class.

Needless to say, I see it as essential that every teacher checks these, and other non-consumable items on a regular basis.

Signed... Rupert Pritchard, Headmaster.

The teachers discussed the memo at the end of the School day.

'Here we go again!' Mary groaned. 'It's only two days since the last one. He's been here for three months now and still we await our first Staff Meeting. Instead, his contribution to the life and activity of the School is still largely confined to these silly memos. That man's a damn bureaucrat, not a real head teacher!'

'Hold on,' Tom put in. 'I agree with you, of course, about the absurdity of sending memos. But Pritchard is quite entitled to ask questions about our use of stock so that he can continue to ensure that we are regularly supplied with it. And we are, aren't we? He's a pain in the neck in all sorts of ways, but he doesn't do too badly about that and other routine admin. matters.'

'I suppose not,' Mary reluctantly agreed. 'So is this a memo that we should take seriously and implement?'

'Yes. Why not? It won't take a few minutes to count your stock of scissors. I suggest we all do it as soon as we can. Our policy is, let us remember, to co-operate whenever it is reasonable to do so, but to oppose all *His Lordship's* requirements that we think are ill-thought out or just plain daft.'

'OK.' Malcolm grinned, 'so long as we don't afterwards get memos about rulers, compasses, inkwells, and all the other non-consumable stock. Otherwise I shall revolt! Life gets very busy towards the end of the Christmas Term.'

'It's already busy enough,' Caroline pointed out. 'I agree that we must carry out Pritchard's request, but it's an untimely imposition. That wretched man always ignores essential issues and concentrates on trivia!'

It was certainly not the most appropriate time to foist an extra task on the teachers. Caroline was busy with her Nativity Play, Mary's class was involved with the production of 'Cinderella,' Malcolm's recorder group, with children from several classes, was working on some pieces by Bach, Handel and Telemann which would complement the singing of carols at a School concert, and Tom's older children were practising for some kind of variety show.

Back in his classroom, Malcolm located his box of scissors and counted them, hoping that they were all there. There were sixteen pairs, which he believed was the same number that he had counted when he arrived at the School about a year earlier. He couldn't afford to blot his copybook in any way with Pritchard, who had the power to make or break his probationary period over trivialities, as illustrated by his threat over time-keeping. He checked with his stock book. All seemed well. He prepared a note for Rupert Pritchard and had it delivered before ten o'clock the next day. The other teachers did likewise.

***

Billy Green, like his pals, did his level best to avoid Rupert Pritchard. To him, the man meant trouble. Keeping out of Pritchard's way was not normally particularly difficult since he did not move around the School anywhere near as frequently as his predecessor William Rogers, or Tom Bates when he was Acting Head.

It was an unwelcome surprise to him, therefore, when he received a message that he should go to the Head Teacher's room.

'What? Me? He looked questionably at the monitor who had brought the message.

'Yes, it's you he wants,' he was told. 'He told me he wanted to speak to Billy Green.'

'What for?'

'Search me.'

Billy made his way with extreme reluctance to Pritchard's room, his emotions a mix of apprehension and defiance. Once outside the door, he stood wondering nervously what he should do next – wait outside or just walk in. He had never been put in this position before; no-one had ever told him the right procedure or what constituted good manners. Mustering his courage, he decided to walk boldly in.

Pritchard glowered at him as he approached. Billy was shocked to see how angry he looked.

'Don't you know that you should knock and wait outside my door?' he growled. 'Haven't you been taught anything?'

'Sorry sir.' Billy felt that he had committed a terrible sin, and his nerve collapsed. He reddened and felt his heart pumping. He hoped this ordeal would soon be over.

'Now, Green, I'd like to ask you a few questions.'

'Yessir. I'll do my best, sir.'

'You don't speak very well, do you Green. Aren't you being taught to speak properly?'

'Yessir. Mr Brown helps us a lot. I've learnt a lot with 'im, sir.

'It doesn't sound like it.'

Billy was crushed. 'No sir, but I try. I can write better'n I speak, sir. I speak like me Mum and Dad. But I fink I'm getting better.'

'Think, boy, not fink. When you speak to me, speak properly.'

'Yessir. Sorry, sir. I'll try.'

'So you think you are learning with Mr Brown?'

'Yessir. Definitely, sir.'

'But he hasn't taught you to speak properly, has he? Does he correct you, as I did just now, when you make a mistake?'

Though loyal to his teacher, Billy had to be honest.

'Well, sir, not always.'

'And don't you think he should?'

'I don't know, sir. I know I make a lot of mistakes. If Mr Brown corrected me every time, sir', – a brief, embarrassed laugh escaped his lips –'well, sir, the other kids wouldn't get much attention, would they? But I fink I'm getting better all the time, sir. Mr Brown's a very good teacher. We all like 'im.'

Rupert Pritchard decided to terminate the interview. He clearly wasn't going to get the response he was looking for with Billy Green. There would be other opportunities. What he wanted was something with which to challenge Malcolm the next time that young teacher failed to accord him the respect and deference that his position required.

Chapter 9
5 December 1954

In addition to their normal meeting during the daily breaks, the teachers at Haselmere now met regularly, immediately after school, or as soon as Pritchard had departed. The primary purpose was to exchange accounts of any worrying experiences they may have had with their Head Teacher, or to discuss their joint response to his latest action. Increasingly, however, they now began their meetings by chatting about something more relaxing – often the national or international news. Malcolm was an especially voracious reader of newspapers. Today, he had an interesting announcement to make, which he knew would be welcomed by his colleagues.

'Have you heard that later this month the BBC is going to broadcast for the first time *Under Milk Wood* by Dylan Thomas? It'll be read by another Welshman – Richard Burton. Should be great.'

'Sounds good,' Mary responded, 'Richard Burton is one of my heart throbs and I love his voice. I won't miss that. By the way, I've got some arts news, too. I've been reading about three books that have just been published. It's said that they're all going to make a great impact.'

'What are they?' Caroline asked.

'Well, there's William Golding's *Lord of the Flies*. That's about the reversion to primitive barbarism of a group of boys marooned on an island. It sounds like pretty strong stuff, but should be very thought-provoking. Then there's Ernest Hemingway's *Old Man of the Sea* which, some people think, might win him this year's Nobel prize for literature....'

'But you mentioned *three* books,' Malcolm broke in.'

'Oh, yes. The other one is Kingsley Amis's novel *Lucky Jim*. All three should be a very good read.'

'I've read the reviews of Amis's novel, Tom said, 'and they're pretty good. It's one I'm planning to read. Now, let me lower the tone a little. Have you heard about *Liberace,* Malcolm?'

'No. Who's he?'

'He's an American pianist who plays mainly classical music.'

'So you're not lowering the tone, after all?'

'Well, perhaps I am. Liberace is also a flamboyant showman who dresses up in colourful costumes – lots of glitter, that sort of thing. The other day one of his performances was highly criticised for that reason, and he was asked how he reacted to the criticism.'

'And what did he say?'

'He said, "Well, what they said hurt me very much. I cried all the way to the bank!" '

***

The following afternoon, Mary Prince received a note from Rupert Pritchard. He would be glad if she would see him in his room at 3.15 p.m. when the children had they afternoon tea.

Mary was slightly irritated because a mid-afternoon break was precious. By 3.15 p.m. she normally welcomed a short respite from the hurly-burly of teaching, and the chance to have a relaxed chat with her fellow teachers. A confrontation with Pritchard was unlikely to be relaxing! However, she was outside his door at the appointed time, knocked, and was invited to enter. As she opened the door, it occurred to her that this would be her first face- to-face meeting with Pritchard since his arrival in September. He had never once spoken a friendly word to her. What on earth was on his mind now?

Pritchard was behind his desk, and there was an empty chair facing him. She noticed that there were two armchairs in the room. Evidently they were not regarded as appropriate for what was about to take place. They were for friendly *tête-à-têtes.* This was going to be something else! Mary rapidly evaluated the set-up.

This arrangement is quite outmoded and undemocratic. It's hardly the way one colleague speaks to another! My 'superior' is sitting in his smart, upholstered armchair while the interviewee – me – is to sit on a plain, hard, wooden chair, facing him. So that's the way it's to be! A formal interview. He wants me on the ropes! We'll see about that!

'Thank you for coming,' Mrs Price,' Pritchard purred. 'No doubt this is a very busy time for you.'

'Yes, it certainly is,' Mary replied. She was determined not to be cowed, and to speak her mind.

'Well, now, first of all I would like to know how many children you have in your class?'

'Twenty two.' She wondered why he didn't know that already. Perhaps he did, and this was simply part of his 'warm up.'

'I see. Quite a small class. Now, you can probably guess why I have asked you to see me.'

'I really have no idea.'

'Well, Mrs Prince, I received your note this morning regarding the number of round- headed scissors you hold. The figure that you have given me is seventeen but the records show that you should have nineteen. Are you able to account for the discrepancy? Two pairs of scissors seem to have disappeared.' Mary blushed.

Is he implying that I have <u>stolen</u> two pairs of scissors? If he is, then he has a damn cheek. I'll have to tell him the facts of life about being a teacher and handling stock such as scissors.

'Mr Pritchard, she began, allowing a trace of irritation to colour her tone. 'I have worked in this School for the last five years, and recollect that for most of that time I have held seventeen pairs of scissors. I do not personally check them every day. There is no time to do so. They are always, however, counted by one of the children when they are given out and when they are collected. If the numbers do not tally, I always ask the children to search for the missing ones, which are usually found to have fallen on the floor. At other times I allow individual children to help themselves when they need to use them in their craft work or for some project. I think it is important to trust them sometimes.'

Rupert Pritchard had listened with an air of serious and concentrated attention. Then his little smile, twisted and insincere, appeared.

'Thank you, Mrs Price, for your explanation. The problem is, however, that we must account for those two missing scissors.'

'Must we, Mr Pritchard? I don't know how far back you have examined the records, but it seems to me not unreasonable if, over several years, a couple of pairs of scissors are written off.'

'Written off, Mrs Prince? I don't propose to "write off" anything. My responsibility is to <u>account</u> for stock, not write it off.'

'That's quite unrealistic, Mr Pritchard, as you must know, as I believe you have had some teaching experience.' Pritchard's face began to redden, as Mary continued.

'In time, well-used school scissors become blunt. They are never sharpened. So after a while they are not fit for their purpose. And we are working in the open air, so scissors will gradually become rusty. Again, scissors may separate into their two parts and therefore become useless.'

She gave Pritchard a rather defiant look which well expressed the thoughts racing through her mind:

Well, that's enough points to be going on with. They're all simple, straightforward and obvious ones that I shouldn't have had to explain to you. Every teacher is aware of them so why aren't you?

Pritchard coloured.

' Mrs Prince, your points admittedly have some validity, but, you know, scissors in schools have a habit of disappearing' – his mouth widened into a toothy, humourless grin that Mary found quite repellent – 'and Head Teachers who wish to run their schools efficiently must account for them.'

'And I think you are making a fuss about very little, Mr Pritchard. You are making a mountain out of a molehill.' It was Mary's turn to redden. She took a deep breath, her heart thumping. She'd had enough, her constraint was evaporating, and she was ready for an explosive outburst. It soon came...

'And what on earth do you mean by telling me that scissors have a habit of disappearing? Do you actually imagine for a moment that I want to steal a pair of school scissors?' Her breath was now coming in deep gulps; she was thoroughly upset.

'I am the Head Teacher here, Mrs Prince, and you will speak to me with due respect. I will decide how matters should be dealt with,' he shouted. 'In future, all broken or otherwise useless scissors should be returned to me so that I can adjust my records accordingly. In the meantime, you will endeavour to trace the two missing scissors.'

'I will do no such thing. You must learn to trust your teachers. If you want my co-operation about anything, Mr Pritchard, you will have to change your tone – which I find offensive – and make a greater effort to discuss all issues with me in a reasonable, sensible and democratic manner. And as for respect, that must be earned – always. It doesn't automatically come with your position. That's all I have to say to you!'

Mary stormed out of his room, red in the face, close to tears, with her heart pumping, and with her mind crowded with indignation.

It was obvious as I entered his room that he had planned to interview me formally, treating me like a probationary teacher applying for her first post. He was fully prepared to dominate, with his own bullying style, coupled with sarcasm and innuendo. And it was all about two pairs of round headed scissors! Incredible. I just had to stand up for myself, and now I feel like crying. It's time for the last lesson of the day with my class, but I must talk to Tom as soon as possible after School.

***

All four teachers came together as usual in Tom's room, but Mary addressed Tom in particular. She explained what had taken place.

'What upset me particularly was the way he treated me, sitting me on a hard chair while he sat on a comfortable one behind his desk, and then formally questioning me – interrogating me – about two pairs of scissors which he alleged were missing. Of course I was also amazed that he was making so much out of something so trivial. A mountain out of a molehill. When he ought to be concerning himself with issues of key importance such as the health and welfare of our children, the curriculum, and so on, he focuses on two pairs of scissors that may well have disappeared years ago, when they were very old and broken, and were then disposed of. What's wrong with the man? How on earth did he ever become a Head Teacher. I doubt that he has ever been even a competent *class teacher*. He is far too cold and remote. And his whole attitude to me was unacceptably disrespectful. He talked about scissors in schools having a habit of disappearing which seemed to me a snide suggestion that I might have stolen them! I will not be spoken to like that Tom. I'm afraid I told him a few home truths, but only made myself very upset by doing so.'

'I'm sorry that you have had to put up with all that unpleasantness, Mary. You ask how Pritchard came to be selected as our Head Teacher. Well, I often ask myself the same question. I know the normal procedure of course. He was chosen by the Governing Body of twelve fairly elderly Councillors. Two thirds of them represent the Party which has a local majority on the Council, and the other one third represent the minority Party. I've met most of them. Although two or three are quite bright and knowledgeable about education, there is certainly some dead wood there. The majority seem to have favoured Pritchard above the other candidates, so one certainly wonders what *they* were like. Of course, Pritchard can talk quite fluently and he was probably able to answer the questions put to him with a certain amount of assurance.'

'But Tom, wouldn't Ronald Parham have been present to make various educational points and to sort of steer the Committee along so that the right decision might be made at the end?'

'Well, up to a point, Mary, but it's not quite as simple as that. Parham was certainly present, and he's pretty shrewd, but

I don't suppose he played a very active part. His role would have been to answer any educational questions that the Governors might have wanted to put – not to interfere unduly with the democratic process. Yes, he probably put a question or two to each candidate, but he would have left most of the deliberations to the Governors and the guidance of the Committee to the Chairman. That's the system. But Mary, I do sympathize with you. I, too, have had to endure Pritchard's diatribes- and Malcolm, too, of course.'

'I know, Tom, and I mustn't make too much fuss, but I wanted to get all that off my chest.'

'I'm very glad you did! And you say you told Pritchard a few home truths. Splendid! You gave as good as you got. Well done. And now.' (he turned towards the other teachers) 'I have a proposal to make to you all.'

All eyes were now on Tom. They knew that he wanted to give them every support.

'Pritchard accused me of undermining his authority, at a time when nothing further was on my mind. I was prepared to be loyal and to work with him to the best of my ability. But after both Malcolm and I had had our brushes with him, we agreed that I should become what I'd been accused of – a *de facto* Head Teacher – and take the lead in developing strategies aimed at keeping the School functioning well in spite of him However, things now seem to be going from bad to worse. It appears that we are never going to have a Staff Meeting, there is increasing evidence of his incompetence as a Head Teacher and now we have a further example of his unprofessional behaviour. Three of us have now been at the receiving end of his unpleasant strictures– and he hasn't yet been here for a complete term! We must think about further action.'

'But you've made a start,' Malcolm observed with a grin, 'and I'm glad you have. You are our *de facto* leader. With you we can have the Staff Meetings on professional matters that Pritchard won't arrange. What else do you propose?'

'Well, I'm now inclined to undermine Pritchard's authority a little more,' Tom replied with a smile. 'I don't think this sort of meeting, just after school, while better than nothing, quite fills the bill. It's a bit furtive and it's necessarily far too short. I think we should meet regularly *outside* the School for future discussions both on professional matters – as Malcolm reminds us we mustn't forget those – and on future objectives and strategy in relation to Pritchard.'

'Fine,' Mary said, 'provided I can make the necessary domestic arrangements. But where would we meet?'

'I suggest we meet at my house,' Tom replied. 'Like yours, Mary, it's not far from the School. What do you think?'

There was a very positive chorus of approval of the idea.

'Good.' Tom consulted his diary. 'And I'll have some refreshments ready of course. How about 6 p.m. on 10 December ?'

The date and time were agreed and Mary felt much happier than she had a short time ago.

I'm sure I can manage to arrange for my boys to be looked after. So much has happened this term that needs to be fully discussed, and we've just got to work out how we're going to cope with Pritchard. Somehow we must try to keep up standards in the school in spite of him! What a state of affairs! It's funny that he was suspicious at the beginning that we were plotting his downfall – and now I'm more than ready to do just that!

Chapter 10
7 December [h] 1954

'How is your Recorder Group getting on, Malcolm?' Mary asked, during the mid-morning break.

'You mean, in regard to the Christmas programme?'

'Yes.'

'Well, we're practising every lunchtime and as we have pupils from three classes, it's pretty hard going. But we're getting there. My children are playing descant recorders and the older children have the tenor and treble ones that need their longer fingers. I've arranged some pieces by Bach and Handel – mostly gavottes and minuets – so we're playing harmony, by courtesy of J. S. Bach, Handel and M. Brown – sorry for that! – (he grinned) and all the children are reading the music, which is great. Oh yes – and two of the best players are going to play a descant that I've written for them.'

'Well done, Malcolm! Baroque counterpoint sounds really good with recorders. And your players are all volunteers?'

'Of course. And aren't you organising a pantomime? That's some project!'

'That's true. Maybe I've bitten off more than I can chew, but the children are having a wonderful time. We, too, are rehearsing whenever we can, including lunchtimes, and almost everyone in the class is involved.'

'How have you managed that? Surely they can't all act?'

'Of course not, but we need stage managers, scene painters, some children to arrange for sound effects, others in charge of costumes, and so on.'

'That's good. The children in this School have often had to miss out because of their various medical conditions, so it's wonderful when we can get them all involved, including those without any special talents.'

'I absolutely agree with that.... By the way, Malcolm, it's already 7 December so we have hardly any time left for rehearsals. We've all got to pull our socks up – especially me!'

'Too true.'

***

In fact, all the various Christmas preparations were now reaching their climax. Tom had taken charge of the school's programme during the week of entertainments, co-ordinating performances so that they took place on different days and dovetailed in with other activities. He had also arranged for the production of programmes and invitations, the latter being sent to the other teachers, parents, Rupert Pritchard, and members of the non-teaching staff.

Tom had suggested to Rupert Pritchard that the Governors might be invited, too, but had been informed that they would come 'only if the standard of performance is high enough, and I will decide that.'

Pritchard made one appearance at the rehearsal of each teacher, listening with an unsmiling face, and saying little or nothing to staff or children – not a single word of encouragement. He then decided that only the music concert matched the exalted standard that he had set. So members of the Governing Body received only one invitation: to attend Malcolm's recorder concert, given in association with carol singing conducted by the peripatetic music teacher, Philip Thomas.

In fact, the music concert was the only performance that would be attended by Pritchard himself. That news dismayed the teachers. They knew that although he was by no means popular with the children, many of them would be disappointed when they learned that their Head Teacher would not see them in action in the other performances. And having put in so much hard work they would have appreciated some words of commendation and a pat on the back: but encouragement and motivation had no place in the managerial repertoire of Rupert Pritchard.

***

8 Dec

Malcolm was so completely absorbed in his music concert preparations that he needed to have his memory jogged that another important event would be taking place that evening.

'It's your music concert this morning, Malcolm, isn't it?' Caroline remarked during their breakfast. She knew the answer of course.

'It certainly is.'

'Have you managed to get the Recorder Group up to scratch?'

'Well, I hope so. They've all worked pretty hard.'

'So have you.'

'I know, but I've enjoyed watching them improve almost every day, and I really think they've learned a lot about music. I also believe they've learned to appreciate some of the great composers, like Bach and Handel.'

'I'm sure they have. They're all reading music now, aren't they?'

'Yes, though they're having to cope with only two different keys. Previously they had no knowledge whatever of staff notation, and some of them are now quite fluent readers. That's what's particularly satisfying.'

'That's marvellous.'

'I've only got one worry.'

'What's that?'

'Well, there are a couple of key players who are sometimes *hors de combat*. We have plenty of descant players and if one or two of those are sick we'd hardly notice, but there are only four players of the larger instruments – trebles and tenors – and if even one of those doesn't turn up, we're sunk!'

'I shouldn't worry. They're all so keen that they'll be determined to be there even is they are a bit out of sorts.'

'No, Caroline. If they're sick, they won't be able to take part, especially the tenor player in Mary's class who has frequent asthma attacks.'

'Well, let's keep our fingers crossed.... Now, there's something else'

'What's that?'

This evening there's my party at Mary's.' Malcolm gulped and reddened.

'Oh, I am sorry Caroline. I'm afraid that hasn't been at the forefront of my mind lately. And it's your farewell party. I really am a shocker!'

'I know,' Caroline smiled. But don't worry; I quite understand. I just want you to bear it in mind. And don't forget to take along a bottle of Cabernet Sauvignon.'

'Right. But Pritchard's going to be there, isn't he? That might put a damper on it.'

'He said he would, but it's up to all of us to make sure the party goes with a swing, whether or not he comes. Let's all do everything we can to make it a great success.'

'I certainly will. Coming after the strains and stresses of the concert, it will be a time to relax – to let my hair down! And they'll be enough of us to keep His Lordship in place.'

***

Rupert Pritchard arrived in the School Hall a few minutes before the music concert was due to begin, chatting deferentially to Mr Bartlett, chairman of the Governing Body. The other governors followed behind in a stately, if somewhat straggly procession. Malcolm watched a little impatiently what he saw as *their painfully slow progress* along the aisle. He was more than ready to begin with the rousing overture – as *allegro* as possible! – that headed the programme.

So these are the governors who preside over our School. I hardly know them, though I recognise one or two who've occasionally visited my class. Today, dressed in their Sunday best, they look very smart. We're honoured! But as the children see the governors moving along, conversations are hushed. The noise level is dropping dramatically, and we must all stand to show our due respect until all the governors have completed their carefully measured journey down the aisle and are comfortably seated ... And now, they are both seated and settled. Hooray! Time to start! The children are all looking directly at me as I raise my baton ...

***

As the concert came to an end, there was a burst of unexpectedly loud and enthusiastic applause. Malcolm's surprise was coupled with both relief and pride. The children had done well and risen to the occasion. He was proud of them. Happily, they had all turned up, too. Caroline was right. Nothing could have kept them away!

But at the first opportunity Malcolm approached Mary. He needed her assurance that the audience had not just been polite; that the standard reached was really as high as it had seemed to him.

'Mary, did you enjoy it? Do you really think it went pretty well?'

'More or less, Malcolm. But I couldn't help noticing that one of your players kept playing an F sharp instead of an F natural.'

'Oh, is that right? I didn't notice that. I hope no-one else did.'

'Blockhead! Of course they didn't. I was only pulling your leg. I'm just not capable of focusing on just one player who's a semitone out! You don't think I've got perfect pitch, do you? Actually, if you really want my opinion, it was a wonderful concert. Everyone loved it! Many congratulations!'

***

'As they meandered untidily out of the hall, Billy Green and the *Scallywags*, all of whom had taken part in the music concert, exchanged verdicts.

'Well, we was 'onoured, Billy said with a grin. 'Old Pritchy and the governors came just to hear us play. An' wasn't it nice to 'ear all that clapping. It gave me quite a funny feeling inside. A bit of a thrill! I've never been clapped like that before. It felt really good.'

'Yeah. That was great. I liked it too. But I 'ear ' that 'e aint going to see the Nativity Play,' Tim Owen complained, 'an' that's the one thing our School's doin' that's really about Christmas, ain't it? An' I 'ear 'e aint goin' to nuthin' else, either. That don't seem fair on all the others.'

'Who's complainin',' asked Lucy Pym. 'We'll all enjoy the other entertainments and the Nativity Play more 'cause 'e won't be there.'

'You're right there, agreed Billy. But we might see the ol' geezer again before Christmas. 'e might be plannin' in secret to give us all a nice surprise by dressing up as Father Christmas, and give us all a Christmas present.'

'Some 'ope', observed Lucy, and they all exploded with laughter.

***

Tom Bates was on his way to enjoy a cup of tea with his colleagues during the afternoon break when he was handed a note from Rupert Pritchard requesting his immediate presence. He made a brief visit to the other teachers.

'Sorry, I won't be with you. I've been summoned to appear before His Lordship.'

'We're sorry, too,' Mary said. 'You've been up to your eyebrows recently organising Christmas activities and you need a break now and again. You'd think that on the day we've had a wonderful music concert, to be followed this evening by a party, this is not the right time to be summoned before "the presence".' But good luck, Tom. 'Don't let him get you down.'

'Don't worry. I won't!'

But Since Tom's previous *tête-à-tête* with Pritchard had been anything but pleasant, he expected nothing better this time as he strode rapidly up the stairs to the Head Teacher's study. Certainly there would be no cup of tea waiting for him!

He took in the scene as he opened the study door. Clearly the interview was going to be stage-managed a little differently from last time. Perhaps it was going to parallel Mary's experience because instead of two armchairs in close proximity there was the formal set-up that had awaited her: Pritchard seated in his comfortable leather chair behind his desk and a hard, unwelcoming wooden chair on the other side, for the School's senior teacher.

This blithering idiot makes his intentions so blatantly obvious. Not that our seating arrangements will make the slightest difference. I'm quite ready to be interviewed in a rigidly formal manner about anything at all. He'll set out to belittle and degrade me, but as I have very little respect for him now, I'll give as good as I get. I have nothing to lose. I'm the most experienced teacher in the School, including him, and I could give this self-important little ass a few tips about how to run Haselmere, too.

Since the men nursed a mutual dislike, there was no exchange of pleasantries – not even a formal greeting. Pritchard simply waved Tom to a chair and then spent a minute or two pretending to finish attending to some papers.

Tom was unmoved. He considered that the weird character before him was simply exposing his inadequacies, both as a Head Teacher and as a human being – as in fact he had been doing ever since his arrival in September.

Once seated, he looked directly at Pritchard, who avoided meeting his gaze. At first his half-open eyes looked restive and furtive. Then they appeared to focus on the wall behind Tom, and the interview began.

'Mr. Bates, I believe I am a reasonably tolerant man. I have allowed all the teachers in my school a great deal of latitude in regard to their teaching methods, for example, and also in regard to the way they conduct themselves. That tolerance has, of course, been extended to yourself....But Mr Bates, tolerance and patience must have their limits.'

What on earth is all this leading up to? In fact it's the teachers who have been incredibly patient, waiting in vain for a Staff Meeting, for some guidance about the curriculum, for his thoughts about various teaching methods, for some indication about how he sees the future development of the School, etc. He talks such utter rubbish! He lives in a different world from the rest of us.

'You will recall our discussion on October 20th. That was nearly two months ago. I made it abundantly clear to you on that occasion that you were to discontinue holding daily staff meetings. You were undermining my position here and sowing the seeds of distrust and discord. You were making my task here very difficult. I had expected your loyalty and support but you were going behind my back. The situation was intolerable. At first you appeared to be following my instructions, and that was very encouraging. But recently I find that the situation is as bad as it has ever been. Let us be clear, Mr Bates. Those meetings must cease forthwith!'

A red flush had crept over Pritchard's face and he had begun to perspire while his eye movements had become increasingly agitated. Tom had also noted how the Head Teacher was clenching and unclenching his fists.

This man is seriously unbalanced – and very nervous and unsure of himself. He has some sort of psychological problem. He seems aware of only his own narrow, selfish perspective. He lives in his own little capsule! Yet I don't think he is completely ignorant of his limitations, for there are also signs of an inferiority complex. He's a very complicated individual, but also a very dangerous one, because he threatens the quality of life and education of the children in the School. I must try to get some outside and expert advice about all this before much longer. Meanwhile I'll at least try to straighten him out on a few matters!

'Mr Pritchard, I confess that I find it difficult to follow your very odd line of reasoning, but I gather that you object to my enjoying a cup of tea and a chat with my colleagues during my free time. Is that correct?'

Pritchard was shaken. He hadn't expected this. A counter attack! The man was defying him again. Insubordination! He resumed the offensive.

'If your response is to be impertinent, then I shall certainly take the matter further, to the detriment of your career. Let me say it again. Your daily staff meetings are to cease forthwith. As Head of Haselmere I am in authority, and that is my decision. I will not have my authority undermined. I am supported by both the Governing Body and the inspector. If you defy me, you defy them!'

Tom kept his eyes on his adversary, while he collected his thoughts.

'Well, let me tell you a few things, Mr Pritchard.' He inched his chair close to the desk. He was now within striking distance.

'Firstly, your threat to take the matter further does not concern me in the slightest. You can speak to anyone you choose, and I would welcome the opportunity to discuss with them your very strange ideas in regard to the management of Haselmere. I think it's probably high time that we let some outsiders into Haselmere to see for themselves what is going on – Ronald Parham, for example, is surely due to make one of his routine inspections. I can hardly wait for that. In fact, I may well get in touch with him, and ask him to bring forward his next visit. I have much to discuss with him!

Secondly – and I'm finding it difficult to get you to understand this – if I want to relax with my colleagues and enjoy their company during the breaks, I most certainly will do so. It is my own free time and I can spend it how I choose! It is nothing to do with you, so stop bringing it up!

Thirdly, I am the one who has exercised patience, tolerance and restraint since your arrival here. I began by giving you the normal support and co-operation that I have always given to whoever is running the school. I would have given you much more had you given even a small measure of support and encouragement to any member of the staff. In fact, you have not even had a single constructive and helpful discussion with your bright young probationer, Malcolm

Brown. You have virtually ignored him, with the exception of that disgraceful scene in the playground. And that, Mr Pritchard is a particularly serious lapse of your duties. It is your responsibility to give a probationary teacher every encouragement, assistance and support, not just to sit in judgement. And you have done absolutely nothing! A very serious lapse indeed. Of course there have been many other lapses, but there is no time to discuss them all now. The fact is, Mr Pritchard, you are not running the school properly at all, are you? You haven't even had a single Staff Meeting. That alone is quite disgraceful. Also there's been no guidance on any aspect of the curriculum, or anything else for that matter.' He paused ...

'How dare you speak to me like that. I am entitled to respect ...'

'No. Respect has to be earned.'

'I have the authority in this School, and I order you to discontinue those daily meetings.'

Tom smiled grimly.

'And I will continue to relax during break times with my colleagues. And if your harassment of staff and general mismanagement continue, I may contact the National Union of Teachers. In that case, you will hear from their lawyers. We've all had more than enough of you!'

With that, Tom rose abruptly, whirled round and strode out of the room before Pritchard could frame a reply.

Well, it was high time he was told a few home truths. Let him come back to me at any time I'll be ready for him!

Chapter 11

8 December . Evening

In spite of his enthusiasm for a farewell party for Caroline, the thought of it left Tom feeling very uncomfortable. Two of the invitees simply couldn't stand each other: himself and Rupert Pritchard. How could they possibly socialize at a party? He had hoped that Pritchard, following their recent bruising encounter, would find some excuse not to attend, but learned to his dismay that that was not the case. His arch enemy would be there, and the party was not an event that Tom would think of missing, Pritchard or no Pritchard.

But I mustn't dwell too much on my differences with that man. He has also upset both Malcolm and Mary so they probably feel just as uncomfortable as I do about mixing socially with him. Unless there is some miraculous change in Pritchard's behaviour towards us, I'm afraid we'll all try to avoid him as much as possible. Some party!

Tom was certainly not alone in his concern. Mary, who had just prepared a buffet supper, confided to Len, her husband, that in view of her recent unpleasant confrontation with Pritchard, she was worried that the atmosphere at the party might not be as relaxed as she had hoped! He was not at all sympathetic.

'Well, you didn't have to invite him, did you? I mean, if he is such an ogre – and I've no doubt he is – then surely you could have omitted him from your guest list. The rest of you get on like a house on fire and would surely have a much better time without him.'

'Yes, we would. But he is the Head Teacher of our school and it wouldn't seem right to leave him out. He has certainly behaved abominably towards some of us, and created a lot of bitterness, and I confess that I dislike almost everything about the man. But surely we should make some effort towards normalising our relationship with him whenever we can, don't you think?

'I suppose so. My hope, though, is that he doesn't stay too long!'

'Yes. That's my hope too. Now Len, being a dab hand at it, you're in charge of drinks.'

'Good. That's the kind of responsibility I like!'

'Give Pritchard a really generous glass, or two or three, of whatever he wants, and we may see him metamorphose into a mellower individual, perhaps even a human being!'

'Right. I'll do my best!' They hugged and laughed.

***

At around 7.30 p.m. the guests began to arrive and all except Pritchard were soon present. The party was soon in full swing, with plenty of laughter and animated conversation.

The doorbell sounded at 7.45 p.m.. In spite of the noise level, several partygoers heard it. There was a hush in conversation, coupled with a distinct tailing off in the general level of hilarity. Looks were exchanged. No-one had any doubt about who was on the doorstep. Len left the room quickly and strode into the hall. He had decided to be first to greet the Head Teacher about whom he had heard so much negative comment.

As the host, it's my job to be friendly to everyone. This guest seems to be universally unpopular but I don't know him personally. I'm neutral, so I'll make a very special effort to show him oodles of goodwill and warmth! Here we go!

He opened the front door, gave Rupert Pritchard a wide, friendly smile and welcomed him with a warm handshake. As the two of them entered the sitting room, several guests nearby, following Len's lead, also gave Pritchard a broad smile as he was guided to a chair and provided with a large glass of red wine.

Mary felt relieved. Pritchard had arrived without incident, and the party soon resumed something like its earlier atmosphere. So far so good!

At his side, Len continued to engage Pritchard in conversation. He said afterwards that it was hard going. Whatever topic he raised was met only with brief or even monosyllabic responses, so it was difficult to get to know the man. He was therefore relieved when Pritchard told him that he would like to say a few words. Len responded immediately by tapping his wine glass with a spoon handle. The loud, musical ring had an immediate effect: laughter and conversation faded, and all eyes turned towards Rupert Pritchard. He rose rather slowly and cleared his throat as he prepared to speak. Mary watched him anxiously.

For crying out loud! He's still in 'Head Teacher mode.' He doesn't seem to know how to party! Evidently Len hasn't yet had time to soften him up. I fear we're going to hear something as stilted as his address to us on his arrival at Haselmere in September.'

'Ladies and Gentlemen,' he began, 'this is both a happy and a sad occasion. It is a happy one because we are enjoying the kind and excellent hospitality of Mr and Mrs Prince and also because Mrs Brown is going to start a family and that is, naturally, an occasion for rejoicing. On the other hand, this is a sad occasion because Haselmere is going to lose Mrs Brown, a dedicated and gifted teacher, who has contributed much to the life and work of the School. Ladies and gentlemen, let us all toast Mrs Brown and convey our best wishes to her for the future.'

A warm response to Pritchard's words floated round the room, in spite of his formal style and delivery, and Mary whispered to Caroline that it was the first time they had heard him sound something like a human being! She wondered whether he might follow it up by moving round and chatting to one or two guests.

But it was not to be. After a word of thanks to Mary and her husband, and a brief beam directed vaguely towards the assembled guests, Pritchard swiftly departed. Almost instantaneously, as if switched on, the party again exploded into life and glasses were refilled. The buffet supper encouraged a further circulation of the visitors.

One of them, not originally on the guest list, was the School Doctor, Alan Hargreaves, who was universally respected and popular. He sat next to Tom, whom he had known for many years. He had no inkling of the situation that had developed in the School

'Good to see you again, Tom. A pity Mr. Pritchard couldn't stay longer!'

Tom swallowed. 'Well, Alan, to be absolutely honest, his departure has my unconditional approval. Frankly, it will be much happier and more relaxed without him.'

Alan gave him a quizzical look and hesitated before replying. 'Tom, we've been friends for a long time now, and I'm about to retire so surely we can be completely open with each other. Has Mr Pritchard settled in well? Is Haselmere just as happy as I've always believed it to be? Are <u>you</u> happy under the new regime?'

'Happy?' Tom's laugh was derisory and bitter. Then, embarrassed, he hastened to apologize.

'Sorry, Alan. I just couldn't help that. Actually I'm not at all happy with things as they are – and nor are my colleagues.'

'I'm very sorry to hear that, Tom. Why? What's happened?' Tom lowered his voice almost to a whisper.

'Well, rather a lot, actually. Mary, Malcolm and I have all had rather unpleasant altercations with Pritchard. In fact, I had a very disturbing session with him today. I think it's fair to say that we can't stand each other!'

'Tom, I had no idea. Although I see him regularly at the medicals, I don't really know him. He just watches and listens while I deal with the children. Though, come to think of it, he's very remote and takes very little interest in individual cases. What's the main problem?'

'Alan, you don't know him; and, amazingly, nor do we! Pritchard is a very queer fish. He is cold and aloof and doesn't mix at all with the teachers. He's an absolute *loner*. There are no Staff Meetings; nor even informal contacts.'

'Good Heavens! What a funny way to run a school.'

'It is, Alan. But he doesn't actually run the School. He's little more than a figurehead. But that's only part of the problem. I think he needs psychological help.'

'Perhaps he does. Tell me more about his behaviour.'

'Well, he focuses on minutiae and comes down like a ton of bricks on anyone who might, for example, have lost a small piece of minor equipment, or who might ring the School bell a minute or two early. He is very suspicious, and when he sees a group of teachers laughing, he imagines that they are laughing at him and perhaps planning to undermine his authority. He's been especially suspicious of me and obviously thought that as I'd been Acting Head I was a threat to his authority.'

'Tom, that's very worrying, and I'm very sorry to hear it.' Hargreaves paused for a few moments. 'But we'd better continue this chat another time because it's time to circulate. I'd certainly like to hear more some other time about your problems.'

'You're right, Alan. We must move around. But can I take you up on your offer? Are you free to come to my place on the tenth? Sorry for the short notice. We're going to have an unofficial Staff Meeting – a discussion about how we're going to cope with Pritchard in future. It'll start at around 6 p.m. They'll be some grub, of course!'

'Yes, I'd like to join you. I may be able to help. And now I really must move around. I'll see you later.'

'Thanks Alan. That's great!'

Tom was soon talking to Mary who referred to his talk with Alan.

'He's about to retire, isn't he? You certainly had a long and earnest conversation with him.'

Tom outlined briefly what had been discussed.

'He asked me how we were finding Pritchard, and I'm afraid I gave him an uninhibited answer! I unburdened my soul! He thinks he may be able to help, and he's coming to our meeting on the tenth.'

'That's fine. I'm sure we'll all be glad to see him again.'

The guests left around 10.30 p.m. and as Mary and Len were washing up the dishes, Len gave his reaction to Haselmere's Head Teacher.

Poor you, and poor everybody at Haselmere. Now I have some idea what you've all had to put up with. That man is an automaton. He has serious personality problems. I could detect no trace of humour or common humanity. Even his little formal speech lacked conviction. You know, I hardly expected him to be the life and soul of the party, but nothing could have prepared me for the reality. He is not fit to be in charge of anyone, let alone a whole school community, including ninety five delicate children! I'm very glad that you're going to be given some medical advice about him! He's a serious psychological case!'

***

10 December

When the children arrived this morning they saw a school that was not entirely unfamiliar but exciting in its glittering beauty. Everything sparkled in the sunlight: every branch on trees and shrubs; the lawns and the flower beds. And there were even more glittering spiders' webs on the bushes than there had been when it had snowed a few weeks earlier. This was one of those beautiful frosty days that accompany a high pressure system and a cold, clear night. To Malcolm, the day presented another great opportunity for environmental exploration; to open the children's eyes to the beauty and marvels of nature.

At the earliest opportunity, he led his children, all well wrapped up, around the School grounds, stopping from time to time to observe, explain and discuss. They pointed out with excitement the blackbirds feeding on bright red pyracantha berries, while others pecked into the ground for insects, and they watched blue tits and greenfinches hungrily attacking seeds on the bird table. They discussed how beaks had different shapes according to the type of food the bird needed.

They studied the patterns in the spiders' webs, gazing at them in wonder, and talked about how the webs were made and what was their purpose. At one time they crossed a lawn to inspect a bird's nest half-hidden in a shrub, and discussed the materials of its construction. They spent about half an hour altogether exploring the grounds and Malcolm felt that it was time well spent. It would lead to further discussion in the classroom, some drawing and creative writing, including the writing of poems.

Both art and written work would be considered for the class magazine, produced at the end of every term. Processing all that creative work would involved Malcolm in a considerable amount of extra work with the Gestetner duplicator, but the magazine was a good motivator, as the children were always delighted to see their work in *print* and copies were provided for parents, teachers and, of course, Rupert Pritchard.

By lunchtime a variety of work had been completed and Malcolm was well pleased with it. But then something happened that caused his pleasure to evaporate quite suddenly; it was replaced by growing indignation, dismay and then anger. The cause of his change of mood was another memo. It was received by all the teachers but Malcolm felt that it was directed towards himself.

MEMO NO.4

From: Mr Rupert Pritchard, Headmaster

To: All Staff at Haselmere Open-Air School for Delicate Children

10 December, 1954

A particularly attractive aspect of this school is its gardens. Our part-time gardeners work hard to keep them beautiful all the year round. Visitors have often commented to me on the richness of colour in the borders and beds and on the immaculate condition of the lawns.

We should all ensure that our pupils, too, enjoy the gardens, but also that they keep strictly to the pathways.

In this connection, I have observed that some teachers escort their classes onto the lawns, no doubt for what they see as legitimate purposes. However, that is not acceptable. In frosty conditions it is harmful to walk on grass, which can easily be damaged.

I would be glad if you would ensure that in future children are taken only along the paths, and are discouraged from setting foot on the lawns.

Signed... Rupert Pritchard, Headmaster.

Like the previous memos, this one had an ostensibly rational basis, but the teachers had had more than enough of being reprimanded by pompously-expressed written communications. Malcolm expressed his anger to Mary at lunchtime.

'He's getting at me! This morning I took my children around the gardens so that they would gain some appreciation of the beauty of a frosty morning and learn a little more about their environment and nature. At one time we *had* to go on to the lawns so that we could examine the frost-covered spiders' webs and the birds' nests. If we often did that it might not be good for the lawns, but we only left the paths briefly for what was, after all, an educational purpose. Why can't that man simply talk to us in a normal way instead of sending these ridiculous memos?'

'Because he's not a normal man, as you well know. Actually, Malcolm, I, too, took my children out just as you did, and for the same purpose, but later in the morning. And I'm afraid we, too, went on the grass! Don't worry about the stupid memo. I won't!'

Tom had approached and heard the last few sentences spoken.

'Mary's right. Don't worry your head too much about it, especially as this evening we'll all have an opportunity at my place to discuss Pritchard's odd behaviour. Get it off our chests. We're going to have a nice, relaxed discussion on future strategy and we'll have with us Alan Hargreaves who wants to hear all about our experiences. I think he may be able to analyse – or should I say, diagnose – Pritchard's mind, and that will be very useful. We'll then have some clearer ideas all ready for 1955.'

'Amen to all that,' said Mary. But surely the crucially important thing is that we have no effective leadership. We're like a well-rehearsed orchestra that has an incompetent conductor thrust upon it. We just carry on doing our job as we know it should be done. But we can't carry on like that indefinitely!'

Malcolm cheered. 'That puts it in a nutshell. Well done!'

'But I think it's even worse than that,' Caroline broke in. 'There are signs that in time Pritchard may prevent you doing your job as well as you can. He's a soulless bureaucrat. You're going to have to operate within a mesh of petty restrictions. They will slow you down, annoy you, and make you less effective as teachers.'

'Hold on dear,' Malcolm protested. 'If you go on like that, you'll frighten us all to death! We're going to make plans tonight so that things don't get as bad as that!'

'I know. I was painting the worst possible scenario. Sorry! Actually, I'm sure that with Alan's help, we'll start to make some progress this evening with the Pritchard problem. And I won't be at School next Term, so I should really keep my mouth shut!'

'No, love; not that. Your warning is timely.'

'And shrewd,' added Mary.

'Sorry everyone.' Malcolm said. 'Our break's come to its end. My class is waiting for me with ill-concealed impatience!'

They all dispersed with a laugh and headed towards their classrooms.

***

Malcolm remained quite upset about the memo and was resolved to see Pritchard about it at the earliest possible moment. He decided to go during the afternoon break when Pritchard was normally in his room.

Shortly after 3.15 p.m. he knocked on his door. His reception replicated that of his colleagues . Pritchard appeared engrossed for a few minutes in studying the papers before him. Meanwhile, his visitor was not invited to sit. Finally, Pritchard looked up enquiringly and with a frown, as if some vitally important work had been interrupted. Malcolm came quickly to the point.

'Mr Pritchard,' he began. 'I'm sorry I must bother you at this busy time, but there is something that I need to discuss with you.'

His opening was met with a look of puzzled wariness.

'Indeed. Well, I hope it won't take too long because I have a number of urgent matters to attend to.'

'No, sir. It shouldn't take more than a minute or two. You have sent out a memo. about pupils walking on the grass.'

'What about it? Isn't it clear?'

'It's perfectly clear, sir, but I'd like to emphasize that on the rare occasions when I have taken my class on to a lawn, it has been for a specific educational purpose. This morning, for example, we had an exceptionally beautiful morning. I wanted to open the children's eyes to a truly fascinating winter scene, with the sun producing a glittering environment, especially on frosty spiders' webs and the birds' nests. I wanted to draw their attention to the various ways in which birds locate different types of food in freezing conditions, and so on. It was all well worth while because it excited and thrilled the children, and stimulated some exceptionally good creative writing in the form of both prose and poetry. You may like to see some of the children's work.'

'All very worthy, Mr. Brown, but I am not convinced that you cannot do just as well using the many pathways throughout the gardens. The preservation of the lawns must be a priority, so keep your class away from them in future. My memo is quite clear about that.

I must also reiterate what I have said previously. You are a young, inexperienced teacher – and not a well- qualified one –

still in the middle of your probationary period. You should follow my instructions, not question them. In due course, I will have to decide whether your probationary period has been satisfactory. Remember, I have previously had to complain about your cavalier attitude to time-keeping. That is all, Mr Brown.'

He then turned over a few papers on his desk and appeared to study them as before.

Malcolm's face reddened. He turned and strode out of the room.

What a pompous little ass he is! He showed no interest in seeing the creative work undertaken by my class. I shouldn't be surprised because he's never seen any of their work! I could have told him that standardized tests of reading and mathematics given to my class this week show they've made excellent progress since last term. But I know he wouldn't be interested. He never is! What a so-called Head Teacher!

***

At about 6.15 p.m. that evening the teachers, and Dr Alan Hargreaves, met in Tom's house and were soon settled in comfortable armchairs. Tom opened the discussion by referring to his various brushes with Pritchard and their deteriorating relationship. He wanted Alan to have a complete picture of the chain of events.

'Initially, I had a strong sense of loyalty to the new Head. Although I felt humiliated and embarrassed after our first encounter, I was reluctant to make too much of it. Pritchard, I reasoned, was settling in, finding his feet, and our relationship would surely improve. I actually thought – we all did – that he would wish to learn as much as possible from me since I'd been Acting Head. In fact, he rejected my approaches to be of assistance. Then his subsequent behaviour – his brusque dismissal of any points put to him, his rudeness, his failure to interact with the staff – we still await our first Staff Meeting –, his failure to outline his views on the curriculum or teaching methods, his apparent lack of interest in the welfare and progress of individual children, and his general incompetence as a Head Teacher, etc. have convinced me that he's a calamity, a pernicious influence that threatens our job satisfaction and the happiness of both teachers and children. It's a struggle to maintain standards in the present climate. He is cold, arrogant, insulting and dogmatic. Apart from Caroline, we've all had similar experiences with him. I should also mention, Alan, that Pritchard has nursed a delusion that I am trying to take his place, that I'm scheming against him. He even accused me quite early in the term of acting as a *de facto* Head Teacher. He was referring to our chats during break time when we enjoy a cup of tea! I had to tell him that it was our free time. Hilarious! – though I didn't see it as funny at the time, just absurd. He seems to make up his mind about something and then stick to it, in spite of all evidence to the contrary. But that's enough from me. Let's hear from the others.'

Mary and Malcolm then related their own experiences with Pritchard, both emphasising the obsession of Pritchard with minor details while ignoring larger, more important issues.

'Now Alan,' Tom said, 'would you like to comment on what you have heard so far?'

***

Dr Alan Hargreaves, quietly-spoken and friendly, was small and compact, with short grey hair and heavy-rimmed spectacles. He always appeared, as now, alert and concerned.

'What you have just told me, following what Tom said at the party, has come as something of a shock,' he began. 'I simply had no idea that anything of the kind had occurred. Now, I'm a GP, not a specialist. Perhaps a clinical psychologist could tell you more, but I'm fairly confident that your Head Teacher is suffering from some form of *paranoia.* Two symptoms stand out especially: the irrational focus on minutiae and the delusion of persecution, that there is collusion among you to bring him down. ...'

Mary laughed. 'That's no delusion, Alan. We want him out!'

Tom corrected her. 'I think Alan knows, Mary, that Pritchard nursed his delusion from the outset: our wish for his early departure has only recently peaked'

Mary concurred. 'Sorry, you're quite right, Tom.'

'My ideas about *paranoia*, Alan,' Malcolm said, 'come from a film: The Caine Mutiny. Humphrey Bogart was the captain of a US Navy ship, and he worked himself up into a frenzy over some missing strawberries, insisting that the whole ship be thoroughly searched for them. That meant, of course, that many essential tasks had to be postponed.'

'Yes, I saw the film,' Alan responded, 'and it was a wonderful performance by Humphrey Bogart. Yes, he certainly was suffering from *paranoia* and the film provides a very good example of it.'

'Well, there are various form of *paranoia* but I would say that Mr Pritchard has *paranoid personality disorder,* which would account for the characteristics of remoteness, the focus of minutiae, and the irrational suspicion and undue concern about anything he perceives as undermining his authority. But I suspect there are other aspects of his personality that have little to do with *paranoia.*'

Tom thanked Alan for his diagnosis of the problem.

'You've obviously listened to us all very carefully, Alan. It's very helpful to have that kind of information. Now, as to future strategy, I suggest we resolve to act jointly in future rather than respond individually. Let's examine together any future memos, for example. We'll then decide whether they are reasonable or not, and act accordingly. Sometimes we may need to go to Pritchard *en masse.* That will give him no scope at all for bullying or intimidation of any one of us. What do you think?'

'Fair enough,' Mary opined, 'but what are we to do if Pritchard refuses to act on any of our reasonable requests?'

'Well,' Tom replied, 'if we think he's being intolerably difficult about a vitally important issue, we may have to bring in Ronald Parham. He's pretty shrewd and I have a feeling that he may have already formed a poor impression of Pritchard. Our revelations may not come as a complete surprise!'

'You could be right,' Caroline agreed. 'After all, no-one could converse with Pritchard without concluding that he is a very weird person.'

Malcolm grinned. 'Except our governors, of course!' That provoked a round of caustic laughter among the teachers who remained mystified about Pritchard's selection. As the laughter died down, Malcolm continued: 'Actually, I think we should bring in Parham as soon as possible. We've got to bring matters to a head!'

'I agree,' Mary said, 'but perhaps future developments will work in our favour. A new teacher will be joining us in January. Won't Ronald Parham want to see how she is settling in?'

'That's a good point,' Tom said. 'He may even want to call on each one of us at the same time. That would give us our chance. ... But I think we've devoted enough time to Haselmere and Pritchard. Many thanks, Alan, for your insights into his mental state. That was very helpful. And now it's time for grub and a drink – wine or beer – and let's all relax and avoid all serious topics!'

In a surprisingly short time, all five were well loosened-up and laughing at anything remotely funny. It left the teachers in good heart. After a term of worry and trauma, they now felt equipped to face whatever the New Year might bring. It was to bring a few surprises!

Part Two: The Showdown

Chapter 12
10 January 1955

It was the first day of the *Spring* Term. That designation always intrigued Malcolm. There was no *Winter* Term. Today was not untypical for January, with temperatures well below freezing point, producing a hard frost and a world of whiteness. Having enjoyed a Christmas Holiday of over two weeks with Caroline, and all the comforts of home, such as a glowing coal fire, he'd been thoroughly spoilt! But now, he reflected, he would again spend every day in the open air, whatever the challenges posed by the weather! Well, he'd soon adapt to it. The ink in the children's inkwells would be frozen, so all writing would be by pencil. That hardly mattered. The first priority today would be to keep the children active and happy – and warm! He would take them outside the classroom for a little jogging, and perhaps a few vigorous games, before they returned, with glowing cheeks, to sit at their desks wrapped in their blankets.

He had been happy to exclude Rupert Pritchard from his thoughts while at home, but now the challenges of the New Year flooded into his mind.

Thank Heaven we're going to work together to counter any further irrational or spiteful behaviour by Pritchard. So far, we've managed to keep up our standards, especially in literacy and numeracy. No thanks to him! But now we really need some outside support. The Governing Body won't help us. Pritchard's cosy relationship with it precludes that. I expect his reports to the governors present a ridiculously biased account of School developments – with himself playing a key role! – giving the impression that he is running a happy and efficient institution. They can't have much idea of what it's really like here!

Ronald Parham is our best hope. Perhaps he'll come to visit the new teacher. I wonder what she'll be like? I doubt that

Pritchard will introduce her to us so I'll go and see her as soon as possible. An introduction to open-air teaching in freezing conditions is quite a challenge! And I hope she'll fit easily into the teaching team.

Arriving at Haselmere shortly after eight o'clock, Malcolm greeted Tom and Mary. Following a brief chat about their various experiences of Christmas, with Mary providing a hilarious account of her skirmishes with assertive in-laws, they talked about international affairs. Tom had been reading his newspaper and couldn't wait to discuss the latest news.

'I see that the Mau Mau atrocities are still taking place in Kenya.'

'Yes. They're ghastly,' Malcolm commented. 'There's a substantial number of white people in Kenya, mostly farmers, and many of them are being attacked and sometimes murdered.'

'Yes, and I'm afraid that will continue until Kenya is granted independence,' Tom observed. 'And talking about Africa, did you see that South Africa's apartheid Government proposes to evict all black people from Johannesburg."

'No, I didn't. But that's disgraceful!'

'I agree.'

'So do I,' said Mary. ... But it's not all bad news for coloured people. The first black singer is going to perform at the Metropolitan Opera House in New York.'

'Who's she?' Malcolm asked.

'Someone called Marion Anderson.'

'I must admit I've never heard of her,' Tom said, 'but she must have a truly wonderful voice – so outstanding that she simply had to receive the recognition she obviously deserves, in spite of her colour.'

'And there was something else that caught my eye in today's newspaper –something very peculiar,' Malcolm continued. 'France's Interior Minister, Francois Mitterand has just made a really crazy proposal. He wants to integrate France and Algeria. He actually wants them to form a single country, one part in Europe and the other in Africa! A barmy idea!'

'It sounds pretty daft,' Tom agreed. I think the Algerians want independence – nothing less. The large number of Frenchmen who live there will just have to get used to the idea.'

'But will they?' Malcolm said. 'I've read that they'll fight if they think independence is on the cards. They have arms, you know.'

'I know, but I think Algerian independence will come.'

***

A little later, when the group had broken up, and he had prepared his classroom for the first lesson of the day, Malcolm discovered that he still had plenty of time before the children arrived. Suddenly, and impulsively, he decided to do the unthinkable. This was, he decided, just the time to show goodwill, even to the man responsible for so much misery. He would go to Rupert Pritchard and wish him a Happy New Year. With someone like him there were times when one simply had to turn the other cheek!

He knocked on the Head Teacher's door, was invited to enter, and was soon face to face with the man with whom his confrontations to date had always been disagreeable.

'Sorry to break in like this, sir,' he began, smiling, with an outstretched hand. 'I just wanted to wish you a Happy New Year before the new term gets underway.

Pritchard's expression suggested that Malcolm's initiative was just about the last thing that he had expected. Then Malcolm felt a cold, clammy hand in his, and was very glad that it was swiftly withdrawn.

'Thank you, Mr. Brown,' he responded. 'I trust that your good wife is keeping well.'

'Yes, very well indeed, sir. Thank you. I think the usual term for her present condition is "blooming."' He grinned.

Pritchard nodded, said 'Good,' and signified, in his usual manner, his wish to terminate the interview. Malcolm smiled and departed.

What a very cold fish he is! And what a wet and floppy handshake! Ugh. Still, at least he'd been polite, or marginally so, and he'd even enquired after Caroline. That's progress of a sort! And now, the coaches are arriving.

***

During the mid-morning break, Malcolm ran along a garden path to speak to the new infant teacher, who was replacing Caroline. Miss Susan Carter was fortyish, short and plump, with mousy hair in a bob. She wore no make-up and was very plainly dressed, but looked pleasant, alert, and ready for action. Her personality was soon manifest: spirited, forthright, confident and down-to-earth. An experienced teacher, she had already evaluated all her classroom resources, and knew precisely how much paper, cardboard, paint and other materials she needed for her young children.

She gave Malcolm a friendly smile and a warm, surprisingly strong handshake as he introduced himself.

'I'm pleased to meet you, Malcolm. Most of my experience has been in normal schools, but I've taught in a school for the Partially Sighted, so I know how different a *Special School* can be. But I'll be glad to pick your brains while I'm finding my way around.'

'Of course, I'll be happy to help you settle in,' Malcolm responded, 'but I must say that you are highly organised. I see you've already made some teaching aids, including word labels. Are they *flash cards*?'

'They could be, but some of them will be placed, or hung, on various objects – for instance: cupboards, blackboard, desk, table, books, etc. The children will regularly put them in position so that they learn the words.'

'So you use *Look and Say*?'

'Oh no! On its own that wouldn't work. I teach reading using *phonic* methods as well. Both *Look and Say* and *Phonics* are essential.'

'I absolutely agree.'

'I'll see you again when we have coffee which I believe is available in the hall, but now I must go to the stock room. Is it open?'

'Yes, it should be. See you later then.' Malcolm hurried across to the hall, thinking about Susan.

She's a good, professional teacher, with a no-nonsense approach – probably as outspoken as Mary! It's going to be a lively term! But she'll fit in well with us. How she'll find our paranoid Head Teacher is another matter altogether!

He was soon to find out. Susan approached him during the lunch break, full of indignation, bordering on anger, with tears not far away.

'My God,' Malcolm thought, 'surely Pritchard hasn't already upset his newest member of staff!' He was immediately sympathetic.

'I'm upset,' she announced, biting her lip.

'Let's sit down while you tell me about it,' he suggested. They sat in a corner of his classroom while Susan poured out her concerns.

'I went to the stockroom and was glad to locate about half of what I need. The rest, I thought, could be ordered. I was about to leave, carrying a fairly heavy load of consumables, when a harsh voice behind me shouted,

"What do you think you're doing?"

'I was really shaken by the sudden interruption. It was Mr Pritchard. My heart pounded, my face was burning, and I was really shattered. I still am. No Head Teacher has ever spoken to me so rudely before. I told him that I was taking materials that I need for teaching aids, and he said,

"You've got far too much there. No-one has ever taken so much stock before and I don't think it's necessary. I must ask you to put at least half of what you are carrying back on the shelves, immediately!"

'Well. I was dumfounded. Obviously a new infant teacher needs a large amount of material at first, to make new teaching aids, and to build up a good working stock. When I'd recovered sufficiently, I explained – in spite of my resentment – how and why I needed the stock, and fully expected that he would then calm down, and even apologise for his intemperate interruption. Not a bit of it. He was stubbornly insistent. I had to do what he ordered, and I'm not at all happy about it. I know that all stock has to be carefully regulated, or we'd soon run out of it, but Mr Pritchard wouldn't even listen to my arguments. He seems to have no idea how to deal with professional colleagues. And what a way to treat a new member of staff!'

'I'm sorry, Susan,' Malcolm sympathized. 'Pritchard has behaved abominably. He should be giving you every support and encouragement, and have been as friendly and helpful as possible on your first day. The way he treated you is shocking. Unforgiveable! We've all had our ups and downs with that man. That's why we're working together to try to neutralize his more harmful activities. We'll all give you as much help and support as we can. I think you'll find all the staff very friendly.'

Susan, now recovered, smiled and thanked Malcolm for his kind words, which were certainly of some consolation, although it occurred to her that she would have never accepted a teaching post at Haselmere had she suspected that she would have to work with such an awful man as Pritchard.

But a further shock was not long in coming.

A little later another memo was circulated.

MEMO. NO.5

From: Mr Rupert Pritchard, Headmaster

To: All Staff at Haselmere Open-Air School for Delicate Children

10 January, 1955

No doubt most of you are aware how important it is that the distribution of consumable stock should be carefully managed. Otherwise, we could find ourselves short of particular teaching materials before new supplies become available.

Therefore, from now on, all staff will submit to me a list of their requirements for my approval. The list should be sent on a Monday, and before 11a.m. My initials at the bottom of a list will signify that that amount of stock and no more may be taken in the usual way.

Signed... Rupert Pritchard, Headmaster.

When Malcolm saw it, he burst out laughing. It was the phrase ... *from now on all staff will submit to me* ... that sparked his merriment. But there was nothing else that pleased him, or his colleagues. When the teachers met at 4.40 p.m. Tom opened the discussion.

'I'm sure we're all very sorry, Susan, that your first day here was spoilt when you found yourself embroiled in an argument with our Head Teacher.

Sadly, the way he spoke to you doesn't surprise us. We've all experienced his rudeness. Perhaps we should also brief you about Pritchard's other shortcomings?'

'Yes,' Mary agreed, 'but we should also tell Susan about our plans for the future. We should show her that we're thinking positively!'

'Yes,' Tom said, 'let's do that, too.'

'Right,' Malcolm said, 'Susan, we have a wacky Head Teacher, whom we only see occasionally, and who governs by memos that he refuses to discuss.'

Tom smiled. 'That's a fair summary,' he said. 'And he doesn't like to see informal gatherings of staff, when he imagines that we're all conspiring against him. In particular, he sees me as the arch enemy who wants to replace him. So we are forced to be secretive; that's why we're meeting here after school. But we also have meetings at my house; more about that later.'

'You see,' Mary pointed out, 'we don't have any Staff Meetings with Mr Pritchard.'

'You really don't have any at all?' Susan was aghast.'

'Well, we haven't had one yet. So he doesn't feed any ideas to us, or give us any guidance on anything: curriculum, teaching methods, future plans, etc.'

'So you never have the chance to discuss anything together with him?'

'No. Or to give him any of <u>our</u> ideas.'

Susan was beginning to look horrified. Tom resumed.

'Sorry Susan, but there's more to come. He never talks to us informally, either together or individually, so he remains isolated in a School that he is supposed to be managing.'

Mary suddenly felt overwhelmingly sympathetic to Susan. On her very first day she had first to endure first a bruising encounter with her Head Teacher, and was now hearing how absolutely dreadful and inadequate he is.

I like what I've seen of Susan and I feel we could be very good friends. We've had to tell her a few facts about Pritchard so she'll be on her guard, but we mustn't depress her or make her want to leave. I'm sure she'll fit in here very well. I'll be as positive as I can.

'Susan, in spite of what you've heard, we all love working here, and find it very rewarding. I'm sure you will too. We've managed to keep up standards in spite of Pritchard, and we plan to maintain them. We all work together very well, and help one another with everything. I hope what you have just heard doesn't worry you too much. Life here is much, much better than any impression you may have got after your experience with Pritchard and what we've just told you.'

Susan smiled.

'Don't worry, Mary. Actually, I've found this meeting very useful. I can see that you are all united and that's great. After my row with Mr Pritchard, I was certainly hot under the collar, but I'm quite re-assured now. I'm sure I'm going to enjoy working with you all, and I have a really lovely class of children to teach. I just have one immediate worry, and that's about this memo. What are we going to do about it?'

'Well, I've been thinking about that,' Mary said. 'You must get the stock you need, but let's be careful how we respond. It's a nuisance to have to make a list, but there is a certain logic in the memo. Let's think about how it would seem to the Governing Body or to the inspector. They'd see it as a bit formal but quite sensible, wouldn't they?'

'Probably,' Tom said, 'so how do we get round it?'

'First of all,' Mary answered, 'we should all troop in to Pritchard's study, tell him that the *open access* system of taking stock has always worked well because we are responsible professionals, and ask him to retain it.'

'Fine,' Malcolm responded, 'let's do that. But suppose he behaves to us *en masse* just as he has to us individually. What do we do then?'

'In that case,' Mary answered, 'I have an alternative plan. But let's go ahead with the meeting first.'

'Right, 'Tom said. 'How about 8.15a.m. tomorrow? We'll together walk into the lion's den!'

The teachers chuckled as they dispersed and returned to their classrooms for the day's final teaching session.

***

That evening Malcolm expressed his concerns about the proposed meeting.

'Pritchard doesn't hesitate to bully and insult us when we see him individually,' he pointed out. 'How will he react when we face him together? I suppose he might cave in, become a reasonable, rational being, and show some willingness to compromise. But, frankly, I don't think so. Our visit may reinforce his persecution complex. He may lose his self-control and make a scene.'

'Just take care,' Caroline warned. 'That man is dangerous!'

Chapter 13
11 January 1955

The next morning, all four teachers met outside Pritchard's study, knocked, heard a reply, and entered. The others had briefed Susan on Pritchard's invariable rudeness on such occasions. He was true to form, pointedly ignoring them for a few minutes while they stood awkwardly, feeling rather nervous, ill-at-ease and self-conscious. Finally, he looked up, reddened and frowned. Malcolm felt that his worst fears were about to be realized.

He interprets all meetings as confrontational, and sees them as a threat. He is definitely stressed whenever anyone faces him. Even before we start he looks as if he is about to break a blood vessel! What an unhappy wretch he is!

'What's this?' he questioned. 'This is highly irregular. I have not sent for you. Mr Bates, as the senior teacher here, I would like you to explain what this is about.'

'Certainly, sir, 'Tom replied, calmly and politely. 'We've received your latest memo and would like to discuss it with you.'

'Mr Bates, when I send a memo. I do not equivocate and I make sure the content is crystal clear. The last one was concerned with the conservation of stock, which is clearly essential, so I cannot see that there is anything to discuss. I send copies of all memos to the governors for their approval. They appear to understand them without further clarification, and always readily endorse them, so I always have their full support. Do I make myself clear?'

Mary groaned inwardly.

It's interesting that he mentions his support from the governors. A sign that he is becoming more defensive? But the meeting could hardly have had a worse start. Pritchard's antagonism towards Tom will prevent any progress unless we try a new tack. Perhaps a little bit of soft soap?

'Mr Pritchard,' she began, 'we are very sorry to have burst in upon you like this. We know you are very busy. Regarding the memo we all appreciate the need to conserve stock and to use it carefully. It's in all our interests to ensure there is always plenty of material of every kind available for our teaching needs.'

'Quite so, Mrs Prince. So you understand the message in that memo?'

'Yes, Mr.Pritchard, but up to now we've had an *open access* system that has always worked well. We have been able to take teaching materials as and when we want them. In open –air conditions some stock can deteriorate rapidly so we don't take too much on any one occasion. And we always keep an eye on the amount of stock left so we've never run short. In other words, self-regulation has been successful. In view of that, do you think we could we retain the *open access* system at least for the time being. Should you find after, say, a month's trial, that it is not working satisfactory, then it could be changed. We could revert to the system that you have proposed.'

Malcolm was impressed.

Mary has explained the situation very reasonably and has put a watertight case. How can Pritchard possibly dismiss her arguments?

He was about to find out.

'Mrs Prince,' Pritchard began, in a tone of controlled irritation, 'I am glad we agree that stock should be carefully monitored. That is precisely why I have issued the memo. I am not, by the way, *proposing* a system. I am *stating* the procedure that I wish to be followed. So the answer to your question is no. I have devised a system that is rational and should work well.'

Susan now entered the discussion.

'Sir, I'm afraid I seem to have been the cause of our present difficulties. I believe you thought that I was taking an unreasonable amount of teaching material yesterday, but as a new infant teacher, I wanted to produce some visual aids that will be in use for many months. I won't need so much in future. I know we all have a responsibility to regulate our use of stock very carefully, but I'm not happy that a system that has always worked well in the past is now going to be changed because of me.'

'Miss Carter,' Pritchard retorted, raising his voice appreciably, 'I dealt with what purported to be your stock requirements yesterday, and I see no reason to return to the subject.' Susan reddened.

This is confirmation of what the other teachers told me yesterday. He won't discuss anything. He really is a dictator! He's unpleasant, arrogant and rudely dismissive. He has no idea how to motivate staff.'

Malcolm, ignoring Pritchard's intransigence, now attempted a compromise.

'I wonder, sir, whether you would consider some modification of your procedure. Writing a list of required stock, to be in your hands by 11a.m. on a Monday morning, might sometimes be difficult if we are having a particularly hectic time. I wonder whether you would mind if we submit our lists any time on that day? That would give us a little more flexibility.'

Pritchard replied angrily.

'Mr Brown, you should know that there are always good reasons for my decisions, and I do not expect to have to explain them to a junior member of my staff. However, I will deal with your point. I wish to consider all requests for stock simultaneously, so that I can assess the total demand on each occasion. And I expect you to implement my instructions, not question them, Mr Brown!

Now, Mrs Prince, it is time for you to begin the children's exercises, and I must return to my work – and so must you all! Mr. Bates, I would like you to stay behind for a few moments.'

The others hesitated before moving. After all, they had agreed to act together. They looked anxiously towards Tom, but he seemed quite unperturbed. Having no doubt whatever that Tom could look after himself, they shuffled out. As they did so, Tom fixed his attention on Pritchard.

I must tell my colleagues how well I think they've spoken. They brought up proposals that any reasonable Head Teacher would have been willing to discuss. But Pritchard's always determined to have his way. He's now perspiring freely and his hands are shaking. He's nervous and unsure of himself as he prepares to shape up to me. And I, too, am ready for a fight if it comes to that!

Pritchard now glared at Tom before he began.

'How dare you! You organised that protest. As the senior teacher you have full responsibility for it. You thought that if you all arrived together you'd be able to get your way. Well, it didn't work did it?' He drew in several deep breaths. 'In your favourite role as the teachers' leader, you arranged for me to be intimidated in my own room. Your behaviour is disgraceful...And I will not forget it!'

Tom was resolved to keep his temper whatever the provocation.

'We came here, Mr Pritchard, in good faith. Some of the teachers were concerned that they might need certain materials urgently and then have to wait for your endorsement. They simply wanted to discuss the memo with you. Perhaps all they needed was reassurance or a friendly explanation that all applications would be endorsed by the end of the day. But instead of that, you rejected their sensible suggestions out of hand. In doing so you embarrassed and upset a new member of staff – and, I suspect, a very good teacher!'

'I've had enough of this,' Pritchard shouted.

'But I haven't finished,' Tom insisted, his voice remaining calm and controlled, but colder in tone. 'There is never any discussion or exchange of views between you and the teachers, and you never have a Staff Meeting Instead of motivating your teachers, you insult them. You don't deserve to have such excellent people working under you. You provide no guidelines on curriculum or teaching methods, you never look at the children's work, or discuss with staff the academic and medical progress of individual pupils, and no-one has any idea about your ideas for the future development of Haselmere.

You seem to have no notion of forward planning. I'm afraid that you've lost our respect!' Pritchard shook with fury.

'This is intolerable,' he blustered. 'I shall report you to the Governing Body and to the Inspector of Special Schools, for insubordination, impertinence and non-cooperation ... and for plotting to undermine my authority.'

'Please go ahead and speak to Ronald Parham,' Tom replied evenly. 'I would welcome the opportunity to tell him about your failure to manage Haselmere in the ways I have just outlined, and how your omissions and wrong-headed decisions threaten to undermine our work. I could tell him more. And now, Mr Pritchard, I really must return to my class. I never keep my pupils waiting. Excuse me.' And Tom turned and left before his fuming Head Teacher could respond.

I'm glad I enlightened him about some of his deficiencies. Oddly enough, after that bitter exchange I feel quite elated. There's nothing like getting something off one's chest. But I never thought that I'd have to speak to a Head Teacher in that way. My colleagues were magnificent. Even Mary kept wonderfully calm as she put her arguments quietly and rationally. For the first time we had some sort of a meeting with our Head Teacher. And what a meeting! But now, I suppose, Pritchard will look for opportunities to get his revenge. Let that stubborn bureaucrat do his worst. I'll be ready for him.

***

Rupert Pritchard took out his handkerchief to soak up some of the perspiration that was trickling down his cheeks. His face was burning and blood was pounding in his head, which was cluttered with raging thoughts and emotions.

This is a new threat. They're acting together and advancing on me as a defiant body. I must take some action to thwart them; otherwise matters will soon get out of hand. Bates is the real problem. He is a constant threat. He'll do anything to undermine my position because he wants to take my place. I'll have to deal with him decisively. Then the others will become much more manageable.

In the afternoon the teachers discovered another missive in their pigeonholes.

MEMO. NO. 6

From: Mr Rupert Pritchard, Headmaster

To: All Staff at Haselmere Open-Air School for Delicate Children

11 January, 1955

I would like to make it quite clear that I will in no circumstances permit an unofficial and uninvited gathering in my room. If any individual member of Staff wishes to see me about any matter, he or she should send me a short note requesting an appointment. I will then make the necessary arrangements.

I must also point out that if there is any breach of the above, then I will have no option but to report the matter to the Chairman of the Governing Body forthwith. Appropriate action will then be taken.

Signed... Rupert Pritchard, Headmaster

A meeting was arranged at the end of the day to discuss the latest communication.

Tom summarized what he regarded as its most significant features.

'First of all, you'll have noticed that individual teachers can no longer 'pop in' spontaneously to see His Lordship, something that we have always been able to do at Haselmere. Obviously, too, he doesn't want any more *en masse* confrontations because he thinks they undermine his authority. Secondly, the memo contains a threat. If anyone breaks his new rule, he will report them to the Governing Body.

Thirdly, he is not now mentioning Ronald Parham, the inspector, as someone to whom he might complain about us.

That's probably because I told him that I would welcome Parham's involvement. If Pritchard did bring in Parham, then we could enlighten our inspector about the dire situation here: no Staff Meetings, no guidance on teaching methods or curriculum, no informal contacts between staff and Head, no support whatever for teachers, etc.

'That's right,' Mary said, 'but I think we may well have to defy this latest memo occasionally. Why? Because staff feelings and opinions must be expressed. We can't be gagged. Either Pritchard arranges for Staff Meetings in the normal way or we must again go to him *en masse* with our views – and perhaps sometimes our complaints. There is no alternative. We are not his puppets. We're professional people!'

The others indicated their full agreement with Mary's views.

'Yes,' Tom added, 'and Mr. Parham would agree that we should *act* like professionals. He would be quite shocked, for example to hear about the absence of Staff Meetings. So, if he doesn't visit the school during the next few weeks, I think we should ask him to come here to talk to us as we are very concerned about a number of matters. What do you think?'

'I absolutely agree,' Mary responded, 'and I'm sure the others do, too. But we mustn't wait too long. Let's monitor Pritchard's behaviour closely. If it gets any worse, then we shouldn't wait to get the inspector here. The sooner the better. Let's clear the air.'

'I'm in full agreement with everything that's been said, Susan said, 'but what are we going to do about stock? It looks as if I'm going to be short. Mary, you said that you had an alternative plan if we failed to shift Mr Pritchard – and we did fail didn't we?'

'Yes, we did,' Mary replied, 'and I do have another suggestion – that we put some of your stock needs on our lists of requirements. If, for instance, you wanted twelve sheets of manila card, you put in for, say, six, and Malcolm and I would each request three sheets each. We can do the same thing for any one of us who requires at any time an unusual amount of anything. We've just got to circumvent all unreasonable requirements. What do you think?'

'I think it's a great idea – a reasonable subterfuge to cope with an unreasonable person,' Malcolm responded, and Susan agreed.

'It's fine provided it doesn't get you into trouble.'

Malcolm laughed. 'Don't give it a thought. We've been in trouble ever since that dreadful man arrived here. But we must never trust him, and we should all watch our backs!'

***

'Y'know,' Billy Green said, addressing his little group of friends in the playground, 'there's somefink goin' on, but I ain't sure what it is. I can't put me finger on it. But take my word for it. Somefing's up.

'What's that then?' asked Tim Owen.

'Well, when we was playing just after we left the coaches this morning, all the teachers was coming out of old Pritchy's office. Three came out together, and then Mr. Bates came out afterwards. Now, that's a bit funny. I never see them do that before. I fink somefinks up.'

'What sort of fing?' Tony asked.

'I dunno. Perhaps the teachers don' like somefink old Pritchy's doin'. I wouldn't be surprised.'

'I 'ope you're right,' Lucy said, 'and I 'ope they gave 'im a good talking to.'

'P'raps they did,' Billy responded. 'P'raps they told 'im 'es got to do a lot better, or they won't 'ave 'im as their Head Teacher no more!'

They all laughed.

Chapter 14
23 January 1955

Mary spoke to Malcolm just after they had both arrived at Haselmere.

'Have you tried out the new stock system yet?'

'Yes, and – surprise, surprise, – there were no problems! I drew up my requirements last Friday, after school, so I was ready for Monday. I don't have time to think about them at the beginning of the week when so much is going on.'

'And when did you receive His Lordship's endorsement?'

'Just before mid-day on Monday; one of the gardeners brought it.'

'Good. That's encouraging. Perhaps Pritchard did actually listen to some of our concerns.'

'I doubt it. He never has – at least, not in any genuine way. But he may feel that we can't be subdued so easily these days and he's forced to move a little in our direction.'

***

Ronald Parham chose today to spring a surprise visit. He never advised schools of a visit in advance. He believed that spontaneous visits were far more valuable than *advertised* ones. The latter gave teachers and Head Teachers time to prepare, so he would not see typical lessons or a normal school environment. Efforts might be made to make a school especially tidy, extra care might be taken over lesson preparations, classrooms might be suddenly brightened up with new displays of children's work, and new equipment, that had been under lock and key, suddenly exposed to the light of day, etc. The inspector considered his priorities.

I want to see how the School is run, and I want to see, and evaluate, some normal lessons. I haven't seen Susan Carter since her interview. I wonder how she has settled in at

Haselmere. An open-air school is rather challenging, especially if someone starts work there in the middle of a freezing winter. I'll certainly see her. If time permits, I'll also check up on Malcolm Brown who's now more than halfway through his probationary period.'

As usual, Ronald Parham paid a brief courtesy visit to Pritchard on his arrival. Approaching the Head Teacher's study, he reflected on the interview, which was the last time he had seen the Head Teacher, and he had been by no means comfortable about its outcome.

The six candidates for the Headship of Haselmere were rather a dull, undistinguished bunch. Perhaps I should have recommended a second trawl. The post could have been re-advertised at the beginning of the Autumn Term, when there might have been a better response. Of the six we interviewed, Pritchard was certainly the most articulate. He answered every question put to him in a clear and precise manner. But verbal fluency isn't everything. I had doubts about his suitability for the Headship, but the governors had made up their minds very quickly. They definitely wanted him. It wouldn't have been right to have stood in their way. But he's an odd-looking chap. I wonder how well he is managing the School. I'll soon find out!'

With such thoughts swimming in his mind, Parham decided to open his discussion with the Head Teacher with a few generalities.

'Mr Pritchard, I'm glad to have this opportunity to visit Haselmere, which has always been a great pleasure. You've been here for something like five months, I believe. Is everything working out well for you here?'

Pritchard, having had no idea that the visit was to take place, was immediately suspicious about its purpose. Parham's apparently innocuous question might be leading up to something ...

Nevertheless he beamed at Parham as he answered.

'Yes, I think so. I have already put in place some new procedures and others are under review.'

'Good, and what are they?' Parham smiled reassuringly as he put the question, noticing Pritchard's fleeting expression of alarm.

'Well...I would rather not go into details at the moment as my plans are all in a formative stage. And it will take a little time for my ideas to lead to significant changes.'

'Oh, why is that?'

'Well, I must carry the teachers with me. I have to change well-entrenched ideas ... '

'Of course.'

'And at first I had to spend a little time here just studying the way the teachers were performing, before I was ready to consider what changes are necessary. As you know, I've been here for only one complete term. In that time, I've been listening and learning, as one must to get a clear picture of the situation.'

'Naturally, and now you are ready to move forward?

'I believe so.'

'Well, I'll be very interested to see your ideas come to fruition. But, tell me, how is young Brown getting on?'

'Well, he's enthusiastic. For instance, he now runs a School Magazine and he organised a music concert for our Christmas celebrations. However, he is inclined to question quite reasonable requirements and is not always as cooperative as I would wish. Perhaps his recalcitrance is due to inexperience. I feel that I must monitor his progress very carefully.'

'I see. That's rather disappointing. When I saw him, he seemed to me a very promising young teacher, but we shall have to wait and see. I hope to see him teaching a little later. And Susan Carter? Has she settled in well?'

'Well, it's too early to make any firm judgement. She didn't make the best of starts here by trying to take too much teaching material from the stock room on her first day. I had to point out that it would not be fair to the other teachers if she removed an unreasonable amount. I think she took the point. As with Brown, I'm keeping a close eye on her progress.'

'Right. Well, I'll get on my way now. I may pop in again should my discussions with your teachers lead to any questions which need your clarification.'

In fact, he did not return, because he soon uncovered some disturbing facts that merited immediate and urgent investigation, and the need for probing questions with the teachers. That took up all his time.

Pritchard knew the layout of the Haselmere very well, and he headed straight for Susan Carter's classroom, admiring on the way large groups of snowdrops and winter aconites in some of the flower beds. Nearing the classroom, its openness enabled him to hear and observe the activity within.

Susan Carter, dressed in a smart trouser suit, was displaying large white cards for phonic drill; and then she invited individual children to hang or place a word card on the appropriate object. She used a pointer to indicate words to be read by the whole class. Some words were written on one blackboard and pictures of corresponding objects were pinned on a second one. Individual children were invited to marry word and picture.

The experienced inspector saw immediately that Susan was on top of her job. The atmosphere of the class was impressive: the children, attentive and alert, were learning and also enjoying the lesson. The inspector watched and listened for about half an hour.

At break time, the children made their way to the playground and Susan turned to meet the inspector, who smiled and shook her hand.

'I much enjoyed watching your lesson. You have a happy and lively class, and the children are responding well, aren't they? Are you happy here? Are you settling in well?

Susan was thoughtful for a moment.

'Well, as far as the children are concerned, I'm very happy. I have a delightful class. I learned all their names as quickly as possible and studied both their medical and attainment records. I feel I know them all now. Obviously I'll find out more about each one in time, especially about their individual idiosyncrasies – I've got a few characters in this class! – but that won't take long. I mix up class, group and individual work to cater for the wide age range and an even wider attainment range. You see, some children have spent long periods in hospital when they would otherwise have been attending a school, so they've fallen behind.'

'It sounds as if you are really enjoying teaching this class.'

'Yes, I am.'

'Good. And are you just as happy in this particular School?'

'Well, my colleagues have been very helpful and supportive. I believe we have a good team of teachers here...' She had been speaking with easy confidence, but now hesitated. She looked uncertain about how to continue and a little flustered. Finally, she spoke as if she had just made up her mind to unwind.

'But it would be helpful if we had Staff Meetings here sometimes because there is so much to discuss and we could learn a great deal from one another. We do have brief chats together, of course, whenever we can. ...' She had spoken in a nervous rush and when she paused, Parham pounced on the point that she had just made.

'Do you really mean, Miss Carter, that there are no Staff Meetings, or that you have not had one so far? You haven't yet been here for two full weeks, have you? Perhaps there will be one later in the Term.'

Susan had now regained her poise and her confidence.

'I mean, Mr Parham, that Staff Meetings never take place here. I understand from my colleagues that there hasn't been a single one since Mr. Pritchard's arrival. That really is a great pity. Quite apart from sharing views on teaching and learning methods, we need to discuss various aspects of the curriculum and, of course, the health problems and progress of individual children. There really is a lot to talk about.' She paused to re-group her thoughts.

Have I let my tongue run away with me? I'm very new here so perhaps I shouldn't express my views so positively. Mr Parham is quite stern-looking, but there is something about him that encouraged me to blow my top!

'Yes, of course there is a great deal for teachers to discuss,' Ronald Parham agreed, 'so I expect you chat with Mr Pritchard informally from time to time. You discuss any problems or issues as and when they crop up. Is that the case?'

'No, not really.' Again Susan hesitated. She also blushed and looked nervous.

'What I mean is,' Parham persisted, 'no doubt you have an opportunity to chat with Mr Pritchard when he visits your classroom?' He had noticed that Susan was looking increasingly ill-at-ease but now she perked up and her confidence seemed to be swimming back.

'Mr Parham, as you have said, I have been here only a short time. Mr Pritchard has not visited my class, and I understand from the other teachers that he doesn't ever visit classrooms.'

'And he hasn't spoken to you at all?'

Susan smiled. 'No. Well, only when he reprimanded me on my first day when he thought I was taking too much material from the stock room.' She smiled again. 'It was mainly about the word cards that you saw me using ... Oh, yes, we did speak together when we all went to see him.' She explained what had happened ... and was then worried that she had let the cat out of the bag.

But Parham's response was reassuring.

'Well, thank you, Miss Carter. I've listened carefully to what you have told me and you've give me much food for thought. I hope we'll be able to continue this conversation later, but I must now see the other teachers. Meanwhile, please carry on with your good work.'

In fact, Parham was amazed and alarmed to discover that Pritchard was holed up in his study for much of the time. He felt strongly that in a small school liked Haselmere, a Head Teacher should be active around and about, showing positive leadership. Determined to investigate further, he now strode swiftly towards Malcolm's classroom. Again, its open-air nature enabled him to form a preliminary assessment some time before he arrived. The pupils were writing (he learnt later that they were composing poems, stories, etc. for the School

Magazine) and Malcolm was bending over desks, helping with problems, making suggestions, correcting English, etc. Some children were using dictionaries to check spellings or meanings.

He was particularly impressed by the atmosphere of quiet and purposeful activity. Here was a young teacher, completely in control, relaxed and involved with his pupils, who were thoroughly motivated and working hard. He shook Malcolm's hand and asked him whether he was enjoying the work in an open-air school.

'I do. I love it here. Even the children who have spent long periods of time in hospital and have fallen behind, are making some progress. They really want to learn.'

'Good – and that's partly because you have motivated them. And do you have plenty of opportunities to share ideas with your colleagues?'

'Well, whenever we can – mostly during the breaks – we talk shop, but it would be helpful if we had regular Staff Meetings.'

'And you don't?

'No. We used to have them regularly, but haven't had any since September.'

'I see. And what about informal contacts with Mr Pritchard?

Malcolm laughed but was quick to apologise. 'I'm sorry, Mr Parham, but the fact is that I've had no contact at all with Mr Pritchard, except for those occasions when he has reprimanded me about something.'

'Reprimanded you! And why did Mr Pritchard do that, Mr Brown?'

Malcolm was almost certain that he detected a twinkle in the inspector's eyes. He outlined his playground admonition and the day he took his class out to observe the beauty of a frosty morning.

'I see. Well, those incidents don't sound much like heinous crimes.' And now Malcolm was certain that he looked amused. 'But now, Mr Brown, I must talk to the other teachers.' He smiled. 'You have obviously made a good start here and you are doing some good work. Keep it up.' He shook Malcolm's hand, and went on his way. Malcolm had not heard such words of encouragement from 'above' for some time, and was quite affected by them.

As he approached Mary's classroom, Parham heard quite a commotion. He was startled. Then there was laughter ... and suddenly silence. He wondered what on earth was going on. As he drew near, realisation dawned. A play was being acted. He greeted Mary and asked her about it.

'I divided the class into six groups of three, and each of them has been writing a short play. Each group discussed the outline of a story with three characters, and told me what they had in mind. I made a few suggestions and then they began. Only one in each group did the actual writing; the others fed in ideas, which they discussed before anything was written down. The plays were finished last week. I had them typed and copied so that each child could learn a part. And now two of the groups are acting their plays.'

'Well, they seem to be enjoying the acting.'

'Yes. They thought the last one was very funny; I thought so, too!'

'And though they don't all have any writing practice, they all read the play that they've produced together?'

'Yes. Actually, they read the plays of all the other groups, too. I make enough copies. So they get plenty of reading practice.'

'Splendid! Mrs Prince. Now I have a request. Have you a copy here of any curriculum notes, guidelines, or other documents that you have been given?'

'Yes, here we are. These notes were given to us by Mr Rogers, the previous Head Teacher.'

'And Mr. Pritchard has, as it were, endorsed these?'

'No. I don't think he has seen them.'

'Really? And has he provided you with any other teaching notes or curriculum guides?'

'No.'

'I see. Well, thank you, Mrs Prince. I would like to discuss several other matters with you, but they will have to wait. I must now have a word with Mr Bates. I've enjoyed meeting you.' He shook Mary's hand, and swiftly walked away.

So. Three teachers who are all above average in their enthusiasm and skill, and all doing well in spite of incredibly weak and ineffective leadership. I haven't yet discovered <u>*anything*</u> *that Pritchard has done that's helpful to the staff. I don't need to see Tom Bates teach, but he's the one who will give me the clearest and fullest picture of what's going on here.*

He met Tom just after his pupils had left to go to the home-bound coaches.

'Tom. It's good to see you again. If you're not in too great a hurry to go, I'd be glad if we could have a talk.'

'Let's do that. I'm not in a special hurry and I'd welcome a chat. I've been hoping that you would soon visit us.'

'Tom, I'm relying on you to clear up a few matters. Firstly, I understand from your colleagues that Staff Meetings never take place here now.'

'Yes, that's right.'

'That seems very odd. Is there any reason for that?'

'I think you may like to put that question to Mr Pritchard, Ronald. We teachers have never been given a reason.'

'Now, Tom,' Parham said, and grinned. 'We're old friends. I have a responsibility for this School, and especially for young teachers like Mr Brown. Why do you think there are no meetings?'

'Well,' Tom replied, 'if you really want me to *spill the beans ...*'

'I certainly do,' broke in the inspector. 'With your help I hope to establish all the facts. Otherwise how can I provide the help and support to both staff and pupils that I should?'

'Right. The absence of Staff Meetings is simply part of a pattern. The fact is, we don't have meetings of *any* kind, except for those we arrange surreptitiously for ourselves.'

'Surreptitiously?' Is that really necessary?'

'Oh, yes. Mr Pritchard doesn't like to see us talking together.'

'That's incredible......Well, what sort of contacts do you have, then, with Mr Pritchard?'

'Frankly, there are very few contacts at all! Mr Pritchard stays in his room for most of the time, and he never visits the classrooms or discusses anything with us.'

'Tom, that is really worrying and I must certainly deal with it as a matter of urgency. Do you think there is any underlying reason for Mr Pritchard's strange *modus operandi* if one may call it that?'

'I honestly haven't a clue. But Dr Hargreaves had some ideas. As you know, he has recently retired. He thought that Pritchard suffers from some sort of paranoia. He mentioned two characteristics of paranoia that match at least two types of behaviour that we have experienced.'

'And what are they?'

'He is constantly obsessed with the notion that there are plots to reduce his status, plan his downfall, and replace him. He is especially suspicious of me, and imagines that I am hoping to become the Head. So when he sees us talking together, he thinks that I am acting as a *de facto* Head Teacher and have called the others together for a meeting. And all we are doing, of course, is meeting for a tea or coffee break and chatting together. He has suspicions and delusions that have no basis in reality. Obviously, since there are no other opportunities to talk *shop,* we also discuss individual children's academic or medical progress, our teaching methods, the curriculum, etc.'

'And what is the other chief characteristic?'

'It's giving close attention to trivial matters while neglecting larger, more important issues, such as the curriculum, teaching methods, the medical and academic progress of pupils, staff development, etc. There have been several examples of an obsessive focus on unimportant details that have caused unpleasant incidents with staff, seriously eroding staff/Head relations ... '

Parham broke in:

'Yes. Brown told me about the extraordinary playground incident. He wasn't complaining about it: simply responding to my gentle pressure. And Mr Pritchard also keeps his distance most of the time?'

'Yes, he certainly does. You already know now that he avoids every kind of meeting, formal and informal, and that he doesn't visit our classrooms. No teacher receives any encouragement and he never sees the children's work. He is an absolute *loner*. He doesn't socialise or speak to us at all, unless we go to see him in order to ask for some clarification about something'

'Clarification about what?'

'Well, he sends us memos from time to time.' Tom handed a pile of them to Parham.

'You may like to look through these memos. This is the only way that Mr Pritchard chooses to communicate with us.'

'Extraordinary!'

'I know, but that's the way it is here. And sometimes we've gone to him to discuss some aspect of them. That has angered him and led to unpleasant incidents. I'm afraid we now have little respect for him.'

'I'm not surprised. And you, Tom, how are you coping with this peculiar situation?'

Tom laughed.

'With difficulty. The absence of effective leadership is a worry. As Mary Prince put it, we're like an orchestra that's been well rehearsed in the past but is suddenly confronted by a conductor who is not up to the job. We know what we have to do and we do it to the best of our ability, but in the longer term, we need a real leader who plans ahead with us, and, if possible, inspires us. And Caroline, who left at Christmas, expressed another fear, that these memos and other requirements, may gradually form a bureaucratic mesh that will strangle our creativity, our initiative and our morale. And now, Ronald, I think I've said more than enough. You've got the picture.'

'I have, Tom, and I'm very grateful to you. I know it's not easy for you to talk critically about your Head Teacher. But I had to hear it all. The truth was bound to come out sooner or later, and the sooner the better. And now, I must do what is best for the welfare and education of the children ... and I'm concerned about the staff, too. Now that I have a clear picture of the situation I'm ready to act. But first a word or two of caution. ... This is a delicate matter that I'll have to handle very sensitively. Please say nothing to your colleagues. I don't want to raise false hopes. I'll discuss a plan of action with the Chief Inspector, and possibly with the Chairman of the Governing Body. Believe me, I'm fully convinced of the need for action, and I won't let the grass grow under my feet.'

And Ronald Parham then shook hands with Tom Bates, patted him on the back, and went on his way. Tom was well satisfied. He was glad to have unburdened his concerns, and he was confident that Parham would be as good as his word.

***

Meanwhile, the other teachers had collected a new memo from their pigeonholes. It read as follows:

MEMO. NO.7

23 January, 1955

From: Mr Rupert Pritchard, Headmaster

To: All Staff at Haselmere Open-Air School for Delicate Children

My normal policy is to take a fairly relaxed attitude to the question of staff dress, but I should now like to emphasise that at all times, you must present yourselves in a correct and dignified way that commands respect. This requires a mode of dress that, as well as being neat and tidy, is rather more formal than may be appropriate elsewhere. It precludes, for example, the wearing of polo-neck pullovers or open-neck shirts by male teachers, a tie being essential, and the wearing of trousers by female staff.

Please bear these requirements in mind at all times.

Signed... Rupert Pritchard, Headmaster

This latest missive was discussed by the teachers at the first opportunity the next day. All were indignant, but Susan was furious. She had worn her new trouser suit for the first time that morning. It had seemed particularly appropriate in view of the extremely cold weather. It was fairly expensive, but very smart and well- tailored. She was proud of it. Her three colleagues had all made favourable comments. Now, they all knew that Pritchard must have drafted the memo as soon as he caught sight of her. Her wrath exploded when she met the others.

'How dare that man tell me what to wear! I'm comfortable in this suit and I think it's quite smart. Isn't it?'

'Of course it is,' Mary assured her, 'and it's just the right thing to wear during this atrocious weather.'

Tom agreed, and added,

'He told me last Autumn what I should be wearing. I felt I should go along with his wishes as he was new. We didn't know then just how difficult he could be. My advice is to completely ignore the memo. ... And I will return to wearing my polo-neck pullover. That will endear me to Pritchard for ever I should think!'

'And I'll join the club, too,' Mary said, smiling mischievously. 'Tomorrow morning I'll wear my own trouser suit. It's not half as smart as yours, Susan, but we'll be standing together.'

'Well done both of you,' Malcolm grinned. 'I'm only sorry I can't make a similar protest, but I've only got this *demob* suit from Burton's, and with our baby on the way I can't afford to splash out on a new outfit in order to defy His Lordship. But tomorrow you'll see me without a tie, provided I still look as dignified as I do at present!'

They all hooted with laughter.

Having disposed of the question of appropriate dress, the conversation turned to an exchange of views on Ronald Parham's visit. All the teachers felt buoyed up that the inspector had called in, and that he seemed to approve of what they were doing. They now looked to Tom to enlighten them on the likely outcome of the visit. However, following the inspector's wishes, Tom revealed only that Parham was particularly concerned about the absence of Staff Meetings, and that significant changes at Haselmere were likely to follow.

**

Recent comings and goings had not passed unnoticed by *The Scallywags.*

Who'd yer fink that tall geezer was, the one who went into all the classrooms?' asked Billy Green.

'I <u>know</u> who he is,' replied Tony Seymour, rather proud of his superior knowledge.

'Who?'

''es the inspector.'

''ow d'yer know?'

''because 'es been 'ere before. I remember 'im.'

'Right! Then what's 'e doin' 'ere?'

'Search me,' Tony replied.

'Well,' Billy continued. 'I'll tell you what I fink. I reckon ol' Pritchy may be in a lot of trouble. We all know 'e ain't been doing 'is job 'ow it's been done before. Inspectors come 'ere to check things is alright. I fink 'e must 'ave noticed that somefing's wrong 'ere. It ain't nuffin' to do wiv the teachers. They're smashin'. It's ol' Pritchy. Maybe 'e'll be kicked out. What d'yer fink?

'I fink,' answered Lucy Pym, 'that'd be alright wiv me.'

Ronald Parham was worried, upset and very angry. Though having niggling reservations about the appointment of Pritchard, he had been quite unaware of the state of affairs at Haselmere. He mulled over what he had learned from the teachers.

Pritchard seems to be completely ineffective, with no discernible leadership qualities. The teachers have received no guidance about the curriculum or methods that he wants them to follow. He has neglected to arrange Staff Meetings and doesn't even bother to visit the classrooms or to talk informally to the staff. He has spent an undue amount of time cooped up in his room instead of moving about to keep his finger on the pulse of activities in progress. His contribution to the School has been both negative and negligible. He completely misled me about the two teachers I had gone to visit. I think he deliberately lied to me about them. In fact, he has four teachers, all of whom are good professionals, and it is only due to their commitment and hard work that the School continues to function as well as it does. And then there are those absurd memos!

It would, however, be far from easy to remedy the situation. Clearly, the Governors had given Pritchard their full backing from the beginning, and Parham had no doubt that at the meetings of the Governing Body, he would have provided regular reports that cast him in the best possible light. He would take the credit for every imaginative activity or development that had taken place in the School since his arrival.

In any case Parham knew that it was very difficult to sack an inefficient Head Teacher; even more difficult than to get rid of a poorly performing teacher. The paranoia matter was intriguing. He knew very little about the condition and his instinct was to find out as much as possible about it before taking the matter further. He would need to hurry because the matter was urgent. It then occurred to him that it might be useful to contact the new School Doctor, Clive Mann, who had replaced Dr Alan Hargreaves. Although Mann was, of course, a GP, not a specialist in mental disorders, he would surely know rather more about paranoia than he (Parham) did.

As soon as he arrived home, he rang Clive Mann, who answered almost immediately.

'Hello. I'm Ronald Parham, the inspector of special schools. We haven't met. I believe you've replaced Alan Hargreaves as the School Doctor, so I'm sure that our paths will cross, as we must both visit the same special schools from time to time.'

'Yes, that's right. I'm glad to hear from you. What can I do for you?'

'Well, I wondered whether we might meet for a chat and get to know each other. Neither one of us will have much opportunity to do that while we are visiting. There are times when we'll need to work together very closely. I'm thinking, for instance, of the kind of situation where you may recommend that a child should be transferred to an ordinary school, perhaps because he is now fully fit. In such circumstances I would be called upon to advise upon the educational aspects.'

'I see,' said Dr Mann. 'Well, yes. Perhaps we should meet, as you say.'

In fact, he was puzzled and intrigued about Parham's approach. It had come quite *out of the blue.* He wondered whether the inspector had something in particular on his mind. If so, what could it be?

'Good,' Parham responded. 'Then let's fix up something.'

They exchanged addresses and Parham suggested a pub known to him that was roughly mid-way between their homes. They agreed to meet in the Saloon Bar of *The Three Tuns* at 6 p.m. on the following Friday.

Dr Clive Mann was glad that he had joined a small team of MOs. dealing with children in *Special Schools.* He was required to examine pupils with a wide range of disabilities, including the maladjusted, the emotionally disturbed, the partially sighted or deaf, the educationally sub-normal (ESN), the severely sub-normal (SSN), and children suffering from asthma or eczema. His present post would, he thought, provide for a young doctor a valuable learning experience. And that might be helpful for his future career, whatever form it might take. He judged from Parham's speech that the man was much older than himself, perhaps twice as old! He wondered again what was the real purpose of the meeting. ...

***

As they approached each other in the bar of *The Three Tuns*, the inspector was smiling. Dr Mann swept his eyes over his new companion, taking in the deep lines cut across the forehead and face, and the strong but slightly discoloured teeth. When the inspector extended a large hand, the doctor noticed the prominent veins, and when they were seated, he decided that the man facing him was probably even older than he had imagined.

Surely he must be near retirement age. And what a formidable presence! He looks like a Colonel Blimp, with his military bearing, back straight as a rod, short, clipped moustache and short back and sides.

Parham found himself confronted by a young, very tall, thin, ginger-haired man, with a rather bony, freckled face and a prominent Adam's apple that seemed to bounce about in his throat. The cheerful expression, that included his laughing eyes, seemed to be a permanent characteristic. Parham was disturbed to be confronted by someone so young – and perhaps immature!

He looks more like an undergraduate – and one in his first year – than a doctor. There's too much levity about the man!

However, recovering his composure quickly, Ronald Parham offered to get them drinks, and they each settled for a pint of mild and bitter. The inspector smiled and opened their discussion.

'You have responsibility for the health of children with a very wide range of disabilities and conditions. I imagine that you have to deal with some very interesting cases.'

'Yes, I do. Actually, all my patients are interesting, but I take a special interest in eczema cases, as that is my particular specialism.'

After a few more generalities, Parham decided, much to Mann's relief, to come to the point.

'I must admit that I had a specific purpose in mind when arranging to meet you, apart from the pleasure of getting to know you as a professional colleague, responsible for the same schools as myself.'

Clive Mann smiled. This was confirmation of what he had anticipated.

'And what was that?' he asked, grinning from ear to ear.

'Well, a situation has arisen in one school where there is someone who is said to suffer – if that is the appropriate word – from paranoia. Now, I know almost nothing about that condition, so I would be very grateful if you could tell me something about it – just the basic facts.' He smiled. 'Actually, if you were to give me a full, medical analysis of paranoia, I don't suppose I would follow you too well, but a broad definition would be helpful, with some idea of the normal symptoms.'

Dr. Mann chuckled. 'A detailed account is, in any case, out of the question. I am a GP, not a specialist in psychotic disorders, but I can certainly give you a broad outline of the main features of paranoia.'

'And what are they?'

'It's a very complicated area and there is a wide range of types, from the extremely deluded person to those with a relatively mild form of *paranoid personality disorder,* which is not uncommon. Such people often have a superficial sense of rationality, but in fact lack a sense of perspective or balance. So they make decisions that they perceive as absolutely logical while others see them as totally misguided. In certain situations they may perform quite adequately but they are not at all suited to posts of responsibility.'

'Now, that is very interesting indeed. It is precisely what I needed to know. But why are they unsuited to posts of responsibility?'

'Well, to begin with, they are often what sociologists called *isolates*. They eschew social gatherings, preferring to work, or relax, on their own.'

'I see. Anything else?'

'Yes. They are often suspicious of others who they think may be conspiring to harm them. That can make them aggressive. They may also give undue attention to relatively minor matters, which others think hardly worthy of attention, to the exclusion of really important matters. If they are actually in charge, then that can lead to obvious difficulties and tensions. And they may suffer from depression. Those are the common traits. Now, can you tell me, Mr Parham, who, in particular, you have in mind? I may then be able to help you further.'

Ronald Parham had listened with rapt attention, but was taken aback by the final question. He hesitated. Dr Mann had provided him with precisely the information he needed, but he was in no hurry to confide his problem to this young man with the disconcertingly laughing eyes.

'Well, at the moment I'd rather not if you don't mind. The situation is rather delicate.' Clive Mann grinned.

'Mr Parham, may I make a suggestion? Do you have in mind the Head Teacher of one of your schools?' Again, the inspector was caught off guard. He hesitated for a few moments to collect his thoughts, before replying.

'Yes, I do, as a matter of fact.'

''Then,' continued Mann, with another grin, you must be thinking of Rupert Pritchard. Am I right?' He hoped he didn't sound too triumphant. Then looking closely at Parham, he noted his discomfiture, and wondered whether it was wise to continue with his revelations.

Parham was certainly uncomfortable. The young, inexperienced doctor had now taken over leadership of the meeting and left the older man, an experienced inspector of schools, groping for the right words to respond.

'Well ...you're right, of course. Yes ... Rupert Pritchard is the person I have in mind. So you noticed something that alerted you?'

'Yes. In fact, I soon came to the conclusion that Pritchard had a paranoid disorder. He usually sits nearby while I am examining a child, and when he says anything at all, it's to dwell on minutiae rather than on the broader issues. Then, when I have ended an examination, most Head Teachers say a few words to the child – words of encouragement or humorous remarks. But not Mr Pritchard. He just gazes into space and seems quite remote. Also he has occasionally made remarks that suggests that he feels threatened, and must fight back. Actually, Mr Parham, I think he has a fairly low self-esteem and that he may suffer, from time to time, from depression.'

Parham was now well – satisfied. The doctor had told him more than he had hoped to hear. A second beer was ordered for both of them.

'Well, Clive, you have been most helpful to me, and I am very grateful to you.'

'I'm glad to have been able to help, Ronald. And now, may I put a question to you?'

'Of course.'

'I would imagine that Mr Pritchard is giving you, and the School, a few problems. So I'm rather curious to know, what action, if any, you propose to take?'

Before replying, Parham studied the young man before him. He was certainly open and friendly, and he had been very helpful, but he looked immature and might not be discreet. It would not be prudent to say too much.

'I'm not yet sure, Clive, but I'd like you to regard our exchanges today as strictly confidential.'

'Naturally.'

'Well, this is the position. Mr. Pritchard was selected by the Governing Body, by a large majority, and my feeling is that he still commands its full support. It's the governors who have the power to hire and fire, not me. However, I'll have a few words with the Chairman of the Governing Body, and acquaint him with examples of the Head's poor performance –

and, of course, I will tell him about the effect of Pritchard's behaviour on staff morale. ...And now, Dr Mann, I should like to put a question to you: should Rupert Pritchard be persuaded to see a doctor?'

'No. I doubt that you would be able to persuade him to do that. Paranoiacs hardly ever think there is anything wrong with them. They are convinced it's the people who surround them who have problems.'

Parham nodded. 'Yes. I can see that that would follow from everything you've said about paranoia. But now I must be getting on my way. Thank you again for the useful information you've given me. It was just what I wanted.'

Dr Mann said that he had enjoyed their chat, and that he would be quite happy for them to meet again if the inspector thought he needed any further information.

'Thank you,' Parham said. 'I'll certainly bear that in mind. Well, it's been a pleasure to meet and talk with you.'

And on that friendly note, they shook hands and went their separate ways.

Chapter 16
1 February 1955

Since the inspector's visit, the teachers had felt encouraged, and had grown more confident of their future. They believed that change was on the way. Perhaps Rupert Pritchard would be persuaded to resign from his post and return to teaching. Or perhaps he might be sacked. Tom took part in their discussions and speculations, but felt that a word of caution was in order.

'I'm quite sure that Ronald Parham will follow up his visit here. He knows that Pritchard doesn't measure up to the job– that, in fact – he's pretty hopeless. But the inspector will have problems.'

'As we have,' Malcolm grinned, 'and the biggest one is our Head Teacher!'

'That's absolutely right,' Tom agreed, 'but Mr. Parham really will have difficulties to overcome before he can get some action going.'

'Such as what, Tom?' Mary asked.

'Such as convincing the governors that all is not well here. You've seen for yourselves their cosy relationship with him. You must have noticed how Pritchard cultivated them at that awful drinks party, and again at the Christmas concert. I'm sure that he's set out from the beginning to get their backing; to bolster his position. Parham will also need to bring on board his senior inspector. And when they are all convinced of Pritchard's failures, it won't be the end of the road. Pritchard may appeal to his union for support, and the union will give him legal backing. I don't think that Pritchard will go quietly. He'll fight!'

'So you think we're in for the long haul,' Mary said.

'Yes I do,' Tom replied.

'That's really depressing,' Malcolm said, 'and I was already feeling a bit low after reading the latest news from South Africa.'

'There's hardly ever any good news from South Africa these days,' Mary said.

Malcolm agreed. 'It's about Sophiatown this time. It's been designated a *White Residential Area.* Heavily-armed police have removed 60,000 black people, and razed their houses to the ground. Isn't that disgusting!'

Mary agreed, 'It's terrible to push out all the black people in order to have a whites only area, and to do it in that way, breaking up communities and families.'

She was contemplative for a few moments before resuming. 'I suppose those houses are part of a shanty town aren't they – homes made from planks of wood, cardboard and corrugated iron? Are the black people being offered better accommodation?'

'No, they are not. And I don't know that all the houses being destroyed are part of a shanty town. I expect some of them are. But it isn't a matter of slum clearance. It's a matter of skin colour.' Malcolm became quite heated. 'The black people are not being treated as human beings. It makes me very angry. And think how rich South Africa is! Think about all that gold!'

'And diamonds, too' Susan added.

'But let's not talk only about the bad news,' Tom suggested. 'Have you read about what's happening in the USSR?'

'You mean about the change of leader?' Susan asked. 'I read something about it, but changes like that in the Soviet Union don't usually mean much, do they?'

'No, not usually,' Tom agreed, 'but you never know. Malenkov has been ousted, and someone called Khrushchev is now leader of Soviet Russia. There are hopes that he may improve things a little – move a bit away from Stalinism by carrying out a few reforms. It may mean the beginning of the end of the *Cold War.* Who can tell?'

'Well, let's hope so, Mary said, but a totalitarian state doesn't become a democracy overnight, so we mustn't expect too much!'

***

Later in the day, the teachers were handed another memo.

MEMO. NO. 8

From: Mr Rupert Pritchard, Headmaster

To: All Staff at Haselmere Open-Air School for Delicate Children

1 February, 1955

> *At 4.15 p.m., the end of the School Day, coaches are ready to return our pupils to their homes. It is essential on grounds of safety, that <u>all</u> teachers are present at the point of departure. It is necessary for each teacher to ensure that every child in his or her class is properly supervised and is counted in when entering a coach.*

Signed… Rupert Pritchard, Headmaster.

Normally, the teachers arranged between themselves which one of them would have overall responsibility for the homegoing of pupils on any particular day. That meant that if they wished to spend a little time in their classrooms, clearing up or preparing work for the next day, they were free to do so. In practice, most of the teachers were normally present with their class when the coaches drew up.

The latest memo. did not drive the teachers to distraction. It was just a little irritating, as were some other memos. As usual, there had been no prior discussion, while there was no evidence that anything was wrong with their normal arrangements.

'Here we go again,' Mary sang. 'It's memo time! His Lordship has decided that it's time to give us the benefit of his latest thinking. He feels that sending us a missive like this from time to time keeps us on track! Very Impressive! What would we do without him – or them?'

Malcolm laughed. 'It's just a bit of a nuisance. I like having a little time in the classroom at the end of the day when it's not my time to be on duty.'

'So do I.' Susan said, 'But what's to be done about it? Do we just carry it out or do we ignore it?'

'I think we should just do what Pritchard says in his memo,' Tom replied. 'By all means let's make a fuss when we're really put out about something – go to Pritchard *en masse,* send a copy of an offending Memo to Ronald Parham, etc. – but this one's not that important. It's just a blessed pain in the neck, a confounded nuisance. Believe me, matters will come to a head here and there'll be some quite dramatic developments. In the meantime I think we should just be patient and get on with our work.'

'Dramatic developments? Sounds fine,' Malcolm observed, 'but haven't we got to wait a long time for them? You agreed with Mary that we're in for a long haul, didn't you?'

'Yes, I know,' Tom agreed. 'I wanted to damp down any idea that Parham's visit would soon set the place on fire. I didn't want to raise false hopes – and I still don't. But it's also quite possible that things may move a little faster than we expect. ...'

'Then let's all do as Tom says – just get on with our teaching.' Mary said. We've been doing that very successfully so far, in spite of Pritchard.'

'I agree,' Susan said. 'We don't want a confrontation unless we've got a strong case or there is a development that makes us really angry.'

Such a development was not far away!

***

In Malcolm's pigeonhole the next morning was a request that he should let Pritchard know about his Graded Reading Books, a series called 'Reading for Pleasure.' He wanted to know how many books Malcolm had in his class at each grade.

The series was used mainly by Susan's class and his own, though a few slow readers in Mary's class also used them. Susan stocked books 1 to 5, he had books 3 to 8 and Mary had a few 6 to 8 books. The overlap was essential to accommodate the needs of both Susan's more advanced readers and some slower ones in his own class, who included Billy Owen and other children who had spent long periods in hospitals or clinics.

Malcolm studied the request again, and reflected on its possible significance.

I wonder what's in Pritchard's mind this time. When he asked about the number of scissors we held, it was followed by a memo. And now it's the number of graded readers. Surely he's not going to send us yet another memo. so soon after the last one. I'm getting really fed up with them! But it's easy enough to do what he wants.

Malcolm provided the information wanted by Pritchard, and found that Susan and Mary had received similar requests and had also complied with them. They too, were intrigued, if not suspicious, about their Head Teacher's sudden interest. Previously, he had shown little or no interest in the children's reading progress.

All speculation came to an end the next morning.

MEMO. NO. 9

From: Mr Rupert Pritchard, Headmaster

To: All Staff at Haselmere Open-Air School for Delicate Children

The Graded Reading Series called 'Reading for Pleasure' is currently being used by three classes. I am concerned that some classes are using books at an inappropriate level, books that should really be used exclusively by another class.

It is essential to rectify this situation immediately so that no class is short of those books appropriate to its needs.

I list below the classes and the books that they should be using. Any other books should be returned forthwith to the class that is to use them.

In this way, each class will have a range of books to accommodate the needs of both slower and more advanced readers, and also sufficient numbers at each grade.

Miss Carter.....Books 1 to 3
Mr Brown........Books 4 to 6
Mrs Prince......Books 7 to 8

Signed... Rupert Pritchard, Headmaster.

This memo prompted an eruption of anger among the three teachers concerned. No previous one had upset them to the same extent. To outsiders, it might appear to be eminently sensible. Pritchard himself no doubt regarded it as completely rational, and it probably met with the approval of the governors, who received copies of all memos. But Pritchard, as usual, had failed to take account of the views of the staff, and of the needs of individual children. The furious teachers could hardly wait to express their fury at a meeting held at the end of the day. Tom began by explaining his position.

'Of course, this memo. doesn't affect me. I have a few slow readers, but they are working on another series more suited to their older interests. Like some other memos this one looks reasonable enough, but it was sent, of course, without any consultation. Now tell me more. Put me in the picture about your concerns. How about you, Susan?'

'Well, we've got a flexible system,' Susan began, 'in which we switch books around. We worked it out among ourselves and it works very well. We ensure that every child has a suitable reading book, one at just the right level so that everyone can make maximum progress. We all have to cope with a wide range of attainment. For instance, I have a child who was reading simple books when she was three – her parents taught her – and now, at six years of age, she needs a Grade 5 book: otherwise she'd have to mark time! And I have some other children, not quite so advanced, who need a Grade 4. Under Mr Pritchard's plans, those books wouldn't be available to the children until they are promoted to Malcolm's class. That would be absurd wouldn't it? But I'm also amazed that we weren't consulted so that we could explain what we're doing and why.'

'Well done! You've put the position very well,' Malcolm said approvingly. 'It's absolutely vital that children have access to a graded reading book that is just right for them. Otherwise they lose interest. And making progress through the reading scheme means they can enjoy reading our library books, too. In my class there happens to be a particularly wide range of reading ability – I use standardized tests to check their levels – so I need Books 3 to 8. Some children came to me as non-readers, while I have some excellent readers, children who are ready to tackle almost anything. They are proud of their progress. Children who have books at the right level can be well-motivated and happy because they are making good progress, instead of being baffled and frustrated by having to cope with too many difficult words and phrases. What do you think, Mary?'

'Well, I agree with everything that has been said,' Mary said. This memo is the sort we most feared. It threatens our work as teachers. It could hold back the education of our pupils. It has no merit whatsoever. We should certainly not compromise our professionalism.'

'You mean, we should simply ignore it?' Tom asked.

'No,' Mary replied. I'd like to do just that, but while we certainly shouldn't do what Pritchard wants, we should try once again to knock some sense into that man.'

'Go to see him *en masse?*' Malcolm asked.

'Yes.'

'But that's always a waste of time, isn't it?' Malcolm said.

'Yes, it has always been useless. But I think we should make the effort once again. When Pritchard's scandalous neglect of his duties has been exposed by the authorities, it'll be clear that the staff tried, and tried again, to persuade him to see sense.'

'And you think that will happen? There'll be a full investigation?'

'Yes, I do.'

'I think so, too,' Tom added. 'And on the books question, it's clear to any reasonable person that we have a watertight case for retaining the *status quo.*'

'Good', Malcolm said, 'then let's give negotiation a chance!'

'Right,' Tom said, 'Let's all go to see Pritchard tomorrow morning as we did before. As usual, we'll be polite and explain that we feel that this is a vitally important educational issue. If he is dismissive, obstructive or aggressive, etc. then you can be sure that I'll report the whole episode to Ronald Parham. He asked me to keep him posted. I'll certainly do that. Tomorrow morning, then. Rehearse your speeches!'

***

The following morning, they all met early and made their way to Pritchard's study.

Pritchard looked at his staff with astonishment when they stood in a semi-circle a few feet from his desk, and Malcolm noticed that his incredulity was mixed with fear. The teachers looked ill at ease and a little embarrassed while he looked uncertain and vulnerable. For a moment, his small, malformed eyes darted from side to side and Malcolm thought that for a moment he looked desperately anxious. Then, his face reddened, and he glared at each teacher in turn before focusing his eyes on Tom.

'Mr Bates,' he exclaimed, with rising anger, 'you are fully aware that uninvited intrusions of this kind are forbidden. I have made that abundantly clear. You have again plotted to undermine my authority. You have been a scheming trouble-maker since my arrival here ...'

Tom remained calm but it required a determined effort.

'Mr Pritchard,' he broke in. 'I am very sorry, but it's vitally important that we discuss your latest memo with you, and come to some agreement.'

'You are very sorry,' Pritchard sneered, 'and you will be even sorrier when I report your behaviour to the Chairman of

Governors. My memo does not even affect your class. Make no mistake, your time in my School is limited!'

Malcolm was studying his Head Teacher.

This is not quite the usual Pritchard. He's steadily losing control. His speech is getting wilder. And I've never seen him quite so red in the face. His hands are trembling. He reminds me of a trapped animal!

He decided to take over from Tom.

'Mr Pritchard,' he began, in a tone of quiet reasonableness, 'I am very much affected by your memo so perhaps I may explain how it affects me. You would like me to hold three different types of reading book instead of six, as at present. Now, I happen to have a very wide range of both ability and attainment in my class ...'

'How do you know that?'

'At the end of every term I carry out a standardized test of reading ability, so I know the reading age, or reading quotient, of every child. I want to give everyone a graded reader that is just at his or her level. To do that, Mr Pritchard, I need all six grades, so that every child can make maximum progress.'

'You, Mr Brown,' Pritchard retorted, 'are a young, inexperienced probationary teacher with much to learn. The three different grades allocated to your class should cover all your needs – if you make use of them in the proper way. And,' – his voice rising in pitch as his control slipped again – 'I do not expect young teachers with your very short experience to questions my decisions!'

This was all too much for Susan, who was becoming very agitated.

'Mr Pritchard,' she interrupted. 'I'm afraid I resent the way you have just spoken to Mr Brown. His argument is a valid one, and that has nothing to do with the length of his time teaching, or his age. You are quite wrong and unjust to dismiss his points in such a cavalier and insulting way....'

'I don't want to hear this,' Miss Carter.

'I'm sure you don't, but there are things that must be said. Malcolm's case is very similar to mine. My children are very young and many of them have had a difficult time in hospital.

If I am to use my teaching skills effectively, I must make sure that each child has a book that is attractive and at just the right level. Young children can easily become discouraged. I want mine to enjoy success. We all want the best for our children.'

'I'm not prepared to listen to any more of this,' Pritchard shouted. 'It's outrageous!'

'No,' Susan retorted, 'what is outrageous is the sending out of instructions that affect our teaching, without any discussion beforehand.' And then, after a few moments to recover her breath, she continued.

'I also think that your treatment of Mr Bates has been disgraceful.'

Before Pritchard could make any retort, Mary broke in. She spoke quietly and firmly.

'Susan is right. It is quite absurd to hold Mr Bates responsible for organising this meeting. This latest memo has upset us all. And now that you have heard exactly how it could retard reading progress, are you prepared to withdraw it? Or will you let us continue to practise a scheme that has been working well?'

'Certainly not!' Pritchard shouted, 'and I am going to take all necessary measures against anyone who tries to undermine my efforts to rationalize and bring under control, practices that I, as Head Teacher, regard as unsatisfactorily or inadequate. And now, I must request that you all leave my study immediately.' With his voice steadily rising in pitch, he continued. 'And do not forget that I am the Head Teacher here!' He was now quivering with rage.

The teachers exchanged looks – and then left without a word.

At the foot of the stairs, Tom whispered to his colleagues.

'Well, we did our best, and well done all of you. We got nowhere, of course, but that was what we expected. And now I will write a full report for Ronald Parham.'

Malcolm was looking very serious.

'I found that very worrying,' he said. 'Pritchard is losing control all the time – and becoming less rational. No-one with his state of mind should be in charge of any school, and certainly not one for delicate children. I see him not simply as a hopeless Head Teacher, but as a threat – and a dangerous one.'

Chapter 17
15 February 1955

Ronald Parham was feeling frustrated. He was very worried about Rupert Pritchard's behaviour and failings, and convinced that a terrible mistake had been made when the Head was appointed. Pritchard was quite unfit for his position, and ways must be found to remove him. Parham wanted, first of all, to explain the gravity of the situation to Richard Bartlett, Chairman of the Governing Body. It was vitally important to have him as an ally. It was the Governing Body that would finally have to decide Pritchard's fate.

He had telephoned Barnett several times without getting a reply. Then, to his annoyance, he was forced to abandon his efforts for over a week because of involvement in other tasks: interviewing new teachers, in-service talks, inspections, etc.

Finally, when his work schedule permitted, he telephoned the Council Office and learned that Bartlett was on holiday, cruising in the Caribbean. Parham cursed his luck, but his frustration lessened somewhat when he learned that the Chairman would return in two days.

He reflected that Barnett probably regarded Pritchard with approval, and convincing him to think otherwise would be no easy task.

I am pretty sure that, at the Governors' Meetings, Pritchard's account of his impact on the School has been biased, selective and totally misleading. The governors will have no idea of his isolation and detachment from the day-to-day running of the School, his failure to have Staff Meetings, his failure to give the teachers any guidance on curriculum and methods ,etc. But I'll put Bartlett completely in the picture about the true situation at Haselmere – and I'll take it from there.

Soon after the Chairman's return from holiday, Parham contacted him and they fixed a meeting.

Malcolm was not, as an expectant father, particularly patient, and Caroline could see that he was getting rather edgy. The forecast date of her confinement had been 18 February and now, twelve days later they were still a childless couple! Not appreciating that such delay was by no means unusual, Malcolm feared that something might have gone wrong. Caroline, however, was not unduly concerned. The baby's movements were very evident now, and she found them quite reassuring. They were also exciting.

When her doctor acknowledged that the baby was overdue, and recommended that she should take a specific quantity of castor oil, Malcolm was astonished.

'Castor oil! Why on earth should you take castor oil?'

Caroline enlightened him. 'Well, dear, it's a common practice when babies seem to be in two minds about showing themselves,' she replied with a smile. 'I understand that it's to induce the birth.'

'Really? It sounds a bit radical. Let's hope it works!'

'Well, my GP is confident that it will.'

'Good. And when should you take it?'

'That's up to me, but I thought tomorrow when you come home from school, so you'll be present when it begins to work.'

'Right. And you'll be OK?'

'I certainly will. Malcolm, it could be the most exciting day of our lives!'

'I know you're right.'

***

At the School, everyone was delighted that London was to become a smokeless zone. This development followed a large number of deaths from bronchitis, asthma and emphysema, etc. caused by *smog,* especially in November. Most homes were still heated by coal fires which were very smoky. This added to the pollution from factories and power stations which also burned coal. When there was high atmospheric pressure (an *anticyclone*), there was often a temperature inversion, when smoke from the hundreds of chimneys rose only for a time, and then flattened out or descended. The smoke particles often combined with fog to produce a really dirty fog called *smog* which could have a deadly effect on the vulnerable and the elderly.

Many of the pupils at Haselmere would certainly benefit when a *smokeless zone* was fully established in London, particularly sufferers from asthma. The teachers felt they really had something to celebrate.

***

Malcolm hurried home to find, to his relief, that Caroline was as well and happy as when he had left her that morning. They discussed when she should take the *castor oil,* the potion that promised so much! The decision made, Caroline, in due course, swallowed the approved dose, without much pleasure, and they awaited events. Their excitement grew as the minutes ticked by.

The result was, in fact, quicker and more dramatic than they had anticipated. Within a couple of hours Caroline was violently sick, and in a short time she asked Malcolm to take her to hospital. Her waters had broken and her contractions were beginning. She was sure that their baby was shifting its position more than hitherto, and was convinced that its arrival was imminent! Malcolm tried his best to remain calm, but his heart was thumping.

A taxi took them to the maternity hospital and in a short time, Malcolm found himself sitting in a waiting room with two other fathers-in-waiting, both grim-face and staring into space. Two hours and several cups of coffee later, a nurse appeared to tell him that all was well. Caroline had an eight and a half pound boy.

Some time later Malcolm was overwhelmed when he saw Caroline sitting up in bed cradling their baby. He had long, black hair like his mother, and constantly turned his head as he tried to focus on the strange new world to which he was now exposed. Life would never again be the same for the Browns!

***

Ronald Parham had received Tom's report on the latest clash between teachers and Head Teacher. It was timely. He had finally managed to fix a meeting with the Chairman of Governors for the following day, and here was further evidence of Pritchard's failings: his refusal to consult with staff on key matters, his misguided instructions which could have a negative effect on the education of children, and his arbitrary dismissal of the views of his colleagues.

Parham was now free of other commitments, and so was able to focus his mind exclusively on the critical situation that had developed in what had been one of London's most successful open-air schools. He reflected on the appointment and conduct of Head Teachers.

It's unfortunate that Head Teachers are never normally evaluated. Competent or otherwise, once they have been appointed, they usually carry on from year to year until their retirement. By then, the incompetent ones could have had a detrimental effect on the education of the thousands of children who pass through the school. The only cases I can recall when Heads have been dismissed are when they have committed a major crime such as murder, embezzlement or rape. Well, we'll have to add gross mismanagement to that list!

But first the inspector must engage with Richard Barnett, Chairman of the Governing Body. A great deal would depend on the outcome of their discussion.

Richard Barnett's responsibilities as Chairman of the Governing Body covered a group of Special Schools, all within a defined area of London. Tall and lean, with penetrating, bright blue eyes, bushy black eyebrows and thick, black hair, he was someone who commanded attention in a crowd. Before his retirement he had held a responsible administrative post in a large industrial firm. He impressed people around him with a natural sense of authority.

For many years he had been very active in Local Government. Although he would accept that his work as a Councillor had its tedious aspects, it also had attractive compensations for him. It gave him a recognised status in the community, and people often sought his advice. He was highly respected. He had been mayor of his London Borough three times, and expected to enjoy that distinction once again in a year or so. But above all, he was motivated by a genuine desire to contribute something to the local area and local people. He felt he was of service to his local community – and he was.

There was, it is true, a less noble reason for his busy life outside his home. His wife exasperated him, especially now that he was retired. It was her oft-repeated and vacuous remarks, and her unending stream of gossip, that was particularly galling. It was therefore difficult for him to relax at home, and civic duties were a welcome diversion from domestic boredom.

The Chairman had a wide range of responsibilities: chairing interviewing panels for Headships and teaching posts, and, of course, chairing the regular bi-termly governors' meetings at several schools. His fellow governors appreciated that he was intelligent, articulate and conscientious.

Parham's unexpected contact intrigued him.

I wonder what's on the Inspector's mind – what he wants from me? Normally we only ever meet on Interviewing Boards. Parham is very sound, and I've always found his advice useful, but this present approach is unprecedented. Something must have cropped up; a major problem or crisis.

He found Parham in his office. The inspector had been immersed in some papers, but jumped to his feet immediately when he saw his visitor. Following their cordial, though formal, greeting, Bartlett was led to another part of the L-shaped office, well away from the formally-furnished office to a more relaxed area, with two comfortable armchairs. Barnett was invited to make himself comfortable, and was glad to accept a cup of coffee. The relaxed ambience reinforced his instinct that a matter of some gravity was on the Inspector's mind.

Parham began with his customarily pleasant overtures .

'Well, I must say that you look very well after your Caribbean holiday.'

'Yes. I've had a wonderful holiday, and I do feel refreshed.'

'Well, that's the most important result of a good holiday. The Caribbean is a fascinating part of the World, isn't it? I was there a few years ago. On one occasion I went out in a glass-bottomed boat. We came to where the water was crystal clear. Then someone dived off the boat and swam underneath it to feed the fish. Almost immediately the sea boiled with the movements of hundreds of iridescent and brightly-coloured fish, as they dipped and turned to snap at the food. It was enthralling. You, too, must have had many interesting experiences.'

'I certainly have. We visited a different island every day. Each one has its own character, and we had some excellent excursions, including visiting the huge volcanic crater on the island of St. Lucia.'

'Which other islands did you visit?'

'Let me see. St. Thomas, Tortola, St Maarten, Martinique, Barbados and Granada.'

'I envy you. It must have been really memorable. ... Now, I know how busy you are, so perhaps we should get down to business. But first, many thanks for coming here so soon after your return. You must have a lot of catching up to do.'

'Well, yes, there's plenty of work waiting for me, but I know that you must have something important on your mind.'

'Yes, I have,' Parham said. 'A problem has arisen in one of our schools. It poses a threat to the education of the children there, and it may undermine the morale of the teachers. I'd like to put you fully in the picture and hope that together we can work out some sort of strategy for remedial action. I really do need your full cooperation.'

'Of course. You can count on that. I'll help in any way I can. Which of the schools is having this problem?'

'It's Haselmere, Mr Barnett, and I'm sure you'll be surprised to hear that.'

'I certainly am surprised! Haselmere has always seemed a very settled and happy school, with few problems. The regular reports on school activities that we receive from the Head Teacher haven't mentioned any serious problems. Quite the contrary.'

The inspector swallowed. He paused to think for a few moments; then looked squarely at his visitor before beginning, step by step, the process of disillusioning him.

'Yes,' Parham continued, 'it has in the past been a very successful and happy place, and I have the greatest respect for the teachers there. They are still doing an excellent job. But they are at present extremely worried and there is a risk that their morale will gradually slide downwards, causing standards in the School to fall'

'And why is that?' asked Barnett

'The problem is, I'm sorry to say, with the Head Teacher, Rupert Pritchard.'

Barnett looked stunned as he absorbed this entirely unexpected news, but he quickly recovered and responded.

'Now I really do find that quite astonishing. Mr. Pritchard's reports give us a clear picture of what has been achieved in the School – in the very short time that he has been there. I have always had a high regard for him. What exactly is the problem?'

Parham paused again to marshal his thoughts

This is going to be tricky. I've got to peel off all the layers of partial information, biased accounts and half truths that the governors have been hearing at their meetings.

'I understand your concern,' he replied, with a smile, 'and I fully appreciate that what I am going to tell you will come as something of a shock. But I'm sure that you would like to have all the facts, and then I will value any advice that you are able to offer.'

'Yes, I do need to be put fully in the picture if I am to make any useful contribution. But please tell me what is wrong.'

Parham then outlined some of the main events that had worried the Staff and dealt particularly with the affair of the graded reading books.

'The teachers feel very strongly that when children are making good progress with a particular book, it should not be taken away from them.'

'Of course not. Are you saying that Mr Pritchard has actually done that?'

'I'm afraid that would have happened if he'd had his way. He sent the teachers a memo requesting a redistribution of graded reading books between classes. Its effect would have been to deprive many of the pupils of the books best suited to their attainment, books that matched their reading level.'

'But Mr Pritchard may have simply made a mistake. If the situation is pointed out to him, perhaps he will rectify the mistake.'

'It <u>was</u> pointed out to him, but he rejected all the points made to him.'

'Are you suggesting that he has arbitrarily refused to reconsider?'

'Yes, that is the case, but he should in any case have consulted the teachers <u>beforehand</u> about something that vitally affected their teaching.'

'Of course he should. So there was no prior consultation and when the teachers told him of the problems that would be caused, he refused to reconsider?'

'Yes, Mr Barnett, that sums it up very well. More generally, Mr Pritchard never consults the teachers about anything. He has sent several of these memos requesting changes, without prior discussion, and he never budges when various difficulties in their implementation are pointed out to him. And it's actually worse even than that. He resents any approach by the teachers to <u>discuss</u> a particular memo and has been very aggressive when they go to him with their suggestions.'

Richard Barnett's incredulity was now very manifest, but Parham decided this was no time to pull his punches. He outlined the unpleasant incidents, involving Malcolm, Tom and Mary, and then summed up the situation.

'My investigations indicate that Mr. Pritchard isn't actually managing Haselmere according to normal standards. In fact, he is quite ineffective as a Head Teacher, spends an undue amount of time in his study, never visits the classrooms, never engages with the teachers in discussion on either professional or personal matters and has issued no guidelines or advice or any aspect of the curriculum or teaching and, as a consequence, he is having a bad influence on the School.'

Richard Barnett had been listening with full concentration. He could not ignore the barrage of negative information he had just heard, but wondered whether there were any balancing, or redeeming, factors.

'That is all very disturbing, Mr Parham. You have given me a full account of Mr Pritchard's failures and omissions, but is he doing anything at all in a satisfactory way?'

'Yes. He carries out routine tasks such as ordering stock and arranging for the payment of non-teaching staff, and so on. But frankly, the School Secretary could do that kind of thing.'

'I see. And is there anything else I should know?'

'I'm glad you asked, because I had forgotten something very important. Mr Pritchard never has Staff Meetings.'

'Good heavens! That's extraordinary! They are essential, aren't they?'

'Yes they are. The staff need to meet to exchange ideas, to feed in new ideas to the Head and to discuss a wide range of issues concerning teaching methods, curriculum, the progress of individual pupils, school developments, long–term plans, and so on.'

'I appreciate all that. I really am amazed to hear that there are no Staff Meetings.'

'I must add that Mr Pritchard also takes exception to the teachers meeting informally to talk together.'

'But no-one can do that. Surely the teachers have breaks – their free time – when they're quite free to talk together about anything at all?'

'Yes, of course. No Head Teacher can legitimately ban free speech. However, Mr Pritchard has made clear his disapproval of informal meetings. Having no staff room, the teachers had been meeting in the hall, but such meetings have now been virtually banned.'

'That's almost incredible.'

'Yes, but that's the case. Of course, they must meet somehow, because, without formal Staff Meetings, they are left with many professional matters that <u>must</u> be discussed.'

'Yes. So what do they do?

'They have been forced to meet outside the School.'

'But that's a most unsatisfactory state of affairs.'

The Inspector was entirely in agreement.

'It certainly is. So there is no democratic discussion, and no attempt to take advantage of the experience and educational expertise of the school's excellent teachers.'

'Mr Parham, I find all this quite shocking. Mr Pritchard has always painted a glowing picture of the school's developments and progress as he distributes copies of his memos to show us various aspects of management that have claimed his attention.'

'Yes, I can well imagine that,' Parham responded, rather drily,' – and he looked searchingly at the Chairman as he continued – 'and I'm sure it must have occurred to you that sending written notes of that sort to his four teachers was a bizarre way to manage a small school community. The memos are edicts which are often misconceived. At best they are redundant; at worst, educationally harmful, as in the case of the reading books.'

'Mr Parham, I do, of course, accept everything that you've said. It's an awful state of affairs and I'm glad you have told me everything. Now, what can we do about it?'

'I think we have to proceed by stages, Mr Barnett. First of all, I'll talk to the Senior Inspector of Special Schools, and put him fully in the picture. He may feel that there is no alternative to having a Full Inspection of Haselmere which would look at every aspect.'

'Yes. That would appear to be a good start – and then?'

'Well, I can't anticipate the findings of an inspection. But it will lead to a detailed Report, copies of which will be given to all governors and teachers. Then will be the time to consider the action to be taken. I will keep you informed of developments and will value your co-operation. In the end, the Governing Body's decisions will be paramount.'

'And what should the Board of Governors do in the meantime?'

'I would prefer,' Parham replied, 'that you do nothing at all. I don't think the governors need know anything until they receive their copies of the Report. Partial and premature information could lead to controversy. I'd be grateful if you would carry on with your governors' meetings as usual.'

'I'll do that,' Bartlett agreed, 'and I'd certainly like to know the views of the Senior Inspector.'

'Of course, and I'll be in touch again to keep you fully informed. In the meantime, I must say that I'm very grateful to you for listening so patiently to my detailed account. Thank you very much. Working together we can surely find a solution to this problem.'

The two men then shook hands and parted. Parham felt that he had achieved all his objectives. Richard Barnett, who wielded considerable influence among the governors, was now his ally.

***

Well, that's phase one over. So far so good. Richard Barnett is not easily swayed, but he's now as convinced as I am that Pritchard is not fit to run a school.

I haven't yet told him about the possibility that Pritchard may suffer from a form of paranoia, but that would hardly explain all his failures, and it's certainly no excuse for much of his conduct. It doesn't affect the need to remove him. I'll mention it to Barnett later.

Pritchard is a menace. I must now consult with the Senior Inspector about the whole situation. And as soon as I can.

Chapter 19
21 March 1955

Malcolm's belief in the joys of fatherhood was coming under strain. He had been awakened night after night at midnight, and again at 3.00a.m. by Paul, whose lungs were evidently in perfect working order. In accordance with the prevailing medical advice, the plan had been to breast-feed him every four hours. But at night, he was usually ravenous after only about *three hours,* and he excelled at drawing attention to the fact. Caroline accepted all the haphazard interruptions to her night's sleep with smiling equanimity, and was serenely happy if, following his nourishment, Paul was soon in a deep sleep. When Malcolm left home for Haselmere this morning, the baby was, in fact, in just that state, and looking as peaceful as an angel.

***

Malcolm often discussed the weather with his class, making good use of both their open environment and his experience as an air navigator. He had told them about the troughs of low pressure which brought rain from the Atlantic Ocean, the formation of hailstones, or the various cloud types: cumulus, stratus, altocumulus, stratocumulus, cumulonimbus, etc.

But today there were no clouds – at least at first. It was one of the loveliest of Spring mornings, the sunshine enhancing the beauty of beds of daffodils, narcissi, crocuses, mascari, primroses and reticulata, which surrounded the classrooms.

But it didn't last. Innocent-looking cumulus clouds which formed later in the morning, at first as mere puffs of cotton wool, gave way to darker, larger, more menacing formations towards lunchtime.

The teachers noticed that a huge cumulonimbus cloud had formed and was spreading towards them. Malcolm had often navigated his Lancaster round them and knew that they could grow to an enormous size – over twenty miles in extent and twenty or thirty thousand feet high – and that they were massive generators of electricity which could bring violent electric storms.

All the children were resting on their canvas beds in the hall, some of them sound asleep, while the teachers conferred.

'It's a shame to wake them before the usual time,' Tom said, 'but it looks to me that we'll soon have a terrific downpour. The children won't be able to return to their classroom without getting drenched to the skin.'

'Tom,' Mary reproved him, with a smile, 'surely our senior teacher isn't going to flout memo no.1, which clearly forbids any departure from the normal schedule.'

'You bet I am,' Tom replied. 'Exceptional circumstances you know.' His eyes twinkled. 'Now, let's get our children on to their feet ...and away!'

Malcolm soon had all his children back in the classroom. It was now fairly dark so he switched on the light, let down and secured the canvas curtains and set a task for the children. They were soon settled.

A few minutes later there was a distant rumble, and some of the children looked up momentarily from their books before resuming their work. Another rumble seemed much nearer – and distinctly louder.

Suddenly there was an ear-splitting, explosive clap of thunder which lasted for a few seconds. It seemed to be all around them. A few children appeared slightly alarmed and looked to Malcolm for reassurance; others smiled. Only one child – Tim Owen – looked really scared, and Malcolm noticed Billy Green comforting him with one arm round his shoulder. He had always appreciated Billy's sympathetic instinct.

Then there was a brilliant flash of lightning which seemed to enter their classroom in spite of the protective curtains. It was almost immediately followed by the loudest crash of thunder that Malcolm could remember. It brought back fleeting images of the Blitz – wartime bombing and Anderson air raid shelters, and the particularly massive explosive when a landmine exploded at the end of his road and demolished hundreds of homes, including a block of flats.

Then the rain cascaded. It was torrential. Unlike some previous occasions, however, it fell almost vertically in heavy plops, which bounced up five or six inches on the pathways around the classroom and made such a noise that, for a time, combined with the staccato pounding on the roof and the flapping of the curtains, it was almost impossible for anyone to speak or be heard.

Yet the work of the class was hardly affected, and Malcolm reflected on the uniqueness of teaching in an open-air school.

I really like teaching these children. They're pretty remarkable. Not only does life in the open air improve their health, while they make good educational progress. It also seems to develop their characters. Life here is a bit Spartan for all of us – but it does the children no harm at all!

***

By the afternoon break, the skies had almost cleared and the sun peeped tentatively around patches of mackerel cloud. The children bolted for the playground while the teachers sipped tea in the Hall. After some exchanges about the weather, current affairs took over the conversation. It was more relaxing than discussing the latest Pritchard gaffes.

Malcolm asked Tom whether he thought it was time Winston Churchill resigned as Prime Minister.

'Of course he was a great War leader,' he said, 'but now he's a very old man. Some people think he has carried on for too long. What do you think?'

'Probably the same as you,' Tom replied. 'Anthony Eden's been waiting impatiently in the wings for some time. It's probably time for a younger man to take over.'

'What do you think?' Tom was looked in turn at each of his colleagues.

'I admire Churchill,' Mary said, ' but I remember that he showed how out of touch he had become when India achieved independence . He spoke then of *giving away the Empire*! As independence for India was being negotiated in the thirties – remember Gandhi's visits? – I don't think we had much choice but to arrange for Indian self-government as soon as possible after the War!'

'Yes,' Malcolm commented, 'Churchill's been such a long time in politics, much of it in government. It's amazing to think that he held senior Cabinet posts during the <u>First</u> World War.'

'Enough about politics!' Susan demanded, with a show of mock impatience. Albert Einstein has just died. Unlike your politicians, he was a genius.'

'Probably he was,' Mary said, 'though I don't understand his *theory of relativity.*'

'Nor do I,' Susan replied, 'but he was famous for more than that. For instance, his Nobel Prize was for work on the photo-electric cell – and that's something I do know something about.'

The others looked at her in surprise.

'Well, I do have a Bachelor of Science degree,' she explained, 'and work on photo-electric cells was pretty basic stuff, but I did find it extremely interesting.'

'So we've got a scientist among us,' Malcolm smiled, 'and I suppose each one of us has some hidden skills or knowledge. We really must get to know one another!'

'Right,' Tom said, with a grin. 'Did you know that I'm a skilled parachutist? – though I haven't had much experience since 1945.'

Mary laughed. 'And I,' she said, 'have diplomas in dance and drama, though I'm not in the mood to dance before you right now.'

'While I,' Malcolm chuckled, 'am pretty ignorant according to our Head Teacher, 'but I hope to be awarded a B.Sc.(Econ) of London University quite soon!'

The others cheered, patted him on the back, and returned to their classrooms in good spirits.

Rupert Pritchard, watching them from afar, glared and clenched his teeth.

***

'You don't want to worry about them storms, Tim,' assured Billy Green, 'specially now that sir's told us all about them.'

'I know,' Tim Owen replied, 'and it was int'resting, but I can't 'elp jumping when I 'ear a really loud bang – like an explosion. That's when I jump out of me skin.'

'Yeah, I used to do that.' There was a touch of pride in Billy's voice as if he had benefited from years of experience.

'I liked it 'specially when sir told us about 'ailstones,' Tim continued. Each one 'as layers like an onion. That's 'cause they goes up and down. Every time they goes up they get a new layer of ice. So they get bigger and bigger.'

''Sright,' Billy agreed, 'so why do they come down?'

'That's easy. They get too 'eavy so they just fall.'

'On us!

'Yeah, that's right, on us!'

Chapter 20
24 March [h] 1955

Ronald Parham was keen to build up a momentum in his campaign to remove Rupert Pritchard. But though heartened by his discussion with the Chairman, he had been having difficulty pinning down the Senior Inspector of Special Schools, Dr Charles Mitchell. Mitchell had been attending a seminar in Northern Ireland. After that, his appointments and meetings, many of which had been postponed because of the seminar, were now, according to his secretary, very urgent. Although Parham felt that his own need to see Mitchell was of paramount importance, he fully appreciated his colleague's situation. He himself had urgent commitments beside the one that dominated his thoughts.

Today, however, they were able to meet in Mitchell's office, and Parham explained how matters stood at Haselmere. He informed Mitchell in detail of the various unpleasant incidents that had taken place, emphasized Pritchard's isolation from the life and activities of the School, showed him copies of Pritchard's memos, emphasized the complete lack of any genuine discussion, and outlined the views of the two school doctors – that Pritchard's behaviour suggested some form of paranoia.

'But,' he added, 'that would not explain many features of his odd behaviour. He is hardly managing the School at all, and has minimal contact with the Staff, who have found him dogmatic, unwilling to listen to any reasonable points put to him, and often quite malicious and spiteful.'

'I haven't met Pritchard, as you know,' Mitchell said. 'What is your own assessment of him?'

'In appearance he is most unprepossessing. He's a red-faced, podgy little man, with a nervous habit of darting his little eyes from side to side while he talks. I'm fairly sure that he has a pretty low self-esteem, which he tries to conceal under a fluent barrage of superficially-rational arguments. When under pressure, he doesn't hesitate to lie or mislead. He is not to be trusted, he poses a danger to the welfare and education of the pupils, he long ago lost the trust of the teachers, and he is altogether unfit for his office!'

'Well, that's a pretty comprehensive account. He sounds like the worst possible head for a *special school for delicate children.*'

'That is so ...'

'Well, that's extremely worrying,' Mitchell broke in, rather impatiently. 'Did you say also that there are no Staff Meetings and no informal contacts, either?'

'That's right. All the teachers told me that.'

'Then it's incredible that such a person, unfit for the responsibilities of a Headship, should have been appointed in the first place.' He now sounded rather angry.

'I must agree,' Parham said, reddening with embarrassment, 'and I only wish we could put the clock back. Frankly, we had a pretty poor batch of candidates, and the Governing Body chose the one who was far and away the most articulate.'

'It sounds to me,' Mitchell said, 'that the post should have been re-advertised. A second trawl might have yielded a more promising batch. You were there, weren't you? Couldn't you have persuaded them to make another attempt, to re-advertise?'

'Yes, and with hindsight, I think I should have emphasized to the governors my doubts about Pritchard, more strongly than I did. But they were adamant that they wanted him, so I'm afraid I let matters take their democratic course. No-one could have foreseen just how hopeless Pritchard would turn out to be.'

'Yes, I appreciate that. Well, that's all water under the bridge now, but it's left us with a very difficult problem which will take a lot of resolving. I accept everything you've said about the man's failings, and I don't want him to remain in the school for a moment longer than absolutely necessary.'

'That's exactly what I think.'

'What action have you taken so far?'

Parham told Dr. Mitchell about his discussion with the Chairman of the Governing Body, and of its outcome.

'Well, I'm glad you've got him on board. We'll need his input.'

'Yes, he's well respected by the other governors, and may be able to influence them. They've been told nothing, by the way, but I've promised Barnett that I'll keep him fully informed of developments. I want him as an active ally.'

'Right.' Mitchell thought for a few moments. 'Now this is the plan. I want you and I to carry out a *Full Inspection* of Haselmere, and the sooner the better. We'll begin by interviewing all the teachers, and, of course, watching their lessons. We should also interview the School Medical Officer, the peripatetic staff and all non-teaching staff. That should give us a good overview of every aspect of the School. And of course we'll look at all the resources, the equipment, etc. We'll then confront Pritchard and put some penetrating questions to him so as to expose the full extent of his failures and deficiencies. Finally, we'll publish a Report which will set out our findings in detail – and, of course, our recommendations. A copy of that will go to the Chairman of the Governing Body.

While the Report will need to be seen to be fair, balanced and objective, it should lead any reasonable person reading it, to the inescapable conclusion that Pritchard must go!'

'Good. I'm very pleased, sir, that we see eye to eye on this. I've been very worried about it.'

'Yes – and with good reason.'

'When the Report has been published, there will be the problem of convincing the governors. That could be tricky.'

'But you said that Barnett had a lot of influence with them.'

'He has, but it won't be easy to get a unanimous view. I know them pretty well.'

'Perhaps,' Mitchell said, 'when he has read our Report, Pritchard may choose to go voluntarily.'

'Yes, it's possible. But somehow, I don't think it will work out like that. He's a complex character.'

'If he doesn't, then we'll take further steps.'

'Yes, though the Governing Body must take the final step. Still, I must say I'm feeling more optimistic now that we'll finally get the outcome we want!'

Relations between Pritchard and the teachers were now frostier than ever. If the teachers happened to meet their Head Teacher in the morning, the briefest of formal greetings were exchanged. Sometimes, Malcolm made an effort to unfreeze relations with a smile and a cheerful remark, but Pritchard always failed to reciprocate. His response was always minimal. So, in general, the staff kept out of Pritchard's way and just got on with their work. They were thankful to be left alone. They continued to send their written requests for stock, and there was no trouble getting what they requested. What sustained their spirits and morale now, apart from their mutual influence, was the knowledge that Ronald Parham was now aware of their problems; and they were confident that he would take whatever action was necessary.

Meetings in Tom's house once a month were always anticipated with pleasure. Not only was essential professional business transacted and ideas shared, but serious discussion was invariably followed by well-earned relaxation. Tom was always a generous host. There was plenty of delicious food, and drink flowed freely. The teachers had fun, laughed without restraint, and generally let off steam. After working in an ambience clouded by tension, Tom's hospitality provided a useful safety valve.

Today they would hear of an entirely unexpected event which would provide the central topic for their next meeting.

Meanwhile they were astonished to receive the following request:

2 April 1955

From Mr Rupert Pritchard,
Head Teacher.

I would like to know how many hours and minutes your class spends on each of the following subject activities:

English language/Reading/Writing
Mathematics
Nature Study/Science
Practical work.
Environmental Studies/Geography/History
Games/Outdoor activities
Other

In the case of Art and Music, the main teaching is carried out, of course, by the peripatetic teachers, but if you teach these subjects at all, please mention them in your return.

Rupert Pritchard, Head Teacher.

'What on earth can this mean?' Mary expostulated. 'His Lordship's been here for over two terms and suddenly he wants to know what we're teaching! He should jolly-well know what goes on in our classrooms, but up to now, he's shown little interest. There's something fishy here!'

'Well, of course,' Tom agreed. 'Actually he should have a good knowledge of every subject or activity that is taught at Haselmere. In fact, I suspect his knowledge is miniscule about either what we teach or how we teach it. '

'So why this sudden interest?' Susan asked.

'I've no idea,' Tom answered, 'but I agree with Mary that it seems very strange to make this request out of the blue, without explanation.'

'I have a feeling,' Malcolm added, 'that before long the mystery will be solved. But now, what do we do?'

'No doubt about that, 'Tom answered. 'It's a perfectly reasonable request. We can't possibly have any objection to it. We just do what he wants. In course of time, we'll learn what's behind it – if anything.' He chuckled. 'On reflection, I think Pritchard may be following his usual practice, that is, collecting information from us about something; then identifying an imagined deficiency and finally sending us a memo to straighten us out.'

'Oh dear, I don't want to be *straightened out* by anybody, least of all by Rupert Pritchard.' Sarah said. 'I expect that he'll try, as with the graded readers, to unravel a system that we all know is working pretty well.'

'Possibly,' Tom agreed. 'In the meantime, let's carry out our leader's request without delay.

The *raison d'etre* for Pritchard's letter to the teachers was a communication that Pritchard had just received. It was an official notification that there would be a Full Inspection of Haselmere. It was as follows:

31 March 1955

From the Office of the Inspectorate of Special Schools.

Dear Mr. Pritchard,

Kindly note that on the following dates there will be a Full Inpection of Haselmere Open Air School for Delicate Children:
29th April to 1st May inclusive.
All lessons and activities should proceed in the normal way. Any special preparation should be strongly discouraged.

Signed Ronald Parham
Inspector of Special Schools.

If the brevity and simplicity of the letter were intended to convey the impression that this was to be merely a routine inspection, and not set alarm bells ringing, it was not, by any means, successful. As he read it Pritchard was alarmed and agitated! He was soon in something of a panic!

He stared at it for a few minutes, speculating and worrying about its purpose, with a flow of suspicious ideas chasing one another in his brain.

What is this about? Who is behind it? What is its purpose?

What is involved in a FULL INSPECTION? Is it aimed mainly at the staff or at me? Will my work be inspected? If so, how?

Is someone trying to stir up trouble for me? Bates perhaps? He and Parham have known each other a long time, and get on well. Are they conspiring to get rid of me?

Is it a threat to my position?

What information should I equip myself with that might be useful to me if and when I am questioned?

It was the last question that had persuaded Pritchard to send the teachers a request for information.

He remained stressed for some time, the same questions, always unanswered, constantly returning to torment him. The more he thought about the coming inspection, the hotter under the collar he became. After a while he locked himself in his study and happened to catch his reflection in a mirror. He was perspiring and red in the face. The small group of long hairs on his head, normally aligned and patted carefully into place, were now a dishevelled tangle. He looked just as agitated and alarmed as, in fact, he was. He decided to relax in an armchair until he had calmed down.

Later in the day, he decided to inform the teachers. He would phrase his note to imply that it was *they*, in particular, who were to be inspected. It was as follows:

Please note that there is to be a Full Inspection of all lessons and activities in the school on the following dates:

29th April to 1st May inclusive.

The inspectors wish to see <u>normal</u> lessons, so no special preparations or special arrangements should be made.

Signed Rupert Pritchard.

The teachers received this note at lunchtime, and as soon as they could, they met in the Hall, where they laughed uncontrollably. Their suspicions were confirmed. With an inspection on the way, Pritchard was desperate to acquire even a thin veneer of basic information about the School he was assumed to be running.

Susan, in particular, could hardly contain her laughter. Trying to talk through her giggles she gasped,

'Isn't he pathetic? With the little snippets of information we've provided he's not going to get very far is he?'

'No. he's not,' Malcolm replied, 'but remember that our Master is adept with words. He'll make the most of those snippets of information.'

'Perhaps he will,' Susan continued, 'but in a small school like this, the inspectors will surely expect the Head Teacher to have an intimate knowledge of what is going on: the curriculum, our teaching methods, the academic level and medical condition of individual children, how we assess the pupils' work, how we deal with the retarded ones, how we ensure continuity between the classes, and so on.'

No-one disagreed with that, but Tom added,

'It's reasonable, too, to expect the Head to arrange for Staff Meetings, to have encouraged us to contribute ideas, and to have a clear idea of the direction in which he wishes to steer us – the educational and social goals he has in mind.'

'I think this inspection will prove to be a watershed,' Mary said. 'His Lordship is about to be caught out. He's neglected his duties, and he knows it. He's absolutely incompetent and all his weaknesses will be exposed by the inspectors. I bet he's in a panic!'

'I hope he is, though that sounds too good to be true,' Malcolm commented, with a grin. 'I only hope you're right.'

'Actually, we should remember that it's not only our Head Teacher who is going to be inspected,' Tom added. 'This is going to be a general inspection, and that means it will include us. It will also include all our facilities, including our equipment, books, etc. Now, if the inspectors identify specific deficiencies, that could be to our advantage. We may gain some more equipment , non-consumable stock , as a result.'

'Good,' Mary said. 'That gives me hope that they may see that our poor old Bluthner piano has had its day. It has steadily deteriorated over the past few years and is now hardly playable and it's often out of tune. What can you expect when it has to put up with frequent changes of temperature and humidity.? There's no such thing as an *open-air piano!* I have to play hymns on that geriatric instrument three times a week!'

'To me,' Malcolm said, grinning, 'it sounds like a *honky tonk* piano. Seriously, though, it's time we had a new one, with a new canvas cover to give it better protection when not in use.'

Mary endorsed that ecstatically.

'Hear! Hear! Roll on the General Inspection!'

Chapter 22
29 April 1955

This was the day on which Anthony Eden, who had succeeded Winston Churchill as leader of the Conservative Party, won the General Election. It was also the day on which the General Inspection of Haselmere Open-Air School for Delicate Children was due to begin.

Ronald Parham, accompanied by Dr Charles Mitchell, knocked on the door of Pritchard's study. The Head Teacher moved with alacrity to the door and beamed at his visitors, but there was, in his eyes, a fear and uncertainty that did not go unnoticed.

The Chief Inspector was introduced and the three men then had a short, formal meeting. On this occasion the inspectors were simply making a courtesy visit, at which they intended to say as little as possible. It would be on the third day, when they had spent two days listening to a variety of lessons, interviewing the teachers, and examining the books, equipment and all the facilities of the School, that they intended to give Pritchard a thorough grilling.

Accordingly, Dr Mitchell began with a few general observations.

'You will know, Mr Pritchard, that the Inspectorate normally carries out a Full Inspection of every school at five – year intervals. According to our records, it is some years since Haselmere had its last inspection. In the next few days, we will try to see everything here, including lessons, meals, outdoor activities, equipment, and all your facilities. We hope you will welcome that, because we can often identify deficiencies in equipment or facilities, etc. In such cases we can put in a strong recommendation for that deficiency to be put right.' He paused and smiled. 'And we hope that our activities will not cause any undue disruption.' He again smiled reassuringly at Pritchard, who smiled and nodded in return. He continued,

'We will not bother you personally until 1st May when we will probably wish to clarify some points arising from our interviews with the Staff, or from what we have observed. I feel sure that you will offer us your full cooperation.'

Pritchard beamed. 'Of course.'

The fairly soft approach of the inspectors – courteous though formal – made him feel a little more relaxed, and he was quite happy with the brevity of the visit, though the last thing he wanted was to have the two of them prowling around his school unaccompanied. So he put a question to his visitors.

'Would you like me to escort you to the various classes? I'd be happy to do so.'

Parham almost groaned. Pritchard must be kept away from their work at all costs! His presence was the last thing they wanted. They had to be completely free to wander about the school as necessary, to talk to both children and adults, and to converse confidentially together at all times.

'No, thank you,' Mr Pritchard,' he responded. 'That would be quite unnecessary. As you know, I am quite familiar with the layout of Haselmere. I should be. I've been visiting here for many years. No.' He looked directly at Pritchard and spoke firmly. 'We must be free to move around on our own, as and when we think fit, so that we can carry out an *independent evaluation.* I'm sure you understand.'

Pritchard coloured with embarrassment and resentment. He realized that he was being put in his place. Suspicions again welled up in his mind as to the real objectives of the inspectors, and questions persisted.

Why is this inspection taking place now, when I have not yet had a full year in this post?

Whose idea was it?

Are they trying to trap me?

Dr Mitchell had been studying Pritchard intently. He now added his closing assurances.

'We won't look in again today, then, Mr Pritchard. I am glad we are to have your full cooperation. Without that our task would be very difficult indeed.' He smiled again, Pritchard contrived to smile back, and the two inspectors left.

As soon as they were well clear of the building which housed Pritchard's study, Dr Mitchell spoke quietly and confidentially to his colleague.

'That man's a bundle of nerves. I'm sure you couldn't help but notice those queer eye movements – some sort of nervous twitch, I suppose – , but did you also see that his right foot was constantly tapping the carpet while his hands were shaking. And he was perspiring. He's really under considerable stress. I suppose our visit is partly responsible for that. In my experience, a certain amount of concern by Head Teachers is not uncommon when inspections are about to take place, but I've never seen anyone look so worried about the prospect!'

'Nor have I,' Parham responded, 'but I suppose that's because he has plenty to be worried about!'

The inspectors had planned their programme very carefully. Parham would first carry out an inspection of Susan's and Malcolm's classes, while Mitchell would inspect Mary's and Tom's.

Each inspection would involve interviews; the listening to lessons; an examination of all textbooks, reading books and exercise books; a survey of the equipment; inquiries about forms of assessment; and a reading of any guidelines relating to the curriculum and teaching approaches and methods. Talks with teachers would include questions about opportunities for the exchange of ideas, the support and guidance received from the Head Teacher, etc.

Both inspectors actually enjoyed their visits to classes during the first two days, and were impressed by the lessons they observed. They found the children alert and involved, the teachers had a good relationship with their pupils, there were no serious disciplinary problems, and standards were generally high, bearing in mind the loss of many months of schooling by some children, on medical grounds.

However, Mitchell was puzzled and intrigued.

'How is it,' he asked Parham, 'that a relatively high standard of teaching is taking place in a school where there is no evidence of genuine educational leadership?'

Parham suggested one answer to that conundrum.

'Haselmere had an inspirational Head Teacher for many years. William Rogers took great care in his selection of staff, and was himself completely devoted to the school. He was a born leader and an outstanding educationist, who spent much time encouraging pupils, supporting teachers and often teaching himself. He was a wonderful role model for everyone in the school. He built up an ethos of cooperation, helpfulness, humour, close attention to the needs of the children, and constant striving for higher standards. Happily, the legacy of that ethos still exists. It's the teachers, of course, who have kept it alive. They were always good teachers, and they happily absorbed all the guidance they had from Rogers. It's greatly to their credit that they've maintained standards in spite of the lack of management and any proper supervision from above.'

'But the danger is that they could, in time, become demoralised and depressed under Pritchard, and that standards could plummet?'

Parham thought carefully before answering.

'I don't think it would be quite as dramatic as that,' he replied, 'because these teachers are real professionals with a love of teaching. But yes, if the absence of effective leadership were allowed to go on for too long, I doubt that it would be possible to maintain the present high standards.'

'Well, we must hope to get this School once more on the right track under good management.'

Mitchell had more to say about his inspection of the classes.

'I found the teachers reluctant to say too much. What emerged very clearly, though, was confirmation of everything that you had previously noted. They receive virtually no guidance from Pritchard on the curriculum, or, for that matter, on anything else, and no support whatever. He keeps well clear of the classrooms. Incredible!'

'Yes it is,' agreed Parham, 'and since young Brown is still a probationer, the lack of guidance and support for him is a serious dereliction of duty.'

'Agreed. But considering the kind of odd creature that Pritchard is, I don't suppose for a moment that Brown wants him around too much!'

'No. By the way, sir, you've seen all the memos?'

'I have, and I've discussed each one with the teachers. Sending them was bizarre. They were never discussed beforehand with the staff. Some were redundant and others, though superficially rational, actually threatened to unravel something that was working quite satisfactorily. Now, Ronald, I think we've achieved our objectives for the first two days. Tomorrow we must interview Pritchard. He remains the main focus of our efforts, and we should go to the meeting with several key questions in mind.'

'Also,' put in Parham, 'we must put Pritchard on the defensive early on. He's very slippery and clever with words.'

'Well, yes, we should do that. Above all we must get enough evidence which, added to what we've already established, will give us a watertight case to present to the Governing Body.'

'Yes, and we want unanimity there, sir, and that won't be easy. A few of them are his devoted fans. I believe Pritchard has been careful to foster good relations with them. And, of course, they *selected* him so they will need some convincing! '

'And you think they will hold out even if the Report is absolutely damning?'

'I think,' Parham replied, 'that it may be touch and go.'

***

'Somefing's up. I knew somefing was up.'

Billy Green stood at the centre of his friends during the afternoon break.

'What d'yer mean? asked Jimmy Knox and Jack Miller almost in unison. Over several years they had together attended clinics for children with only one lung, and, as a result, they had become bosom friends. Malcolm thought they were like non-identical twins.

'Well, it stands to reason, do'n't it?' Billy replied. The tall geezer who looks like Colonel Blimp 'as been visiting the classes. He came in ours, didn't 'e? So 'as the other man. I fink they're both inspectors. Somefing's up. I fink we're bein' inspected. It don't look good for old Pritchy!'

'Then I 'ope,' put in Lucy Pym, 'that when they've inspected old Pritchy, they decide to chuck 'im out. Wouldn't that be smashing?'

'Not 'alf,' Billy replied.

Chapter 23
1st May 1955

The inspectors were glad that they had brought their umbrellas with them, as there were no covered walks between any of the buildings at Haselmere, and they were trapped in a sudden downpour, the rain splashing up around them and soaking the turnups of their trousers. Attempting a sprint towards cover, it occurred to Parham that this was a normal hazard here. The children had to move from one building to another, throughout the day, always unprotected. How did they manage?

Evidently they managed very well. The inspectors paused once they had passed the threshold of the admin building, their attention caught by a phalanx of children on the move, each one armed with a colourful umbrella. They moved along calmly, chattering and laughing, though wasting no time, to their various classrooms.

With their own umbrellas still dripping in spite of a vigorous shaking outside, they mounted the stairs to Pritchard's study. He stood outside the door, awaiting their arrival, fidgeting with worry but beaming nonetheless.

After mutual greetings, the inspectors declined the offer of armchairs, and the three men were soon sitting on what Parham afterwards described as *those dreadful polypropylene chairs*. They faced one another in an equilateral triangle, their chairs about two yards apart. It was the format they had planned. This was clearly to be no cosy chat, but what Parham saw as *an eyeball to eyeball confrontation.*

Pritchard looked tense. Studying him, Parham was satisfied. The Head Teacher would soon feel the heat as their questions penetrated to the heart of the school's malaise. Mitchell, however, began in his usual courteous fashion.

'Well,' Mr Pritchard, 'we've taken a close interest in the work of your teachers, and I must say that we have been favourably impressed by their competence, their dedication, and their well-planned lessons. All the teachers have a detailed knowledge of their pupils – their medical histories, their past school experience and their present attainment levels.'

Pritchard almost purred. He was pleased to lap up any praise for his staff, and ready to take full credit for any virtues or achievements attributed to them.

'That is very gratifying,' he responded.

'Yes,' Mitchell continued, 'and you are very fortunate to have teachers of their calibre in your School. You should be proud of your staff.'

Pritchard smirked, though he remained somewhat apprehensive about what was going to follow.

This seems to be getting better and better, but I suspect that these two have some nasty surprises up their sleeves.

'Now,' the Senior Inspector continued, 'there are a few matters on which we would like to have your views. Let's begin with your talented teachers. Each one has no doubt plenty of ideas of value to the others, and also to the School in general. Do you agree?'

'I certainly do,' Pritchard replied. 'As you have said, they are gifted teachers with plenty of ideas.'

'So,' Mitchell said, 'regular meetings between the teachers, and between the teachers and yourself are essential, aren't they?'

'Oh, yes,' Pritchard readily agreed.

'Then,' Mitchell continued, 'we would first of all like to know about the opportunities the teachers have to share and to contribute ideas.'

Pritchard frowned, and reacted with heightened colour and quickened eye movements. Was this request designed to trap him? But he recovered quickly with as confident a tone as he could muster.

'Well, there are, of course, plenty of occasions when the teachers can talk together. As you have just indicated, they are all performing at the same high level, and clearly sharing ideas, techniques and approaches with one another.'

'I'm sure they are,' Mitchell responded, and I suppose that they not only *share* ideas but are encouraged by you to *contribute them* at Staff Meetings. Do staff meetings, by the way, take place on a fairly regular basis – I mean once a month or something like that?'

He looked steadily at Pritchard, and his eyes conveyed only an innocent wish for enlightenment. Pritchard, however, reddened still further, his heart pumping furiously while his discomfiture increased. With his eyes racing from side to side, Parham thought he looked like a trapped animal. Then he recovered and was ready with his answer.

'I'm sure you will appreciate,' he began, in a reasonable-sounding voice, 'that because this is a small, friendly community, formal meetings of the kind that take place in larger schools would not be appropriate here. After all, there are only four teachers.'

Parham had to admire Pritchard's cunning answer, which had some validity, though he deplored the man's disingenuousness. He had warned his colleague that they were dealing with a slippery customer!

But Mitchell persisted relentlessly. He knew that he would have no difficulty punching holes in Pritchard's response.

'You don't have any Staff Meetings at all then?'

'No.'

'But you have already agreed, haven't you, that your teachers need regular opportunities to share and contribute ideas.'

'Yes, of course.'

'Perhaps, then, you would please explain to us, how, and with what success, that objective is achieved informally.'

Pritchard's rapidly sought a form of words in response.

'The nature of informal contacts obviously means that there is no record of them, so I'm afraid I can't give you a precise answer, but the standards achieved by my Staff are evidence that they do share ideas, information and techniques.'

Mitchell now decided to change to a higher gear.

'Exactly. But if a teacher has, for example, an excellent and innovative idea, that could benefit the whole school, it may or may not be discussed at all by the teachers meeting together – perhaps only by two of them – secondly, it will not be recorded, as in the minutes of a formal meeting – so it may easily be forgotten – and thirdly, you, as Head Teacher, may never hear about it. Is that the case?'

Again he smiled, but Pritchard could feel the net closing around him.

'Yes, I suppose so.'

'So perhaps formal meetings do have some advantages?'

'Yes.'

'Now, let us think about the informal contacts, the importance of which you have emphasized, and quite rightly. If you are in fairly regular contact – I mean, on a daily basis – with your teachers, discussing various ways of doing this and that, then you would soon learn of their ideas, and you would be able to pass on your own ones, wouldn't you?'

'Yes, of course.'

'And are you? Do you see, and speak to your teachers most days?'

'Yes, I suppose I do.' Pritchard saw no alternative to lying. After all, they couldn't prove that he didn't contact his staff regularly.

The two inspectors exchanged the briefest of looks. Pritchard was lying. There was, as all the teachers had confirmed, no regular contacts at all between Pritchard and themselves. In fact, they saw very little of him. It was time to move on to a new topic.

'Now, as Head Teacher,' Mitchell continued, 'you are appointed to provide leadership in all educational area, aren't you?'

'Yes, that's right.'

'Now, suppose you had a plan or idea that you wanted the teachers to consider, how would you communicate it to them?'

'Well, as we have just said, "informally".'

'And have you, since your arrival here in September, had occasion to call all the teachers together – perhaps informally – to discuss a new idea, a new direction, or some plan that you would like them to consider or to carry out?'

'No, I haven't.'

Dr Mitchell raised his eyebrows and looked surprised and puzzled.

'You mean,' he continued, 'that you haven't had in mind any ideas, developments or plans for the future – all based on the kind of school you want Haselmere to be?'

Pritchard paused before replying. He was feeling the heat.

They're trying to outwit me, but I too, can play that game. I must craft my responses with the same degree of guile as my interrogators are using.

'I agree with what you said earlier,' he began, 'that the teachers here are all highly competent, and I consider myself very fortunate in that respect. I established early on that the School was running well, and it would have been presumptuous and foolish of me – even arrogant – to propose any sudden departures. I don't believe in the concept of the new broom, the Head who wants to sweep away everything that has stood the test of time, in order to introduce his own ideas.'

Pritchard studied the inspectors' faces, looking for clues to their reactions, but both had impassive expressions. He felt that what he had just said was incontrovertible, and wanted acknowledgement of that, but they were silent for a few moments. Then Mitchell resumed:

'I see. So you have been content to let things, as it were, tick over?'

'Well, that sounds as if I've been inactive, which is by no means the case. I've spent a long time observing and studying. I've been learning every day – so that any proposed developments that I finally put to the staff will be soundly based.'

Another look passed between the inspectors, and this time it was noted by Pritchard. Ronald Parham now took over the questioning.

'Your youngest member of Staff, Mr Pritchard, is Malcolm Brown, a probationer. When I last spoke to you about him, you indicated that you had to monitor his teaching carefully, especially as you felt he had not been entirely satisfactory. Would you tell us how you have been doing that?'

'Well, I've been keeping an eye on him. His time-keeping had been rather slack, for example.'

'Oh, in what way?'

'On one occasion he rang the School bell two minutes early although I had sent a memo emphasising the importance of keeping to certain times.'

Both inspectors had difficulty keeping a straight face, and Mitchell found it necessary to press a palm against his mouth. Parham continued:

'Probationary teachers need support and encouragement, don't they?'

'Yes, they do.'

'And you have been supporting young Brown. In what way?'

'As opportunities have occurred, I've given him every help.'

'You've had regular chats with him about such matters as curriculum, methodology, assessment – that sort of thing?'

'Yes.'

Ronald Parham was beginning to wonder what was the use of questioning a persistent liar. He tried a new topic.

'You said just now,' he began, 'that you found the School *running well.*'

'Yes, I did.'

'Wasn't that was a tribute to the teacher who had been Acting Head during the previous, rather difficult period – Mr Bates. He obviously did the job very successfully. Would you agree?'

Pritchard paused again for a few moments. The subject of Tom Bates was one he had very much wished to avoid. Perspiration glistened on his forehead and his hands shook as various points flashed through his mind.

What the devil can I say about Bates? They don't know that he's scheming to take my place. He's been my enemy from the start, planning to undermine my position. Mitchell and Parham are trying to do that, too. I'm sure they want to get rid of me, and put him in my place? That's something I'll fight!

But only one answer was possible.

'Yes,' he replied.

Chapter 24
1st May 1955 (Continued)

Dr Mitchell and Ronald Parham felt that their interrogation had now reached a watershed. Pritchard had acknowledged two important facts: that Haselmere had been running well when he took over as Head, and that the credit for that should go to Tom Bates. Parham now sought to build on those admissions.

'So you were aware from the beginning that Mr Bates had performed well as Acting Head, that he had a thorough knowledge of how the School should be managed, and that he had made a significant contribution to the life and work of Haselmere?

'Yes, I knew all that.'

'And have you been able to draw on his experience?'

'I'm not sure what you mean.'

'Then let me put it this way. I would think that, bearing in mind his experience here, you would have been anxious to talk at length with him, to learn as much as possible about the School: its recent history, its day-to-day management, its teachers and pupils; any problems that might crop up from time to time, and so on. Would you agree?'

'Yes.'

'And you spoke with him?'

'We've had some talks. Yes.'

'About the sort of matters I've referred to?'

'Not exactly.'

'I see.' Parham now smiled before putting his next question, in a quietly persuasive manner. 'Why was that? Did you think his experience was of little relevance, and that you had nothing to learn from him?'

Pritchard was now sweating profusely. He had an urgent need to remove his tie, which he felt was strangling him. After a moment's hesitation, he asked his visitors to excuse him while he did so. That gave him a brief respite, and time to marshal his thoughts, but obfuscation seemed the only course open to him.

'Obviously,' he began, 'in the world of education, we can all learn from each other. I certainly appreciate that Mr Bates has had valuable experience here, both as the senior teacher and as Acting Head. But basically, I wanted to discover things for myself, at first hand.'

'I see,' said Parham. 'And how did you set about doing that?'

'By moving around the School, observing what was going on and talking to the children.'

'And the staff?'

'Sometimes, yes.'

Again, since the man was lying, the inspectors decided to move on to the next subject, and, following a brief look between them, Mitchell again took over the questioning.

'What sort of guidelines do you provide for the staff on curriculum matters, Mr Pritchard?'

This was an area in which Pritchard felt particularly weak and vulnerable. He took his time about answering, and found it impossible to control his deep gulps of breath, while he cobbled together some kind of answer.

'Well, of course, our curriculum here is rather restricted. Unlike ordinary schools, we have breathing exercises, a rest after lunch, three meals a day, medical inspections, etc. all of which take up a lot of time.'

'I agree,' Dr Mitchell said, and added, in a quiet, even voice, 'but I would be obliged if you would answer the question, which I think is an important one.'

'I think,' floundered Pritchard, desperately, 'the answer follows from my earlier response. I found the school functioning well, and I want to wait until the end of a full school year before I decide my next move.'

He then remembered his recent request to the teachers.

'I can give you precise information on how much time each class devotes to the various subject areas. You will find that we cannot, for instance, teach science, because we haven't got the facilities.' His face now wore a rather helpless expression.

Mitchell was becoming more than a little irritated.

'I gather that you have provided no guidelines at all, then.'

'No.'

'Then tell me what sort of guidelines are *presently* in existence, and what you think of them.'

Pritchard now asked whether he might get a glass of water. Mitchell smiled, said, 'Of course,' and the Head Teacher quickly disappeared into an adjoining room, normally used by his part-time secretary. As he resumed his seat, clutching a glass, he attempted a pleasantry–

'It's now May and warming up.' He smiled, and the inspectors smiled in return. He now had his answer ready.

'I am not aware that any curriculum guidelines exist,' he said. 'As I said just now, I know how each teacher divides his day between the various subjects and activities, and I am currently considering whether they have all got the right balance between them. I propose to focus increasingly on curriculum matters at the end of this school year.'

Mitchell now dropped his bombshell.

When you do that,' he mentioned quietly, 'you would do well to examine the excellent folder of curriculum notes written by your predecessor, William Rogers, copies of which are kept and used by all your teachers!'

Parham noted Pritchard's immediate reaction.

He is puzzled, startled and thoroughly stressed. And no wonder! He had no idea of the existence of the curriculum notes. That's absolute proof that he's never discussed any aspect of the curriculum with the teachers – otherwise they would surely have spoken to him about them. We discovered them after only two days but he knew nothing about them after two terms. Clear evidence of his incompetence.

Rupert Pritchard certainly looked thoroughly disconcerted for a few moments, but he once again proved his ability to bounce back after a setback, and, to some degree, he regained his composure.

'Yes, I will,' he said. 'Thank you for mentioning it. It had not been brought to my attention before.'

The inspectors could not refrain from smiling, and Dr. Mitchell felt he had to draw attention to the obvious implication of Pritchard's admission.

'Perhaps you might have learned about it before if you had discussed any curriculum area with Mr Bates, or with any of the other teachers,' he suggested.

This time Pritchard was really lost for words. He flushed, and the perspiration glistening on his forehead began to run down his face. Parham added a few words.

'And you could usefully study it to see whether you wish to consider modifying it in any way, after consulting with the Staff, of course.'

'Yes, thank you. I will certainly do that.'

Dr Mitchell now dipped his hand into his briefcase and brought out a sheaf of papers. Pritchard recognised them and speculated.

My memos! Well, there's not much that they can find wrong with them. They are all quite logical and based on facts. They show that I have kept my finger on the pulse of the school, and tried to make some changes aimed at improving various systems.

Mitchell looked briefly down at the notes in his hand; then raised his head and focused his eyes on the Head Teacher.

'Mr Pritchard,' he began, 'I have here a sheaf of memos that you have sent to the teachers. I wonder if you would mind explaining to us their purpose?'

'Purpose?' echoed Pritchard. He was indignant. Surely their purpose was obvious.

'Each one has its own purpose,' he said. 'Sometimes it is to rationalize a practice that has got out of hand or needs tidying up. For instance, I had discovered that the series of Graded Reading Books had strayed between classes so that their distribution was irrational. One class actually had six different books in that one series! I wanted them re-distributed so that each class had books appropriate for its pupils. I also saw to it that each class retained a good range of books to cater for the various levels.' He was well satisfied with his answer.

Well, I've given them a good and comprehensive answer. I'm glad I carried out that particular reform. The facts are incontrovertible.

Ronald Parham now put the key question.

'But before you sent out that memo, Mr Pritchard, did you discuss it with the teachers, so that you would be able to take account of their views or concerns?'

'No, I did not.'

'You didn't think it was necessary to do so?'

'No. I knew that it needed to be done so that each class would have more of the books that it actually needed.'

'And you, not the teachers,' persisted Parham, 'decided what each class needed to use?'

'Yes, I did.'

Parham frowned and shook his head.

There's so much this man doesn't seem to understand about normal educational practices. He really is a liability. It was easy for me to discover the range of books each teacher here needs, and why. He could have done the same. His misconceptions and failures are so blatant. We've now got him on the ropes, and I think we should keep him there!

Chapter 25
1st May 1955 (Continued)

There was a long pause, and a tense atmosphere.

Then Parham said, 'Let us be clear. You thought that it would be entirely unnecessary to talk to the teachers about the changes you had in mind?'

'Yes,' Pritchard acknowledged. 'What would be the point? If something is the right thing to do, then good leadership demands that it should be done.'

'But suppose it is actually not the "right thing to do". Suppose the teachers know about factors of which you are completely unaware, factors that make the proposed changes extremely unwise. Did that possibility not occur to you?'

'No, it didn't.'

'Then I must point out to you, Mr Pritchard, that the teachers were fully aware of the reading needs of every child because they have an intimate knowledge of every child's ability and attainment, based on their day-to-day contact with them. They had worked out together how best to distribute the books, and they were naturally horrified that you wanted to upset a system that was running well.'

Rupert Pritchard did not look at all convinced.

'Mr Parham, in my view, teachers need time to accept new procedures,' he said. 'They are reluctant to change their routine. Change is often resented.'

'But because you failed to consult the Staff, you were unaware of all the thought and effort that lay behind the current arrangements, weren't you?'

'I proposed a well-thought-out change.'

'No, Mr. Pritchard, you proposed nothing of the kind; you issued an edict.'

'I'm sorry you put it like that.'

'All right. Now let me tell you the full rationale behind the teachers' arrangements. In the two lower classes, the teachers regularly measure the reading age of every child, using standardized tests. They revealed that Mr Brown's class, which has a three year <u>chronological</u> age range, has a much wider age range of reading attainment. He needs those six different books, Mr Pritchard, so that the reading progress of every child can continue. The children were enjoying and benefiting from those books that you wanted to take from them. Once a child has mastered a particular book in the Graded Series, he is ready to tackle library books of parallel difficulty before moving on to the next book in the series.'

'But Mr. Parham, you will appreciate that I was not given the full picture that you were able to obtain.'

'But don't you think that the full picture would have emerged, Mr. Pritchard, had you discussed your proposals with the Staff?'

'Possibly, but my proposals were not, I think, unreasonable. I allowed for a range of three different books for each of the lower classes. I thought that would be enough,' he finished weakly.

Parham now made a dismissive sign and showed signs of irritation. Mitchell decided to continue with the questioning.

'So,' Mr Pritchard, you sent a memo. And what do you think happened afterwards? Do you think the reading books were redistributed in accordance with your memo?'

'Yes, I suppose so.'

'Did you, in fact, check that the books had been redistributed?'

'No. I trust my Staff.'

'In fact, Mr Pritchard, nothing happened. The teachers felt bound to follow their professional judgement – they were right in my view – and to continue the flexible arrangements that they had carefully worked out, rather than change to something they saw as detrimental to the children's education. Don't you think they were right?'

'Perhaps they were.'

'And do you think, Mr Pritchard, that sending your memos – especially without prior discussion – is the best way to manage a small school such as Haselmere?'

'I think it is a reasonable way to rationalize procedures and systems.'

'No, Mr Pritchard. We have studied all your memos, and it seems to us that while each one may have some logical or theoretical basis and may have been well-intentioned, some were completely unnecessary, and others were potentially harmful, as in the case we have just discussed. Every one should, in any case, have been the subject of prior discussion.'

He paused for a few seconds.

'Now, Mr. Pritchard, in a school of this size, don't you think that the regular interchange of ideas, suggestions, comments, etc. between the teachers and yourself, is absolutely essential?'

'Yes, I do.'

'But it doesn't happen does it?'

'Not all the time. No.'

'But it would be more effective than sending written communications, don't you think?'

'I think there's a place for both.'

Both Mitchell and Parham were now beginning to look both weary and frustrated.

'Now, Mr Pritchard,' Mitchell continued, with an air of resignation, 'let us move to another area. Managing a school also involves motivating the staff, by encouraging good practices, praising outstanding efforts or achievements, and so on. Would you agree?'

'Yes, of course.'

'And do you think you have been doing that?'

Pritchard thought for a few moments.

They just want to continue to embarrass me. I've been Head Teacher of this School for only two and a half terms. I'm a new Head. Yet they expect me to have got everything right in my first year!

'Well,' he began, 'not as consistently as I would wish. I would not claim that I got everything right all the time. After all, I am a new Head Teacher, and I have not yet been a full year in my post. Yes, I admit that I am still learning.'

Dr Mitchell continued.

'No-one, Mr Pritchard, would expect you to get everything right in your first year, but we are simply doing what is our duty – making an assessment of practices, procedures and performances by everyone concerned in this School.

And now, Mr Pritchard, I would like to refer once again to your answers to Mr Parham when he questioned you about Malcolm Brown. You said that you had given him advice and support, but his recollection is that you have not spoken to him at all about his teaching. That discrepancy is, you'll appreciate, rather worrying.'

'Yes it is. I've done my best, but I suppose I have tended to treat all the teachers the same.'

'But surely you have a clear obligation to give particular support to Brown because he is a probationer and relatively inexperienced. To have failed to do so is a dereliction of duty, don't you agree?'

Pritchard reddened.

'No, I don't accept that. Mr Brown is doing quite well. You have said so yourself.'

'Indeed he is, but that is no thanks to you, Mr Pritchard. That young man is a natural teacher, and his colleagues have supported him where necessary. Your involvement in his professional development has clearly been entirely negative. I'm afraid that is a damning indictment.'

'I'm sorry to hear you say that.'

'Secondly, what on earth made you think, Mr Pritchard, that you could manage Haselmere by spending most of the time in your study, and taking little active part in the life of the school?'

'I don't accept that, either, Dr Mitchell. I have already explained to you that, since the school was functioning well, I decided to limit my activities while I worked out the best way to proceed.'

'I see.'

There was now an almost palpable tension in the atmosphere, which was partly lessened when there was a knock on the door. It was Jenny, the part-time School Secretary. When she heard a response, she entered the room and enquired whether the visitors would like a cup of tea or coffee. They turned to her with a smile and said that a cup of tea was just what they needed. Pritchard now asked the others to excuse him and bolted for the toilet.

As he returned a few minutes later, Jenny entered with a tray carrying three cups of tea. The atmosphere now became a little more relaxed, and Mitchell decided that it was an appropriate time for winding up the interview. It was also the time to lower the temperature, and resume normal civil intercourse. He again addressed Pritchard.

'I think we have covered as many areas as we reasonably can, bearing in mind that we still have some further tasks to carry out here, including interviewing your peripatetic music teacher, Philip Thomas, and your Secretary. I'll have a talk with Dr Clive Mann when the medical inspections are over, and we may need to clear up some further points with your full-time staff. Thank you for your cooperation, and I hope we haven't taken up too much of your time.'

'No. Not at all. But what will happen next?'

Pritchard's voice betrayed his anxiety.

'Well, all Full Inspections are followed by a detailed Report, copies of which are made available to the Chairman of the Governing Body, the Chairman of the Education Committee, yourself, and each of the full-time teachers. There will be a number of recommendations which we would like you to consider. Mr Parham will visit you soon afterwards to discuss your response to those recommendations.'

'And that's all?'

'Oh, no. Obviously, the Governing Body will wish to discuss the Report, and its recommendations.'

'I see.'

'Thank you again, Mr Pritchard. We'll leave you now.'

All three rose, and both inspectors shook Pritchard's hand, and departed.

Pritchard now rushed to a mirror at one end of his room. Normally immaculate, he saw himself dishevelled in appearance, red –faced, wild –eyed and perspiring. He sat down while a growing anger enveloped him until he was shaking violently and breathing heavily, overwhelmed by what had taken place.

They come in here for a few days and think they know it all after that, and can sit in judgement. Obviously they've been listening to Bates who has been scheming against me and plotting to replace me ever since I arrived. I haven't been given a fair chance. And now, they're all against me! If there's any criticism in their report, I'll respond to them, and I'll also defend myself at the meeting of the Governing Body. The governors have always given me their full support. They know more about me, and about the School, than those two. They appointed me. They make all the main decisions. They'll be on my side, as always, so no-one will be able to touch me!

Only time would tell whether Pritchard's 'confidence,' in that respect, was misplaced. It was clear that both sides would be preparing for battle, and the outcome was by no means certain.

Part Three: Crisis and Change

Chapter 26
1st May 1955

As the inspectors, with undisguised relief, left the building, they were glad to note that it was no longer raining. Grey clouds were still scudding across the sky, but there was also a little hazy sunshine. They relaxed and chatted.

'What a really slimy character he is! He's worn me out,' Dr Mitchell observed. 'It was such long session. And those oscillating eyes! '

'Yes,' Parham agreed, 'and they almost seem to register his stress level.'

'You mean an *eyestressmeter?*

They both laughed. Any silly joke would do. They just felt they needed the relief of humour after their long and trying interview with Pritchard. Ideally, they would have both repaired to the nearest hostelry for a pint!

Mitchell became serious once again.

'His stress level was pretty high at times,' he said. 'I suppose we were rather ruthless with him, weren't we?'

Parham shook his head. 'I don't think so, sir. We *had* to ask those questions, and we had to be frank. We know that Pritchard can be difficult to pin down. If we hadn't put him thoroughly on the rack, and cornered him into a series of admissions – though he rejected some points – then we'd have achieved nothing.'

'I'm sure you're right,' Mitchell agreed, 'but I never want to be in that position again. I felt like a barrister in court whose relentless questioning has pushed the accused on to the ropes, and kept him there until the truth emerged. It's hardly the way I usually work.'

'I know, sir. Nor is it not my favourite *modus operandi* but we had no option.'

'True'

For a few minutes, the two men walked along in silence, each meditating on the lengthy confrontation that had just taken place. Then Dr Mitchell spoke again.

'Ronald, it's very difficult to remove a Head Teacher, even one as incompetent as Pritchard, isn't it?'

'That's right. It's very problematical. But he has to go. Pritchard has twelve to fifteen years before he is due to retire. Think of all the damage he could do in that time!'

'An alarming thought! The main problem, though, will be to persuade the Governing Body.'

'Yes, they'll make the ultimate decision, so we must have a really watertight case!'

'Then let's make sure we do just that.'

***

After their lunch with the teachers and pupils, Parham listened to Philip Thomas giving a music lesson, while Mitchell talked to the School Secretary.

Philip Thomas was thirtyish, of medium height and build, with the reddest hair that Parham had ever seen. His round face was creased in ways that suggested that amusement or laughter was never far from the surface.

The children sang some folk and national songs. Parham recognised 'Men of Harlech', 'The Grand Old Duke of York,' and 'Begone Dull Care.' He had himself learnt those same pieces as a child, and saw them as part of our musical heritage. He was no musician but he appreciated that the children were enjoying their singing, that clear enunciation was insisted upon, and that they were gaining musical insights and knowledge.

Afterwards, he spoke to Philip.

'I enjoyed listening to those traditional songs.'

'I'm glad to hear that, sir. But you may have heard a few *growlers* in this class. They are the children with no sense of pitch.' He grinned.

'Can you help them with that?'

'Sometimes, and gradually, but I have to deal with each one separately, usually for a few minutes after each lesson.'

'What about the piano? I can see that it's well protected with a canvas cover when not in use, but it's exposed to rapid changes in temperature and humidity, isn't it? How do you find it?'

Philip laughed. 'Very frustrating! No-one has ever manufactured a waterproof piano. They were never designed to be treated like this. Tucked away in a corner of the hall, and under its all-enveloping cover, it's just about playable. But with its cover off during a lesson, it can often go out of tune. Sometimes the keys stick! When it's out of action, I use my flute, especially when teaching a new song, phrase by phrase.'

'And that works well?'

Philip laughed again. 'Well, most of the time. But when I blow it on a cold winter day, I'm blowing hot air into a cold instrument. My breath condenses inside, so the flute is soon full of water which I have to shake out. And the children hoot with laughter.' He laughed again.

Parham smiled. 'I appreciate your problem. Is there anything that can be done about the piano?'

'Frankly, no. This old Bluthner is clapped out. We need both a new piano – a restored one would do – and a new, and better cover, with a more effective waterproof lining. Better ones are now available.'

'Right. I'll make a note of that,' Parham promised.

Philip Thomas looked very pleased.

***

Dr Mitchell, meanwhile, was interviewing the School Secretary, a petite brunette in her mid-fifties, with wide, black-rimmed spectacles, who exuded an air of quiet competence.

After some introductory remarks, including a few words about confidentiality, he continued:

'Jenny, you've worked with two Head Teachers here. Now, no two Heads work in the same way, so I expect you've had to be very adaptable, haven't you?'

I doubt that she'll be willing to answer that one. Her sense of loyalty to her boss may inhibit her response. Anyway, I hope we'll be able to have a friendly, relaxed chat. She must have a good idea of what's been going on in this School

But he was pleasantly surprised to find her very ready to confide. The words tumbled out.

'Oh, yes Mr. Rogers was always warm and supportive, and he had a good sense of humour. We often laughed together. And he spent a lot of time visiting the classes, talking to the children and teachers, and taking lessons. I think he was a wonderful Head Teacher. He was closely in touch with everything that was taking place.'

The she hesitated for a moment or two, wondering whether she had said too much, studying Mitchell's face, as if seeking reassurance. Then she said, very thoughtfully:

'I found Mr Pritchard very different. Frankly, it wasn't easy for me to work with him at first. He is much more remote than Mr Rogers was. I used to discuss all sorts of School matters with Mr Rogers. He often consulted me. But Mr Pritchard usually makes up his mind about something, and doesn't change it, whatever anyone else says. Well, he's the Head Teacher, so he's in charge. He likes to feel that he has the right solution for every problem.'

'And does he?'

'Well, I don't know, but I think he would probably find it helpful sometimes to talk to the teachers. They've had plenty of experience of open-air schools.'

'And talk to you as well?'

'Well, not about educational matters. But I talk a lot with the teachers so I do sort of have a finger on the pulse of things. I know what's going on. I know about their problems.'

They talked about other matters, including accountancy procedures, stock management, etc. Then Mitchell glanced at his watch. It was time to keep his appointment with the School Medical Officer, Dr Clive Mann. He thanked Jenny for giving up her time to talk to him and hurried off. On the way he mulled over what had transpired.

She obviously welcomed the opportunity to talk – Pritchard hasn't given her much scope for that. Yet I think she was constrained a bit. She didn't grumble, but she's clearly had an uncomfortable time with Pritchard and could have said much more than she did. But her account fits in with the general picture that we're building up.

Like Parham, Mitchell thought that Dr Mann was the youngest-looking doctor he'd ever seen. Masking his surprise, he greeted the doctor warmly.

'It's kind of you to spare a few minutes at the end of a busy day,' he began. 'How many medical inspections have you carried out today?'

'Twenty, I think.' Clive Mann wondered what on earth the inspector wanted from him, and waited for that to emerge.

'Hm. That's pretty impressive. Well, you really have had a long day, so I'll try to be brief ...I'd like to discuss with you a rather delicate matter that you have already mentioned to my colleague, Mr Parham.'

'Oh, yes. You must mean Mr Pritchard's paranoia?'

Mitchell was rather taken aback by the directness of the young doctor; but if he had something useful to say ...

'Yes. I understand that you have noticed some characteristics that suggest paranoia?'

'That's right. I could hardly ignore them.'

'I see, but you only see Mr Pritchard once a week when he attends the medical inspections of children, and you haven't been here very long, have you?'

Clive Mann looked amused.

'All that's correct. I don't see a lot of him – and I'm rather glad I don't! He grinned and his eyes twinkled. 'His paranoia was very apparent from the very first day I saw him. After examining each child, I normally explain the symptoms, treatment and progress with Heads. There's always very little reaction from him! In fact, he never seems particularly interested in the overall condition of a child, but nick-picks and fusses about points of minimal significance. '

'I see, and that, you think, indicates paranoia ?'

'Not alone. It's one of several symptoms. It shows some lack of balance, or lack of proportion.'

'Anything else?'

'Plenty. Let me now give you an example of his behaviour in a normal social interchange. When I make a joke, or a light-hearted remark – and I'm afraid my sense of humour often bubbles to the surface – he doesn't respond in any way one might expect – with a smile or similar remark. He looks wary, as if he's misunderstanding my humour, or is looking for some special meaning in it, or even that I am implying something sinister. That's very off-putting! It's quite impossible for me to relax in his company.'

'I'm sure it is.'

Clive Mann continued:

'At the end of an examination I always talk warmly and reassuringly to the children. I pat them on the back, make a joke or two and ask about their favourite activities. Then they go out happily.'

'And Mr Pritchard?'

'Well, that's just when he, too, should join in and be friendly and relaxed – but he keeps his distance and is as aloof as ever. Frankly, Dr Mitchell, that's very odd behaviour!'

'Yes, it would seem so.'

'He lives in a world of his own. His rigid concepts and opinions, however misguided, become a fixed reality in his mind, so he's impervious to any other ideas or suggestions. Once he feels he has the solution to a problem, he sticks to it like a leech.'

'Well, I said that you've had a tiring day, and it's not been a very relaxing day, either.'

'No. It hasn't ...Oh, one further thing. I've had no special training in psychiatry, but my feeling is that Mr Pritchard probably suffers from depression. That's hardly more than a guess, though. It's just the impression I get. ...I could tell you more, but I'm afraid I've got to hurry now to catch my train, or there's a half-hour wait. I can contact you again if you like.'

'That probably won't be necessary. But you mustn't miss your train. Dr Mann, you've been very helpful and I'm very grateful to you.'

The two men exchanged a few pleasantries, shook hands and parted.

***

The two inspectors had arranged to meet following their staff discussions, and they chatted as they strolled around the grounds of Haselmere.

'Well, Dr Mitchell said, 'that's the end of our final day here, and I think we've done all we set out to do. Now we must put our heads together and write an Inspection Report that will present a full and comprehensive picture of this School. It must surely present a convincing case for fundamental changes to management.'

'Amen to that!'

Chapter 27
20 June [h] 1955

Baby Paul, pink, round and thriving, at three months, was smiling at his parents as if he had a secret source of amusement, and showing undiluted pleasure when something delighted him. On such occasions, he would kick his legs wildly, wave his arms about like windmills and utter strange sounds, the meaning of which was known only to his inner self.

How dramatically that could all change! Paul seemed to become suddenly aware that he was truly ravenous, and expressed the urgency of his appetite in the only way he could: his face crinkled, his mouth opened wide, his face appeared to puff up like a red balloon, he sucked in huge breaths of air, and the air was soon rent with his heartfelt, earsplitting cries.

Thankfully, Caroline was at hand. She quickly arranged herself so that his desperate appetite could soon be assuaged and the previous relatively peaceful atmosphere soon restored.

Malcolm glanced at his watch. The babe would soon be in a deep sleep. It was time to leave for Haselmere. Caroline received a kiss on the lips, and Paul one on the top of his head. Quietly, he let himself out.

***

Unlike Rupert Pritchard, the teachers at Haselmere had all enjoyed the visit of the inspectors. All quietly proud of what they had been achieving, the Staff had been glad to exchange views with two pleasant and well-informed outsiders, who could offer them ideas gleaned from other open-air schools. Their exchanges were lively and punctuated by humour. Malcolm had described them as 'Great fun!' Moreover, the inspectors seemed genuinely interested and concerned with the teachers' problems.

There was also the hope that the resources and facilities of the School might be improved following the Inspectors' Report.

Therefore, unlike Pritchard, the teachers were not *on edge* awaiting its publication though, when they thought about it at all, some questions floated into their minds:

Would the report lead to an improvement and expansion of the School's facilities? If so, of what kind?

Should the report be strongly critical of Pritchard – and no other outcome seemed realistic – would he simply be admonished and strongly advised that certain changes in management style were essential?

Or would he be sacked for gross incompetence?

Would the Governing Body, over which they believed Pritchard had some sway, support him, whatever criticisms were in the Report?

If Pritchard were to be dismissed, who would take his place?

In the end, what would the Inspection, and the subsequent Report, mean for Haselmere, and its staff and children?

The arrival of the Report was imminent, but it would answer only one or two such questions. Others would be debated fiercely once the battle lines were in place.

***

It finally arrived, in each teacher's pigeonhole, during the afternoon. All the copies intended for the school had been sent in a single parcel to Pritchard, but inside were separate envelopes addressed to each teacher. Pritchard had been fretting about what might be in the report ever since the Inspection. Now, once he had arranged for Jenny Martin to distribute the envelopes, he locked his door, and sat down in his study to peruse its contents.

School Inspectors in the 1950s – and for some time afterwards – were adept at writing reports couched in a particular kind of language. Some teachers called it *Reportspeak.* While messages were clear to the perceptive reader – who could *read between the lines* – there was often an absence of direct and candid criticism. The language was usually diplomatic and generalised. It had to be interpreted.

Thus, comments such as, *'We wonder whether the useful practice of ...has been considered.'*

Or, *'It may be educationally desirable to ...'* etc. were commonly used.

In most of its pages, the report followed this style, especially when discussing various types of lesson that had been observed. The general idea was to avoid being over-prescriptive, but to suggest points for the teachers to consider and discuss.

In regard to Rupert Pritchard's work as Head Teacher, however, the Report strayed repeatedly from this diplomatic mode of expression, and the Inspectors' views were explicit and were forthrightly expressed. There was no equivocation and no room for misunderstanding.

As Pritchard focused on particular phrases, his eyes bulged, his face reddened and his anger grew.

Staff/Head relations were described as *steadily deteriorating.* This was said to be attributable to many causes, including *the inexplicable absence of regular contacts, both formal and informal, between Head and staff, and the self-imposed isolation of the Head Teacher.*

They pointed out that the teachers had plenty of ideas to contribute for the potential benefit of the whole School but the absence of dialogue meant that *the Head Teacher was unaware of what they had to offer.*

In regard to the question of a long term educational strategy for the school *the inspectors could not identify any sign that this was being developed or was even being considered.* They felt that there was instead *an undue focus on matters of minor concern* ,as illustrated by the content of some of the memos they had examined.

The memos themselves were described as *an unfortunate feature of the Head Teacher's management style.* It was felt that they sometimes dealt with issues better left to face-to-face contacts, where an exchange of views would have been possible before any action was taken. At other times, their content was seen to be *negative or detrimental to the children's education, as illustrated by the memo on children's graded reading books.*

They were particularly critical of the fact that *there was not only no prior discussion of any of the memos but also that no discussion was permitted afterwards.* They were, therefore, edicts, and it was expected that they would be implemented in full *however misguided or misconceived their message might be.*

On curriculum matters the Inspectors' observations were equally scathing. They could see *no evidence that any curriculum guidance of any kind had been provided.* The teachers, they said, made good use of some folders of curriculum notes written by the previous Head Teacher, which provided a good framework without inhibiting the initiative or enterprise of the staff in any way. The Inspectors were surprised to note that the present Head Teacher was quite unaware of the existence of these notes, *having failed to make the necessary enquiries or even attempted a discussion on curriculum questions with the teachers.*

In summary, the Inspectors expressed their concern for the school's future *unless radical action was taken in the short term. The present unsatisfactory situation should not be allowed to continue a moment longer than necessary.*

In the meantime, the teachers had been managing well, in spite of *the lack of adequate leadership*, partly because of their own gifts and training and partly because the excellent school ethos developed by the previous Head Teacher was still felt. However, it was emphasized that the teachers could not be expected to continue teaching at such a high level if their work and morale were *constantly undermined by unwise action at the top.*

Rupert Pritchard had read more than enough. His frustration had mounted as each page was digested. Staring in front of him, eyes bulging, and red in the face with pent-up fury, he pounded his desk and vented his anger in a loud outburst.

They haven't said a good or kind word about my work here. They might have acknowledged that I order the stock regularly so that we are never short of anything. How could the teachers work as well as they do unless I facilitate their work? The criticisms are unfair, especially those about the memos. Some things had become slack and I tried to rationalize them, to tidy things up. The Inspectors don't realize how important attention to detail is in a small school. If you get the small things right, the bigger things fall into place. I may have got some things wrong. Well, I haven't been here a year yet. They can't expect me to have got everything right in such a short time. That gives the game away. There's been a conspiracy against me. It started with Bates and he's spread his poison to the others. What the Inspectors have said must have come from the teachers. They were consulted before I was. When the Inspectors came to me, their minds were already made up!

The cathartic effect of this outpouring made Pritchard feel a little better, but he was left exhausted and breathing heavily. His head fell forward on to his chest and he closed his eyes for several minutes. He then decided to tidy up before his lunch arrived.

***

'Seen 'ol Pritchy lately? 'Billy Green enquired of his pals.

'Yes,' Tim Owen answered. 'I seen the 'ol geezer a little while ago.'

'Lucky ol' you,' said Billy. ''ow'd'e look?'

'Well, 'e was in a bit of a state.'

'What d'yer mean?'

'Well, sort of 'ot, red and rough.'

'I bet 'e did. You know what? A little bird 'as tol' me the Inspectors' Report 'as come. That's can't be good news for ol' Pritchy.'

'Why's that?'

'Stands to reason. I bet there's things in that Report that ol' Pritcy don' like.'

'What're you sayin'? Lucy Pym piped up. 'Do you think the ol' geezer 's goin' to get the 'igh jump?'

Billy turned to her and spoke with quiet authority.

'Only time will tell,' he said, 'but I reckon we're sort of movin' in that direction.'

Lucy shrugged. 'I s'pose that somefing,' she conceded.

***

The teachers were in no position to drop everything and read the Report with the close attention to detail that it merited. Their children had priority as usual. But they did manage to scan the *Summary of Recommendations* during the lunch break, and again during the mid-afternoon break. It set hearts beating. A meeting in Mary's classroom at the end of the day was hurriedly planned.

Tom chaired it in the normal way. He invited immediate reactions. They were all delighted with the complimentary observations on their teaching but were also keen to distil implied criticisms from minor qualifications, of which there were a few.

They welcomed the remarks about deficiencies in equipment or resources, Mary focusing especially on the section dealing with the piano.

'I'm really pleased about that,' she said. 'It strongly recommends that the old Bluthner be replaced by a reconditioned piano with a more substantial waterproof cover. Philip will be really pleased. And though I use it only for morning hymns, I'll be glad, too, to have a more reliable instrument.'

Malcolm noted with satisfaction that his School Magazine received generous praise, with a recommendation that the old Gestetner duplicating machine should be replaced by a more modern, labour-saving model.

A cheer went up from all the teachers when they read that a covered way should be erected between all the classrooms and the hall. Getting caught in the rain had been a part of life!

'You know why that bit got in?' Mary chuckled. 'It's because, if you remember, it rained cats and dogs on the third day of the Inspection!'

They all laughed.

'Now,' Tom said, 'let's get down to the *nitty gritty*. Have you all read the criticisms of Pritchard?'

'I think we all have,' Mary answered, 'and I, for one, agree with all their comments and criticisms. It was obviously a thorough investigation, and they've got to the heart of things.'

'They've used some pretty blunt language, haven't they? Malcolm remarked. 'The Report hasn't pulled any punches.'

'And,' Susan added, 'it doesn't seem to hold out much hope that things can improve under the present management.'

'That's right,' Tom agreed. 'They seem fully aware that Pritchard just isn't up to it. He's both incompetent and inadequate.'

'And especially for a Headship in a special school,' Mary said. 'Yes, they've hit the nail on the head several times. I like the bit about the need for radical change.'

'Like the dismissal of Pritchard,' suggested Susan.

'That can't be ruled out,' Tom said, 'but, you know, it's very hard to get a really bad teacher dismissed – it hardly ever happens, though we've all had to work with some really weak ones – but it's even harder to get rid of a completely inadequate Head Teacher.'

'I reckon there are only two grounds on which a Head is normally sacked,' Mary said, 'and they are financial or sexual irregularity. If Pritchard is to go, it will break new ground!'

'Suppose Pritchard does go,' said Malcolm thoughtfully. 'We'll all cheer ...and then what? Who will take his place? The Governors will choose someone else and we may go from the frying pan into the fire!'

They all laughed.

'We'll take a chance on that,' Susan said.

'Right.' Tom said, 'We can't say any more just now as we all want to get home. We're agreed, I think, that's it's a good report, and that it fills us with hope.'

Four happy teachers nodded and smiled.

Rupert Pritchard was preparing to leave for home. He had put on his trilby hat and raincoat and had almost reached the door when the telephone rang. It was Ronald Parham.

'Hello. I just thought I would confirm that all the copies of our Report arrived safely.'

'Yes. They all arrived.'

'And the teachers all have a copy now?'

'Yes. I gave them out just after they arrived here.'

'Good. The other point,' continued Parham, 'is that I thought I would call in to discuss possible outcomes.'

'Possible outcomes?' Pritchard's fears bubbled to the surface and he felt his heart pumping.

'Well, yes. Dr Mitchell and I have expressed our concerns in the report, and I would like to hear how you respond to them, what you think about them. That's normal procedure.'

Pritchard was not convinced that it was.

What's the real purpose of this meeting? Is he going to sack me? No, he can't do that. The Governing Body are the only ones with that power, and I get on well with them. They'll always back me!

Ronald Parham had waited long enough for a response.

'Look', he said quietly, in a tone of marked reasonableness, 'I appreciate that you've only just received our report, and you need time to study it before we meet. Shall we make it in about a week or two?'

'Yes.'

Excellent. Now, I'm free on 5 July . Will that suit you? Say, about 10 a.m.?'

'Yes. That'll be alright.'

'Fine. I'll see you then. Thank you. Goodbye.'

And he rang off. Pritchard, still wearing his hat and coat, sat down, and mulled over this latest development.

They think they've got me cornered, but I'll show them. They want to know how I respond, do they? Right, I'll give them more than they're expecting. I'll respond in a way that will take the wind out of their sails. They'll have a big surprise! They'll find out that I can fight!

Chapter 28
5 July 1955

Ronald Parham was not one whose jaw dropped when he was confronted by the unexpected, but he would probably have admitted to being unsettled when he next met Pritchard. He had never seen the Head Teacher of Haselmere look or sound remotely like this. He had *never* before confronted this person!

Setting out that morning, he had been glad that he had arranged the meeting. It would help to keep up the momentum. Both inspectors were keen to do that.

Inevitably he had speculated on how Pritchard might choose to respond to the damning criticisms in the Report. Perhaps he would just recognise that he was quite out of his depth and resign. In that event he would be offered a teaching post in another school. According to the records he hadn't been a completely hopeless teacher.

The first surprise met him on arrival at Pritchard's door. He was greeted with excessive *bonhomie*, the Head Teacher smiling radiantly and paying exaggerated attention to his comfort and well-being as he seated him in a comfortable armchair. Where was the neurotic wretch he had witnessed on his last visit?

Pritchard's absurdly relaxed and over-attentive demeanour disturbed Parham. It made him feel uneasy. He certainly wanted to preserve the civilities – a veneer of politeness, even pleasantness – and to have a productive exchange of views. But this was not the atmosphere he had planned. There was hard and serious business to be discussed. Obviously, Pritchard had decided on a new strategy, and was feeling decidedly complacent and confident – far too confident – about it. That was worrying. But perhaps he had already decided to go, and was feeling relieved, happier and more at ease with himself now that the decision had been made!

What a bizarre character he is! And full of surprises! But what's in his mind? He's worked out something which he thinks will be his salvation. We'll see. This dialogue should expose his plans!

'Thank you for agreeing to see me this morning,' he began. 'It seemed to me, on reflection, that Dr Mitchell and I had written a fairly critical Report and that it was only fair to give you an opportunity to come back at us, as it were. Above all, we have to decide on the next step.'

'Yes, and that was most considerate of you,' purred Pritchard. 'Well, I have studied the report in depth, and I've given a lot of thought as to the best way to respond to it.' He paused and smiled. 'I've prepared a detailed response for the Governing Body, and I would be happy to give you a copy of it for you to read at your leisure.' As he spoke he extracted from a drawer below his desk, a very substantial, most impressive-looking document.

Parham tried hard to conceal his astonishment. This was entirely unexpected. What on earth was in the document? He had never imagined that anything like it would be produced as an *answer* to the points in the Report. Such a thick document must have required many hours of work so as to present a coherent and convincing case – or so he supposed. It was, no doubt, full of specious arguments.

'This is it,' Pritchard said, with a beam that Parham found intensely irritating. 'It's a statement of strongly-held values and beliefs, and outlines a programme of action. I won't try to cover, here and now, everything that's in it, but I'm sure you'd like to be aware of some of its main provisions.'

'Yes, I certainly would ...'

'Well, I'll summarize some of the salient points. But may I say, first of all, that I found your Report very helpful and timely, in that it provides a valuable basis for future planning at the end of my first year here.'

'Oh, you think so?'

'Yes, I do.' Pritchard was looking and sounding supremely confident now. 'I fully appreciate that during my first year as a Head Teacher I may well have made some mistakes. There are many things I wish I had done differently.' He shook his head sadly. 'I expect most new Heads feel the same way at this point. And, of course, this is an Open-Air School with very special problems so there was even more to learn.' His voice brightened. 'But your Report, I'm glad to say, could hardly have been more timely. Now ... before I get too involved about it, may I get you a cup of coffee?'

Parham said that would be very nice. The break, and Pritchard's temporary disappearance, enabled him to reassemble his thoughts.

I'm hearing a lot of claptrap. It hardly relates to what has been going on. Pritchard has neglected every opportunity to learn how to manage the School – he could have learnt a great deal about that from Tom or exchanged ideas with his very knowledgeable staff. It's they who have successfully held the School together while his actions have often threatened to undermine their efforts.

But I'll hear everything he has to say, because we must understand the kind of strategy he's developing to stay in post. Obviously he intends to do so – and that's very depressing.

Pritchard returned with a pot of coffee, milk and sugar, and proceeded to pour two cups. He resumed the conversation.

'You know, Mr. Parham, I've had no special training in school management, except as a deputy, but I'm a great believer in the value of learning skills on the job. As I've mentioned before, I always intended to make some changes, to steer in a particular direction, once I felt I had enough experience. And then, your valuable Report arrived. Just at the right time! It provides a catalyst for those improvements that I had been contemplating, and which you will find fully outlined in the document.'

While he listened, Parham was hoping that his expression did not reveal the slightest trace of the cynicism he felt.

What a metamorphosis! His eyes are shining with evangelical fervour, and if I didn't know him better I'd be swept along in his current of lies and half-truths. He's rehearsing for his crucial meeting with the Governing Body. Face to face with the governors, he'll use every kind of facile argument, to gain their powerful support. He'll urge them to look to the future as he has envisaged it in his 'progressive' plans for the years ahead.

It mustn't happen. It would be a disaster!

'I wonder,' he said, quietly, 'whether you'd like to tell me exactly what you have in mind.'

Pritchard's shining eyes again revealed his excitement.

'Certainly. Let me give you some examples,' he responded eagerly. 'You have raised the key question of Staff Meetings. I think, on reflection that I was mistaken in thinking that formal meetings are not really appropriate in a small school. On the contrary, they are, of course, vitally important. I am proposing to institute regular monthly Staff Meetings from the beginning of next term. They will be completely democratic in character. Not only will the teachers be invited to propose items for the agenda; they will, also, in rotation, chair the meetings. That form of procedure has always appealed to me, but I couldn't introduce it earlier, before I had really settled in.'

Parham was almost speechless. Pritchard had caught him off balance by proposing the most radical arrangements for future Staff Meetings.

'That's very interesting,' he managed to say. 'And is there anything else to which you which you would like to draw my attention?'

'Yes, another area of vital concern is the curriculum. I have drawn up a framework which embraces all the subjects and activities appropriate to a school of this size and character. Now, I won't, of course, issue is as a *fait accompli*. My preference is to let the teachers study it, and then discuss it at a special Staff Meeting. It will be a framework for discussion. Nothing more. I've played my leadership role by drawing up precise objectives for each subject and for each age group. They, too, will be discussed and possibly amended. Finally, I will work out with the teachers a detailed curriculum for each age and subject. It will take a little while but I would hope to draw in every teacher's expertise and experience in the process. Working together, the flesh that we put on the bones of my framework, will lead to curricula that command every teacher's support.' He leaned forward and looked eagerly and expectantly at Parham, who almost snorted with disgust.

Words! Words! Words! He's not only done nothing about the curriculum for nearly a year. He hasn't even discussed with his probationary teacher a single one of his lessons, or given him the slightest help or encouragement. It makes it worse that he knew what he should be doing, yet did nothing!

He listened to some further proposals that were in Pritchard's report. In every case, the measures proposed were both enlightened and forward-looking. Inwardly he fumed.

All this is a smokescreen, a desperate attempt to hold on to the Headship. There's no limit to this man's duplicity. To some degree, I suppose, his behaviour is explained by his paranoia, but he's blatantly disingenuous anyway. In fact, he's a pathological liar!

He turned to face Pritchard.

'Thank you,' he said, in a voice of quiet, controlled politeness. 'You are quite right to select Staff Meetings and curriculum as critical matters demanding urgent attention. There is also the question of regular contacts with the teachers – that sort of thing.'

'Indeed,' Pritchard responded, with a smile, 'and I think you will find that I have comprehensively covered that ground. I fully appreciate the need for continuing dialogue if Haselmere is to flourish.'

Parham had had enough. It was clear that if he spent a further hour with the Head Teacher, he would be given, with impressive consistency, fluent and comprehensive answers to every point he might raise. The gap between words and performance was more than he could stomach.

'Well,' he said, standing up. 'I don't think I need detain you any longer. You have obviously put a lot of thought and work into your document, and I can assure you that Dr Mitchell and I will give it our full attention very shortly. Goodbye, then. I'm sure we'll be in touch again in the very near future.'

They shook hands and Parham went on his way. He was not a happy man.

Damn! That lying bugger has stolen the initiative. I always knew he would be difficult to pin down. Yesterday, he had to respond to our Report; today he wants us to respond to his report. A clever strategy! He's prepared to promise anything to save his skin. No doubt his report will impress the Governing Body, which already looks on him favourably – perhaps with the exception of the Chairman. If any doubts are expressed by the governors, he'll emphasize that he has tried to respond to every issue in the Inspectors' Report. He simply wants a fair opportunity to make the kinds of changes that everyone agrees are necessary, and that he is fully prepared to implement for the benefit of the whole school. Rubbish!

On his return to his office, Ronald Parham rang Dr Mitchell, and outlined to him the essence of what Pritchard had told him. While doing so, he could hear the sharp intake of Mitchell's breath. When he had finished, the Chief Inspector's reaction was explosive.

'Oh, my God!' he almost shouted. 'I didn't expect this. It seems he's going to play this as cleverly as he can. He's preparing the way for the Governors' Meeting. He wants to groom them as his saviours. That meeting will now be even more important than we thought. Now, Ronald, you'll be there won't you? Obviously I can't attend it. You can? Good. That meeting will probably decide Pritchard's fate one way or the other. We can't let him win, Ronald. We've got to stop him!'

'Of course. I'll do everything I can.'

'You've already spoken to the Chairman of the Governing Body, haven't you?'

'Yes, I have. I found him very cooperative.'

'Yes, well I suggest that you now have another talk with him. He's read the Report and will want to discuss it. We must keep him absolutely on board about this, Ronald.'

'I agree.'

They arranged to have regular conversations, to discuss progress on a day-to- day basis Then Dr Mitchell rang off and Parham telephoned Richard Bartlett.

'Yes, I've read the Report,' the latter said, 'and I find it very disturbing. I had no idea that Mr. Pritchard had performed so badly as a Head Teacher, even after our previous talk.'

'Yes, I can understand that. You've had to rely on his own selective accounts, in each of which he has put his own gloss on happenings in the School. And it's what he's omitted that is so important.'

'Yes, I appreciate that. The teachers seem to have done very well, though, don't they?'

'Yes, they have. That's because they are all gifted, highly-motivated teachers . Now, Mr Bartlett, I wonder if you and I could meet to examine the Report in detail, and also, and in particular, discuss how to respond to the case that Mr Pritchard will probably make.'

'Certainly. I'd be glad to discuss the Report with you. We have a meeting of the Governing Body next week, and Mr Pritchard will, of course, be there. I'm rather worried about how to handle it in the circumstances. Mr Pritchard, as you know, has a way with words, and he may be able to sway the governors in his favour.'

'Yes, I understand that,' Parham sympathised, 'and I hope we'll be able to thwart him. Well, could you come here tomorrow so we can discuss how that might be done?'

'Certainly. At what time?'

'10am. If that suits you?'

'Yes. I can manage that.'

'Good. I'll see you then, in my office, tomorrow morning at 10 a.m.'

They exchanged a few more pleasantries and then rang off. Parham collected his thoughts.

Things are moving quickly. Thank heaven I've been able to fix a meeting with Bartlett at such short notice. We must correlate our approach to the process of ousting Pritchard.

***

'What's 'appened to 'ol Pritchy?' Tony Semour asked of no-one in particular.

'What d'ya mean? Tim Owen asked.

'Well, today he's looking so 'appy – not like our 'ol Pritchy at all.'

'I don' know what 'es got to be 'appy about,' Billy Green put in, ''cause I reckon 'es in trouble. One of them inspectors was 'ere again today and 'e went up to see the ol' geezer. I 'ope 'e brought 'im some bad news.'

'What sort of bad news?' asked Lucy Pym.

'That 'e aint been doin' 'is job prop'ly, so 'es for the 'igh jump.'

'You reckon 'es goin'?'

'Yeah – an' I 'ope it won't be long.'

Chapter 29
5 July 1955 (Evening)

The teachers were all gathered in Tom's house for one of their regular meetings.

'Has anyone seen *The Caine Mutiny*, yet?' Malcolm asked. 'You'll remember that I mentioned it briefly when we met with Dr. Hargreaves.'

No-one had. He continued:

'I think you would find it very interesting. You'll remember Dr Hargreaves' confirmation that Humphrey Bogart, as Captain Queeg, was suffering from paranoia? I think the film will help you to understand our weird head teacher a little more. It really is a great film, and Humphrey Bogart, gives probably his greatest performance as commander of a run-down U.S Navy warship. His behaviour to the crew forms the kernel of the story. Queeg gets everything out of proportion, and neglects the essential work to be carried out in the running of the ship, to the extreme frustration and anger of some of the senior officers. He focuses on trivial matters, such as the absurd search for a few strawberries that are missing. Shades of Pritchard's round-headed scissors! In fact, Queeg's behaviour reminds me very much of Pritchard's antics. It's a film not to be missed.'

Susan was not entirely convinced about that.

'I like to see all really good films,' she remarked, 'though I don't really want to be reminded of Pritchard while I'm being entertained!'

They all laughed.

'He's an enigma,' Tom said, 'but Malcolm's account of the film is very interesting. It may provide us with some further insights into Pritchard's behaviour. ... But let's now get down to business. I think it's your turn to take the minutes, Susan. Let's go through the Report, chapter by chapter, examine its recommendations, and decide on its implications for us – how we should react to it.'

Tom's proposal was accepted and they went carefully through the Report, discussing all the major issues that were raised. Then Tom summed up his own reactions.

'It puts the cat among the pigeons. I'm sure the inspectors want Pritchard to go, and the best way would be for him to resign. But suppose he won't oblige? He may dig his toes in and concentrate on building up support among the governors. They have the power to make or break.'

Malcolm found that hard to accept.

'You're saying Tom, that even though the Report is highly critical of Pritchard's work in the School, and clear that he's incompetent, yet the inspectors can't insist that he goes. Is that right?'

'That's right, Malcolm,' Tom replied. 'The Governing Body appointed him and the Governing Body has the final say in any question of dismissal.'

'Although the inspectors have more knowledge and experience of educational matters than they have?' Susan persisted.

'Yes, in spite of that,' Tom said, 'but don't despair because Ronald Parham will probably be present when the crucial meeting takes place and, if he is, I'm confident he'll make sure that the Report's criticisms are fully understood and appreciated by all the governors.'

Mary frowned.

'If he's there. But he may not be. I believe the inspector normally attends a governors' meeting only when it's for the interviewing of candidates for a post.'

'That's right, Mary,' Tom said, and Mary continued,

'And even if he does attend this one, the governors may choose to ignore him and continue to support our wretched Head Teacher. Besides, as you have pointed out before, Parham must always be very circumspect at governors' meetings and he can only advise. The meetings must be democratically conducted.'

'Quite true,' Tom agreed.

'So, bearing in mind Pritchard's powers of persuasion I'm not feeling at all optimistic,' Mary declared firmly.

'Nor am I,' Susan said. 'I can see him twisting the Governing Body round his podgy little finger.'

'Who will have a copy of the Report?' asked Malcolm.

'I believe only the Chairman,' Tom replied.'

'That doesn't make much sense,' Susan pointed out. 'Every member of the Board should have a chance to examine itt *before* the meeting so they are fully briefed. Otherwise it will be easier for Pritchard to use all his unscrupulous arguments. They should have the complete Report in front of them so they can study all the issues themselves.'

The others agreed, and Tom promised to forward their views to Parham.

'Something else is worrying me,' Malcolm said. 'We, the teachers, know everything that's been taking place in our School. We're the experts, as you once said, Tom. So isn't anyone going to ask for our views on the vital matters that are going to be debated?'

'A very good point,' Tom agreed. 'It's quite possible that Ronald Parham or the Chairman of the Governing Body, Richard Bartlett will consult us at some stage.'

'But must we wait for that possibility?' Mary asked.

'I don't think we should,' Susan responded resolutely. 'I think we should express our agreed views quite unequivocally in a document to be circulated to all the governors – they should certainly be aware of our feelings -, and the two inspectors should have copies, too.'

'And don't forget Pritchard. He should see it too,' added Malcolm. 'We must be seen to be fair.'

'Yes,' agreed Susan, 'though that should not inhibit us from saying exactly what we think. Now, how we go about this could be of key importance. I think we should draft an agreed *Statement* addressed to the Chairman of the Governing Body, with copies to all the others. The gist of it should be that we agree wholeheartedly with the inspectors' findings, have no confidence in the present School management, and feel that a change of Head is essential.'

The other teachers looked at Susan with surprise and admiration registered on their faces. They felt that she had summed up their views perfectly and they liked the boldness of her plan.

After a lengthy discussion, the teachers agreed on the following:

We, the teachers of Haselmere Open-Air School for Delicate Children, have studied carefully the Report, following a General Inspection of the school. We regard it as fair, balanced and accurate in its assessments and criticisms insofar as they refer to the management of the School.

In the past year, we have had no opportunities whatever for democratic exchanges of opinion with the Head Teacher because of the absence of both formal Staff Meetings and informal exchanges. In fact, we see very little of him. Consequently, no-one has been given any support or encouragement where that might well have been timely and beneficial. We have had no opportunities to put forward our own ideas and suggestions, based on our considerable combined experience, and we have received no positive ideas or guidance from the Head Teacher, on methods, curriculum, discipline, assessment procedures, or any other aspect of our teaching.

This absence of creative dialogue and hands–on management is threatening to undermine or stifle our work as teachers, and must in time affect its quality.

Our four classes should be bound by common objectives, a common curriculum, and a common ethos. To that end, we should regularly discuss and review every School practice and procedure, including pupils' assessments, records, timetables, future developments, etc.

We have received a series of memos, none of which have been discussed with us. We regard them as either, at best, only marginally relevant or, in some cases, actually detrimental to the education of our children. They have often been based on misconceptions which would have been exposed had discussion taken place. We are convinced that the friendly interchange of ideas is always likely to be much more effective in a school of this size than written communications.

We have received no guidance from the Head Teacher on curriculum matters, so we have been using some notes provided by the previous Head Teachers, but from time to time they should be revised and updated, with our involvement.

Our approaches to the Head Teacher, singly or en masse, to discuss a problem or for clarification of some matter, have been met with discouragement, rejection and sometimes unpleasantness. A genuine discussion is never possible.

We have tried to maintain standards in these difficult and unhelpful circumstances, but in time it will become increasingly difficult to sustain high morale and motivation.

We feel very strongly that only a change of Headship can provide the positive leadership that is so clearly lacking at present.

Finally, we would add that we all share an instinct of loyalty to anyone appointed as our leader, but developments at Haselmere call for an exceptional response. We feel that the true situation here must be fully understood and appreciated if essential changes are to take place. Nor is it our habit or wish to complain, but we are compelled by the circumstances outlined above to state our position on the various issues raised in the Report.

Signed: Tom Bates, Mary Prince, Susan Carter, Malcolm Brown.

'Do you think we've got it about right?' Malcolm asked Tom.

'Yes, I do,' Tom answered. 'It's a bit wordy but I think it will serve its purpose. If we tinkered with it any longer it might lose some of its impact.'

'I think it puts our combined views quite succinctly,' Susan maintained. 'And what is important now is that we should deliver it to the Chairman as soon as possible, with copies to all the other governors, to the two inspectors and to our beloved Head Teacher. Then we'll have put all our cards on the table, face up!'

'Hear! Hear! That's the idea!' Mary grinned delightedly.

'Absolutely,' said Malcolm. 'We'll have done our bit, and then it's up to the others.'

'I agree,' Tom said. 'I'll see to the distribution.'

He looked in turn at his colleagues, and joined in their smiles.

'Many thanks to you all for your contributions, and especially to Susan for her excellent proposal which really got us going. We've taken a vital step, and I'm sure we've done the right thing.'

The drafting of the *Statement,* which had taken longer than expected, had left all the teachers feeling tired but exhilarated. The debate over its content and wording had had a cathartic effect on them. Instead of simply waiting upon events they had taken the initiative, and although the final decision would be taken by others, they were happy that their views would not now be ignored.

Chapter 30
6 July 1955

Once again Ronald Parham sat in what he called the *loungy* part of his office with Richard Bartlett. Comfortably seated and relaxed, they sipped coffee while discussing strategies and tactics to be employed at the forthcoming meeting of governors. Their views and attitudes, following publication of the Report, and their phone conversation, had largely coalesced. They were co-conspirators.

Parham wanted confirmation of the date and time of the next Governors' Meeting.

Bartlett's face clouded fleetingly and he frowned.

'It will be in six days' time, on 12 July . he answered, 'and I confess I'm very worried about it. You see, my colleagues have been quite impressed by Mr Pritchard over the past year – as, indeed I have, too. Perhaps we've all been rather naive. We accepted all the information provided, taking it on trust. We listened to Pritchard's accounts of developments taking place in the School – he put his own gloss on everything – and the School seemed to be flourishing. Of course, he always gave us only *his* version of events and *his* opinions.'

Parham nodded, and smiled with understanding.

'I'm sure he did! You've had to take his word for everything, though I presume you've all taken turns to visit the School regularly to see things for yourselves?'

'Yes. We all take part in rota visits, but they have limited value, you know. Mr Pritchard always accompanies us everywhere and he selects what we see.'

'So you have never found the rota visits particularly useful?'

'No, I haven't.'

'May I ask you about the memos. I believe Pritchard gave you copies, didn't he?'

'Yes. We were each given copies of all of them,' Bartlett replied, 'and Mr Pritchard explained the purpose of each one. We didn't appreciate the reality and accepted that they were a useful administrative tool. I can see now that it was a very odd and inappropriate way to communicate to colleagues in such a small school.'

'It certainly was, especially as there was no genuine exchange of ideas, face-to-face. Now, Mr Bartlett, how do see the meeting developing?'

The Chairman's face puckered as he thought for a few moments.

'Well, governors who have been 'drip fed' a superficial and rosy version of developments at Haselmere, won't necessarily change their minds in a flash on the basis of your Report, will they? Some may feel angry that they've apparently been given a very partial or one-sided view; others will take some convincing.'

'I appreciate that. Now, as Chairman, Mr Bartlett, how do you envisage your own role during this crucial meeting?'

'Well, I suppose I must quote from your Report to persuade my colleagues that Pritchard has been a pretty hopeless Head Teacher. That'll be quite a task! I'll need some help! And, by the way, Mr Parham, at the moment I'm the only governor who has a copy of this highly-critical document. Do you think that's good enough?'

He looked squarely at the inspector, raised his voice a shade, and there was a new edge of determination in his voice.

'I really do feel, Mr Parham, that every governor should have a copy so they can digest all the arguments before the meeting rather than just hear them from the Chair.'

'You're absolutely right,' Parham agreed. 'Frankly, I'm sorry I didn't do that at once. As a matter of fact, the teachers made the same point, and I immediately sent copies to all the governors, by first-class post.'

'Good. I'm relieved to hear that. The report will help to gear them up for the meeting and hopefully shift their minds in the right direction.'

'I agree. Now, Mr Bartlett, what else is on your mind?'

'Well, I'd like your confirmation that you will definitely attend the meeting.'

'Oh, yes. If it's your wish that I should attend, then I'll certainly be there. To justify my presence, perhaps you'll explain that it is an extraordinary or special meeting, and that you have invited me, as an educational professional, to provide any information or clarification that may be needed.'

'Oh, I'll certainly do that.'

'And that will be acceptable to them?'

'I'm sure it will. I would expect them to welcome you on that basis.'

'Good. Anything else?'

'Yes. It's a really fundamental question. Can you confirm that a change at the top is absolutely essential? There's no question of a second chance?'

'Yes. We need a new Head Teacher at Haselmere. It would be disastrous to allow Pritchard to remain in post for another year. For one thing, it would be unreasonable to stretch the tolerance of the teachers any further. If Pritchard were to stay, I think they would probably want to leave, and that would be a disaster, for they are one of the most dedicated special school staffs in London.'

'Right,' Bartlett smiled with satisfaction. 'That clears up an important matter.'

'Good. Any other issues that need to be aired?'

'Well, my main worry now centres on Pritchard. Some of my colleagues find it difficult to challenge him on educational matters, especially because of his use of educational jargon. He can impress, as he proved when we appointed him. He's very articulate and appears to be quite knowledgeable about education. There's such a chasm between theory and practice in his case, isn't there?' He smiled ruefully. 'I'm afraid he can tie us all up in knots.'

'But I recall,' Parham pointed out, 'that you have two or three colleagues who are actually quite well informed on educational matters, and will surely be strongly influenced by our Report.'

'Yes, I think that's right, Leslie Burgess, in particular is very discerning, and Miss Forster, too, has a very clear mind. She'll put her points explicitly and forthrightly. She's very effective at spotting weaknesses in arguments.'

'Good. Then they should help to tip the balance a little in our favour. Now, how many of the others, do you think, will stick by Pritchard through thick and thin?'

'At least two, possibly three.'

'And there's a reasonable chance that most of the others will be persuaded by the arguments in the report.'

'Well, I think it'll be touch and go. And even if a majority become convinced that Pritchard has had a really bad year, they won't necessarily decide he should be sacked. They may say something like this:

Mr Pritchard has acknowledged his initial shortcomings, and has produced a most impressive plan for the future. Why not give him the chance to carry out his well-thought-out plans? The inspectors could then carefully monitor developments over the second year to ensure that he was kept on track.'

'Yes, but I hope that it is not a view that will prevail.'

'So do I. But others may feel that Pritchard should be allowed to carry on provided he takes note of all the criticisms in the Report. And they may add that another inspection could take place after a further year, to assess the progress that's he's made.'

Ronald Parham's expression clearly registered his concern.

'Mr Bartlett, you really are beginning to frighten me!'

Bartlett laughed.

'I think it would take more than that to frighten you. But seriously, I'm just trying to think of all the possibilities.'

'Yes, and you're quite right to do so. Actually, I think we have a good idea of Pritchard's plans.'

'Really, has he confided in you?'

'In a way. You've seen the comprehensive document he has produced. When I saw him recently, he really let the cat out of the bag about his strategy He was bursting with excitement about its contents, anxious to convince me that it provided a complete answer to all the concerns expressed in our Report. He thinks he has an answer to everything! He'll try to persuade the meeting on the lines you've suggested. He'll admit to shortcomings but emphasize that he has been learning all the time, and that his Report is evidence of that. He'll press the meeting that what matters is the *future*, and that his proposals are what is needed. And they are! The question is: will he get away with it? It's up to the governors to question him on all the issues covered in his own version.'

'They'll have to balance the two won't they – your Report following the inspection, and his one?

'Yes, and they'll be a third document – one from the teachers which sets out their views. Tom Bates phoned me this morning to tell me that copies are on their way, to Dr Mitchell and myself, to all the governors and to Rupert Pritchard. So everyone at the meeting will have been briefed with a full sheaf of documents well before the meeting.'

'Now that, Mr Parham, is really encouraging. I still can't say that I'm feeling exactly sanguine about the meeting – I remain convinced that it will all be on a knife edge, – but you've given me hope.'

'Good, then it's time for a drink. Whisky, gin and tonic, or whatever? What's your favourite tipple?'

'A small whisky would be nice.'

***

Rupert Pritchard was satisfied that his meeting with Ronald Parham had gone exactly as planned. He had seized the initiative and taken the wind out of the inspector's sails. The key factor was to overwhelm the governors with detail, to present an incontrovertible case. He'd told Parham about only a small part of his document, just enough to demonstrate that he had a complete answer to that outrageous report. And their meeting had been an opportunity to rehearse some of his arguments as he geared himself up for the important Governors' Meeting.

The governors would surely like his emphasis on the future. They would appreciate that he had thought through every issue very carefully before drafting his plans. He'd made clear that he knew precisely what he wanted to do at Haselmere, and everything he proposed was based on the most enlightened of educational practices. The governors would surely be persuaded. They had always given him their full support. There was plenty of goodwill towards him. They were his friends.

But I won't read out any part of my report. That wouldn't be the most effective 'modus operandi'. Instead, I'll memorize it, master it, so that I'll be able to look round the table and make eye contact with every governor in turn while I am apparently ad-libbing and speaking with emphasis and conviction. With all the details at my fingertips I'll be able to convince them that I just need a fair chance to put my ideas into practice. I'll rehearse my arguments over and over again until I am word perfect.

When there is any criticism of the past year, I'll accept with a rueful smile that not everything may have worked out exactly as I had hoped, but my report shows just how much I have learned during the past year. I will constantly emphasize that what surely matters is THE FUTURE.

The more Pritchard thought about the meeting, the more his confidence grew.

He then decided to study once again the Inspectors' Report to see whether he had missed anything of significance, and whether there were any other ways he could counter its arguments and bolster his case. He must leave no turn unturned.

It was a mistake. This time, the inspectors' scathing criticisms began to bite deeply into his psyche and undermine his self-regard. The incriminating words and phrases seemed to pose an insidious threat. His confidence plummeted and his self-esteem evaporated. Becoming increasingly pessimistic and dejected, he nevertheless ploughed on stubbornly, though the criticisms burned into his consciousness as he agonised over them. He was especially crushed by such phrases as, *detrimental to the children's education, the inexplicable absence of regular contacts, no curriculum guidance had been provided*, and *steadily deteriorating.*

A wave of despair began to envelope him, he began to shake uncontrollably and to suck in quick gulps of air, while his heart beat rapidly and his face became wet with perspiration. Then quite suddenly he became thoroughly exhausted and could read no more. He slumped in his armchair. He wanted to do nothing and to see no-one. Motionless, he was gripped by an extreme lethargy and felt that he was descending into blackness.

When, some minutes later, he did stir, and his mind began to clear, he began to consider seriously, for the first time, whether he was, after all, the complete and utter failure described in the report.

But the mood of despair was eventually succeeded by the earlier one of defiance, which reasserted itself. Once again he saw all the events at Haselmere since his arrival through the distorted prism of his own perceptions. He now pumped himself up with a new determination.

No! I won't give in to Bates, who has plotted my downfall from the start, and poisoned the minds of the other teachers against me, causing insubordination and disobedience. He has turned the inspectors against me too. When the opportunity arises, I'll get even with him!

Some of the governors will definitely be on my side. Certainly Tom Hawkins and Mrs. French, and probably a majority of the others. That's all I need: a majority. I think I'll get it. I'll have a few surprises for everyone!

Chapter 31
12 July [h] 1955

At last it had arrived! Today, the Governing Body would discuss the Inspectors' Report and its implications for the school, its staff and its pupils. And the future of Rupert Pritchard would surely be in jeopardy. It would certainly be on a knife edge. Everyone at Haselmere knew how much was at stake. Attitudes to the governors' meeting was a mixture of curiosity, anxiety and hope, the dominant reaction varying from one person to another. But tension was felt everywhere.

In the early afternoon, his class being absorbed in project work, Malcolm darted a glance across from his classroom towards Pritchard's study, looking for signs of activity. He was intensely curious! And suddenly, there they were! Some governors were arriving in ones and twos. He felt a tingle of excitement! This was it! Today, the events of the past year would surely reach a climax. The inspectors had done their work well by preparing the ground for change in their report. The teachers had agreed a comprehensive *Statement* of their experiences and agreed opinions. What would be the outcome? With all that evidence, would the governors reach a clear-cut verdict or would equivocation and indecision prevail?

But Malcolm's curiosity would remain unsatisfied for some time, the Governing Body being closeted for the whole afternoon in the Head Teacher's study.

***

Pritchard received his guests at the top of the stairs, greeting each one with a smile and a handshake, and ushering them into his room. He looked relaxed and supremely confident. He had every reason to be, for he had not left a stone unturned. His preparations for the meeting had been meticulous, and he was sure he could overwhelm the governors with the impressive weight of factual material at his fingertips, and the evidence he would provide of enlightened educational practices that he was anxious to introduce. Hadn't the Governing Body not only appointed him, but had also always supported him loyally and enthusiastically? He felt that he was, in general, among friends, and that impression was confirmed by the warmth of their greeting. Their smiles suggested that this meeting would hardly pose a threat. His enemies were surely outnumbered. Let battle commence!

In his study was a large, rectangular table, (actually a number of adjoining trestle tables) covered by a green cloth. Around it twelve chairs had been arranged by Jenny Martin, and name tabs placed in each position. It was always a tight squeeze to fit everything and everyone in but it all looked appropriately formal and businesslike.

With only a few minutes to go before the meeting was due to begin, Pritchard was surprised to see Ronald Parham climbing the stairs towards him. At first he was not unduly concerned. Hadn't Parham listened attentively when he had outlined his plans and aspirations to him, at their last meeting? In any case, the inspector did not usually say very much at governors' meetings, usually adopting a neutral position on most issues. 'That was,' Pritchard thought, 'as it should be.'

But then, some of the most trenchant criticisms in the Report flashed through his mind and began to gnaw into his confidence.

Perhaps Parham has something up his sleeve! After all he was co-author of that disgraceful Report that's given me so much worry. It was an unjustified attack on my first year as a Head Teacher. Most of the criticisms were grossly exaggerated, unfair and biased. So Parham has proved that he is my enemy, threatening my future. Why has he come to this meeting if not to try to seal my fate?

His mind flooded with such thoughts, Pritchard suddenly felt uncomfortably hot and began to perspire. He took out a white handkerchief and dabbed the beads of sweat on his brow. His handkerchief was soon damp and he fiddled in his pockets, searching in vain for a spare one.

Ronald Parham, observing the Head Teacher's restless, nervous activity, wondered what had caused his sudden agitation. Pritchard's mood swings, he thought, could be quite sudden and there was no obvious reason for this one.

It didn't last long. A few minutes later Pritchard was chatting amiably to one of the governors, and his confidence appeared to have been restored.

Richard Bartlett, Chairman of the Governing Body, sat at the head of the table with Jenny by his side to take the minutes of the Meeting. He studied the other governors as they arrived and shuffled to their places around the table. Some stopped to greet old friends; others simply acknowledged the others and hurried to their places to study or review the documents that would provide the basis for their deliberations.

There were twelve governors altogether, including himself, but three had sent their apologies for absence. Of the eight others present, four usually said next to nothing, and made little impact on the others, while the other four could be expected to express their views unequivocally. The Chairman was well aware of their potential impact.

They are the 'movers and shakers' whose views will determine the outcome of this meeting. Each one of them can argue passionately and shift the balance of opinion decisively one way or the other. They are all strong personalities. I must ensure that none of them has the floor for an undue length of time.

The Chairman's eyes focused on each of the governors in turn, but especially on the four whose contributions, he anticipated, would be of crucial importance.

One, Tom Hawkins, was in his early 60s. He was a local builder, a short, strongly built, bald-headed, burly individual. At meetings he always wore a smart, dark grey suit. Bartlett noticed that his well-rounded stomach seemed to protrude more than usual, because he was quite unable to draw his chair close enough to the table. The long period of food rationing, that had ended only the previous year, had apparently had little effect on his waist line! The Chairman smiled to himself.

Tom Hawkins was of limited education and ability, but was motivated by a genuine desire to serve the local community. At meetings he could be pugnacious and stubborn, especially when he identified a particular point of principle. He was a useful person to have on one's side, and a formidable adversary. He could wear down the opposition with rather bombastic assertiveness. There had been times when he had reiterated an argument so forcefully, that some members had become exhausted and abandoned their opposition. A few had even sought refuge in a short nap, thereby leaving the tireless Hawkins to carry the day. The sturdy builder, the Chairman reminded himself, should not be underestimated.

Next to Hawkins was Miss Georgina Forster, a librarian in her late forties. Tall and thin, bespectacled, sharp-eyed, sharp-nosed and rather gaunt-looking, with grey hair, swept back severely, she was an entirely different personality from her neighbour, but was another member who could be relied upon to take her duties seriously and to make a positive contribution. Articulate and precise, if occasionally pedantic, she could usually absorb the details of a complex situation, and could be relied upon to comment on it helpfully and constructively – and often critically.

Opposite her was Mrs Cecilia French. Seventyish, straggly haired, shabbily and unfashionably dressed, and devoid of make-up, her personality was as unattractive as her appearance. She was the longest-serving governor and a local councillor, well-respected for her work with charity organisations. She was never reluctant to speak up, and though not always in complete command of all the facts, her passionate advocacy could make her a formidable debater.

The fourth member who would certainly have something interesting to say was Leslie Burgess. In his early '50s, Burgess was incredibly tall and thin. Bartlett thought he must be about 6 feet 9 inches in height. The constant necessity to bend forward so that he could listen and converse easily with 'normal' people had given him a permanent stoop. Articulate and lucid, he was probably the most intelligent of the governors. He was also very knowledgeable in regard to educational developments, and he had previously been a distinguished Chairman of the Board. Burgess had the reputation of being of absolute integrity and of always speaking his mind. Bartlett had a strong feeling that his contribution this afternoon might well be of critical importance.

It was now time to begin. The Chairman brought down his gavel, and the many conversations, in full spate round the table, were soon hushed. Heads and eyes turned towards him. He sensed an atmosphere of tense expectation.

Bartlett was prepared for a meeting of many ups and downs, with arguments, counter-arguments and shifting sentiments. Though he could have no concept of the drama to come, he braced himself for what he anticipated would be the most confrontational and turbulent meeting of the year. He hoped he would be equal to the occasion.

His confidence was stiffened by the sight of Ronald Parham at the far end of the room – tall, stern and commanding. It was good, he thought, to have such a reliable ally.

Sweeping his eyes round the room and smiling, the Chairman began his introductory address.

'Good afternoon ladies and gentlemen. I'm very glad that so many of you were able to come here today, at very short notice. This is, as you know, an Extraordinary Meeting so a normal agenda is unnecessary. The meeting is to be devoted entirely to discussing the recently-published Report, following a Full Inspection of Haselmere School, and I will suggest the key topics arising from that Report that I feel we should discuss. Members will, of course, be free, to bring up any other relevant issues that occur to them.'

He paused, smiled and again looked in turn at each of his fellow governors.

'I'm also very pleased,' he continued, 'that Ronald Parham, the Special Schools' Inspector, and a co-author of the Report, has been able to join us. His expertise and professional advice has long been available to us, and he has been a good friend of this Board and of the School, for many years.'

There were murmurs of agreement and a few 'hear hears.' Bartlett continued,

'Mr. Parham has sent each of you a copy of the Report and I hope you have all found time to study it in detail, as most of our deliberations will be based on it.'

Leslie Burgess now raised his hand.

'I think we are all very glad to have our own copies of the Inspectors' Report, Mr Chairman. But each of us has also received a copy of both Mr Pritchard's own report and a "*Statement*" signed by the four members of the teaching staff. Are we going to consider the arguments raised in all three documents at the same time? Are we, for instance, going to take each issue in turn and then consider what each document has to say about it before we discuss that particular issue?

Pritchard frowned. As the Head Teacher of Haselmere, attending a meeting with his governors, he felt he was of central importance here, and his views should command commensurate attention. He therefore considered that his own report should certainly be considered on equal terms with that of the Inspectorate. But in regard to the teachers' *Statement,* that was an impertinence, and he hoped that he could ensure that it would be largely ignored. After all it was a product of the conspiracy against him.

Bates must have been behind it. He probably wrote it himself and persuaded the others to sign it!

Ronald Parham, who had read the teachers' *Statement* with great interest, and noted how much common ground there was with the substance of the Inspectors' Report, observed with satisfaction, Pritchard's renewed discomfiture.

'Yes,' Richard Bartlett responded, we should certainly consider all three documents at every stage. They deal with the same aspects of school management and complement each other. While the Inspectors' Report is an expert appraisal from outside the School, the *Statement* provides us with the teachers' perspectives and feelings – and then there is Mr Pritchard's response paper.'

Tom Hawkins' reddening features and angry frown suggested that he was getting rather worked up, and bursting to made a point.

'Mr Chairman,' he began, 'we have seen the Inspectors' Report and also the other paper by the teachers. So,' and now his tone was of utter contempt, 'we know what some people think. But there is also the very thoughtful document from Mr Pritchard, in which he answers several, if not all, of the criticisms that have been made against him. He must have put a lot of work into that document. It makes it clear that he has a lot to offer. He's been in his post for only a year so he hasn't had much time to make a difference. I think we should encourage him to express his views. He should be allowed plenty of time to put his case. He has concentrated on the future, and it is the future that matters. I'd like him to elaborate some of the points he's made.'

Hawkins had sounded very determined and he now swept his eyes defiantly round the table.

The Chairman smiled to himself.

Tom's as down to earth and belligerent as ever. He's made his usual categorical statement at the outset. We all know exactly where he stands.

Support for Hawkins' position was immediate.

'I agree,' Mrs French stated loudly and emphatically. 'Mr Pritchard was appointed by this Board to manage Haselmere, and until I read the Report, I must say that I thought he was making a good job of it. He's given us plenty of evidence of developments and activities in the School, and he's kept us fully in the picture. I suppose the inspectors must have some grounds for their criticisms but there are two important points I would like to make. One, that Mr Pritchard has been here for only a year – hardly enough time for him to reveal his full potential , and two, that he has provided us with a very full and interesting report of his own. He has clearly built on his experience during the past year to produce a blueprint for the future. I found it very well argued and very convincing.'

There was a sympathetic murmur of agreement around the table and two or three governors tapped the table in support.

Parham had to mask his concern. The governors seemed to have made up their minds before the discussion had got under way.

There was worse to come.

The theme of fairness towards the Head Teacher was taken up with unbridled enthusiasm – and not a little passion – by a very obese lady with deeply-etched lines in her sagging jowls. Naturally pale, she was well –rouged, with generous purple eye make-up. Her hair had been henna-dyed but near the roots it was clearly grey. She wore cheap, heavy and very colourful jewellery on her podgy fingers, wrists and neck, and a cheap perfume. She was Alice Peabody, whose contributions at governors' meetings were rare in number and unpredictable in content.

'I really don't understand all this, Mr Chairman,' she began. 'Mr Pritchard, as has been pointed out, has been Headmaster for only a year. Have any complaints been made about him in that time? I certainly haven't heard any. And I don't think anyone else has either. We've all found him to be very satisfactory, haven't we? And yet we are suddenly told that everything is not as it should be. That's very odd, isn't it? Mr Pritchard is someone we've got to know quite well. He has kept us very well informed about what is going on in the school, hasn't he? We can't suddenly take a different view. Thank goodness Mr Pritchard is here to tell us the facts of the matter and to reassure us. ...'

As Alice Peabody was getting into her stride, her tone rising in a steady crescendo, she began to repeat her points and the .meeting showed signs of becoming restless and inattentive. The Chairman therefore seized a moment when she paused for breath to assure her that her points had been well made and that Mr Pritchard would have every opportunity to address the meeting on all substantive issues.

Ronald Parham groaned inwardly and fidgeted. Sitting next to Alice Peabody, he had been all too conscious of the perfume wafting in his direction, especially when she gesticulated wildly to make a point, which she often did. But now the lady, to everyone's relief, resumed her seat. She had made her contribution and would take no further part in the deliberations.

Richard Bartlett now decided to get the meeting on track.

'May I tell you, ladies and gentlemen, about the procedure that I would like us to follow. We're here to concentrate mainly on *key issues*, in regard to the management of Haselmere School, insofar as they relate to Mr Pritchard's first year in office. Those *key issues* have all been highlighted in the Inspectors' Report. Is everyone in agreement with that?'

There was a general murmur of consent.

'Good. Now, I suggest there are four major fields of activity on which the inspectors have made stringent criticisms. We should look at them in turn, and at the same time refer, as appropriate, to the teachers' *Statement* and also to Mr Pritchard's document.

The first is Curriculum. It is dealt with on page four. I will give you a few minutes to re-read it – to refresh your memories – and you could also look at references to the Curriculum in the other documents.'

At the end of the allotted time, Bartlett brought down his gavel.

'Thank you,' he said. 'I hope that was long enough to refresh your memories. The key passage here states that there has been no guidance from the Head Teacher whatever on any aspect of the curriculum. As you know, the word curriculum embraces the entire teaching content of the various subjects and activities taking place in the School. It has also been said that none of the teachers has had the opportunity to discuss with the Head Teacher any aspect of teaching and learning. Now, let us, as Mr Hawkins has proposed, hear Mr Pritchard's response to those accusations. 'And,' turning to Rupert Pritchard, 'you may, of course, wish to refer to the appropriate sections of your own document.'

Rupert Pritchard rose. He nodded, smiled, and looked completely at ease. Tom Hawkins' sturdy contribution, reinforced by those of Mrs French and Alice Peabody (even though the latter appalled him!) had helped him to recover his poise. He had always found it relatively easy to persuade the

Governing Body to accept whatever line of reasoning he chose to take.

'Thank you very much, Mr Chairman,' he began. 'I welcome this opportunity both to comment on the Inspectors' Report and to outline to you my plans for the future. May I say, at the outset, that I found the Report a most useful document in that it helped me significantly to clarify my own ideas. And may I add that I entirely endorse your view on the importance of the curriculum which embraces the totality of the pupils' learning experiences.'

He paused and looked round at his audience. He had their rapt attention. He continued:

'As you know, I have held the Headship of Haselmere School for a little less than a year. Perhaps I have taken rather a long time to assemble my plans, but I wanted to structure them on a firm foundation. I wanted to get everything right, so it was important not to rush things. This first year has been for me a period of careful observation as my plans have evolved, and as I have put the various elements into place. I had never taught in an Open-Air School and, in fact, I had not even set foot in one until I came here. So I had much to learn. That is why I gave myself a full year to draft comprehensive guidelines for every aspect of the curriculum. But now I have completed that task. I have prepared what I hope is a useful framework for every subject and activity that I think is appropriate for this school. It has been a major undertaking. I call it a framework because I want to put it to the Staff for a full discussion. I think that would be the right democratic procedure. The best of the ideas contributed by the teachers can then be incorporated, so they will have the confident knowledge that they have all had a hand in it. I'm sure that they will then be ready to give it their wholehearted support.'

He again studied his audience to assess their reactions, focusing on each governor in turn. Then, satisfied that they – or most of them – were suitably impressed with his words, he continued:

'If you would kindly refer to page five of my report you will see a full outline of my curriculum framework. I think that you will find that it incorporates modern approaches to the curriculum adapted to the special needs of a Haselmere Open-Air School for Delicate Children.'

There were muffled sounds of approval, accompanied by the nodding of heads and again some banging of the table.

At this point, he decided that it would not be prudent to continue and possibly risk losing the attention of his audience, especially as one of two governors tended to doze in the afternoon. He was confident that he had them, as usual, in the palm of his hands. There was the rustle of pages being turned and several member were now completely engrossed in studying the text of his report. Pritchard sat down. His supporters would surely speak up once again! He hadn't long to wait.

Tom Hawkins indicated his wish to speak.

'It seems to me, Mr Chairman,' he began, 'that Mr Pritchard has put up a good case. The inspectors had a duty to write their Report, but Mr Pritchard, too, has a point of view, and it makes good sense to me.'

'I think that's right,' added Mrs French. 'I must confess that I don't know much about curriculum, but Mr Pritchard has given up a great deal of time to produce a most impressive document. I think he's gone about it the right way, too. He has demonstrated good leadership by drafting only the main elements, and leaving the details to be drafted only after democratic discussion. He has given us a well-considered document, and should be congratulated on all his hard work. We should now give him the opportunity to put all those exciting ideas into practice. May I put a question to him, through you, Mr Chairman?'

'Yes, certainly.'

'Will Mr Pritchard keep the Governing Body fully informed as and when he develops and implements his curriculum?'

'Richard Bartlett nodded to Pritchard, who rose and beamed at his audience.

'I can give Mrs French my full assurance that the governors will be kept fully informed at every stage,' he said.

Both Ronald Parham and the Chairman were now feeling somewhat dejected. So far everything had gone Pritchard's way and they were anxious to get the Meeting back on track. They hadn't yet discussed any of the criticisms in the inspectors' report.

But now Miss Georgina Forster indicated her wish to speak. Would this be the turning point?

Chapter 32
12 July 1955 (Continued)

Georgina Forster was not one to accept half-baked ideas. Her expression as she rose suggested to Parham that a strict Headmistress was about to deal with an errant child. He smiled at the thought.

'I was surprised to hear Mr Pritchard's suggestion that he needed a full year in which to put together a simple curriculum framework,' she began, 'I find that difficult to understand.'

The meeting stirred uneasily, and all the governors were now alert and attentive. She continued:

'I am, of course, very much in favour of developing the curriculum with experienced teachers, but nothing of the kind happened during a whole year, did it? The teachers were anxious to know something about Mr Pritchard's views, but he told them nothing. I really find it extraordinary that they were given no curriculum guidance at all. They were left in limbo! Shouldn't they have been given some idea of the Head Teacher's thoughts soon after he took up his post? The younger teachers especially – and I understand there was one on probation – surely needed detailed advice and support about subject content and recommended teaching methods, etc. from the beginning of the school year.

Miss Forster paused and looked around. Then, satisfied that her fellow governors were listening intently and absorbing her arguments, she continued.

'And shouldn't the views of experienced teachers have been sought from the beginning? Curriculum development is not simply a matter for the Head Teacher's arbitrary decisions. There appears to have been no democratic discussion whatever, either of the curriculum or, for that matter, of any other aspect of education – extraordinary in this day and age! What Mr Pritchard is proposing, even now, is a top-down approach.'

Richard Barnett managed with some difficulty to conceal a smile of satisfaction. Georgina, he felt, had started well. He turned to the Head Teacher, and looked suitably grave.

'I wonder whether you would like to respond to those points of concern, Mr Pritchard?'

'Well, yes,' Pritchard began, clarifying his thoughts with some urgency while he rose. 'Thank you, Mr Chairman.' He managed a rather unconvincing smile. 'Miss Forster has posed some interesting questions. I think she will find, however, when she has had time to study my document carefully ...'

'I have done just that,' the lady interrupted.

'... that I have addressed many, if not most, of her concerns,' he continued, ignoring the interruption. 'However, she is quite right to point out that the teachers needed an interim curriculum. And that's just what they had. The teachers haven't been teaching in a vacuum, you know, because my predecessor had issued some curriculum notes which have proved to be reasonably satisfactory for the time being. And, of course, I've had informal contacts with the teachers.'

Ronald Parham started and frowned when he heard the last remark. It contradicted evidence from all the teachers, and Pritchard had not even been aware of the curriculum notes. He wondered whether any of the governors would challenge Pritchard on that. He did not have long to wait.

Leslie Burgess now indicated his wish to speak.

'I'm puzzled, Mr Chairman,' he began. 'The Head Teacher talks about *informal contacts,* but the inspectors, in their Report, refer – and I quote – *to the inexplicable absence of regular contacts, both formal and informal* – and Burgess stressed the key words – *between Head and Staff.* They also refer – and again I quote – *to the self-imposed isolation of the Head Teacher.*' He paused, with a significant look at his colleagues before continuing. 'And the teachers' *Statement* says ... *in the past year we have had no opportunities whatever for democratic exchanges of opinion with the Head Teacher because of the absence of both formal staff meetings and informal exchanges.* And, to reinforce the point, they add that they see very little of him. Now, Mr Chairman,' and he paused again, 'what conclusions can we draw? That neither the inspectors, nor the teachers are telling the truth? Surely not.'

The Chairman now addressed Ronald Parham.

'Mr Parham, that does seem a contradiction, doesn't it? As a co-author of the Report, perhaps you would like to comment?'

Ronald Parham was satisfied that the two most articulate governors were going to maintain an effective and highly critical barrage of questions. There would be no need, therefore, for him to depart from his usual neutral stance.

'Certainly, Mr Chairman,' he began. 'My role here is simply to try to be useful, to facilitate the discussion, by clarifying, where necessary, particular educational issues or problems.' He now raised his voice a notch and looked round the table. 'My overall concern,' he continued, ' has always been the same as that of the Governing Body – the maintenance of the highest professional standards in a school where children have for many years achieved good standards in both health and education.'

That evoked a response of warm murmurs from his audience.

He went on, 'My colleague, Dr Charles Mitchell, and I examined the school very thoroughly. On most occasions we carried out separate enquiries, but our findings were always identical. Our Report simply tried to record those findings as fairly as possible. Now, I had no idea that the teachers intended to prepare a joint *Statement* about their concerns, until they sent me a copy, but I was very interested to see that their views and ours also largely coincided. The governors will, of course, draw their own conclusions, following their study of all the documents and the outcome of the present discussion.'

Bartlett thanked the inspector. He thought that it was now time to move on. He smiled as he began.

'May I now sum up your views by saying that while some of you are impressed by the curriculum outline, and plans for the future, that Mr Pritchard has provided in his own report, others feel very strongly that there should have been support and guidance for the teachers throughout the year, as well as opportunities for the teachers to contribute their own ideas.

The next topic is one that has already been mentioned: Staff/Teacher relations.'

Leslie Burgess now pointed out that before leaving the subject of Curriculum, he would like to refer to a significant passage in the Inspectors' Report. The Chairman invited him to make his point.

'Mr Pritchard has told us,' he began, 'that the teachers were able to make good use of curriculum notes already in existence, but the inspectors have expressed surprise that the Head Teacher *seemed unaware* of those notes. I find it difficult to square those two accounts.'

There was a pregnant silence in the room as the governors absorbed the fact that Pritchard appeared to have been misleading them on at least two matters.

Bartlett allowed a minute to pass, and took some satisfaction from the quiet, but disturbed buzz that floated round the table. He could then see that the point made by Burgess had gone home. He decided to move on.

'Now, Staff/Head Teacher relations covers both formal and informal contacts. As Mr Pritchard has readily acknowledged, there have been no Staff Meetings during the past year, and the inspectors were concerned that the teachers had no forum in which to share their ideas with both their colleagues and with their Head Teacher. Perhaps, Mr Pritchard, you would like to comment, and also to elaborate your views on Staff Meetings.'

Pritchard's plan was to say as little as possible about the past year and to concentrate on plans for the future, as set out in his document. He now downplayed the importance of most traditional Staff Meetings and related, with all the enthusiasm he could muster, the ideas in his document that he had rehearsed with Parham, emphasizing his wish to institute innovative, democratic and regular Staff Meetings, chaired by the teachers themselves, in rotation.

Mrs French was impressed.

'I am very much in favour of Mr Pritchard's plans,' she announced in a strong voice. 'I like the fact that every teacher will be able to contribute to the agendas of the meetings, and that they will also, in turn, chair them. It's an excellent, democratic plan.'

Miss Forster then observed that while she fully supported the Head Teachers' ideas for democratic Staff Meetings, she could not understand why no meetings of any kind had been held during the past year.

'Nor can I,' added Burgess. 'The plans put forward by Mr Pritchard are to be welcomed. But for a whole year the teachers have not been able to share ideas or to contribute ideas to the Head Master which may well have benefited the school, the staff and the pupils.'

Ronald Parham stole a glance at Tom Hawkins to see how he was reacting to the criticisms. The sturdy builder was looking uneasy and uncertain. He had great respect for the calibre of both Forster and Burgess and their arguments disturbed him. He wanted some answers.

'Perhaps, Mr Chairman,' he said, 'Mr Pritchard would like to respond to the points that have just been made.'

Parham smiled to himself

This is a good development. One of Pritchard's staunchest supporters now shows signs of doubt and uncertainty. He wants a clear cut answer. I wonder how Pritchard will wriggle out of this one!

Chapter 33
12 July ^h 1955 (Continued)

Pritchard was dismayed that one of his staunchest supporters was pressing him in one of his most vulnerable areas.

What's got into Tom Hawkins? I can usually rely on him. If he deserts me, I'm not going to get the backing of the Governing Body as a whole! They've cornered me, but I'll try the line I put to Parham the other day.

'I'll be very pleased to answer those points, Mr Chairman,' he began, 'but may I first of all confess something? I do not hold the view about Staff Meetings that I held at one time. My earlier view was that it was not appropriate to hold formal Staff Meetings in such a small school as Haselmere. I felt that discussions on an informal basis would be preferable. But I was wrong, Mr Chairman. I am now convinced, as you will see in my report, that both informal and formal contacts are vitally important. Both therefore have a place in my detailed plans for the future.' He paused, and then resumed in a voice of passionate appeal – 'On the basis of my experiences in the past year, I've tried my best to develop rational plans for regular Staff Meetings which, I believe, will benefit Haselmere, both its staff and its pupils, for many years to come.'

Pritchard hoped that such an emotional ending might divert his listeners, who would fail to notice that certain questions remained unanswered. He would discover later that such hopes were futile.

Leslie Burgess and Georgina Forster decided to leave it at that. The Report had been quoted and they had made their points, and hopefully stimulated the minds of some of their colleagues. They would have further opportunities to hammer home their points.

Richard Barnett then proposed that the meeting should discuss that general question of *informal contacts between Head Teacher and the staff.* He invited the Meeting to turn to page seven of the Inspectors' Report from which he quoted the inspectors' phrase *The self-imposed isolation of the Head Teacher.* Then he summarized the inspectors' findings in this area, i.e. that informal meetings between Head Teacher and teachers were apparently frowned upon, and they were therefore forced to meet secretly.

He turned to Pritchard, 'I am sure that you would like to say something about that.'

Parham was not sure that Pritchard would. Honest answers to the points being made would amount to an admission of guilt. The Head Teacher was now perspiring freely, his face red and his hair dishevelled. He mopped his brow, loosened his collar and rose slowly, while trying to pump up his confidence by thinking about his supporters.

I've got the backing of most of the governors and I must build on that. I'll continue to ignore the most outrageous suggestions that have been made.

'Mr Chairman, may I correct some misunderstandings about my position on informal contacts between a Head Teacher and his staff? I do not underestimate the value of such contacts. On the contrary, I value them very much. I appreciate, of course, that I probably did not talk enough with my colleagues during my *learning period.* I may have been concentrating too much at that time on developing my future plans, and neglecting other duties. But now I would like you to turn to page twelve of my document where you will see that I have tried to develop a well-considered plan for the future. In that plan, I intend every teacher to be fully involved in discussions about all the school's activities. I will take every opportunity to exchange ideas with my professional colleagues on a daily basis, because I value their experience and their various viewpoints.'

Parham, who had heard it all before, marvelled at the man's insincerity and level of hypocrisy.

Are the governors really being persuaded that their Head Teacher has become the supremely enlightened educator he purports to be? Are they going to ignore all the evidence to the contrary? Are they going to insist that he should be given more time? How many of them, if any, have now changed their minds about him? I can't be sure about anything at the moment. The meeting could still go either way.

Bartlett thanked Rupert Pritchard. Then he looked at his watch, smiled, and said he was sure that everyone would now welcome some refreshments. He had received a message that tea was ready. It was too late for Alice Peabody. She had been slumped in her chair for some time, and now her head had sunk on her bosom and her irregular snores were sometimes audible to everyone. Two or three governors were looking embarrassed.

'I think we should adjourn for tea,' the Chairmen said. 'We have already discussed some key issues, and time is getting on. After tea I hope we can review the memos and consider the question of long-term educational strategies. After that there will be time for further discussion, after which you may wish to put a motion or motions to the meeting. Before we finish today, I hope that we will reach a firm decision. one way or the other.'

'Amen to that,' said Parham to himself.

***

While the governors were having their refreshment, normal daily activities were taking place in the School. And some less normal ones too. As Malcolm's class poured out of their classroom for the afternoon break, an incident took place that was similar to others that had occurred from time to time.

Tony Seymour was suddenly extremely upset, in a way familiar to those who have had to deal with emotionally-disturbed children. It all happened in a split second. It was impossible to identify precisely the cause of the disturbance. A pupil in another class had made an apparently innocuous remark which Tony had interpreted as making fun of his eczema condition. His was all-too-conscious of his red, blotchy, and itchy skin. He suddenly exploded with fury, shouting aggressively and throwing his arms around wildly, while his friends all tried to reassure him and calm him down.

Billy Green, a leader, as usual, seized a moment when Tony paused for breath, to divert his attention.

'Tony, guess what?

'What?'

'The inspector – you know, the tall geezer who was 'ere the other day – 'e's been at a meetin' with the governors for hours. I told you before that something was up, didn't I?'

'Well. What's 'appening?' Tony was fully attentive now.

'It's what I was tellin' yer the other day. Ol' Pritchy's goin' to cop it. Take my word for it.'

Lucy Pym followed up Billy's initiative by singing, quite unmelodiously, the following lines to the tune of *Lily Marlene.*

Let's chuck out ol' Pritchy,
The man that everyone 'ates.
Let's chuck 'im out of 'aselmere.
And bring back Mr. Bates.

Billy laughed, noted that even Tony was looking amused, and said, 'That's not bad, Lucy. You didn't make it up yourself, though, did yer?'

''Course I did,' responded the spirited Lucy. 'I made it up yesterday and I've been singin' it to meself ever since. It makes me feel good!'

'Well,' said Billy, I really fink it could 'appen, but we'll 'ave to wait an' see.'

Tony now spoke up, his recent burst of aggression completely forgotton.

'I 'ope you're right Billy. It'd be nice wivout 'im!'

***

Among the teachers, the afternoon break provided an opportunity to discuss what was uppermost in their minds.

'How do you think it's going?' Malcolm said, addressing no-one in particular.

Tom laughed. 'Like hammer and tongs,' I should think,' he replied. 'If you mean, what sort of outcome is likely, that's anyone's guess. It could go either way, I suppose.'

'That's right,' Mary agreed. 'But we don't know enough about the governors, do we? If the majority are as bright as we should expect them to be, then they'll be persuaded by the arguments in the Inspectors' Report, won't they?'

'Perhaps,' Susan said, 'but don't forget that Pritchard has his loyal backers, who've been carefully cultivated during the year. One Report won't necessarily shake their confidence in him. I'm sure that, in the end, everything will be finely balanced. But forgive me' – she broke into a smile – 'I see little point in this speculation. We'll all learn soon enough how matters stand. If you don't mind, I'm going to change the subject.'

'Oh, come on, Susan,' Malcolm chided her. 'You know how vital to us this meeting is. We can't help being a bit anxious about it.'

But then his curiosity asserted itself.

'All right. What's the new topic, Susan? I can see you're bursting to tell us something.'

'Well, you know that Ruth Ellis has been found guilty of murdering her lover?'

'Yes,' Mary replied, 'and she's going to be hanged tomorrow, isn't she?'

'That's right. Isn't it awful?'

'It's barbaric,' Malcolm answered. 'Especially as the House of Commons voted by only a small margin a short time ago to retain the death penalty. I'm sure it'll soon be abolished for good.'

'Maybe,' Susan said, 'but meanwhile we've got this grisly taking of life. I'm shocked! It shouldn't be happening in the twentieth century. Especially here in Britain. Perhaps she'll be the last person to be hanged here! Perhaps she's innocent!'

The others agreed and sympathized. As Malcolm pointed out, juries do make mistakes sometimes. There have been some famous miscarriages of justice. A young woman was going to be hanged and it was just possible that she might be innocent. ...

But they were now ready to discuss a new topic.

'Have you heard that the dock strike is over?' Mary asked.

'Yes, I read it in the papers,' Malcolm replied. 'I think it's lasted for six weeks. There's a massive accumulation of goods at the dockside waiting to be exported, and dozens of ships are standing by.'

'It'll take weeks to clear the backlog,' Tom observed.

'And our *Balance of Payments* will look worse than ever,' added Malcolm. Now, I wonder what's happening right now in the meeting?'

Chapter 34
12 July 1955 (Continued)

After a fifteen minute break for tea and biscuits, during which there were some noisily animated discussions punctuated by raucous laughter – which Parham felt was singularly inappropriate in the middle of a critically important meeting – the Chairman returned to his seat and brought down his gavel. The sound resounded in the room.

Though some governors appeared reluctant to abandon their pleasantly relaxed chats, they all drifted slowly back to their seats. As they did so, Bartlett studied their faces and expressions. Some of the older ones were looking tired. In particular, Alice Peabody was dragging her unwieldy body with difficulty. As she slumped into her chair with a sigh of relief, he was resigned to the possibility of her dropping off again. She would be needed if it came to a vote! The Chairman resolved to bring the meeting to a conclusion after an hour or so. Otherwise some of the others might take a nap!

'The next topic,' he announced, 'will be the memos. Members may like to spend three minutes of so looking again at page eleven of the Inspectors' Report.'

After the allotted time, he rapped down his gavel, and continued:

'As you have seen, the memos are described as – and I quote – *an unfortunate feature of the Head Teacher's management,*' and it is suggested that some of them may even have been detrimental to the children's education. That is, of course, a very serious charge. The teachers have made similar points. All members of the Governing Body received copies of those memos at the times when they were issued, so you are familiar with their content. However, you could not have known of their impact, if any, on the children's education. But now you have both the Inspectors' Report and the teachers' *Statement.* They make clear how the memos were regarded both by the teachers and by the inspectors. But let us hear what Mr Pritchard has to say about them. May we have your observations, then, Mr Pritchard?'

The Head Teacher had listened to the quotations with increasing resentment and fury. He was feeling the pressure and his head felt strangely congested and heavy with tension. Nevertheless, he felt more confident about this topic than some others, and had a growing contempt for his critics.

What do these people know about managing a school? They couldn't even manage a whelk stall!

The latter was an observation made during a fierce House of Commons debate that was for some reason lodged firmly in his memory.

Overcoming his growing lethargy and despair, he rose to his feet and spoke boldly and confidently.

'Mr Chairman, I welcome the opportunity to speak about the memos.' he began. 'Yes, I sent the teachers a number of them. And why not? I was a new Head Teacher who had identified a number of irregularities. The memos were a quick and efficient way of addressing those irregularities. The memos dealt with matters that would concern anyone responsible for the smooth management of a school. You will recall that I always provided copies of them to every governor. I wanted you all to see and approve them. You had shown faith in me by appointing me as Head Teacher of Haselmere, and I was very grateful for your confidence. I believe that every one of those memos was fully approved by you all when their purpose was explained. I was always glad to have that endorsement, and the support of the whole Board.'

Pritchard now paused and looked round the table to assess the reaction of the governors. He was satisfied that he had their complete attention, and that his point had gone home. They had approved every memo and so, in a way, they shared responsibility for them. It had never occurred to any one of them, even the more critical ones, to question the rationality of a single one. Some governors were now looking at him quite sympathetically. He found that encouraging. But now he felt it was time to show some humility. He continued:

'Now, there may well have been times when, as a relatively inexperienced Head Teacher, I did not tackle some of the problems I identified in the best possible way. Arguably the memo was not always the most appropriate procedure. But have no doubt that there were problems and I was making an honest attempt to deal with them.

There was, for example, the question of the daily timetable. I had noticed after only a few days, too many unjustified and unacceptable variations in the timing of school activities. To be blunt, things had become rather slack during the previous term, the interim period following the death of William Rogers. I wanted to put matters right as quickly as possible. I was also reminding the teachers that they now had a new Head Teacher who was determined to bring in some order.'

He paused, smiled again and swept his eyes from governor to governor before continuing:

'With every memo I hoped to improve a system, and to make everything rational and predictable. I suppose I like tidy arrangements that make good sense, not ones that vary according to a teacher's whim. I like to be well-organised, and to be in charge of a well-run School. The use of memos has been queried, and their disadvantages alleged. But are there not some advantages, too? I always tried to express my requirements in them in the plainest and simplest English that admitted of no misunderstanding. My memos were unequivocal. And as they were in writing they could be referred to at any time. Everyone knew where I stood on each particular issue. They were therefore a useful tool.'

Pritchard now sat down, still smiling. He was confident that he had won some points. Ronald Parham was still full of doubts and worry.

Pritchard can certainly put a persuasive gloss on his actions, though his case is flimsy and full of holes. Will the governors spot the holes in his arguments?

He looked across at the two key governors, the shrewdest and most perspective of the group. So far, no-one else had made a single penetrating criticism so a great deal depended on

Forster and Burgess. He was relieved that both seemed anxious to speak.

Georgina Forster had the first opportunity.

'Mr Chairman,' she began, 'I would like to make two inter-related observations. Firstly, I am not at all convinced by the explanations that we have just heard. Mr Pritchard seems to have chosen a very odd way to communicate his wishes. This is a *very* small school. There are only four full-time teachers. Why not simply speak to them, either individually or together about any matter of concern? That would have been the best way to get to know them, especially in the early days. Why try to manage such a small school at a distance? Formal written instructions can easily be misunderstood and in this small community it seems very unwise that there was such dependence on written communication. What was needed was not one-way written communication but plenty of lively interaction and a healthy exchange of views. Regular discussion and debate, Mr Chairman, should have been the way forward.'

Secondly, while it is true that the Head Teacher explained the *raison d'etre* of each memo to us, we could hardly judge their relevance. And I hadn't realized earlier that not one of them was ever discussed with the teachers, either before or after they were sent. Isn't that extraordinary? Surely the teachers' views matter. They are, after all, the ones in closest contact with the children. They know better than anyone else what is needed to enable them to teach effectively, don't they?'

Miss Forster now sat down while the meeting digested her arguments. Parham had had to resist the temptation to nod and mutter his approval. It was very difficult for him to play a neutral role in such a clear case. Leslie Burgess was now ready to follow Miss Forster. He thought it was time to focus on a particular memo.

'One memo, Mr Chairman,' he began, 'seems to have really upset the teachers, particularly those teaching the younger ones. I refer to the one about Graded Reading Books. A redistribution of books between classes was requested, quite arbitrarily. Now, the teachers had carefully and thoughtfully, allocated those books between classes, following discussion among themselves, to ensure that every child had the one best suited to his level, and therefore the one that would help him to make maximum progress with reading. The children were enjoying those books, and benefiting from them. So why take them away? Remember that here we are talking about teachers who are regarded as outstanding professionals. The inspectors have praised their expertise. Fortunately that particular memo was never implemented. Otherwise, as the inspectors recognised, the children's education would have suffered. The teachers were not going to allow that to happen. Good for them!' He allowed himself a grin before regaining his seat.

Miss Forster wished to make a further comment.

'Mr Chairman, that particular memo well illustrates the point I have made. The teachers have an intimate knowledge of their own pupils and of their educational needs. They should certainly have been consulted before any changes were made to a system that was clearly working extremely well. In fact they were just ignored and they must have been very frustrated and angry about that.'

The Chairman asked Pritchard whether he would like to reply to what he had just heard. The Headmaster seemed to hesitate, but then indicated that he would. Yet as he rose to his feet he was not at all sure how to deliver an effective response. He decided on a tone of quiet reason and sympathetic understanding.

'Mr Chairman, I would not like Miss Forster to think that I saw my memos as an alternative to face-to-face discussions. As I have previously emphasized, I regard both as essential. But there are, in my view, some carefully-selected areas when putting something into writing has much to commend it.'

He now decided, in spite of the arguments just put by Burgess, to reiterate the case for re-arranging the Graded Reading Books.

'I wanted each class to have the right number of books of the right sort. It was clear to me that some of them were in the wrong place. But I took care to arrange that each class had a wide range of books to cope with its wide range of reading

attainment. So each class had books at three different levels.'
Burgess now broke in angrily.

'But that wasn't enough, was it? The range was, according to the teachers, greater than you thought! They knew. You didn't!'

Pritchard ignored the interruption and ploughed on. But he had decided that once again a touch of humility was due.

'However, with hindsight, I think that, in spite of my good intentions and logical approach, that particular memo may not have been the best way forward. The range of reading attainment in one class was unusually wide. As a newcomer I could not possibly know that.'

Miss Forster now pounced to reinforce an earlier point that had not been answered.

'Exactly!' She sounded forthright, with a note of triumph. 'Had prior discussion taken place with the teachers,' Mr Chairman', she began, 'the Head Teacher would have discovered, in good time, that it was better to leave the books where they were. A proper discussion would have revealed the folly of what was proposed.'

Pritchard inwardly fumed as he heard those words. He felt the blood rushing to his head as his embarrassment and anger increased.

Damn the woman. She's always been a pain in the neck and a bloody nuisance.

But help was at hand in the form of Mrs French

'I think we should all remember, Mr Chairman,' she began, 'that Mr Pritchard has always been absolutely open with us about the memos and that a sound case has been made for each one. He has now told us quite frankly that he may have been mistaken about one of them. I commend him for his honesty and frankness. It is not easy to admit that a mistake may possibly have been made. Is the man to be condemned because of a slip made during his first year as an inexperienced Head Teacher when there were so many difficult decisions to be made?' she demanded challengingly. 'Mr. Chairman, may I now suggest that it is time to move on to another topic?'

Richard Bartlett was happy to oblige, but first he wished to summarize the arguments.

'Some governors have views very similar to those expressed in the Inspector's Report, that sending memos was not the best way to deal with perceived problems in a small school, especially without prior discussion with the teachers. But others appear to accept the Head Teacher's view that, in most cases, it was a simple and clear-cut form of communication.

'The next topic,' he began, 'is the question of whether the Head Teacher provided the teachers with any idea of the kind of school he wanted Haselmere to be. Did he give them any notion of how he saw the future? Did he have any long-term educational strategy? The inspectors thought not. They thought he was focusing on relatively trivial matters, and not giving enough attention to the bigger picture: how Haselmere should develop in the second half of the twentieth century. Now, I am sure that you have a point of view about that, Mr Pritchard.'

The Head Teacher, now red-faced and perspiring freely, had had enough. He suddenly felt drained of energy. He was sure that his blood pressure had risen to dangerous levels. He felt he was on trial and having to answer questions put by people with an inadequate knowledge of the reality. The worst aspect was that he didn't know what to expect next, which was unnerving. Nevertheless, he knew that his future was at stake, and that he was on a sticky wicket! He rose and looked around him defiantly before attempting a response.

'Mr Chairman,' he began, 'it seemed to me to be of key importance that I should study every aspect of an Open-Air School – a type of school of which I had no previous experience – before I could begin to think about the longer term. I wanted to plan for the future on a sound, well-considered basis. I wanted to get the basics right. You have all had an opportunity to study my ideas in my document. Do you think those ideas are evidence that I wasted my time, or do you think they reveal that I have spent a considerable amount of time thinking and planning to good effect? I hope I will not appear to be immodest if I say that, in my report, I have comprehensively covered all the areas of concern that both the teachers and the inspectors have expressed: democratic staff meetings; a well-rounded curriculum, drawing on the rich experience of my teachers; regular discussions between the staff and myself on all matters of concern; measures to enhance the care of our pupils, together with ensuring their maximum progress both academically and medically; the fostering of good school/parent relations, and so on. Mr Chairman, I needed time to develop such plans, and I submit that I used my time well.' As Pritchard regained his seat he felt well-satisfied with his latest oration.

Some of the governors were certainly impressed with that! Good! Burgess and Forster may nit-pick but the others will see that my plans have been well-constructed and are enlightened and incontrovertible. I've produced an impressive document. No-one can deny that. Perhaps the tide may now turn my way.

Leslie Burgess now indicated his wish to speak and the Chairman concurred.

'Mr Chairman, the Head Teacher has just explained that he needed a full year to shape his ideas on the future development of the school. That doesn't sound unreasonable does it? But consider what he did not do while his plans were being developed. He did not, at any time, liaise with his teachers so that they would be fully involved in the process, although he has indicated that he respects their expertise. He didn't even consult the very experienced senior teacher who had twice been a successful Acting Head. In fact, every time that teacher tried to initiate a discussion with his Head Teacher he was repulsed, often rather rudely.'

Pritchard now shook his head vigorously. Burgess, ignoring him, continued:

'I am glad that Mr Pritchard has finally produced a report on the future development of Haselmere, but the teachers have had no hand in it. Yet all of them have had useful experience in open-air education and each one has much to contribute. They all know more about it than their Head Teacher. Yet, as we have heard, instead of encouraging creative discussions, Mr Pritchard chose isolation in his study for much of the time. He ignored his staff.' He now paused, looked around the table and raised his voice for his final sentences. 'Mr Chairman, I regard that as a quite extraordinary and unacceptable state of affairs. It is no way to run a school!' He glared at Pritchard.

As the words of Burgess echoed round the room there were a few moments of shocked silence. Ronald Parham, still anxious about the outcome of the meeting, assessed Pritchard's reaction and that of the governors.

His face is redder than ever, and his jerky eye and body movements suggest that he is near the end of his tether. He's a bundle of nerves. He was so bouncy when the meeting began but now he looks dejected and beaten. His swings of mood have been extraordinary. Yet he has certainly shown remarkable resilience and he probably still has some support in the Governing Body. But how much? How many of them are changing sides as they weigh up the arguments?

The Chairman now looked at his watch, and was considering how best to move forward when suddenly a new hand was raised. It had gone up very positively as if its owner was most anxious to make his point without delay. Eyes around the table suddenly stared in his direction, for this was a governor who rarely spoke at meetings. Bartlett was curious to know what had moved him to intervene at this stage.

The hand belonged to the oldest member, Humphrey Cooper, who had worked in local government before retiring. He was a small, inoffensive-looking gentleman in his mid-70s, neatly-dressed in a dark blue serge suit. Although he regularly attended all meetings, and listened intently to all contributions, he was one of that rare breed who speak only when they have something of particular significance to say. Because of that he was widely respected. He might not be a 'big hitter', but his contributions always commanded attention. The room was now charged with an atmosphere of tense expectation. What was Humphrey going to say? Would he come down firmly on one side or the other? Would this last-minute intervention make any difference?

Chapter 35
12 July 1955 (Continued)

All eyes were focused on Humphrey Cooper as he rose to speak, none more so than those of Ronald Parham, who barely knew the little man, but appraised him rapidly.

He looks as if, normally, he wouldn't say boo to a goose, but at present there is a look of firm resolution in his eyes and bearing. He seems determined to have his say. He must feel very strongly about the situation, one way or the other. Which way, I wonder?

Humphrey Cooper would soon indicate which way. He would express his conclusions unequivocally. He now swept his eyes around the table, smiled and began.

'Mr Chairman, we have all studied the Inspectors' Report. I thought it was very fair, clearly expressed and cogently argued. We have also seen the *Statement* representing the unanimous view of the teachers. Those two documents reach very similar conclusions, don't they? I find that very significant indeed. Now, I am quite sure that the teachers were *driven* to state their views by sheer desperation. Their *Statement* is a *cri de coeur.* They obviously felt that things could not go on as they had during the past year. School standards were at risk. The children's education was likely to suffer. Somehow they had managed during that crucial year to keep things going, to continue with their excellent work, but they felt under threat and apprehensive about the future. We all know why. The Head Teacher was hardly ever in touch with them. He spent much of the day isolated in his study. He failed to consult them about anything. He made no attempt to make use of the wisdom and experience of his Staff. He even rejected – rudely I believe – advice from the very experienced senior teacher who had been a successful Acting Head. He issued memos demanding arbitrary changes which were either irrelevant or misconceived, and were never discussed with those who had to implement them. He told his staff nothing about his philosophy of education, or, if you like, his ideas for the future of Haselmere. He gave them no curriculum guidance. He did not even give any advice or support to a probationary teacher. In summary, he did not perform satisfactorily as a Head Teacher. There was a total absence of effective leadership.'

Mr Cooper paused to study the faces of his listeners before continuing. Many looked quite shocked or stunned. That was hardly surprising. He had wasted no time outlining to them, with no softening of the edges, some of the worst features of the school's management during the past year. They had already heard much of it before, but now it was all being brought together along with its harsh implications. There was worse to come for Rupert Pritchard as the speaker continued.

'Mr Pritchard has spoken with spirit in defence of his work, but frankly, his record is indefensible. He has had to bat, of course, on a sticky wicket. So, in order to divert our attention from his dismal record, he has produced a rather idyllic plan for the future. Now, Mr Chairman, I would ask all my fellow governors to ask themselves this question. Do you really think that someone who has seriously neglected his duties for a whole year – as has been clearly established – is capable of carrying out effectively the changes envisaged in his report?' He looked challengingly at his audience and shook his head. 'I'm quite sure he could not. As far as Mr Pritchard is concerned, those proposals are completely unrealistic. They have been devised in order to spread a cloud over the actual situation, the reality, as set out clearly in the official Report of the Inspectorate. Mr Pritchard is obviously desperate to save his position, but we would be neglecting our duty as governors, to the staff and pupils of Haselmere, if we were to fail to take appropriate and forthright action now.

Time is getting on, Mr Chairman, so may I respectfully suggest that it is time to bring matters to a head? In a few moments I would like to put a motion to the meeting, but before I do I would like to draw the attention of my colleagues to some extracts from the documents which entirely accord with the views I have just expressed. The conclusion in the Inspectors' Report states:

The staff cannot be expected to teach at such a high level if their work and morale are constantly undermined by action at the top.

Now, while that is pretty strong stuff, the teachers go even further. They have dared to articulate what the inspectors have implied. They are, of course, the ones closest to the action. Now what do they say? Here it is:

... we are carrying out our work without the benefit of any advice, guidance or support from the Head Teacher.

Mr Chairman, I think we should all consider those words very carefully indeed – NO ADVICE, NO GUIDANCE, NO SUPPORT.

They are a damning indictment. And those words are followed by:

Only a change of Headship can provide the positive leadership that is so clearly lacking at present.'

Bartlett felt that the silence in the room was almost palpable. But Humphrey Cooper had not finished. He now continued with his summary, approaching its climax:

'Isn't it clear to us all, Mr. Chairman, that no-one at Haselmere has any further confidence in Mr Pritchard? For the good of the School, I strongly suggest that Mr. Pritchard should therefore be relieved of his duties.'

He now paused again to look meaningfully at his fellow governors.

'May I now put my proposal to the meeting, Mr Chairman?' he asked.

Bartlett invited him to proceed, and he did so:

We, the Governing Body of Haselmere Open-Air School for the Delicate, having taken note of the critical and deteriorating situation in the management of the school, as outlined by the inspectors, Dr Mitchell and Mr Parham, and by all the teaching staff, recommend that Mr Pritchard should be relieved of his post as soon as that can be arranged.

Soon after Humphrey Cooper had sat down, the Chairman asked whether someone would like to second the motion, and

Leslie Burgess did so immediately. Bartlett now invited the meeting to discuss the motion.

Tom Hawkins spoke first.

'This is a very sad day for me,' he began. 'I have always had the greatest respect for Mr Pritchard and it had seemed to me that he was doing his job reasonably well. But I have read and re-read the Inspectors' Report and listened carefully to all the criticisms. I now see that we governors were not, in fact, kept fully aware of what was actually happening in the school. In certain respects we were misled. I have therefore decided, however reluctantly, to support the motion.'

Mrs Cecilia French then said,

'I very much agree with Mr Hawkins. I think that Mr Pritchard meant well, but probably his talents would be better employed elsewhere.'

Mr Bartlett scanned the faces around the table which were focused on him.

'Would anyone else like to make a comment?' he asked.

'There was no response. Presumably everyone felt that further observations would be unnecessary. In any case, everyone was anxious to bring the meeting to an early conclusion.

'Well then,' he said, 'let me put the motion to you without further delay.' He turned to Jenny.

'To make sure that we've got it right, would you please read it out to us.'

Jenny nodded, turned to her notes and read out the motion, trying hard to keep any suggestion of a nervous tremble out of her voice.

The Chairman turned and thanked Jenny. Then he said,

'Would all those in favour of the motion kindly raise their hands.'

Every governor raised his or her hand.

'Thank you,' said Barnett. 'Now to be absolutely positive, would those against the motion raise their hands.'

No-one stirred.

The Chairman said, 'Thank you very much. The motion has been carried unanimously. I will discuss with Mr Parham and the Education Office, as soon as possible, the correct procedure to be followed in implementing your decision.

I am afraid it has been a long afternoon, ladies and gentlemen, and I am sorry about that, but I will shortly bring the meeting to an end. Before doing so, I would just like to say that this is a very sad day for all of us. (There were murmurs of 'Hear! Hear!') On a personal level, I have worked very happily with Mr Pritchard over the past year, and the Report of the Inspectors came as a shock to me, though, like you, I have become convinced by its arguments. I'm sure we all hope now that Mr Pritchard will be given opportunities elsewhere commensurate with his talents, and I'm sure that we all wish him well in any future appointment that he might have.' A murmur of agreement floated round the room. The Chairman continued: 'I will write to you all in connection with today's meeting. Thank you.'

Richard Bartlett then rose and prepared to depart as did most governors. Others, apparently still in shock, were slow to move, but gradually did likewise. Ronald Parham stayed in the room for a few minutes to have a confidential word with the Chairman, and then turned and hurried away. Both he and the Chairman were immensely relieved, though they realised that a new vacancy for a Head Teacher, after only one year, would arouse widespread speculation, and the filling of that vacancy would be problematical.

For a time there remained a quiet buzz of conversation in the room as a diminishing group of governors engaged in inconsequential chatter. From time to time the gossip was interspersed with banter and occasional laughter, the latter affording them some relief after a stressful day.

But in a short time, the exchanges faded and the room gradually emptied. It suddenly seemed unnaturally silent. There now remained only the hunched, solitary and forlorn presence of Rupert Pritchard, who remained in his chair, seemingly hardly aware that two or three governors patted his back as they departed.

Head buried in his hands, he stayed slumped and motionless for another half hour. Then he removed his hands and sat upright, staring in front of him, as, face reddening and lips compressed, despair gave way to a rising and uncontrollable anger, focused on those he held principally responsible for his downfall. Wild eyed, he began to pound the table with his fist until it ached, while his face became wet with perspiration, the sweat running in irregular channels down his face. The few long strands of hair on his head, previously arranged with care, now hung raggedly about him.

Finally, exhausted both emotionally and physically, he staggered to his feet, dragged himself across the room to a metal filing cabinet, pulled out the top drawer, and took out an address book. He flicked through several pages, scribbling the information he sought on to a note pad. At one point, he examined his list, thought for a moment, and then decided to add another item. Finally, after another brief look at it he tore off the top page and pocketed it.

He sat down again, immersed in his thoughts, brows knitted. After some minutes, he looked up, and stared ahead, his features gradually relaxing, until a twisted little smile played on his lips. He knew what he had to do, and was determined to do it without delay.

Chapter 36
13 July 1955

Malcolm Brown was about to leave for Haselmere but Caroline would not let him go without raising the subject at the forefront of their minds. She plucked his sleeve.

'Today, dear, you should manage to learn something about yesterday's events, don't you think?'

Malcolm grinned. 'You mean, what exactly happened at the meeting of the Governing Body?'

'Don't tease. Yes, of course. That's the great issue of the day, isn't it?'

'It certainly is. Well, I hope I'll find out something. We're all on tenterhooks. Jenny Martin usually attends as a minute-taker, and she may pass on a hint or two, though I wouldn't expect her to breach confidentiality by saying anything specific – unless, of course, something really sensational happened which could affect us all?'

'Well, whatever you hear, you must give me a full report when you get home. The suspense is awful.' She smiled. 'And try to make it good news!'

'Yes, I'll do that,' he grinned. 'I'll put the best possible complexion on whatever I hear.'

'Oh, no you won't!' Caroline affected a scolding manner. 'Just give me the unvarnished facts, please.' She was thoughtful for a moment, and then spoke with quiet seriousness.

'Malcolm, I've been thinking about what's been going on, and I want to warn you to be very careful. You and the other teachers have an enemy and we know he can be malicious. He's a nasty piece of work. We may yet find out just <u>how</u> nasty'

'You can't be referring to our Rupert.'

'I certainly am. That *Statement* you sent to the governors was dynamite. It must have infuriated Pritchard. It lines up all

302

the teachers against him. It told him just what you think about his record, about his failures and about what you all think of him altogether. It makes it clear that you all want him to go. Whatever happened at the meeting, for the rest of the term he'll be hating you all. He'll be bitter and resentful and looking for ways to take his revenge. There's something about him that frightens me, Malcolm. I'm worried!'

'Well, don't be worried, dear. Look, we don't have any idea what happened yesterday at the meeting. But we do know that the Inspectors' Report was damning and Pritchard may have decided that the game is up and that he'll resign. In that case we'll all celebrate!'

'But if he got the governors on his side, he may be the one celebrating!'

'I doubt it, dear, but wait till I come home. I'll find out all I can. Honestly, there's no need to worry.'

They kissed and Malcolm departed for Haselmere.

***

Mary Prince, who was habitually one of the first to arrive at Haselmere, normally caught a glimpse of the arrival of Rupert Pritchard as he strode along the garden path leading to his study. But during the mid-morning break it suddenly dawned on her that she had not seen him at all. As everyone in the School was still bubbling with curiosity about the outcome of the meeting the day before, she wondered whether she had missed his arrival, or whether he had not turned up. As usual, she met her colleagues in the hall for tea or coffee, and a chat.

'Morning, Tom. What a wonderful, sunny day! This is when teaching in an open-air school is a real pleasure. Now, I've got two questions on my mind and you may know the answer to at least one of them. First of all, have you heard anything about the future of our Head Teacher? And secondly, do you know whether he came in today? I usually see him arrive, but I didn't this morning.'

Tom smiled. 'As to the first question, Mary, I wish I could enlighten you. I just haven't heard a thing. Jenny will know, so perhaps one of us should go to her office. She's only a part-time secretary but she should be in now. And I'm afraid I don't know whether or not Pritchard is here. As soon as I got in this morning, I started preparing for my first lesson and then did some marking before the children arrived. So I've had a very busy morning so far. Pritchard may have gone off to attend a Head Teachers' meeting, or he may be unwell. He may simply be suffering from a headache or exhaustion after the meeting. But again, Jenny should know.'

'Right,' Mary said, 'I'll go and speak to Jenny, and at the same time, see whether His Lordship has arrived.'

Mary hurried away. Before she returned, Malcolm and Susan joined Tom and they chatted, inevitably about Pritchard and his apparent absence. An air of nervous uncertainty permeated their discussion.

'I doubt that he's unwell.' Susan said. 'I can't remember him being ill at all since I've been here. Not that that's very long.' She gave a short, embarrassed laugh.

'I expect he's doing what he does for most of the day,' Malcolm joked, 'sitting comfortably at his desk practising the art of bureaucracy.'

But he wasn't. Mary returned shortly with the news that Pritchard had not put in an appearance, and that Jenny had no idea why. He had not telephoned Jenny either to tell her that he might be late, or that he would not be coming in.

'That's very odd,' Tom said, 'especially as it's the day after the Governors' Meeting.

The others agreed. The break period was drawing to an end and they would soon have to return to their classes. Tom quickly made up his mind.

'I think there's almost certainly a link with yesterday's meeting,' he said. 'Now, if the governors recommended Pritchard's dismissal, he would normally not leave us until the end of the term, and we would expect him to be here today, as usual. If, on the other hand, nothing as dramatic as that happened, we would still expect him to turn up. So his non-appearance is a mystery! Look, you all go back to your classes. I'll give mine a task to keep them busy, and then try to find out what's happened.'

The group dispersed. As they walked together, Malcolm commented to Susan that whenever there was any particular problem in the School, they could always rely on Tom's leadership. Susan agreed.

Tom found Jenny busy at her desk.

'Still no news, Jenny?'

'No, Tom, and I'm getting rather worried. He's always kept me informed of his movements.'

'Have you tried to telephone him?'

'Yes, three times. There's been no reply.'

'And can you tell me anything about yesterday's meeting?'

'Oh, yes. The Governing Body voted unanimously that Mr Pritchard should be relieved of his duties. That's what makes his absence now so worrying.'

'Relieved of his duties? Given the sack?' Tom could not conceal either his delight or his incredulity.

'I'm amazed that they were unanimous,' he said. 'That's really dramatic news!' Although the dismissal was not entirely unexpected, it stunned him for a few moments, and his mind flooded with its implications. Recovering quickly he said, 'Then his absence really is worrying. Now, if I may use your phone, Jenny, I will do two things: inform Ronald Parham, and then get in touch with the police.'

'The police? Really?'

'Yes. Don't be alarmed. It's just a precautionary measure. I'll ask them whether they would be prepared to send a policeman round to his house just to check that everything's alright. You said that he was punctilious about informing you of his movements, but this time he hasn't, so we must find out why.'

'But it does seem rather early to bring in the police. We don't want to waste their time.' Jenny protested.

'No, we don't. But we teachers are worried about what's happened, and so are you. The outcome of yesterday's meeting, involving someone as unstable as Pritchard, opens the door to all kinds of possibilities.

Jenny was startled. 'Is he unstable? I know he can be rather odd.'

'Well, on the basis of everything that's happened here over the past year, I think he is,' Tom replied. The police will decide whether they think a check-up is justified and a proper use of their manpower.'

'I expect you're right, so please go ahead and phone.'

Tom phoned the inspector first. Parham was in his office. He sounded quite alarmed when he heard that Pritchard was not at the School.

'His absence the very next day after the meeting is significant. It's a worry, Tom. What's he up to? What's going on? I'm sure he's very bitter, upset and angry at the moment. That's very understandable of course. But how yesterday's decision will affect his overall behaviour, well, that's anyone's guess, but it's certainly worrying. It was an extraordinary meeting, Tom, with a very dramatic and unexpected climax...' He gave Tom a brief account of the events preceding the vote.

'At one time, everything seemed to be touch and go. I was more or less a passive observer, and becoming increasingly worried about the outcome. I had no idea how it would all end. At times, I wondered whether I should intervene more positively to move things in the right direction. The debate was quite well balanced, too much so for my peace of mind. Then, a little old fellow I hardly knew, named Humphrey Cooper – normally shy and unobtrusive – my word, he virtually took over the meeting. He summed up the case against Pritchard so precisely and succinctly that everyone fell into line, even the stalwarts who had previously given Pritchard their wholehearted support. ... Now, what are we going to do about his non-appearance?'

Tom told him about Jenny's efforts to contact Pritchard, and that he proposed to contact the police and to ask them to check whether Pritchard was, in fact, at home. Parham approved of that, and asked to be kept informed of all developments.

Parham was particularly concerned because of Pritchard's paranoia, the possibility of depression, and what he had heard from the school doctor about the occasional relation between paranoia and a preoccupation with death and suffering. His instincts told him that the situation was fraught with potential danger.

By lunchtime there was still no news of Pritchard, but Tom was now able to brief his colleagues on what had happened at the meeting. Like Tom they all looked stunned when they heard about the dismissal.

'I'm really flabbergasted!' Mary said. 'I really didn't think the governors would act so decisively, in spite of all the evidence before them. And they were unanimous! That's amazing!'

'It's also wonderful news,' Susan commented, 'especially as we all thought that he had robust support among the governors.'

'That's right, he did,' Tom agreed, and he told them about the final hour of the meeting and the timely and effective contribution of Humphrey Cooper.

'Good for him!' Malcolm said. 'Well, now that's settled, where do we go from here? What happens next?'

'Well, they'll be some urgent telephone conversations between Parham and Roger Bartlett, the chairman, about that.' Tom explained. 'And the Education Office will be involved. It's a rare thing for Head Teachers to be relieved of their duties, and the authorities need to be quite clear about the right procedure. Lawyers will need to be consulted, too, especially as Pritchard may appeal to the National Union of Head Teachers for support and legal protection. In any case, I don't think Pritchard will actually be relieved of his post until the end of the term.'

'Anyway, first we have to find him,' Susan reminded them, with a smile.

Malcolm agreed, and added, 'It does look as if Pritchard's absence is somehow linked to his dismissal, doesn't it?'

'Yes, it does,' Tom said. He explained to his colleagues how worried Ronald Parham was about Pritchard's absence. 'I think he fears,' he added, 'that yesterday's events may have pushed him over the top, that Pritchard's persecution complex may have led him to imagine that he is the victim of a plot to get rid of him, and that he may feel betrayed or persecuted.'

'You mean, he thinks Pritchard's gone round the bend?' Malcolm asked. 'Isn't that a bit exaggerated, a bit over-dramatized?'

'Perhaps it is,' Tom agreed, 'but that's the way Parham's thinking. He's gone into this paranoia question pretty thoroughly, and he really thinks it links up with quite a lot that we know about Pritchard's behaviour. Not everything, of course. There's no link, as far as I know, between paranoia and really malicious behaviour. But Parham may be right. Remember that Pritchard has always been suspicious of me, and has imagined that I covet his post and have been plotting to replace him? So Ronald Parham may not be so far from the truth. If so, the question is, if Pritchard feels victimized, what is he planning to do, if anything, about it?'

'I don't like the sound of all this,' Susan said. 'It sounds ominous and threatening. He's such a very unpleasant man!'

'Don't be alarmed,' Tom said. 'This is all speculation. We'll soon find out the facts. The police want us to phone them at three o'clock to tell them whether Pritchard has been in touch. If not, they'll send someone round to his house to check. Then they'll phone Jenny. We can't do anything else at the moment. By break-time this afternoon we may know something.'

Malcolm, too, sought to reassure Susan. 'I think there may be a simple explanation to the mystery of Pritchy's absence,' he said with a grin. 'Perhaps he was so exhausted after the meeting that he decided to spend much of today in his bath, relaxing.'

Mary laughed. 'If he's in the bath when a policeman knocks at his door, he's going to get a shock. Serves him right!'

Malcolm joined in the laughter. 'I can see him, stepping naked from the bath; then, wrapping a towel round him, and hurrying downstairs, water dripping from every part of him – he mustn't keep the police waiting!- ...and then ...'

'Don't go on! I can't stand any more!' Mary was laughing helplessly. 'Oh dear, I'm afraid I was imagining all that in graphic detail! Naughty me!'

***

'It's 'appened! It's 'appened! Old Pritchy's got 'is comeuppance!' Billy Green's triumphant announcement ensured that he was surrounded by grinning faces and shining eyes.

''ow d'yer know?' asked Jack Miller.

'Well, stands to reason, don't it? 'e ain't 'ere, is 'e? Billy replied defiantly. 'I reckon 'e's been chucked out.'

'We don't know though, do we?' Jack responded. One day's nothin'.'

'But if Billy's right,' Tim Owen commented, 'that'd be really smashin'', wouldn't it? What's that little rhyme? Sing it Luce!'

Lucy needed no further encouragement. 'We'll all sing it,' she said, 'but don't forget the tune is "Lily Marlene", and she reminded them of the words.

They all burst into song, each beginning at a different pitch, but more or less aligning their various keys after the first few bars.

Let's chuck out ol' Pritchy,
The man that everyone hates,
Let's chuck 'im out of Haselmere,
And bring back Mr.Bates.

Pretty good, Lucy,' Billy said approvingly, 'but "Lily Marlene" goes on a bit longer so we need some more words.'

'OK. Lucy responded, 'I'll write some more words when I can.'

***

It was probably a few minutes after four o'clock when a middle-aged, portly constable rang the doorbell at Pritchard's house. For good measure he also rapped the knocker loudly. It was in a very quiet street and the constable's actions were followed by an emphatic silence. He waited patiently for a few minutes and then repeated his actions. This time he was fairly certain that he heard some movement inside the house. He waited for a few more minutes, and was about to ring and knock again when he heard footsteps approaching along the passage leading to the hall.

Suddenly the door was opened. A short, podgy man, largely bald, except for a few, long wisps of hair, so disarranged that his appearance was rather dishevelled, stood before him. His eyes were bloodshot and appeared to be unfocused. The constable was puzzled. He was checking the presence of a Head Teacher, and this unimpressive, scruffy individual, who looked as if he had only just left his bed, was not the kind of person he had been expecting.

'Excuse me sir,' he began. 'I'm sorry to disturb you in this way, but may I ask you a few questions?'

There was apprehension in Pritchard's eyes. He wondered what on earth the man wanted. 'Of course, constable', he said.

'Then may I ask you whether you are Mr Pritchard, the Head Teacher of Haselmere Open Air School?'

'Yes, I am.'

'Well, sir, there has been some concern because you didn't turn up there today. I understand that you normally contact your secretary if you are likely to be away for some reason. She has been trying to contact you by telephone and couldn't get a reply. Is there anything that you would like to tell me, sir?'

Pritchard had listened carefully to the constable. After a moment or two, he smiled. He had watched the man's approach from an upper window, and had prepared his response to the inevitable questions.

'I really am sorry that I have put you to so much trouble, constable,' he began. 'I must tell you what happened. Yesterday I had some particularly distressing news which I found quite upsetting.

Consequently, when I went to bed, I found it impossible to get to sleep. I became increasingly restless, and so I finally decided to take a sleeping tablet. I don't know exactly what time that was but it was probably around three or four in the morning.'

Pritchard now looked searchingly at his visitor to assess his reaction, but the constable's expression was impassive. He continued,

'It was really rather foolish of me because I know that sleeping tablets always send me into a very deep sleep which goes on for far too long. Anyway, I took it and it did its work. I must have dropped off fairly soon afterwards and I'm afraid I just slept and slept. I suppose I woke up and dressed just before you rang.'

'I see. And are you perfectly all right, sir,' the constable asked.

'Yes, thank you constable. I'm fine. I'm just sorry to have put you to so much trouble.'

'Don't worry about that, sir. The main thing is that you're alright. These things happen. Well, I'll report now to the Station that everything is alright, and no doubt someone there will tell your secretary. Thank you, sir.' He turned and left.

Rupert Pritchard smiled to himself. The constable had been very understanding but, surprisingly, he hadn't even enquired whether the Head Teacher would put in an appearance at Haselmere the next day. 'Well,' he reflected with a grim smile, 'they would soon find out! And they would shortly have some rather unpleasant surprises, too. And so would a few others!'

Jenny normally left Haselmere at around 4.30 p.m. That was about 30 minutes more than her half-time hours allowed, but she was conscientious and liked to have a tidy desk and to have cleared up any outstanding matter before she left. She had just buttoned up her coat and was about to leave when the 'phone rang. She shivered nervously. She didn't think school secretaries should be subjected to the sort of stress that she felt. However, if it was news at last, that would be welcome.

She picked up the telephone with a shaking hand. It was the local police sergeant. He informed her that a constable had called at Mr Pritchard's house. The Head Teacher was apparently quite well though he had had some difficulty in sleeping the night before and had taken a sleeping tablet that sent him into a deep sleep until well into the afternoon. He was very sorry for any inconvenience that had caused.

Jenny immediately ran out to pass on the news to Tom who had been assembling his class for their departure on the coach, and he quickly told the other teachers.

'So our Head Teacher has simply had a day of rest,' Malcolm observed. 'Like most of his days really, except that he didn't spend it here!'

The others laughed. 'But I wonder if that's the whole story,' Mary pondered. I don't suppose Pritchard told the constable everything, but just some story that he'd thought up.'

'What have you in mind?' Tom asked.

'Well, knowing, as we all do, the kind of person Pritchard is, I wouldn't be surprised if he spent part of the day plotting his revenge.'

'You really think that?' Tom asked. 'You think he's going to respond to what's happened by scheming to get his own back in some way.'

'Yes, I do. I don't think he'll take it lying down. He'll be bitterly resentful and full of malicious intent.'

'I'm going home,' Susan said. 'That kind of talk makes me nervous.'

'Well, if I'm right,' Mary responded, 'then perhaps we should all be nervous. But don't worry too much, Susan, there's only one Pritchard and four of us. We've been involved in a struggle with that man for a whole year, and it's a struggle we're going to win!'

***

At home, Malcolm related the day's events to Caroline. She was just as puzzled, and as sceptical, as some of the teachers.

'Do you think that Pritchard could really have been sleeping for most of the day,' she asked.

'I think it's unlikely,' Malcolm answered, 'but not impossible. 'Mary is very sceptical but his story may be true. My mum hardly ever takes sleeping tablets – she doesn't normally need them – but occasionally she has taken one only, and then gone to sleep for up to fourteen hours. Of course, most people don't react to that extent.'

'Of course not. But I'm inclined to think that Mary's right, that Pritchard told a cock and bull story to the constable, and that there's more to his absence than meets the eye. Bearing in mind his paranoia, his solitariness, his obsession about plots and being betrayed, and perhaps his depression, I think we should brace ourselves for some bad news. He's always seemed unbalanced. Yesterday's events could have made him desperate, and quite out of his mind. I don't suppose for a moment that he thought he would be dismissed. He was so confident that the Governing Body would always stand by him. They didn't, and he's in shock. We know how vindictive he can be. All those nasty, spiteful characteristics that he has shown over the past year will have bubbled to the surface. I'm quite sure that the Pritchard we know is now obsessed by feelings of revenge against those he perceives as his enemies.

And, oh my gosh, he's made plenty of those and no friends. Yes, I think he could be very dangerous!'

Malcolm had listened with rapt attention.

'Caroline, you've almost convinced me! And who, in particular do you think is in danger?'

'Oh darling, all of you! Don't forget that *Statement* that you all made. That must have had a very decisive influence on the meeting.'

'Yes, I must agree. All four teachers may be at risk, if you're right. Who else?'

'Well, all the governors because they voted unanimously for Pritchard's dismissal, but especially those who made the strongest criticism.'

'That sounds reasonable. And what about Ronald Parham and Dr Mitchell. Their report was fundamental to the whole process.'

'Yes, it was, so they, too, may be in Pritchard's sights.'

'Well, then, I'm reassured. There are so many of us facing this deranged man that I can't see him getting very far!' Malcolm chuckled.

Caroline laughed. 'You mean there's safety in numbers? Possibly. And I'm probably quite wrong anyway. You've said it's possible to go to sleep for a long time so Pritchard's story may be quite true. And perhaps he'll be back at School tomorrow, as usual.'

'I wonder.' Malcolm said. 'Somehow I don't think he will be. Things may not be as bad as you've suggested, but I have a strong feeling that many more dramatic events will take place before the end of the Summer Term!'

Chapter 38
14 July 1955

Some unpleasant surprises were certainly in store for everyone at Haselmere. It was the second day after the meeting of the Governing Body, and some of the worst fears of the teachers would soon be realised.

Malcolm arrived as early as usual, and went to his classroom to prepare for the day's lessons. It was around 8.15a.m. so he had about half an hour before going to the playground for the children's breathing exercises. He had much to do so there was no time for a chat with his colleagues.

At nine o'clock, the exercises over, it was time for the pupils to go to the hall for breakfast. Malcolm was following them in, and was about half way there when Jenny Martin ran to him, almost out of breath, with the news that neither Rupert Pritchard nor Tom Bates had arrived. Malcolm was taken aback and, for the moment, dumbstruck. This was completely unexpected news. Troublesome thoughts chased through his mind. Then, realising that Jenny was waiting for him to respond, he promised her that he would inform his colleagues of this latest development.

He had been intrigued to learn about Pritchard's absence, but not unduly concerned. He had half-expected it. Pritchard was, after all, a lame-duck Head Teacher, a liability and a drag on progress in the school. The school was a happier place without him and every day he was absent was to be savoured.

But Tom's absence was quite a different matter. He had never been late and Malcolm couldn't remember him ever missing a day at school. His absence at the same time as Pritchard was surely significant. All the talk about him being a threat, however obscure the notion, now began to loom large in Malcolm's mind as he hurried towards his fellow teachers who were chatting in the hall and about to join their pupils at breakfast.

He poured out the latest news and his colleagues were visibly upset, though they realised that there could be a simple explanation for Tom's non-appearance. Mary, as usual, was the first to respond.

'Oh, my God! The absence of both Pritchard and Tom on the same day, in the present circumstances, seems pretty ominous to me.'

'But perhaps,' Susan said, 'it may be nothing to worry about. Perhaps Tom's not feeling too well, and he'll soon get in touch with Jenny to explain why he can't come in today.'

'I've never known him to be ill,' Mary pointed out, 'and if he were, he would have telephoned as early as possible. I also know,' she continued, 'that normally nothing would prevent Tom coming in. He's only too aware that there'd be no –one to teach his class, and that in any case his presence here is especially vital at the present time. He's our rock! He knows we need him in the present crisis. We need his advice and support. Even if he was off –colour, he'd make the effort.'

'Yes,' Malcolm agreed. 'Tom loves teaching here, and he loves this school. I can't imagine anything keeping him away. You know, about the only thing Pritchard and Tom have in common is that they are both good time-keepers and that they never fail to turn up – normally. Now, are their absences connected? If so, in what way? Has something happened between them? Is Tom alright?'

'It's a worry,' Mary said, 'but now we'd better join our classes or they'll be finished breakfast before we've even started! And I've just had a thought: if Tom hasn't arrived by 9.45, something will have to be done about looking after his class.'

'That's right,' Malcolm said. 'I'll have a word with Jenny. If there's no news by 9.30 then she should inform the Education Office, and ask for a supply teacher to come here urgently because, unlike bigger schools, we have no spare cover. But of course, if we do get anyone, it won't be for some time later, so in the meantime I'll keep an eye on Tom's class. They're older children and they're pretty sensible and know how to work on their own. I can settle them with a task and shuttle between classes until a supply teacher arrives.'

'Thanks, Malcolm,' Mary said. She welcomed Malcolm's initiative, and he ran off quickly to speak to Jenny while the others sat down with their pupils. On the way Malcolm decided to ask Jenny to inform Ronald Parham of Tom's absence. When he saw the Secretary he learnt that she had already informed both the Education Office and the special schools' inspector.

After breakfast, Malcolm explained to Tom's class that their teacher had not arrived. He gave them a challenging task that he hoped would require all their energy and imagination for some time, and then hurried back to his own class.

Facing them in the classroom he made a disturbing discovery. Lucy Pym was missing. He knew that she had arrived that morning on the coach, so he was faced by another worrying situation. He was also aware that Lucy's father had brought a new girl friend into their home a few months earlier, and that her mother had therefore decided to leave, or perhaps she had been forced out. Since then Lucy had not seen her mother at all and had confided to Malcolm how much she missed her. She had run away a few times previously, and had wandered around Streatham looking for her in a part of the town where they had sometimes gone shopping together. Immediate inquiries among the children soon established that Lucy was not anywhere in the School grounds and that no-one had seen her at breakfast. She must have slipped away soon after she arrived on one of the coaches. Urgent action was required, but Malcolm's hands were full. He decided to make another quick visit to Jenny to ask her to inform the police. He hated the thought of a little, vulnerable girl like Lucy wandering around on her own. It would be even more worrying if she were still there in the evening.

***

Jenny had returned to her office after her conversation with Malcolm to find the telephone ringing. To her great relief she found herself talking to Tom. He apologised for not phoning earlier, but explained that so much had been happening that this was his very first opportunity.

'Are you alright, Tom,' were her first words.

'Yes, I'm fine. Absolutely fine. But my wife and I have been very lucky.'

'Why? What's happened?'

'Well, we've had a narrow escape. Our house has been burnt to a cinder.'

'Oh, how awful! Thank goodness you're O.K. What exactly happened?'

'It really was quite a nightmare, Jenny. My wife woke me at about 4 a.m. She told me she thought she could smell burning. So could I, an unforgettably acrid smell. I jumped out of bed and rushed to the landing. Looking down the stairs I could see that the hall was ablaze. There was a cloud of black smoke filling the hall and I could hear the crackle of burning wood. We both dashed back to the bedroom, put on our dressing gowns as fast as we could and hurried down the stairs. That was the really tricky bit. We felt the heat of the flames and our eyes were stinging with the smoke all around us. We were prepared to retreat up the stairs and to try to escape through a bedroom window if our path was completely blocked, but fortunately the flames hadn't yet reached the staircase. We saw a part of the hall that was not yet alight and we rushed through the smoke to the dining room. There was obviously no question of trying to douse the flames so I shut the dining room door, dialled 999, blurted out what was happening, and we escaped through the French doors. I can't tell you what a relief it was to get out and to feel the cool night air on our faces.'

'Oh, Tom, I'm so sorry. But are you sure you're both alright? Did you have any burns?'

'We really are OK Jenny. We were certainly coughing and spluttering when we got outside, and our faces were very red, but really, that was nothing, if we think about what might have been.'

'What did you do then? Tom. You were outside in the middle of the night! You weren't wearing much clothing, and you must have been very cold.'

'We were, but our very kind neighbour, Mrs Adams, a widow, took us in, attended to our minor burns and bruises, and made us comfortable. Later she gave us an early breakfast. She was very sweet. But we didn't want to overstay our welcome, especially as Mrs Adams had to go to work early. I wanted to phone my son Clive who lives only a few miles away, but there was no telephone in the house. So I rushed out, still in my dressing gown,'- he laughed – 'to the nearest telephone kiosk and managed to contact Clive. He came quickly and fetched us in his car, and said he could put us up indefinitely.'

'And did the Fire Brigade come?'

'Yes. They came fairly quickly, but I'm afraid there was no question of saving the house. As we left the scene, there were about three engines around a raging inferno. Everything we had was being consumed by the fire. There would be virtually nothing left. But we were safe! We were alive! We had escaped! Somehow, however irrational it sounds, we felt oddly cheerful! It's funny how, at such times you see things in perspective! We were very, very thankful to be alive! And now, Jenny, I must ring off. A very busy day stretches ahead: contacting my insurance company, etc. But I'll be back at Haselmere tomorrow, as usual.'

'Are you sure that's wise, Tom, after what you've been through?'

'Yes, why not? I'm not injured or anything.'

'Right, we'll look forward to having you with us again. Is it all right to tell the others what has happened to you?'

'Oh, yes, please do that. They'll be worried.'

'All right then, Tom. 'Bye.'

'Cheerio. I'll fill you in with more details tomorrow.'

***

Jenny sat back and tried to sort out her thoughts. She now realised how thoroughly exhausted she was. Normally, she was not required to do anything that was not under the heading 'General Administrative Duties,' but now she was to facing one stressful situation after another. However, it was not in her nature to feel sorry for herself, and, realising that her normal work had been accumulating, – there was a pile of unopened post on her desk – she was just considering her priorities when Malcolm hurried in to tell her that Lucy Pym had disappeared during the morning. She promised him that she would inform the police, but first she gave him a brief summary of Tom's news, which stunned him. Then she 'phoned the police.

She was soon talking to the constable who knew Lucy well since he had found her twice before, wandering around the town. Malcolm stayed for a brief moment, listening, and then hurried off to his class.

He found time to send a brief message round to his colleagues about the fire at Tom's house, and soon everyone at Haselmere knew what had happened.

At break time the teachers gathered in the hall and Jenny joined them. She realised that they would want to know much more than Malcolm had been able to tell them.

'It's really shocking news about the fire,' Mary said. 'Are you sure that Tom and his wife are quite alright? We all know that Tom would never make a fuss about anything.'

'That's right,' Jenny agreed. 'Well, he says he'll be in tomorrow, so I suppose he's OK, though I suspect that both Tom and his wife have some minor burns.'

'Tom's tough and resilient,' Malcolm said. 'He was a commando during the War. I'm sure that helps him to face crises calmly. After what he's been through, many people would be in a state of shock and need several days at least to get over it.'

'That's right,' Mary said, 'but I must say that I'm glad that he'll be back tomorrow. We've needed his support throughout the past year, but now that events seem to be approaching a climax, we need him more than ever!'

The others agreed, but Susan was anxious to know more about Tom's plight.

'Can you tell us as much as you know?' she asked Jenny.

The Secretary gave the teachers a full account of what had taken place.

'It sounds as if they've lost everything,' Malcolm observed. 'That's awful. To see your house savagely destroyed by flames!'

'Yes,' Jenny said, 'and they had lived in that house ever since they were married, twenty six years ago. They brought up their three boys there. There must have been so many irreplaceable things of sentimental value that have gone up in smoke.' She dabbed her moistening eyes and Malcolm noticed how weary she looked – weary and distraught. 'I'm sorry,' she said. 'We mustn't let all this awful news get us down. Anyway, I must get back to the office now. There's sure to be someone else on the telephone soon.' With that she hurried away.

'Poor Jenny, 'Susan said. We're all teaching our children, and that takes our minds off other things, but Jenny is at the centre of things. She's expected to do all her normal work and also keep in touch with everyone involved.'

The others agreed. As they returned to their classrooms their minds were fully occupied with recent events and their significance: the dismissal and subsequent absence of Pritchard, the fire at Tom's house, Lucy's disappearance. How, if at all, were those events related? Some of them wondered briefly whether it really was possible that Pritchard had carried out the ghastly crime of setting fire to Tom's house – a revenge attack, an attempted murder? After all, he had always seemed to hate Tom, as someone who, he thought, wanted to take his place as Head. But the idea sounded too far-fetched, too implausible. Pritchard was certainly a very weird, and often unpleasant character, but surely he couldn't be as evil as that? So, to a degree, they didn't dwell on that notion. Except for Mary, who had darker thoughts.

Everyone felt, however, that a drama was unfolding, and that they were only in the middle of it.

***

Since Pritchard had neither put in an appearance – as he had assured the police he would – or been in touch, Jenny decided to try to telephone him. As there was no reply, she telephoned Parham to tell him about both the Head Teacher's absence and the fire at Tom's house.

As he listened, Parham was filled with dread, but he was also instantly alert and plied her with questions.

'Is the cause of the fire known?'

'Not yet. Tom hopes to learn from the Senior Fire Officer's Report in due course about that.'

'And Tom and his wife managed to escape without injury?'

'I believe so, except for some scratches, sore eyes and perhaps some minor burns. They were patched up by a neighbour and apparently there was no need for hospitalisation.'

'Where are they now?'

'They are staying with their son. I can let you have the telephone number. She read it out.'

'Thanks. I'll get in touch with Tom fairly soon.'

'Where did the fire start?'

'In the hall, 'Jenny replied. 'It was ablaze, and I think it's a wonder they managed to get downstairs safely.'

'It certainly is. A wonder and a blessing. How did they get out of the house?'

'Through the dining room and then out through the French doors.'

'Well, thank you Jenny for putting up with all my questions. I'm afraid you're having a trying time, and I'm sure that everyone at the School, as well as myself, is very grateful to you.

Now, at the moment I'm not sure what conclusions to draw about Pritchard's absence. If I call the police again – before we've heard about the cause of the fire – they may be somewhat sceptical that anything is amiss, in view of his disarming demeanour when the constable called at his home yesterday, although he did say that he would be back at Haselmere today.' He considered the situation for a few minutes before finally making up his mind. 'Jenny, I won't take any action just at this moment. I'll wait for news from the Senior Fire Officer. I should get that very soon, and then I may need to move very quickly indeed. But, in the meantime, please let me know the moment Pritchard turns up- if he does – or if there are any further developments.'

'Of course, Mr Parham,' Jenny replied. 'And there is something else I should mention. Mr Brown told me that one of his pupils – Lucy Pym, a very vulnerable little girl – has walked out of the School, and may be wandering about in Streatham. He's worried about her welfare. I've informed the local police, who know her, as she has walked out before. They have always found her and brought her back.'

'Do we know why she walks out? Is she unhappy at School?'

'I believe she's very happy at Haselmere, which gives her some security; she doesn't have any at home.' She gave the inspector a brief account of Lucy's family background.

'I'm glad you've informed the police.' Parham said. Let's hope the girl is soon found. Now, I'll leave you to get on with your work. If any further information comes your way about Pritchard, the fire or Lucy you will be able to contact me at my office.'

'I'll certainly do that, Mr. Parham.'

'Thank you very much, and should I discover anything of interest I'll let you know. Goodbye, Jenny.' The inspector rang off. He thought for a few minutes and then decided to phone the School Doctor, Clive Mann. The Education Office knew his whereabouts, and he was soon in touch.

'Clive, this is Ronald Parham ... I'm fine, thank you. I think you may be able to help me. You'll recall our talk about Mr Pritchard?....Good.' He outlined recent developments and expressed his fears about the Head Teacher's state of mind.

'When we met, you expressed the view that Pritchard is definitely suffering from *paranoia*. Now, it seems to me highly probable that he may have set fire to Tom' house. If so, that would amount not only to arson, but also to attempted murder. Would that link up with *paranoia* in any way?'

'Not exactly,' Dr Mann replied, but there is, I believe, a condition called *Schizophrenic Paranoia*, and anyone in that state would be capable of a murderous attack. But I must say, Ronald, that I'm out of my depth here. I'm only a general practitioner, and a rather inexperienced one.'

'Of course,' Parham said, 'but thank you very much. 'I'm trying to find out as much as I can about Pritchard's state of mind, and you've been very helpful.

***

Parham had hardly put the phone down when it rang again. He picked it up, and soon learned of another event, a very grave development that appalled him and at the same time, crystallized his thoughts about the horror of what was happening. The caller was Richard Barnett, Chairman of the Governing Body.

'Mr Parham,' he began, 'I'm afraid I have some very sad news, and I thought you should know about it immediately. Poor Mr Cooper – you'll remember how well he spoke up at the Governors' Meeting – has had a terrible experience. He's in hospital suffering from burns.'

'Oh, no! Do you know what happened?'

'Yes. His wife has just telephoned me. She was naturally very upset, but thankfully not herself suffering from burns. I don't have all the details, but I understand that Mr Cooper usually gets up two or three times during the night – he has a prostate problem – and he was out of bed at about five o'clock. Returning to his bedroom, he thought he smelt burning and went to investigate. At the top of the stairs he saw flames lighting up the hall. They didn't seem to have spread very much, and Mr Cooper's immediate reaction was to try to put out the flames. He rushed down the stairs, took a bucket from the utility room, filled it with water, and returned to the hall where the flames were now beginning to gain a hold. He had to move very quickly and at his age that wasn't easy. However he began to pour water on the flames, and had some success. Then, when shifting his position a little, and leaning forward, he was suddenly off-balance and fell forward. In doing so he may have put out more of the flames, but he also sustained burns to his face and arms. Nevertheless, he was able to get to his feet, and, in spite of the pain from the burns, run to the telephone in the dining room and call the Fire Service. His wife was with him by this time. As soon as Mr Cooper had put the phone down, he dialled the local hospital, and told the receptionist that his burns were rather painful and needed attention. (His wife had got through the smoke and flames without undue difficulty) Since the hospital was only a mile or so from his house, he was then told by a lady with a very brisk and business-like voice, to make his way there and his burns would be attended to! Fortunately, following a short conversation at the other end of the line, someone else spoke to him and asked about his age. He said that he was seventy seven, and was told immediately that an ambulance would shortly arrive for him.

Well, Mr Parham, I thought you would wish to hear that very unhappy news about Mr Cooper, especially as he made such a valuable and timely contribution at the governors' meeting the other day.'

Parham's worst fears were now realised. His mind was in turmoil. He knew that the incredible was happening and he would need to act very quickly indeed. He thanked the Chairman of Governors for giving him the news so promptly, checked that Cooper was in the local hospital – Streatham General Hospital – said that he would be in touch shortly, and rang off.

He was shattered. His emotions felt drained, he was perspiring, and his hands were shaking. Normally active and energetic, he now felt like an elderly man more than ready for retirement. His mind was racing with ghastly possibilities. Two attacks. He was certain that arson was involved and was equally certain about the perpetrator. He forced himself to be calm and considered the situation.

Is Prichard a Schizophrenic Paranoid? Is that really a medical category? How many more attacks might be attempted or have already taken place? Twelve governors and four teachers could be at risk. Tom Bates and Humphrey Cooper were selected as targets and it's quite clear why. Then there is young Brown. Pritchard doesn't like him. There's also his wife and baby. Oh my God! And, to crown it all, a small and vulnerable pupil has disappeared. ...

Chapter 39
14 July 1955

The Fire Officer's Report would be vitally important. It could provide evidence that would settle all doubts and trigger concerted action. Parham was soon in contact with the Senior Fire Officer, a John Foster, to whom he explained his concerns. He mentioned that in connection with the two fires that Foster's men had recently attended, one house owner was the teacher of a particular school, and the other a governor of the same school.

Foster listened with close attention and mounting interest, and then told Parham that both fires had begun in the hall, and that his crew had discovered, in both cases, traces of rags soaked in paraffin. They had concluded that the same person had committed arson in the two houses. The inflammable rags had apparently been posted through the letter box and somehow set alight from outside. He had already informed the police, but suggested that Parham should also get in touch with them, as he had significant information that would assist them in their inquiries.

Parham did so, and was soon speaking to the duty sergeant who knew about the two fires and the evidence of arson. Parham informed him that both house owners were connected to Haselmere School, and also that he knew who was likely to be responsible. He was asked to call at the Station as soon as possible to give the Detective Inspector a full briefing, covering everything he knew. Parham said he would get on his way immediately. Before doing so, however, he remembered to phone Jenny to give her three pieces of information: firstly, about the fire at Howard Cooper's house and his stay in hospital; secondly, about the Senior Fire Officer's report explaining that both fires had been arson attacks; and thirdly that he was on his way to the Police Station to tell the police all he knew.

Jenny Martin was severely shaken when she heard the latest news, and deeply concerned about both victims. Howard Cooper had impressed her as a very polite and inoffensive gentleman His burns, she thought, must have been very painful. At the meeting of the Governing Body she had greatly admired his spirited and very articulate contribution which, she felt, had definitely tipped the balance. Had he now been punished for his efforts? If so, Pritchard, she felt, was a monster! She trembled and suddenly felt very weak. She reflected that she had been working closely with that awful man for a whole year!

On the way to the Station, Parham couldn't help worrying about how many more arson attacks might take place. Were other teachers and other governors going to be targeted? Were there going to be further cases of attempted murder? He hoped the police would act rapidly to prevent any more attacks. On arrival at the Police Station, he parked his car and strode rapidly inside.

**

'Thank you for coming so promptly,' Detective Inspector Phillips said, with a smile. 'I understand that you are the School Inspector who visits Haselmere School from time to time?'

'Yes, that's right.'

'And you know both the victims of attacks, one of whom is a teacher at the school and the other a governor?'

'Yes. The teacher is Tom Bates and the governor is Howard Cooper.'

'Good. Now, are you able to fill me in with the possible background to these attacks?'

Parham did so.

'And do you know who might have carried them out?'

'Yes, I do.' Parham explained as briefly as he could how matters had developed at the School over the past year and how there had been rising tensions. Then he outlined the pattern of events at the meeting of the Governing Body, which culminated in their unanimous decision that Pritchard should be relieved of his duties as Head Teacher.

'And you believe that Mr Pritchard has some sort of paranoia?'

'Yes, but I'm not a medical man. That information comes from two doctors who have worked at the School, one of whom has retired, the other being his replacement.'

'But people with paranoia are not necessarily aggressive, are they?'

'Oh no, not at all. Pritchard seems to me to be a very complex character with strong emotions. His paranoia is no doubt a factor in his mental make-up, and a factor in these outrages, but obviously he also has other characteristics of an unpleasant nature. I understand that he may be a *Schizophrenic Paranoid,* but, not being a medical man, I don't even know if that is the right term.'

'Right. We'll leave the doctors to sort out that one. ... You have been very helpful, Mr Parham, and now we must lose no time in bringing in Mr Pritchard for questioning. I'll leave immediately with two of my detective constables. If you'll leave your telephone number, Mr Parham, I'll keep in touch with you, and I'd be grateful if you would let me know of any other information that comes your way.'

'There's one further matter of concern,' Parham said. 'The School reported earlier today that a little girl had run away, shortly after arriving there by coach with the other children. It's thought that she has made for the busiest part of Streatham. Her name is Lucy Pym. She wanders around the shops looking for her mother who no longer lives at home. Her disappearance has already been reported to one of your sergeants, who knows her from earlier happenings of the same sort. We are very concerned about this little girl, especially in view of our suspicions of Pritchard and our worries about his future actions.'

'Understood. We'll do everything we can to find her.'

They shook hands and parted. It was now 11.15 p.m., and Ronald Parham needed to collect his thoughts.

Thank heaven that Tom and Howard Cooper are alright, although Cooper may have sustained more serious burns than he has admitted. Both men could have died, so the attacks amount to attempted murder. To what extent are other members of Staff in danger? If they are attacked they may not be as lucky as Tom and Mr Cooper. The Police have now been alerted and will take all necessary measures to thwart any further planned attacks. He shuddered. *What is Pritchard doing now? What is his state of mind? What will he do next?*

Ronald Parham was profoundly affected by the ordeal of Howard Cooper, whom he saw as a courageous and spirited gentleman who had set an example to all the other governors with his ability to separate the wheat from the chaff, to draw out the essential facts and to evaluate them. Cooper's oration, well-reasoned and rational, had finally brought all the governors together and made possible the unanimous vote that meant the end of Pritchard's term as a Head Teacher.

And now, he reflected, the poor fellow was in hospital, the victim of an unbalanced, bitter and revengeful man. Parham resolved to do everything in his power to help to bring him to justice. He hoped he had given the police all the information he had that might be of use. In connection with Cooper there were questions to which he wanted the answers as soon as possible.

Exactly how bad are Howard Cooper's burns?

How serious is his pain?

Is he getting good and appropriate treatment?

Is he likely to recover?

It was the last question that gave Parham particular concern. Cooper was seventy seven and, apart from his burns, had endured a horrifying experience that might well have some permanent effect on his well-being: his nervous system, his self-confidence and his general health. The inspector decided to phone the hospital to find out all he could. Later he would visit to see for himself. He dialled the number and waited.

Unfortunately, the nurse who answered the telephone was not among the most helpful of human beings. She conveyed, in a bored, monotonous voice, little more than that the patient was "comfortable" and as well as could be expected. She would not enlarge on that or give him any other information.

The elderly Schools Inspector, extremely tired and emotionally drained after all the excitement of the past couple of days, found that his patience was wearing thin. Groaning inwardly at what he regarded as "pure hospital speak," which he saw as a minimum of information, released by bureaucrats, he swore freely with his hand on the mouthpiece, and then enquired rather wearily:

'When may I see him?'

'Visiting hours are between 3 p.m. and 5.30 p.m. in the afternoon, and between 7.30 p.m. and 9.00 p.m. in the evening,' was the primly-expressed response. The line then went dead.

He decided that he really must try to fit a visit into his afternoon schedule in spite of the demands of his office where there was an intimidating accumulation of paper-work. Recently, Haselmere had monopolised his attention to the exclusion of almost everything else. But other schools had problems too, and two or three were overdue for a regular visit. He was required to attend an interview board later in the day, and he had to prepare for a series of lectures which were looming ever closer. Altogether, he felt swamped by the demands of his job, and he was reminded of his age! He fervently hoped that the *confounded Pritchard affair* would soon come to an end so that normal duties could be resumed!

***

Meanwhile Jenny had wasted no time informing the teachers of the fire at Howard Cooper's house, of the Fire Officer's Report and of the involvement of the police in the investigation. The news that both fires were the result of arson attacks with paraffin-soaked rags they found both horrifying and upsetting. They had already sought assurances about the condition of Tom and his wife. Now, their concern and sympathy focused on Howard Cooper. They hardly knew him personally, but they were aware that he was elderly, and had

had played a decisive role at the meeting of the Governing Body. They saw him as a friend and supporter. They met for an exchange of views in the hall at lunch-time.

'What happened to Howard Cooper, stumbling into the flames while they were leaping up around him, must have been a frightening experience,' Mary said.

'Especially at his age,' Susan added. 'And we don't yet know how badly burned he is. She felt an intense sympathy for him, and a spasm of emotion overwhelmed her for a few moments. Her eyes moistened and tears ran down her cheeks. She dabbed them with a handkerchief, and struggled to regain her composure.

'As far as you know, is there much damage to Mr Cooper's house?' she asked Jenny.

'I'm not absolutely sure,' Jenny replied, 'but my impression is that the damage is relatively minor.'

'And now we know, beyond any doubt,' Malcolm stated, 'that Rupert Pritchard was responsible. He set fire to both houses!'

'I suppose you're right,' Susan said, 'but we don't know that for certain, do we?'

'Well, it's clear enough to me.' Mary spoke very firmly with a grim note in her voice. 'The fact that the houses of both Tom and Mr Cooper, both connected with Haselmere, were set on fire in the same manner, while our Head Teacher, who has reason to hate both of them, is absent, is surely proof enough.'

'Yes. It's convinced me,' Tom agreed, 'though I suppose the police will need the kind of evidence that can be evaluated in court, and not simply what we have at present, which is what they would call *circumstantial evidence.*'

Jenny now reminded the teachers about another matter.

'I'm afraid,' she said, 'the police have not yet managed to find Lucy Pym.'

'Oh blast!' Malcolm exclaimed. 'For the moment I'd forgotten completely about poor little Lucy. If she hasn't been found by the end of the school day, I'll join in the search!'

Jenny was now anxious to get back to her office. 'I really don't think I can tell you anything more at the moment,' she said. 'If I do hear anything more I'll let you know, but I think I'd better go now.' She hurried away.

It would appear,' Mary said, 'that our Head Teacher is filled with an insane hatred against all those he suspects of plotting his downfall.'

'Yes,' Malcolm agreed, 'and I hate to say it, but I wonder if Pritchard has other targets in mind?'

'Exactly,' Mary added. 'All the governors voted against him, so they're all potential targets. And what about us? We all signed a *Statement* setting out a case for his dismissal.'

Suddenly the penny dropped for Malcolm. A vision of baby Paul and Caroline at home flashed through his mind and he paled and felt quite sick. 'Oh my God!' he groaned. 'I just hadn't given a thought about that. I think we should telephone the police immediately. That madman may have us all in sights. And our families!'

'That's right,' Mary said, 'but Ronald Parham has already spoken to the police and I'm sure they are fully aware of the danger to us all.'

'I'll contact the police, anyway,' Malcolm replied. 'I'll mention our concerns, and I may learn a bit more about the latest developments.' He dashed away to Jenny's office to make his call.

He returned a few minutes later.

'I can't tell you much,' he said. 'The police seem to have the situation well in hand. At present they are on their way to Pritchard's house. Once he's in custody we'll be able to relax!'

'Good. And is there any news about Lucy?'

'No. The police are still looking for her in Streatham. The poor little thing has an urge now and again to see her mother. I wonder whether her mother ever thinks about Lucy...'

Chapter 40
14 July 1955 (Continued)

Detective Inspector Phillips was one of the youngest policemen in the country holding his – fairly senior – rank. He had entered the Force as a graduate and had been rapidly promoted following some early successes. Younger policemen usually worked happily under him, recognising his ability, and responding to his natural authority. But a few older ones regarded his early promotion with misgiving and felt that whatever successes he had had, he was still short of the width of experience essential to those of his rank. Philips was conscious of these doubts, and his response was to demonstrate by sheer hard work and a constant striving for success, that he was fully up to the job.

He was now on his way to Pritchard's house, in a car driven by a detective constable, with another constable – the one who had called on Pritchard the day before – by his side. Arriving at the house, the driver parked the car on the opposite side of the road, and the three officers crossed over, and opened a wooden gate leading to a small front garden filled with a variety of shrubs. Standing by the door of the house, they looked around and paused to listen. The semi-detached house was in a quiet, suburban road, and it was hardly distinguishable in appearance from others nearby.

They rang the bell and waited. No sound came from within the house. They rang again, and also rapped loudly with the door knocker. After a few minutes they decided that there was definitely no-one at home. Looking through a window at the side of the garage they could see that it was empty, and they knew that Pritchard had a car so it was highly probable that he had driven away in it. Phillips had half –expected that; to him, it was just a setback.

He looked through the garage window, but there was nothing to see, except for the usual shelves full of tools, paint, etc. and some garden implements at one end. He then told his men to search the area outside the house, including the garden and a shed that could be seen through a side gate. The door of the shed was held by a latch but was unlocked. They opened the door and entered. Inside they made their first significant discovery; there was a workbench on which was a pile of towelling. Some of it had been torn into smaller pieces, and those smelt of paraffin. There was no sign of a can or any other kind of vessel that might have held the paraffin. Nevertheless the police were satisfied that they now had some concrete evidence. They felt encouraged.

Phillips telephoned the station and reported to his superior officer, Detective Superintendent Collins, who said that in view of their discoveries, they should break into the house and carry out a thorough search. Collins was one of those who saw Phillips as an over-promoted young man, who still had to prove himself, and do much more to widen his experience. Phillips, in his view, looked hardly out of his teens! He was too wet behind the ears!

It was not necessary for the policemen to break down the front door as none of the windows had locks, and it was not difficult to smash a small pane of glass in the kitchen, at the back, and then to open the window latch from the inside. Phillips joked with his constables that all that was needed was for them to break in with the same technique and efficiency as common criminals! They chuckled as they did just that. Soon they were all inside the kitchen. Phillips then instructed his two colleagues to examine carefully everything in the upstairs rooms while he concentrated on the ground floor.

A thorough search of that kind can take a considerable time, but it was after only about fifteen minutes that one of the constables called down to the inspector.

'Would you come up and see, sir. I think I've found something interesting!'

Indeed he had. He had been examining miscellaneous papers in the drawer of a bureau on the landing, and found one with five names and addresses on it. The names were as follows:

Bates.

Cooper

Bartlett

French

Hawkins

It was the list that Pritchard had made in his study immediately after the meeting of the Governing Body had come to an end.

On the face of it, the list was extremely alarming. Bates and Cooper had already been victims of an attack. Their position at the head of the list was understood by the police, who had been briefed by Parham, both about Pritchard's hatred of Bates and Cooper's key role at the meeting of the Governing Body. But there were three other names. The Police would need to ask Parham why he thought those names had been added. But there was one question uppermost in their minds now:

Was Pritchard preparing to set fire to three more homes, those of the other three named?

And there was a second question that worried them.

Were those five just the beginning, a sort of stage one, since the police understood that, for instance, the teachers had combined to call for Pritchard's dismissal?

And a third:

Where would he strike next? Was Pritchard adhering to the order on his list? In that case, Bartlett, the Chairman, would be next in line for attack.

Phillips had a vision of Pritchard hiding somewhere in the area and waiting for the cover of darkness to provide an opportunity to continue his serial arson attacks. Perhaps he had taken with him, in his car, some rags and the can of paraffin that they had not been able to find in the garden shed. They would need to act quickly to foil any planned attacks, and they must apprehend Pritchard without delay or they might have more arson attacks, and perhaps a series of murders, on their hands!

Before doing anything else, Phillips decided to phone Parham to obtain, if he could, some information about the three people named: Bartlett, French and Hawkins. He would ask whether they were teachers or governors. Parham might have a good idea why their names were on the list, whether they had done anything to offend Pritchard, etc. Were all three specially connected, in some way, to the recommendation that he should be dismissed?

Parham was still at his desk, trying to catch up with an accumulation of forms, references and letters in his in-tray, when the telephone rang, and he found himself talking to the Detective Inspector. He was horrified to hear that there was a real possibility of further arson attacks, and that the police had found Pritchard's house empty, and his car missing. Phillips told him about the list of five names.

Parham was momentarily puzzled about the inclusion of the last three, until it dawned on him that at first Pritchard had probably regarded them as his firmest and most reliable supporters – and they certainly were, at the outset. The Chairman, of course, had been convinced by Parham before the meeting took place. But the other two stalwarts had been influenced by the arguments presented at the meeting. Pritchard no doubt regarded all three as traitors who had let him down. If they hadn't switched sides, he would have reasoned, he might have defeated his opponents.

Parham explained his theories about their inclusion on Pritchard's hit list, and the Inspector thanked him for the information, which he was sure would prove useful to them. Then Phillips phoned Detective Superintendent Collins to update him. His line manager could become very tetchy if he was not kept fully informed at every stage of an investigation, but Phillips always found his surly superior 'a pain in the neck!'

However, they agreed that the houses of the three governors should be watched during the hours of darkness unless the police managed to apprehend Pritchard in the meantime. They also agreed that there was a threat hanging over the teachers, though they had not been listed. In their case, a police car would patrol past their houses at regular intervals. All the houses were in a well-defined area, within which it should be possible to observe any suspicious activity, or perhaps spot Pritchard's car.

There would be a nationwide search for Pritchard's car. It was appreciated that he might have decided not to continue with the attacks but to drive out of the district, even to attempt to travel to some overseas destination. His car was a pale blue Morris Minor *Traveller.* Information about it, including its registration number, and a recent photograph of Pritchard, found at his home, were circulated to all police forces. Later in the day, the same information was circulated to garages, port authorities, the BBC, newspapers, airports, etc.

Collins had been as irascible in tone as ever. Phillips had listened patiently while he was told, 'Make sure that Pritchard is brought in without delay, and the car, too, should be located quickly. Pritchard can't carry on with this madness without his car. I don't expect to be let down over this case, Phillips. I want results. Fast!'

The Detective Inspector had smiled grimly at the bullying tone used towards the end of that communication. Collins never concluded any instructions with a word of encouragement, or a light-hearted comment. What he knew about man-management, Phillips mused, would hardly cover a postage stamp! The Detective Inspector would do everything possible, but whether he and his team had some early success might depend on the alertness of other police forces, or of any one of a wide range of ordinary people, including petrol pump attendants and newspaper reporters. Sooner or later – and he prayed that it might be sooner – someone would phone the police with a sighting. They might receive several calls. Some, perhaps most, would be useless. There were always cranks and publicity seekers who provided 'information' that later proved to be worthless. But everything had to be followed up. At any time, a member of the public might phone with some crucially-important information on which his team would act with alacrity.

***

During the afternoon, Parham decided to abandon what he regarded with disdain as 'a pile of damn bureaucratic red tape' on his desk. He left his office, walked briskly to where his car was parked, and drove to the local hospital to check on Howard Cooper's condition.

He walked through several wards before he found the one he wanted. Walking between the rows of beds, he hoped that Howard Cooper, with his facial burns presumably bandaged, would be recognised without undue difficulty.

Suddenly he saw him. The elderly gentleman was looking quite relaxed and sitting up in bed reading a novel. There were some dressings on his face, which looked red and raw where it could be seen, and some, too, on his arms.

Cooper looked up as he approached, and immediately smiled, though any movement of his facial skin was obviously rather uncomfortable, or even painful, for him. Parham showed his concern, but Cooper seemed quite unconcerned about his own condition. He was in good spirits and emphasised to Parham that he was lucky because he and his wife had escaped serious injury, and because the firemen had been able to put out the flames very quickly, so that damage to their house was only superficial. He was much more worried about Tom whose house had been almost completely destroyed. He was, he said, being well looked after, but he was anxious to leave the hospital as soon as possible to get back to his wife and their home. He seemed to have been fully informed about recent developments, probably by the Chairman and had unequivocal views to express about the Head Teacher:

'I think Pritchard must be thoroughly deranged,' he said. 'He's gone completely crackers! I fervently hope he is soon found before he can strike again. You know, as a member of the Governing Body, I feel ashamed to admit that I played a part in his selection, but there it is. We were all taken in. He could be such a smooth operator, and he twisted us all round his little finger.'

Parham agreed that Pritchard had certainly been a clever manipulator. And now he was attempting murder! He also agreed with Cooper that the Head Teacher was now thoroughly unbalanced and driven by a fanatical urge to settle scores with those perceived as his enemies. He assured him that the police, now fully briefed about the background, were doing everything possible to trace both the man and his car. He told him that a well-organised manhunt was taking place. The police were desperately anxious to arrest Pritchard before he had the opportunity to attack anyone else. He added that he was delighted to see Cooper in such good spirits, and looked forward to seeing him again, looking his normal self, in the very near future. The two men then shook hands, and Parham then went on his way. He was glad that he had seen Howard Cooper and relieved to discover that he had sustained only moderately-severe burns. His lively chattiness suggested that his morale was high, too. Parham appreciated, however, that Cooper was not a person to exaggerate his ordeal: quite the reverse. The poor man had, without doubt, had a horrifying ordeal.

He drove back to his office. It had been a long day, and he hoped that the Police would not need to call him again. No news would probably mean good news! He needed a rest.

Suddenly, he felt the need to speak to Dr. Clive Mann in the light of recent developments. He managed to contact him on the telephone.

'Clive, hello. This is Ronald Parham again. There have been several major developments in this Pritchard business, and I'd be glad to have your thoughts on them.'

'OK, Ronald. As a matter of fact, I'm pretty well acquainted with recent happenings as I've been kept posted by Jenny.'

'You heard all about the arson attacks? Good. What are your thoughts about Pritchard now?

Dr. Mann laughed. "Well, they're unprintable! But seriously, Pritchard must now qualify as a paranoid schizophrenic. To his delusions of persecution, sudden changes of mood, isolationist habits, tendency to get things entirely out of proportion, bouts of depression, etc. we must now add his latest atrocities. If I'm right, he probably has suicidal tendencies, too. Yes, he's a paranoid schizophrenic.'

'Thanks, Clive. He's certainly a very dangerous man, but I'm glad to say that the police are now working hard to capture him.'

'It can't be too soon.'

'No, indeed. Well, I've tried to give the police some indication of the nature of Pritchard's mind set, based on what you told me previously. It's important to them.'

'Of course. Let me know if I can be of any further help.'

'I will. Thanks. We'll be in touch later. 'Bye.'

***

Detective Inspector Phillips had become very frustrated during the afternoon when no information throwing light on Pritchard's whereabouts had reached him. He had arranged for a police message to be included in all radio news bulletins, and all his patrol car officers were keeping their eyes skinned for signs of Pritchard's car.

He knew that Detective Superintendent Collins would expect him to report again fairly soon, although he had nothing of substance to say to him. He rather hoped that Collins would not be in his office so that he would be let off the hook. But he had no such luck. When he telephoned, Collins was at his desk, apparently expecting his call. On being told that there had been no significant developments, the Detective Superintendent expressed his disappointment in no uncertain terms, and emphasized the obvious in his usual way. He said that it was vitally important to apprehend Pritchard before he had the opportunity to strike again. Phillips decided that now that his superior was becoming increasingly agitated about the case was just the right moment to make his request. He must strike while the iron was hot!

'Sir,' he said, 'would it be possible to let me have more manpower, possibly of the Metropolitan Police, or perhaps other police forces outside London?'

Collins at first objected to that. He was always reluctant to approach neighbouring forces for assistance, as he felt, foolishly, that that was to admit the limitations of his own officers. But his anxiety for some early success overcame his reservations, and he said he would do what he could. Within the hour, he telephoned Phillips with welcome news that made it possible to increase the number of patrols, and a watch would now be kept on the homes of <u>all</u> the governors – not just those on Pritchard's list – during the hours of darkness, and to a lesser degree, during daylight hours as well. Police cars would also patrol past the houses of the three teachers at least four times each hour. Those measures would begin at twilight.

Chapter 41
14 July 1955 (Continued)

Malcolm Brown had not forgotten about Lucy Pym's disappearance. In fact he could hardly wait until the departure of his class in coaches at the end of the school day, before striding purposefully out of the school and heading for the centre of Streatham.

He visited, quite systematically, all the shopping areas that he had searched the last time Lucy ran away. He was sure she would be found in one of the busiest parts, where the shops were crowded. It was no easy task, because Lucy was so small that she would be difficult to spot in a crowd. Malcolm was becoming increasingly concerned and was determined to search diligently until he found her, however long it took. He had found time to telephone Catherine to explain what he was doing, and that he would be home much later than usual. She had once taught Lucy in her infant class, and was as worried as he was.

Malcolm now began to focus on particular shops that he thought Lucy's mother might patronize. They included hairdressers and beauty parlours as well as food shops. He had searched such places for some time without success and his mind began to dwell once again on the dangers facing Lucy, especially as the evening wore on. He hoped she wouldn't stray into any Amusement Arcades. Such places were usually decorated with winking coloured lights and seemed designed to attract the young and vulnerable. Some unpleasant characters, he thought, often hung around such places. He decided to include them as he combed the town for Lucy.

Then there was the other potential threat. No-one knew where Pritchard was. The Head Teacher had apparently attempted to kill one governor and one teacher, and might even now be engaged in further murderous attacks on the others. The man was demented and while he was at large no-one could predict what he might do next. He might be snooping around in the Streatham area at this moment. Could he pose a danger to the innocent and susceptible Lucy? Malcolm told himself to dismiss such thoughts as unrealistic but they nevertheless persisted.

***

It was around seven in the evening when Detective Inspector Phillips received a telephone call from John Foster, the Senior Fire Officer.

'Bad news, I'm afraid sir, there's been another suspicious fire.'

Phillips felt himself become taught, with tightened muscles, as he digested the news they had all been dreading.

'Whose house is it?' he blurted out.

The Fire Office paused to take a piece of paper from his pocket.

'It's the house of a Mr Tom Hawkins, sir. We're at his house now, fighting the flames. We have four fire engines here and the crews have their work cut out, I can tell you.'

Phillips was horrified and turned pale. This latest monstrous act was taking place some hours before the new precautionary measures were due to come into force. He had been certain that nothing of the kind would be attempted before nightfall. He had been wrong! He had been glad that those measures had been approved by Collins; otherwise his own position would have been difficult. His superior officer would have made his life a misery!

Phillips brought himself back to the immediate situation, and its implications. He asked Foster:

'But what about Mr Hawkins? Is he alright?' There was a pause; the answer was not reassuring.

'Sorry sir, I can't tell you anything about that at the moment. We've made two attempts to enter the building, but the flames have proved to be too fierce. One of my men tried to enter through the kitchen, the hall being well ablaze, but the whole ground floor is now full of smoke and roaring flames.

It's a real inferno! But we'll try again, sir, as soon as we can – probably in a few minutes.' He paused; then continued. 'Yes. I think I'll ask two of my men to make another attempt now, through a bedroom window. ... I'm sorry for the bad news sir, but you must excuse me now as I must get back to my men.'

'Yes, of course. Thank you for keeping me informed,' Phillips replied, 'especially when you've got so much on your plate.'

As he put the phone down, he reminded himself of the need to keep his superior fully informed. With a sigh, he telephoned. To his relief he was told by the duty Sergeant that the Detective Superintendent was out in connection with another case. The Sergeant took a message and promised to pass on the information at the earliest opportunity.

Phillips also tried to telephone Parham, but he was not in his office, but he found his home number in the telephone directory, and rang it.

Ronald Parham had arrived home and was glad to have showered and changed. It had been an exhausting day for him, both physically and mentally. Sitting now, comfortably, in his favourite armchair, he felt refreshed, though far from relaxed. He had been listening to the news on the radio. The announcer had been relating events at the houses of Tom Bates and Howard Carter. Then came the bombshell!

'Oh, my God!' he shouted. 'Not another arson attack!'

Several questions now jostled into the forefront of his mind:

Who is it this time? A teacher or a governor?

Has he or she survived?

Are there going to be even more of these ghastly attacks?

Why haven't the Police been able to stop Pritchard?

And then the telephone rang, and Phillips told him everything he knew.

'And there's no news of Tom Hawkins? Perhaps he was not at home.'

'I'm sorry, sir, that I can't tell you more at the moment,' Phillips said. 'The firemen are still trying to enter the house, though the building is a raging inferno and it's really too dangerous to make the attempt. But I think they will get in somehow, and then they'll soon ascertain the full facts. I'll let you know if I have any more information, though it may well be not until tomorrow morning before we learn whether Mr. Hawkins is safe, but you must excuse me sir. I must now get back to my duties.'

'Of course.' Parham was breathing heavily and finding it difficult to say anything, but he managed to add, 'Thank you for keeping me in the picture, Detective Inspector. I appreciate it.'

***

Detective Superintendent Collins, who was at home, telephoned Phillips at around 7.30 p.m. He sounded both angry and overwrought.

'Phillips, this is the worst possible news-I mean about the fire at the home of Mr Hawkins, who, I understand was a governor at the School. He was on the list you found, wasn't he?'

'Yes, sir, he was.'

'So you had ample warning that he was likely to be the next victim? Isn't that so?' The last question was barked out.

'Yes, sir,' Phillips responded quietly, 'we knew, as I mentioned to you when we spoke earlier, that anyone on that list could be the next victim. The houses of Bates and Cooper had already been attacked. The next one on the list is, in fact, Bartlett, the Chairman of the Governing Body, and Hawkins is the last name. But we didn't assume that Rupert Pritchard would necessarily make further attacks in the order on that list. All the houses are being watched, but, as agreed with you, we planned the new measures to begin at dusk, assuming that any further attacks would be in the hours of darkness. Unfortunately, this latest attack took place much earlier.'

'All right,' Collins said. And is Hawkins safe and well?

'We don't know yet, sir,' Phillips replied. 'We don't even know whether he was at home. The firemen haven't yet been

346

able to enter the house. The fire is very fierce. We probably won't have any more news until the morning.'

'Oh, my God! This case gets worse and worse. I take it you're staying on duty?'

'Yes, sir, for the moment at least. I've arranged for all the visits and patrols that we agreed. I'll be here to receive reports until midnight. During the night Detective Sergeant Baker will be in charge here. He'll deal with all messages. Should anything significant be reported, especially about Pritchard's whereabouts, then he'll telephone me at home.'

'Right.' Collins seemed to be reasonably satisfied with the arrangements.

'Well,' he added, 'Pritchard has outwitted us by striking during daylight hours, but the measures we're taking should keep him at bay during the night.'

Phillips agreed with his superior.

'So, Phillips, the only significant piece of news that we should expect before long is that our man has been apprehended. Don't you think?' He had reverted to his barking tone.

'Yes, sir. I think we're doing everything we can.'

'I hope you are!' After that less than encouraging observation, Collins rang off.

The Detective Inspector was not at all happy. He had never had a comfortable relationship with his line manager. Collins was always impatient for a quick result, especially when his own involvement was minimal. Phillips was bright, conscientious and hard-working but felt under-valued. He would have welcomed a more supportive and encouraging attitude in his superior officer. He himself did everything he could to motivate his own team and believed they worked well, with high morale, as a result. Harassing one's subordinates, he believed, was counter-productive. But he had noticed that those officers who dominated, rather than motivated those serving under them sometimes gained quicker promotion than their equally well-qualified contemporaries. He himself wouldn't change, he told himself. He believed in team work. In the end, he mused, what mattered were results. He had a good record in that respect and he was anxious to add to it.

***

Malcolm, still in the Streatham shopping area, had twice telephoned the police to check whether they had found Lucy Pym, and, if not, whether they were still searching for her. They hadn't found her, but they said that a constable was still searching somewhere in the town. Malcolm told them that he, too, was looking for Lucy. But he had now been tramping around for several hours, and was becoming tired and despondent. He was afraid that Lucy would still be wandering around as daylight hours came to an end and some dubious or shifty characters may, in the meantime, have emerged from the woodwork!

Suddenly he noticed something he had not seen before. About a hundred yards away, behind the shops, was a field, and as the daylight diminished by subtle degrees, and twilight took its place, lines of multi-coloured lights appeared, twinkling and lighting up the area. As he walked towards them, more came into view along with the sound of fairground music and a sight of the usual stalls, bumper cars, helter-skelters, merry-go-rounds, etc. He hadn't seen a fairground for years, and it all brought back memories of his childhood.

He wondered whether Lucy might have been attracted by the lights and music. If she had not succeeded in finding her mother, which was most likely, she would be very tired, and the sight and sounds of a fairground would perhaps have lifted her spirits.

He walked swiftly towards it. There were jostling, noisy crowds everywhere as he moved rapidly from one stall or fairground feature to another. Again, he reminded himself how small Lucy was, and how difficult it would be to spot her among the crowds.

But suddenly he saw her, and she was with someone. She was riding in one of the bumper cars and there was a man by her side in the driver's seat. He had his arm round her. It was not Pritchard. Who was it? Could it be her father? The man was shabbily-dressed, short and heavily-built, with long, unkempt hair, which flowed behind him as the car shot forward. He had a rather fleshy face and tattoos on both arms. Malcolm watched the pair anxiously, waiting until the session had ended. When it did, the man took Lucy's hand and they made for the exit where Malcolm had taken up his position. As they approached, Malcolm spoke,

'Hallo, Lucy. I've been looking everywhere for you. Are you all right?'

Lucy disengaged her hand and ran towards Malcolm, who bent down to welcome her. She was a little embarrassed but spoke up well enough.

'Hallo, sir, I'm very sorry. I first tried to find me Mum. I ain't seen 'er for a long time, and she's often around 'ere at this time. But I didn't 'ave no luck, did I? Then I see the fair. It looked nice.'

'And who is this gentleman, Lucy?'

'Oh...'e's just someone who came up to me and said I looked lonely, and that 'e'd give a good time, sir.'

Malcolm looked up; the man had disappeared.

He took Lucy home on a bus, and stayed to talk to her father. He wanted, if possible, to try to ensure that she would not be punished, but that could hardly be guaranteed. He also saw the girlfriend and was not favourably impressed.

He had chatted amiably to Lucy on the way to her home. Tomorrow he would have a quiet word with her about various matters.

Chapter 42
15 July 1955

Thoroughly exhausted, Rupert Pritchard had driven his car to the end of a very quiet *cul de sac* where, having secured the doors, he had collapsed into a deep sleep. Waking when the rays of the morning sun shot through the windows of his car, his mind was in a turmoil, full of repugnant thoughts, each of which had a few moments of ascendancy before giving way to another. He could hardly contemplate with equanimity the acts he had perpetrated, but they had certainly given him a grotesque sense of satisfaction, even though that sense was mixed with one of horror and distaste. Sometimes images merged, changed and then returned. They were images of faces and fires, of burnt corpses and other ghastly horrors, all products of his imagination, as he had been unable to see any of the results of his atrocities.

He was unclear what he should do next: whether to continue with his programme of attacks upon those he thought had conspired to disgrace him and take away his Headship, or to escape by putting as many miles as he could between the police and himself. There was no room in his mind for any sort of plan or strategy while he continued to dwell in some confusion on what he had just done. But gradually he began to focus on his main objectives. He believed he had eliminated his main enemies: Bates, Cooper and Hawkins, but the satisfaction that knowledge provided was accompanied by the nagging thought that there were others who should not be allowed to escape.

There's that bitch French, who, like Hawkins, pretended to support me, only to put a knife into my back when she voted against me. She should be dealt with like the others.

Then there is the Chairman of the Governing Body, Bartlett, who seemed to be my friend for much of the year, but who I now know was plotting with Parham behind my back, on the best way to get rid of me. He deserves the same treatment as the others.

Pritchard's small, malformed eyes, restless as ever, now glistened evilly as he began to consider his next move. Hate and the urge for revenge had carried him to this point, but he still had some unfinished business. For a time he debated fruitlessly who should be next and had been driving aimlessly for some time, but now, his mind made up, he turned his car in the direction of Cecilia French's house, while always on the look-out for the police.

He didn't want anything to get in his way now, and he fumed when the traffic lights just caught him and he seemed to be stationary for an inordinate length of time. Stranded between the other cars, he felt very vulnerable. The police might approach him at any moment. It was a relief to get on his way again.

Suddenly he was convulsed by fear. Almost two hundred yards ahead he noticed a police car travelling towards him. He panicked. *They were coming to get him!* Swinging his steering wheel to the left, he entered a side turning and found himself in a street market crowded with stalls and people. The way ahead was by no means clear and he suddenly came to a halt with screeching brakes, and an unintended lurch to the right. There were people everywhere, and those swarming around him turned their heads in alarm. Two or three people seemed to be shouting at him but he couldn't understand what they were saying, and many others were now glaring at him. The road had been closed for the market; he noticed that a number of stallholders were bellowing at him and, he thought, were threatening to bear down on him. He was terrified that they might attack him. He had an overwhelming urge to escape from the crowded area with all its noise and confusion, and to find a clear road along which he could make some progress. While he was stranded, he felt that the net was closing around him All thought of dealing with Cecilia French, as he had planned, was now abandoned. His priority was to escape.

He decided to inch forward along the road, sounding his horn at intervals, hoping that he was not trapped in a *cul de sac.* The hostility towards him, however, then seemed to increase. He was seen as an intruder and the sounding of his horn seemed to infuriate the crowd, while some of the stallholders came up menacingly close behind him. He wondered what they were going to do: to kick his car, or try to open the door and attack him. He increased his speed a little, continuing to sound the horn so that a space would be made in front of him. To his immense relief, most of the stallholders who had appeared to be threatening him, then seemed to give up and return to their stalls, where potential customers awaited them. But two or three remained just behind him, still screaming and shouting obscenities.

Then, to his enormous relief, he saw that there was a T junction just ahead, though there was a wooden barrier across it, to keep out traffic. He hesitated, and slowed down, while making up his mind what to do next. Then, his mind made up, he accelerated, smashed through the barrier, which made a loud, splintering noise, and turned left into a main road. Such was his relief at his escape from the market, with its hostile stallholders, that he found himself shouting crazily with triumph. He maintained a fast speed for a time before realising that he was drawing attention to himself, and that an arrest for speeding would spell disaster for him. He cut down to a steady 30 miles per hour, whilst peering around nervously to check that he was not being pursued.

After driving along the busy thoroughfare for some time, he noticed that he was on the London Road. He knew it as the A23 which eventually, he knew, led to Brighton. He had no clear idea of his ultimate destination, being now obsessed by a desperate urge to escape out of London, wherever that led him. He knew that the police would be after him, and reckoned that they would be concentrating on the South London suburban area. He gritted his teeth and resolved to give the Police 'a run for their money.'

He continued in a mainly southerly direction, through the suburbs. Houses and shops, vehicles and pedestrians, crossroads and traffic light flashed by, but for a time no towns could be identified. He presumed he was still on the Brighton

Road. He didn't know whether or not he wanted to go to Brighton but was content with the thought that he was putting more and more space between himself and London.

But then he began to look about him more and more and he spotted evidence of his location. He found himself passing through Thornton Heath, which he knew was in Surrey. Purley came next, then Whyteleafe. He knew nothing about those places but they signified to him progress of a sort. Sometimes he noticed that the speed limit was 40 mph and he accelerated accordingly. He began to feel much calmer and almost cheerful. He was now, he reckoned, at least thirty miles away from his pursuers!

Whilst climbing up a steep hill, he had another shock. His engine suddenly stopped and he was in danger of running backwards down the hill. Fortunately there was a layby only a few yards away, and he attempted to reverse into it. Several large lorries were taking up most of the space but he managed to manoeuvre his car into a space, applied his brakes and came safely to a halt, just clear of them.

He was once again in a state of panic, and perspiration ran down his red cheeks while he could feel the pumping of his heart. He had no idea what had happened to the car, only that any breakdown could mean disaster. He was now exposed and helpless, and a police car, he thought, might come along at any time. His drive had come to an abrupt halt and all his fears now re-surfaced. Nor did they diminish when a lorry driver left his vehicle and strode towards him.

'What's up mate? Did yer engine conk out?' he enquired.

'Yes, I'm afraid so,' he replied. 'I don't know why. I've got enough petrol.' He tried very hard to sound normal.

'Well, mate,' the friendly voice advised, 'if I was you, I'd phone the AA or the RAC. Which one do you belong to?'

'The AA.'

'Not that there's much difference between them, if you ask me. But they'll soon sort you out, mate. Look, you can see a telephone box near them trees.'

'Thank you very much. I'll get on to them.'

Pritchard crossed the road, entered the telephone kiosk and was soon in touch with the AA. He explained what had happened and gave his approximate location. He was promised that someone would be with him in about half an hour. He returned to his car, and sat in the driver's seat, waiting. He probably did not have to wait much longer than the time given to him, but with his mind in a state of ferment, it seemed much longer. He was hot, worried and exhausted.

Finally an A.A. van pulled up alongside his car and Pritchard told him how his accelerator had suddenly become useless and floppy. It was soon established that his accelerator spring was missing. He was asked where he was on the road when he noticed the problem. He was able to point that out, and after a quick search the A.A. man returned with part of the missing spring. He pointed out that it had probably corroded and had broken off. Fortunately most of it – the part he was clutching in his hand – was undamaged. He continued:

'I'll put it back on for you and you'll be able to drive your car to finish your journey, but you should get yourself a new spring as soon as possible; otherwise the same thing may happen again.'

Pritchard said that he would certainly do so. He thanked the AA man – who drove off to attend to his next customer – started the engine of his own car, and pulled over on to the road. For a second time, he experienced a great feeling of relief, almost elation, as he accelerated to at least sixty miles an hour.

Thank God I'm on my way again!

He drove for several miles, without incident, and his confidence slowly returned. He noticed that he was now no longer on the A23, but driving along the A22. He wasn't at all sure how that had happened but was not unduly concerned. Tyler's Green, Godstone and East Grinstead went past, and then he saw that Ashford Forest was not far away.

The idea of being in a forest appealed to him and he followed the signs to it and finally pulled up just inside a wooded area. He got out, locked the car, and began to wander through the trees. Within the forest environment he had a feeling of peace and security, though he reminded himself that his car was not far from the road and that, at any time, it might be identified by someone, who might then notify the police. Much of the area he was in was not, in fact, forested at all. There were many spacious openings through which he tended to hurry before reaching the next clump of trees. He much preferred to keep within the wooded area where he felt safe from prying eyes. It was increasingly quiet and tranquil the further he walked away from the busy road. This was, he felt, much better than driving. He felt more at peace and had more time to think, though he did not welcome some of his thoughts. He continued walking, rather aimlessly for another quarter of an hour and then he made up his mind what he would do next.

What the hell! I'm well out of the London area. My enemies are further behind me with every mile I drive. I'll head for the South coast. And when I'm there, I know what I'll do. My enemies won't catch me!

***

At about 8.15 p.m. in the evening, a garage proprietor reported to the local police that he had seen a blue Morris Minor on the A22, near Polgate, and that it was heading southwards. The driver, he said, had stopped for petrol, but the attendant had failed to identify either him or the car. He himself had been doing some work inside the garage, but fortunately he happened to come out on to the forecourt in time to see the car being driven away very quickly. Earlier he had listened to a news bulletin on the radio about a car whose owner the police wanted to interview urgently, and he had looked hard at the departing car, noting that the registration number, colour and type matched those of the missing car, as described during the broadcast. He had lost no time in telephoning the police. He was thanked for his alertness, and told that the information that he had provided was extremely useful. The local police were in touch with Detective Inspector Phillips in Streatham within minutes.

This was, for Phillips, a worrying development. He had been fairly sure that Pritchard would stay, at least for the time being, in that part of London embracing the homes of both the governors and the teachers. His entire force, including every patrol vehicle, had been deployed with that in mind. He now needed to adjust his ideas, including his expectations. If Pritchard really was driving southwards towards the coast, then there was no further risk, at least at the present time, to the lives and properties of the other governors or teachers. But his quarry was moving further and further away. He was slipping out of his grasp, and Phillips would be dependent now on the alertness and efficiency of the Hampshire Police. He winced as he contemplated the angry reaction of the Detective Superintendent to the latest news. There was also, he supposed, the possibility that Pritchard was planning to leave the country by sea, perhaps to slip across to France. With this in mind, he hurriedly arranged for the various port authorities and customs officials, etc. to be informed so that they might look out for Pritchard and his car.

It then occurred to him that there was a possibility, even if a small one, that the garage proprietor might have been mistaken. A high proportion of reports from the public turned out, in his experience, to be mistaken. The police, after all, had good reason to expect further arson attacks in view of the list that they had found, though it was appreciated that Pritchard might well have changed his mind. On balance, Phillips considered, it would be prudent to maintain at least a watch on the three listed houses for the time being, as well as on Pritchard's house, in case he tried to return to it.

At about 8.30 p.m. another sighting was reported, and now there could be no doubt about the fugitive's movements. The car had been spotted by a pedestrian in the Eastbourne area who had informed a policeman on foot patrol. The Police there were fairly confident that they had a reliable witness. However, it was some minutes after identification of the car before the policeman was free to telephone his station. A serious traffic hold-up involving an altercation between motorists that had threatened to escalate into a fight, had occurred at just the wrong moment! The policeman had no choice but to deal with the matter as expeditiously as possible, so several vital minutes had elapsed before he was able to make his call, adequate time for Pritchard to travel many more miles before the local police could direct their patrol cars to the area in question.

However, Detective Inspector Phillips, who had now come to terms with the flight of Pritchard, and was getting over his previous despondency, was encouraged. The sighting appeared to confirm the validity of the earlier sighting, and therefore, he felt, the net was closing in.

He telephoned Detective Inspector Collins to brief him on the latest developments. The latter did not seem to share Phillips' optimism.

'What the hell's going on? Why wasn't I told before that Pritchard is now somewhere on the south coast?' he yelled into the telephone.

Phillips explained in detail what had happened, emphasizing that Pritchard had travelled almost to the south coast before there had been a positive identification of his car. He said that he had only just received news of what the local police regarded as a really reliable identification.

Collins was then partially mollified.

'Well, now we know, at least, where he is. I hope the Sussex Police will soon get him,' he said.

'I'm sure they will,' Phillips responded, sounding more confident than he felt. In fact, he thought it likely that Pritchard might continue to surprise them with the unexpected.

***

A young hiker had spent most of the day progressing along a footpath over the South Downs. In places his path was a few miles from the coast, but at other times quite close to it. He had so far walked at least twenty miles during the day, and was feeling fairly exhausted and ready to stop. He did not intend to travel any further than Eastbourne, where he hoped to get bed and breakfast accommodation, and to continue hiking the following day. While walking, he had enjoyed looking out to sea whenever that was possible, and sometimes peeping over the cliff to study the beach, the waves splashing along the shoreline and people enjoying themselves. Once, he had observed an interesting ship well out to sea and had used his binoculars to study it.

Ahead of him was Beachy Head, so he knew that Eastbourne was just a little further away, and he would soon be able to rest his tired limbs. He walked closer to the cliff edge as he came near to the famous landmark, but he was rather afraid of heights and approached to within a few feet from the edge very slowly and carefully. He was then able to look down, which he found both exciting and pleasurable. Looking sideways, he also had a good view of a beautiful coastline and a calm sea stretching far into the distance. Once more he looked directly below, and, thinking about how far down it was, he shuddered.

Suddenly he started. Below him, on the shoreline, there was a strange object. What on earth was it? It seemed quite remote. His immediate thought was that it looked like a rag doll with limbs spread out grotesquely. And then he suddenly realised that he was, in fact, gazing at the spread-eagled body of a man on the sand, alongside some rocks and small pools left by the receding tide. He shuddered, whilst feeling a fool for not appreciating the reality immediately. But at first, he told himself, the object had seemed hardly human.

The need for quick action now galvanised him. He turned, and ran past a blue car parked nearby, and towards the town, looking for a telephone kiosk. Spotting one about a hundred yards ahead, he accelerated toward it and hurried inside, puffing and breathless. He was soon in touch with the local police and told them what he had seen and where. They asked him a few questions and said they would wish to speak to him further; in the meantime, he should stay where he was. They would be with him, they said, in a few minutes.

It was probably in an even shorter time than that, that a police car arrived and a policeman jumped out and spoke to him, asking him a few more questions, including such information as his name and address, and his immediate intentions relating to the hike. He was thanked for his prompt reporting of the sighting.

The police were soon down below examining the body on the shore. It was identified as that of Rupert Pritchard.

Chapter 43
16 July 1955

Listeners to news bulletins and readers of national newspapers could absorb, the next day, a full account of Rupert Pritchard's desperate drive out of London: his unintended intrusion into a road set aside for market traders; his breakdown and rescue by the AA; the sightings, first by a garage proprietor and then by a pedestrian in Eastbourne; and finally the discovery by a lone hiker of his body at the foot of Beachy Head. Some broadcasters and newspaper reporters had even secured, in a very short space of time, interviews with the people involved. Altogether a clear picture was available of the whole course of events.

Ronald Parham felt that a nightmare had ended. Pritchard's death had removed, swiftly and dramatically, the terrible danger threatening both the teaching staff and the governors of the School.

But he remained a very worried man, still not knowing what had happened to Tom Hawkins, whose house was the third to be attacked. BBC news bulletins had made only a brief reference to the fire, which was apparently seen as less important than the capture of the man who had started all three fires. Parham thought that was very odd, and wondered whether anything definite had yet been established about Hawkins. It was, after all, the second day after the fire at his house.

Had Hawkins been at home? If so, I don't think he would have survived the fire. But in that case, his remains should have been identified by now. Why is it taking so long to ascertain the facts?

Suddenly his thoughts were interrupted by the telephone ringing by his side. The sound seemed particularly penetrating in the quiet of the morning. He had experienced a prolonged period of stress and his nerves were on edge. He picked up the receiver.

'Parham here,' he announced.

It was Detective Inspector Phillips. Parham braced himself for some bad news.

'Hello, Mr Parham,' he said. 'You've heard about Pritchard's death? We wanted to catch him, of course, but at least the danger to others has now been lifted, and a lot of people will now be able to get on with their normal lives.'

'Yes,' Parham responded, 'it's certainly a relief, but is there any news of Mr Hawkins? I was told that his house was largely destroyed but that nothing was known about him. It wasn't even known whether he was at home. And now another day has passed and I'm still awaiting news.'

'Yes,' Phillips replied, 'and I'm sorry about that. Yesterday, the capture of Pritchard dominated all our thoughts and actions, and we had no definite information from the fire station. But now there is some news and I'm afraid it's not at all good. As I think you know, while the house was burning, the firemen did their best to enter it. But it was a real inferno, a mass of flames and burning materials, and the heat, flames and smoke always held them back. When the fire was finally under control, and they were able to enter it, the house was a blackened shell – still hot and full of smoke, smouldering timbers and glowing ash. In fact, it was not possible to examine the scene until yesterday when everything had cooled down. The firemen spent a long time on that task, and finally, they found what they took to be Mr Hawkins' charred remains among the ash and rubble. I understand that there was, in fact, very little left of the poor chap.'

'Oh, my God! That's the news I've been dreading.' Parham's spirits sank to rock bottom and he almost fell back into his armchair, overcome with nervous exhaustion. He hadn't known Hawkins well but had respected him as a man of principle and a good citizen who had defended Pritchard loyally and robustly at the crucial meeting. His reward was to be murdered by the man he had championed, a man deranged and obsessed by hatred and a misguided thirst for revenge.

After a pause to allow Parham's emotions to settle a little, Phillips continued:

'I understand your feelings, sir, and I can't tell you how sorry I am to have to give you this news.' The Detective Inspector was genuinely sympathetic. He had come to respect Parham over the last few days, and much appreciated the co-operation that he had been given. He added a few more details.

'It's believed, sir, that Mr Hawkins may have been taking a shower when the fire started, and he was probably quite unaware of it until it had spread widely throughout the house, because it's evident that he didn't leave the bathroom. We'll never know whether he tried to do so. He may have been simply enjoying a shower until it was too late to do anything at all as he was quickly overcome by the smoke. The whole of the first floor collapsed and Mr Hawkins' remains were found in the kitchen area of the house along with charred shower and bath fittings.'

When Phillips had rung off, Parham sat for some time deep in thought. As he dwelt on what he had just heard, the final, and worst, of the terrible events that had taken place, it was all too much even for a man who, as a soldier, had seen much distress and death during World War Two. Exhausted and drained of energy, he slumped in his easy chair and could do nothing to stem the tears rolling down his cheeks.

***

Everyone at Haselmere was soon aware of the events of the previous evening. The national newspapers carried such headlines as *'The Madness of a Head Teacher,' 'Suicide of a Stricken Head,'* and *'Victims of a Head Teacher's Fury.'* The later editions focused on the death of Tom Hawkins' – details of which were released much later – with new headlines, such as *Murder of a School Governor.* There was also much interest expressed in the very concept of an open-air school, and in Haselmere in particular. Reporters had managed, in a surprisingly short time, to winkle out facts from both interviews and their research efforts. They explained to readers the characteristics, including the purpose and function, of open-air schools, much of the information being obtained from teachers, past and present. As the facts leaked out on successive days, the stories dominated the news for about a week.

The teachers at Haselmere, led by Tom, had agreed among themselves to be interviewed, and the authorities had not objected. They hoped that by doing so early on they would then be left in peace to get on with their work. Tom suggested that they should also allow the press, at the end of a school day, to enter the school premises in order to take photographs of the classrooms, etc. if that was approved by the Education Office. The teachers agreed that the information imparted during the interviews should be mainly limited to the nature of open-air education, the medical disabilities of the children and the modifications to a normal curriculum that were necessary. If pressed, they agreed to discuss, in broad detail only, some of the areas of tension and disagreement that had arisen, which culminated in the General Inspection and Pritchard's dismissal. The media were satisfied. They had plenty of information to build on.

Once Haselmere was media-free, Tom called a meeting of the teachers a few days later, at the end of a school day, after the children had been seen off on their coaches.

'The first thing I must tell you,' he began, ' is that Ronald Parham has asked me to be Acting Head until a new Head Teacher has been appointed. I know that you'll all want to talk about the future here, and there's a lot to discuss, but first, let's review the recent past. It's been a pretty grim time for us all, and it might be helpful if we talk about it and get it out of our systems, before we discuss the future.'

'I agree,' said Mary. 'Let's do that.'

Tom continued:

'We've all had a challenging year, and I think you've all weathered the various storms marvellously, so that, in spite of everything, the children's education and welfare haven't suffered at all.'

'Thanks, Tom,' Malcolm grinned, 'but we couldn't have soldiered on under that queer fish without your guidance and leadership.' The others nodded or murmured their agreement.

'Rupert Pritchard was an extremely complicated personality,' Tom continued, reflectively. 'His behaviour to me, even during the first few weeks revealed him to be extraordinarily spiteful and malicious. He saw me as a rival who was scheming to replace him, and so he was permanently insecure. That nagging insecurity was probably behind much of his behaviour.'

'Yes, Tom,' Susan broke in, somewhat irritably, 'but I think we've discussed all that many times. 'It's his behaviour towards the end of the School Year that none of us understands. Of course he was the most inadequate and idiosyncratic of Head Teachers, but look at what he became: an arsonist who succeeded in burning two houses to cinders, and setting fire to another, causing the death of one governor and attempting to murder one other governor and one teacher. Nothing that he had said or done previously could have prepared us for all that! Surely he was mad!'

'He probably was,' Mary said. 'but no-one will ever know for sure.'

'That's right,' Tom agreed, 'though it's been suggested that towards the end, Pritchard was a *schizophrenic paranoiac.* Of course, I know nothing about that, but I suppose the shock of being deprived of his headship helped to push him over the top, into a state where reality and fantasy were indistinguishable.

'What puzzles me,' Malcolm said, 'is why he stopped when he did. There were two more names on his list of targets.'

'Well,' Tom opined, 'I expect he began to lose his nerve. He must have realised that the police were after him, and he probably panicked and decided to bolt!'

'Right.' Susan spoke decisively. Perhaps we can leave it at that – perhaps that's enough about Pritchard. For the moments, at least, can we try to forget about those ghastly events and their perpetrator. What we all really want to know is, what's going to happen now?'

'I agree,' Malcolm said. 'Here we are at the end of the School Year. We don't want a repeat of what happened a year ago when the appointment of a new Head was rushed, with disastrous consequences.'

'Well, I'm afraid we have no power over that,' Tom explained, because that is a matter for the governors,' but I'm absolutely certain that both the Governing Body and Ronald Parham will take the utmost care over the next selection process ...'

'That may be so,' Mary broke in, 'but it's quite ridiculous to go through all that again. You, Tom, are now taking over as Acting Head for the third time. Why on earth can't the governors simply make you the permanent Head? I would have thought that Ronald Parham would have suggested that to them.'

Tom laughed. 'You're forgetting one important point, Mary,' he reminded her. 'I don't want to be the permanent Head. I'm a teacher and I love teaching. I'm not cut out for administrative work at a desk. I don't mind stepping in during an interim period, but that's all.'

'That's a great pity,' Malcolm commented, 'and I hope you'll reconsider that, Tom. You'll remember that when William Rogers was Head, he wasn't cooped up in his study all day. Quite the reverse! He spent most of the time moving around the School – inspiring and motivating us, motivating the children, sometimes teaching a lesson, so that we could do some marking or lesson preparation, and generally being an active, hands-on manager. And when you are Acting Head, you find you can teach your class and clear up admin matters at the end of the day, don't you?'

'Malcolm', Tom laughed, 'I agree about William, but what I do as Acting Head I couldn't do for more than a few weeks. For one thing, it means I work at least an hour or two longer each day. And there are many Head Teacher tasks that I don't do because I have no time. That doesn't matter for only a short period, but, believe me, if I were your permanent Head, I would need to spend more time in that little room than I want to.'

'I appreciate all that, Tom, but like Malcolm, I hope you'll reconsider,' Susan announced.

'So do I! I hope that very much!' Mary turned toward Tom with a smile. 'We all want you to rule over us, Tom. It means a lot to us. Please think it over!'

Chapter 44
17 July 1955

Ronald Parham, like the staff at Haselmere, had been taking stock of all the chaotic happenings of the recent past, especially during the last week, and of the new situation confronting everyone connected with Haselmere School.

It's been the hell of a time during the past few months. For someone like me, nearing retirement, it's been a bit too much! I'm sure I've aged a lot. But there is one thing I must do before I go. I must do everything possible to see that Tom Bates becomes the new Head Teacher at Haselmere, on a permanent basis. The case for that is overwhelming. He has now taken on the task of Acting Head for the third time. He always does well. He has proved his suitability beyond doubt for the role of Headship. I'm absolutely confident that his appointment would have the enthusiastic support of the teachers, the pupils and the parents.

But as Parham well knew, there were two problems about that.

The first was Tom's often-expressed reluctance to seek promotion, even to an established position as Deputy Head at another school. He hated any involvement with administrative or bureaucratic chores, and he valued his daily contact with children. He was, in fact, a born teacher.

The second was that a majority of governors were normally in favour of advertising a Headship in the normal way. It seemed to them that there were clear advantages in carrying out a wide trawl of available talent by advertising the post. Ronald Parham and Dr Mitchell would then study all the applications, and weed out those considered unsuitable or ill-qualified, leaving a short-list of six to be interviewed by the Governing Body To any objections that the system had clearly not worked last time, the governors might admit to some culpability in that they had been unduly hasty or unwise in advertising the post during the Summer Holidays. This time, Parham was sure, they would wait until the Autumn Term was well under way before beginning the selection process. They wouldn't want to rush things this time!

Parham decided to tackle both problems head-on. First of all, he needed to have a serious talk with Tom. It would be best, he thought, to have a chat with him in relaxed and convivial surroundings. With that in mind, he invited Tom to join him one evening in *The Three Tuns*. They would, he thought, sip their pints in a quiet corner where they would be undisturbed. He reflected, with a grin, that the pub had become his favourite venue for discussing matters of a delicate or difficult nature!

Tom was surprised when he received the invitation, and naturally speculated about its purpose. Although the two were old friends, they were by no means *drinking buddies!* It occurred to him that Parham might want to talk to him about the appointment of a new Head Teacher. He said that he would be happy to meet Parham in the pub, and a date was fixed.

Parham was keen to buy the drinks and Tom said he would very much like a pint of his favourite 'Old Speckled Hen.' Parham ordered a pint of 'Mild and Bitter' for himself. The two then settled down to enjoy their drinks and to chat.

For a time they chatted inconsequentially, exchanging a few anecdotes and Tom, while enjoying the cosy ambience, wondered when Parham would come to the point and bring up whatever was exercising his mind.

In fact, they had both almost finished their pints before the inspector suddenly decided to take the plunge. He explained to Tom that, especially after all the difficulties and crises that Haselmere had suffered, it was vitally important for it to be led by someone who would command the confidence of the teachers, the parents, the children and the Governing Body. The School needed someone with similar qualities to those possessed by William Rogers, someone who could continue with that happy and purposeful ethos that had characterized Haselmere for so long, before the bizarre events of recent times.

Tom had to agree that William's qualities were indeed those that were required. Anyone aspiring to take on the Headship, he suggested, should be an inspiring leader and a knowledgeable and open-minded educationist.

'We were very fortunate,' he said, 'to have had someone of William's calibre running the School for such a long time. It will be very difficult to identify anyone half as good.'

Parham smiled. 'Well, perhaps it won't be quite so difficult as that,' he responded.

Tom raised his eyebrows. The inspector, he thought, must have something up his sleeve. He settled back to hear more.

Parham took a deep breath. He now had the task of persuading Tom – and he knew it would far from easy – that he himself had demonstrated, as Acting Head, that he had all the essential qualities in abundance. He came straight to the point. Whenever Tom was in charge, Parham argued, there had been a happy and purposeful atmosphere at Haselmere. On his visits he had seen ample evidence of that. There had been a buzz around the place. Both the teachers and the pupils were well-motivated, and were working together as a cohesive community and achieving excellent results. He knew, too, that the parents had confidence in Tom. The School desperately needed to have a period of enlightened Headship, and Tom, he said, could provide that. It was now time for him to take over the Headship permanently. In regard to the admin side, he pointed out that the part-time secretary was well able to cope with most of it.

Tom was taken aback by Parham's praise, and his wholehearted recommendation. He was gratified that the quality of his work was recognised so positively, though, being of a modest disposition, he inclined to the view that the Inspector was *laying it on rather thick!* In any case, the Inspector's proposition had come out of the blue, and a response shouldn't be rushed. He decided to play for time.

'Mr. Parham, I very much appreciate all you've said, but before we go any further, I see that we both have an empty glass. That won't do, will it?' He grinned. 'I wonder if I might get us both another drink before we continue this conversation.'

'Parham said he'd be glad to have another drink, a half pint this time, and Tom approached the bar to give his order, his mind full of Parham's words and the kind of response he would make to them.

After a few minutes, he returned with the beer, sat down, and the two sipped contentedly for a few moments before Tom spoke.

'Mr Parham, I was very pleased to hear what you've said about my work as an Acting Head,' he began, 'though I don't think I can entirely live up to them. You've said some very kind things, but you have rather taken my breath away by suggesting that I might become the permanent Head Teacher at Haselmere. As you know, I love teaching and I've never wished to become involved in school management. So I've never sought promotion. I've never seen myself as the permanent Head Teacher at Haselmere. That's always been my view and it's unchanged, I'm afraid.'

The Inspector tried to hide his disappointment. He appealed to Tom, in view of the difficulties of the past year, not to rule himself out completely. If the post were to be advertised and Tom applied, he would be one of perhaps fifty. Only six of them would be shortlisted and interviewed, and even if he were one of them, the governors might well prefer to appoint an external candidate.'

Tom wondered whether he had been a little too stubborn. In the unlikely event of his appointment, he reflected, he would still be able to teach part of the time. He could give lessons to each of the classes, and so give some free time to the teachers for lesson preparation, marking, etc.

'Well,' Mr. Parham, you know my feelings, but if the post were to be advertised, I would consider applying for it. I don't actually think I would be offered the post by the Governing Body, even if I were to be short-listed, because, as you say, external candidates are usually preferred.'

'And I think that's normally a wise policy.' Parham said.

Tom agreed.

'Anyway,' Parham continued, 'I'm very pleased that you would think about applying for the post. That's all I am asking. Just take part in the process. I think you would probably be shortlisted, and then it would be up to the governors to select the candidate they preferred. There would be five external candidates and one internal one.'

Parham felt that he had gained a major concession, and that it could prove counter-productive to push matters any further. He would now, he thought, test the water with Richard Bartlett, Chairman of the Governing Body and give his persuasive powers another test! This meeting would not be held, as last time, in his office. He would again prefer to use the intimate and congenial atmosphere of *The Three Tuns*. He had enjoyed his conversion with Tom, and also the pub's, Mild and Bitter'!

***

Richard Bartlett readily accepted Parham's invitation to meet him in *The Three Tuns*. He had not had an opportunity to discuss with the Inspector the dramatic events of the past week, and there was also the question of arrangements for the replacement of Pritchard. He particularly welcomed the prospect of enjoying a tipple in one of the most salubrious of local pubs.

The publican recalled not only Ronald Parham's previous visit with Tom, but also an earlier one with Dr Clive Mann. Now here was Parham again with yet another companion. Convinced that he had gained another regular customer, he greeted Parham and Richard Bartlett warmly, and attended to their needs immediately. Bartlett was soon settled with a pint of his favourite 'Brown Ale', while the Inspector had his usual 'Mild and Bitter'. Parham had ensured that they would be ensconced, as before, in a quiet corner where they could confer in peace.

The two men had very different personalities, but shared crises and difficulties had persuaded them to work closely together. They now had a firm mutual respect and there were clear signs of a developing friendship.

Inevitably, they first chatted about the sensational and gruesome events of the past few weeks and Parham expressed his deep sadness and grief about the attacks on members of the Governing Body: the murder of Tom Hawkins and the injuries to Howard Cooper. Bartlett, in turn, asked after Tom Bates He knew that Tom's house had been reduced to ashes and he asked whether he had now managed to find another house. Parham knew that he had, and told the Chairman about it.

It was Richard Bartlett who now raised the question uppermost in Parham's mind.

'Mr Parham, after all the trauma the School has endured, I'm sure you'll agree that we should take enormous care this time to ensure that we get the right person as Head Teacher.'

'I couldn't agree more. The selection of a new Head is always important, but in this case it's especially so. Thank goodness that the School has held together well during the past critical year, but we can't afford to make another mistake. Haselmere deserves to have a really good Head.'

'Of course, but I would suggest,' Bartlett went on, 'that we defer the advertisement until two or three weeks after the beginning of the Autumn Term, when the schools have all settled down. We should then hope to have a good response – plenty of applications. We should give you and Dr Mitchell ample time to select a short-list of six, before we can fix an interview date. That means that the whole process will take up most of the Term, and the new Head won't be available until January.'

'Yes,' Parham agreed, 'and it could be even later than that. The appointee will have to give in his notice near the end of the term, and we might have to wait until after Easter. That's the timetable if we carry out the usual procedure. But in view of the urgent need to get the School back to normal after all the turbulence of the past year, it would be a great pity if, as you say, the school were to be deprived of a permanent Head until next year.'

'Yes, it would be a pity, but we have no alternative, have we?'

Ronald Parham smiled.

'I think there is an alternative,' he suggested, a note of quiet determination in his voice, 'that I think is worth considering.'

'Then I'll be glad to hear of it,' the Chairman said.

'The alternative,' Parham said, 'is to consider appointing Tom Bates to the Headship and to by-pass the usual procedure.'

Richard Bartlett raised his eyebrows in surprise.

'I think every member of your Governing Body,' Parham continued, 'is now aware not only that this is the third time that he has been Acting Head, but that he is held in the highest regard by all his colleagues and by the parents. And I can assure you that he has all the qualities that we are looking for. He is an exceptionally good teacher and educationist with excellent inter-personal qualities essential for effective leadership, he has a deep knowledge and experience of open-air education and the special needs of the pupils, and he has made an outstanding contribution to the life and work of the school. I really don't think – may I call you Richard – it would be possible to find anyone more suitable for the post.'

The Chairman had listened very attentively and was impressed, but he had reservations.

'I really don't doubt Tom Bates's fine qualities. I understand that had it not been for his steady influence and calm advice to his colleagues, the influence of Pritchard could have been disastrous. But Ronald, I'm also sure that my fellow governors with favour the normal procedure. They will argue that the most effective way to find the best person is to cast the net wide and to try to rope in the best talent.'

'But you agree, Richard, don't you, that next year is really too long to wait, and that Tom Bates has the strength of personality, proven managerial ability and educational insights to command the confidence of everyone connected with Haselmere: staff, children, parents and governors?'

The Chairman laughed. 'How on earth can I argue against all that. You've made a very strong case. OK, Ronald, let me get us another drink now, and I promise I'll put your arguments to my colleagues on the Governing Body. You've convinced me, but I'm only the Chairman! The Governing Body will meet on 25 July as you know. You'll be there, won't you? We'll need your advice.'

Parham assured him that he would attend the meeting. Again, he was satisfied with the outcome of his talk. He was well aware that he had suggested one thing to Tom – the question of applying for an advertised post – and quite another to Richard Bartlett – the direct appointment of Tom. He was unconcerned about that. He was determined to do whatever was necessary to secure Tom's appointment!

Chapter 45
26 July 1955

Richard Barnett sat at the head of the table and surveyed his colleagues thoughtfully a few minutes before opening the meeting. This was the first assembly of the Governing Body since the recent calamities, and the absence of Tom Hawkins was a grim reminder of all that had happened.

Apart from poor Tom Hawkins, I think they're all here. I'm sure they all feel as upset as I am about his fate, the destruction of Tom Bates's home and the injuries to Howard Cooper, but it's difficult to tell. They all seem to be their normal selves: chatting away noisily and laughing at anything mildly funny. As usual, there seem to be more of them talking than listening!

This meeting is likely to be as unpredictable as the last one. Ronald Parham is anxious about its outcome and I hope the meeting goes his way, but if he and I push our views too much, it's likely to be counter-productive. Ah, well .... Here we go!

The Chairman rose, brought down his gavel. The lively conversations that had been filling the room ceased abruptly as he began to address the meeting. All eyes were upon him.

'Good afternoon. I am glad that we have a full meeting, as we have a vitally important issue to discuss: the question of a new Head Teacher for Haselmere. But first of all, we should all, I think, remind ourselves of the recent terrible events so close to us. I would therefore be glad if you would all stand for two minutes of silence as a mark of respect for Tom Hawkins, who was a hard-working and conscientious member of this Body. He will be greatly missed.'

The members rose in silence and stood meditatively. It was true that everyone present had respected Tom's forthrightness and character. Richard Bartlett then continued:

'Thank you. On your behalf, I sent condolences to Tom's widow just before the funeral, which I attended, and yesterday I sent her some flowers with our best regards.' A quiet murmur of approval rose from the members.

'And now I would like you to consider how we should proceed in regard to the selection process. We are faced with two alternative procedures, each of which has both advantages and disadvantages, and we must make a choice between them...'

He broke off when he saw that Mrs French was bursting to make a point. She stood up, looking as dowdy as ever, but she had been a member of the Board longer than anyone else and always commanded respect.

'Mr Chairman,' she said, 'I am rather puzzled to hear what you have just said. Surely there is only one procedure that is always followed when there is a vacancy for a Headship. It must be advertised, and in due course we will interview the short-listed candidates and select one of them.'

'You are quite right, Mrs French,' Bartlett replied, diplomatically. 'What you have said is certainly the normal way of dealing with this matter.' He smiled. 'But the circumstances at Haselmere are not actually normal are they? The School has had an extremely difficult year – we can only imagine how traumatic it has been for the teachers – and we are confronted with a unique situation that may suggest – and I would emphasize *may,* a different approach.' At that point he was aware that there was a rustle of discontent among a few governors, which prepared him for the second interruption which quickly followed.

Alice Peabody rose unsteadily to her feet to support her fellow governor. Parham groaned inwardly as he viewed the cheap and vulgar make-up, jewellery and costume that festooned her overweight body. He had ensured that he wasn't sitting next to her this time. He well remembered, on the previous occasion, the lady's dreadful perfume!

'Mr Chairman, I think Mrs French has reminded us all what we have to do,' she declared loudly. 'We've got to advertise this post as we did before, haven't we? Why not?

How can we get the brightest candidates here for interview otherwise?' She looked round the table defiantly. 'There's no need to make it all complicated, is there? I think we should just get on with it. Why should we waste any more time?'

A ripple of amusement floated round the room, which she acknowledged with a toothy grin before she regained her seat.

Bartlett, ignoring her words, now decided to bring in the Inspector.

'I wonder whether, Mr Parham, you would like to explain to the meeting why it is that this time we might reasonably consider a choice between two possibilities.'

Parham stood up and straightened to his full, considerable height, and smiled as he looked round the table. He was confident of a respectful and attentive hearing, and he spoke persuasively in a voice of unquestioned authority.

'As the Chairman has reminded us, ladies and gentlemen, the teachers at Haselmere have had a real *annus horribilis* – I can hardly overstate my admiration for their fortitude under extreme pressure and provocation – and it ended with a series of ghastly events of which you are all too well aware. We could, of course, ignore all that, and simply go ahead, as some of you may wish, with an advertisement for the post of Head Teacher, followed by interviews, as we did last time. It might work out well this time.' He then explained that it would then take most of the Autumn Term to receive and process the applications, and that there would be other delays.

'The successful candidate would then have to give notice to his present employer. His current post would then be advertised, and it would not be possible to fill that until the New Year, if then. That would be the earliest that our new Head could come here. And I'm afraid it could be longer than that. If, for example, you were not satisfied with the calibre of any of the short-listed candidates brought before you for interview, we would be well advised to re-advertise the post, to have a second trawl. None of us would wish to make the unfortunate mistake that was made last time. That could mean that we would not have our Head until after Easter. Two terms without a Head Teacher!

So, even if you finally select an excellent person to run Haselmere, the School would not have a permanent leader for an inordinate period of time.' He paused and studied his audience before continuing in measured tones. 'Now, I'm sure you'll all agree that after all its disruptive and painful experiences, the School should get back to normal much earlier than that. A really good Head Teacher who can provide effective leadership as early as possible is urgently needed – now, not next year.'

Mrs French now wished to speak further.

'I understand your point about the urgent need for a new Head to take up the post very soon, Mr Parham,' she said, 'but that's simply not possible, is it?'

Parham smiled again. 'Actually, Mrs French, I think it would be possible.'

He then introduced the question of an internal promotion. In recommending Tom Bates for the Headship, he used the same arguments as he had put forward to Bartlett in *The Three Tuns*. He emphasized that as Acting Head, Tom had revealed all the attributes required for responsible management, proven qualities of leadership and a wide knowledge of education. He also had the full confidence of everyone in the School and also that of the parents.

'In many ways,' he reminded the governors, 'it was Tom Bates who kept the School together during a turbulent year. I'm sure,' he added, 'that we are all grateful to him for that.' That earned a murmur of agreement round the room. Capitalizing on that, he concluded with:

'Mr Bates would, I know, be an excellent Head Teacher, and he could take over the post at the very beginning of the Autumn Term. As he is already the Acting Head, he would be able to take over his full duties smoothly and effectively. But it is, of course, for you to decide whether you would like him to do so, or whether you would rather advertise the post.'

Parham then thanked the Chairman for inviting him to the meeting, and said that looked forward to hearing the discussion they would now have.

Mrs French was keen to re-emphasize her position.

'Mr Chairman, I appreciate the points made by Mr Parham, but I must emphasize that we governors have a clear responsibility to select a Head in the usual way, beginning with an advertisement. I have no doubt that Mr Bates has all the right qualities, and I see no reason why he should not apply for the post if he wishes to do so. I hope he does. We certainly owe him a debt of gratitude. But when we advertise, we give every potential candidate a fair chance to apply. And it is fully democratic. We trawl a wide area of talent. We could have scores of candidates, among whom we'll interview only the most promising, so we could have five external candidates and one internal one – all well qualified and fully suitable- and then we'll be certain of getting a good result. What happened last time was the result of a serious mistake. We advertised the post at the wrong time. That won't happen again.

I should also point out, Mr Chairman, that Haselmere is a mixed School, and that this post should be open to both men and women. It happens that we have had two men in succession, the last of whom was a disaster. Personally I would welcome a woman as Head, and I hope we short-list a fair proportion of women.'

As Mr French sat down there were murmurs of approval among the governors. She had made several valid points and the support for her around the table seemed strong. Parham looked a little concerned and swept his eyes around the table to assess how many governors appeared to be as impressed as he certainly was.

Leslie Burgess and Miss Forster then made short contributions that were fairly balanced and neutral. It appeared that they had not yet made up their minds one way or the other. While Burgess said that they should all be very grateful to Mr Bates for all his sterling work as Acting Head, he then went on to praise the normal selection procedure which he felt had very positive merit.

Ronald Parham was both disappointed and surprised at what he regarded as the equivocation of those two very able governors. He had fully expected that both would back Tom's appointment. He thought he had made a strong case both about

Tom's qualities and about the urgent need for someone to take over the leadership of Haselmere at the earliest possible moment. It looked as if Mrs French's powerful arguments had carried the day.

When Howard Cooper rose, there was a stir of interest around the table. His standing among the governors had risen markedly since the critical contribution that had led to a unanimous vote for Pritchard's dismissal. He had recovered well from his burns, though his facial skin still looked rather red and a little raw. All the governors were well aware of the details of his ordeal, and there was a great deal of sympathy for him. The fact that in spite of all that had happened, he had managed to attend this pivotally important meeting was much appreciated.

He smiled as he made eye-to-eye contact with all his fellow governors, and then began:

'Mr Chairman, I am sure that not a single person in this room doubts that, in normal circumstances, we would all agree to advertising this post. Casting the net wide, as some of my colleagues have recommended, has great advantages. Advertising often works well, though, as we found to our cost last time, it doesn't always lead to a successful outcome!'

There was a buzz of agreement among some of the governors, one or two of whom muttered rueful remarks. Cooper continued:

'Also, Mr Chairman, this procedure takes up a considerable amount of time, as Mr Parham has reminded us. Can we afford to wait so long? More importantly, can the School afford to wait so long? Personally, I don't think so. Following all the chaos, unpleasantness, lack of direction ... and drama, of the past year, Haselmere should have a Head Teacher in position as soon as possible. It's a matter of urgency! Exceptional situations call for exceptional measures!

'But is there really a practical and satisfactory alternative to advertising the post? Well, it has been suggested by our good friend and adviser, Ronald Parham, that Tom Bates, the senior teacher might be persuaded to take over the Headship. He could do so without delay. But would he really be a suitable person? Has he all the right qualities? Would everyone in the School support his appointment? Well, we have plenty of evidence to suggest that the answer to all three questions is a positive 'yes.' It is fortuitous that he has been Acting Head no less than three times, if we include the time when William Rogers was ill, and later, the period following his tragic death. So there has been ample opportunity to assess Mr Bates's calibre, and Mr Parham has assured us that he always did an excellent job. Incidentally, I wonder if you all realise that each time Mr Bates took over the reins, he also had to teach his own class. How on earth did he manage that? I can tell you. He stayed on after the end of each teaching day in order to attend to all the admin tasks, while, during the day he made it his business to support his teaching colleagues and give them the benefit of his wide experience.

'Now Mr Bates is widely recognised as being an excellent, hard-working, dedicated class-teacher. If that were all there was to it, the case would hardly be made for his promotion. We all know that many excellent teachers can be out of their depth when confronted by the challenges of managing a school. Not Tom Bates. Mr Parham has told us how he always managed to take over without a hitch, winning the unqualified support of the other teachers and the parents. I'm told that the children, too, think the world of him!

'Mr Chairman, it is probably the case that I have a special bond with Mr. Bates as we were both victims of vicious arson attacks – he, poor man, suffering the complete loss of his family home – but I don't think that that has skewed my judgement in this matter.' He smiled again, and resumed:

'My considered view, then, is that we should seek to appoint Mr Bates as the new Head Teacher of Haselmere Open-Air School as soon as that can be arranged. We are fortunate to have a teacher of proven ability ready to take charge of a School that he understands intimately and that he has shown us convincingly he can manage very effectively.'

Miss Forster now indicated that her position had shifted.

'I, too,' she began, 'am usually very much in favour of opening a vacant post to full competition,' she began. 'We could then have not only candidates from the special schools sector, but also others from normal schools. And, on principle, I would agree with Mrs French on the desirability of having applicants of both sexes.

'However, I also fully accept that we are faced with an extraordinary situation calling for exceptional action on our part. There has been a malignant shadow over the school for a full year, which ended with a series of horrendous events. Our response should surely be to give every assistance to Haselmere, to help it get back to normal with the utmost speed so that those events may begin to fade in the memory.

'As Mr Cooper has emphasized, Mr Bates is much more than an excellent teacher. He is also a leader who has won the respect and admiration of both teachers and parents. We also know that, during the very onerous period under Mr Pritchard, it was Mr Bates's calm influence and quiet leadership of his colleagues that held the School together so that standards were well maintained. Mr Chairman, I would support the appointment of Mr Bates without reservation.'

As Miss Forster concluded, Parham realised that Howard Cooper's speech had undoubtedly had a catalytic effect, as had his contribution last time. The Inspector was beginning to feel more sanguine!

Leslie Burgess now indicated his wish to speak, and the Chairman invited him to do so. He came straight to the point.

'Mr Chairman, I support emphatically everything that has been said by Mr Cooper and Miss Forster. I have enormous sympathy for everyone who has been working at Haselmere. In the course of one year they suffered the tragic loss of their much-loved Head Teacher, William Rogers, and were then led by an unbalanced paranoiac with a malicious nature who might have harmed the School immeasurably had Mr Bates not helped his able colleagues to weather the storm. And you are all well aware of the horrible events that have occurred since our last meeting.

There is an overwhelming need now for stability under enlightened leadership. Mr Bates, we are assured, is fully qualified to provide that leadership. Let us help the School to make a fresh start as soon as possible. That fresh start should be under the leadership of Tom Bates.'

Towards the end of his peroration, Leslie Burgess had spoken with warmth and passion. As he concluded, the room seemed suddenly eerily quiet while the governors digested all the arguments of the last three speakers.

He then requested that a motion be put to the meeting, as follows:

We strongly recommend that, in view of the excellent qualities of leadership displayed while he has been Acting Head Teacher, and the urgent need for someone to provide sound and permanent leadership at the School without delay, Mr Thomas Bates should be offered the Headship of Haselmere Open-Air School with a view to taking up the post in September, 1955.

The motion was seconded by Miss Forster, and the Chairman then invited further discussion. No-one, however, seemed keen to prolong the discussion, and when the motion was put to the vote it was carried unanimously.

Ronald Parham could not restrain a smile of satisfaction. Stage one had been achieved thanks largely to the remarkable Howard Cooper. But they were only half way there. He now needed to talk with Tom in order to overcome his remaining reluctance. He had considered it prudent to say nothing to the governors about Tom's feelings. That might have caused them to have second thoughts! And he had been somewhat disingenuous with Tom!

***

The following day, the Inspector visited the School, and during the lunch break had a long talk with Tom in the Head Teacher's study. Coming straight to the point, he conveyed to him the unanimous view of the Governing Body that he should become the permanent Head Teacher of Haselmere in September.

Tom was staggered and took a few minutes to recover. He had never envisaged such a development. He had been convinced that the majority of the Governing Body would wish to advertise the post. He had, with difficulty, become reconciled to the possibility that he might be one of the six candidates to be interviewed, but he had dismissed any idea that he, an internal candidate, would be finally selected. And now he was being told that the governors wanted him, and as soon as possible!

He was naturally pleased that he had the approval and support of all the governors but he was still not at all sure that he was ready to abandon his classroom teaching in order to manage the School.

Parham was nevertheless encouraged. He reminded Tom that there was no reason why he could not combine the Headship with some teaching. Haselmere was a small school. He would be able to teach each class for short periods and he would therefore have an opportunity to get to know all the children in the School. He also argued that Tom should be honoured to have the goodwill and backing of the whole Governing Body, and that his appointment would be welcomed by pupils, staff and parents.

'I am flattered that the Governing Body has selected me,' Tom said, 'but I really can't understand why. There must be many better qualified people than me who would apply for the post if it were to be advertised.'

'No, Tom,' Parham said. 'The governors have taken account of both your *de facto* leadership during the past year which held the School together, and also your success as an Acting Head. They also feel that the whole business should be settled now because the School needs stability and sound direction now.'

Tom laughed. 'Oh, dear! You mustn't speak of my *de facto* leadership. Pritchard accused me of that, and I always denied it!'

Parham smiled. 'Well, call it what you like. It was effective in calming the turbulence that Pritchard caused, and keeping the School on a steady course, wasn't it?'

'I suppose it was.'

Tom's hesitations and doubts now gradually evaporated. While he would have never considered becoming Head of a large school, he could more easily contemplate being Head of Haselmere, a small community, and he liked the prospect of having an overview of the whole School. He accepted that he had taken the initiative during some very difficult times, and that leading his teaching colleagues, for whom he had enormous admiration, had been a pleasure. He told Ronald Parham that he would be delighted to accept the Headship.

***

At home that evening, Malcolm and Caroline reflected on a tumultuous year that had ended with multiple arson attacks, murder and a suicide.

'Well, at least the School survived,' Malcolm observed, in summary, 'and so did we!'

'Yes,' Caroline responded, 'just about. And if the children's education and care was largely unaffected, and I think it was, that's a great tribute to all the teachers. Well done, all of you! But it's over, thank God. A huge shadow has been lifted from our lives. And now, let's talk about something else, a much happier subject. We have a lovely baby, we're going to buy a house quite soon, and you're going to try for promotion. Right?'

'Absolutely!'

'Well, doesn't all that call for a celebratory drink?'

Malcolm grinned. 'No doubt about it.' He strode over to a decanter of sherry on the sideboard and filled two small glasses. They celebrated their present situation and their future prospects, and then had another glass. Caroline then turned towards her husband, smiled shyly, and said:

'Paul has been sleeping soundly for a quarter of an hour, and I don't expect him to wake up for at least another three hours.'

'That's great!'

'Well, it's the last day of term, and also the last day of a terrible year. We're feeling very happy, and we're deeply in love, aren't we?'

'We certainly are, my love.'

'And I'm quite ready for you to do something about it.' Caroline smiled again, and Malcolm thought she looked quite delightful.

'Yes, of course, my darling!'